CATS' EYES

Michael Eric Stein

S

Streetlight Books

New York

Also by Michael Eric Stein

Continuous Trauma, a novel

All Good Things,
the stage musical story of the Remains

 **Author Michael Eric Stein** has been a novelist, playwright, screenwriter, television writer (*Miami Vice*, the CBS television movie *Higher Ground*), and a journalist writing on film, rock, jazz, and Hawaiian music and culture for *Films In Review*, the *Los Angeles Times*, and *Maui No Ka Oi* Magazine. He is a graduate of Yale University and the New York University Graduate School of Film and Television, and currently lives in New York City.

Additional Praise for CATS' EYES

"A brilliant book, vivid and moving, with an astonishing richness of detail that successfully replicates an overwhelmingly vivid cultural and political era -- not just a child's delight at the World's Fair and the mythic adolescent glories of Woodstock, but other much less benign events like the Newark riot and the clashes at Columbia University. The writing is often mesmeric, and the evocation of rock music is extraordinary. And the characters of **Cats' Eyes** include deeply concerned adults and their perspectives, which is rare in novels of the 1960s. A big, rich, powerful piece of work."

Robert N. Watson, Neikirk Distinguished Professor of English and Associate Dean of Humanities at UCLA, and author of *Back to Nature* and other books on Renaissance culture

"In **Cats' Eyes** Michael Eric Stein takes us on a rollercoaster journey through the Sixties in New York City. It's all here: drugs, sex, and rock 'n' roll – and plenty of all three; returned Vietnam veterans and antiwar activists; Black Power and white panic; the rebellion of the young and the anxiety of their parents; John Lindsay and Abbie Hoffman; Bob Dylan, Jimi Hendrix, and Allen Ginsberg. Stein brings the epoch to bursting life with dazzling language, compelling characters, and an enthralling, multilayered plot. A fascinating tapestry of the era that changed everything – in New York, America, and the world."

Michael Takiff, Author of *A Complicated Man: The Life of Bill Clinton as Told by Those Who Know Him*, and Executive Director, Gravitas History

For further information on Michael Eric Stein, please contact
E-mail: mericstein@streetlightbooks.com
www.streetlightbooks.com

Book Design by Kurt E Griffith,
Fantastic Realities Studio
www.fantastic-realities.com
Cover concept by Kurt E. Griffith and Michael Eric Stein
Illustration by Kurt E. Griffith

ISBN 13 - 978-0692212486 (Streetlight Books)
ISBN 10 - 0692212485

Published in 2014 by Streetlight Books
Printed by CreateSpace, An Amazon.com Company
Available from Amazon.com, on Kindle, and at other retail outlets.

To my sister Susan Stein; my parents Maxine and Arthur Stein; my *hanai* family Pat, Louise, Michael, Mary Anne, Betsy, Henry, and Katherine Tanner; and to all my family and friends who shared the years of this novel with me.

"Lord, help me stay in tune and in time."

— Carlos Santana,

before going on at Woodstock

8

PROLOGUE

When Nate Kovacs saw Danny being led out by the prison guard, he looked so frail in his orange uniform that Nate was reminded again—just a kid.

A kid who had befriended his kids, helped his kids, although now was not the time to think about that. Not the time for the other thoughts that crept in when Danny gave Nate a smile, but swiveled his gaze past him—that weird, jittery gaze, maybe from the wards, maybe from the drugs—that checking for ghostly intruders.

A stare that brought Nate right up to his own shadows, so close...

No. Danny was just a kid. Beyond the flurry of rock music he was known for, beyond the headlines in the Daily News, scrawny, defiant, fallen, and very young.

Danny finally concentrated on Nate's presence, even if his limbs, in reaction to the medication, shifted and twitched relentlessly. Nate now had to face the fundamental obligations, the enormous questions that he had to decide within one lawyer-prisoner visit. Guilt or innocence. Sanity or madness.

His children would have their own questions that he'd have to answer. After all this time, he yearned for his wife to be by his side when they asked them. But had his family, had his world not been cut apart five years ago ... this chasm was their life, its vanishing point their future.

My God, what had they done?

Chapter 1

THE FAIR

Artie watched as Karen looked up to the sky and winged her arms in circles that grew and grew until they embraced the steel globe that loomed above her head, the clouds caught in its meridians, the fountains, the thousands of people all around her. Nate and Becky scrutinized her closely, but Artie just laughed at his goofy kid sister.

It was obvious Karen was just mimicking the orbits that circled the twelve-story-high Unisphere. Now Becky and Nate laughed as well, Becky hugged Karen, and Artie got impatient. The newspaper said it might take a week straight to see the whole Fair. Lines stretched around some pavilions an hour or more.

"Don't miss a thing!"

A beautiful April morning shone through the Unisphere. Karen shouted that it was like an egg. Artie pointed his Instamatic at a red-and-gold Taiwanese palace next to African huts raised on stilts over a pool of water, and clicked off another snapshot: an architectural crazy quilt, the seams of the world knitted together. Then he took a photo of Mom, Dad, and Karen, and they decided to ask someone else to take a family photo of them where they stood.

Nate thumbed through the official guide to the Fair trying to prepare an efficient itinerary, knowing Artie would want to see everything he could in the Industrial and Transportation areas before Becky steered them to the International exhibits. He glanced at a picture of Robert Moses—the man who had built the Triboro Bridge, the expressways that girdled the City, and now the World's Fair—dining with a fashionable woman at the Top Of The Fair Restaurant, the Unisphere way behind them. The photo was also an ad for the Gas Pavilion. "The gasbag in the gas house,"

Nate's boss Ted Schomer had snorted. He'd made fun of Moses's summation of the Fair: "The products of philosophy which is the guide of life, and knowledge which is power." A splinter group of the Congress of Racial Equality had decided the power in question was white corporate America. They'd announced they would stall cars on the highway routes to Flushing Meadow and create the largest traffic jam ever on the Fair's opening day, to remind Fairgoers of the misery of being Negro in New York City. The protest had sputtered—although as a result the subways were packed. But they would have been packed anyway.

Let his boss and CORE mock the Fair. They didn't see the faces of Nate's children.

Around the fountains' rainbow spray were hundreds of families. Kids were everywhere, posing for Bell and Howell movie cameras and waist-level Brownies like the one Nate carried, skittering across the Court of the President of the United States in polo shirts, cardigan sweaters, red-white-and-blue Keds sneakers and baseball caps from the Mets, Yankees, Dodgers, and Milwaukee Braves. They jabbered and pointed and screamed with anticipation. Nate was comforted by the nexus of other fathers' sympathetic and slightly amazed stares. Just look at this brood we've sired, coddled and cooed over in the millions, their pranks celebrated on television, their heroic adventures accompanied by collies (no, son, we can't have a big dog in the city), their foibles calmly ministered to in the "den" (no, son, we can't make a den out of a two-bedroom New York apartment). Floating with the lightest grasp on their parents' sleeves as they worshiped the marvels spread before them.

Becky corralled a French tourist, and as the family gathered for the picture she gripped her cane and bent over to embrace Karen with one arm. Nate could see that it hurt his wife's wrist like hell. She sang the tune from *Mary Poppins* as "It's a jolly holiday with Karey ... " and Karen larkishly giggled.

Look at her, after all the grief of the past year, walking and laughing as if she didn't have a care in the world.... The family stood in front of the Cor-Ten steel pedestal and the western hemisphere. Becky leaned against Nate, who held on tight. It was an hour before they saw their first pavilion, even though kindly Fairgoers let Becky ahead of them as they joined a crowd who filed slowly, one concentric ring after another, before the Ford Wonder Rotunda. At last the family rode in a Mustang convertible down the Magic Skyway between a carload of happy Texans and another of nervously quiet Germans. Artie, gazing out through the transparent panels and a sea anemone wall of pylons at the crowd still lined up by the reflecting pool, felt an enormous, delightful sense of privilege, until the narration on the car radio suddenly turned to Spanish. Artie yelled at Karen. Becky laughed—always pushing buttons, such an imp sometimes. Nate reached forward and clumsily jabbed at the radio until English was restored.

Darkness settled over the line of convertibles. A brontosaurus craned its neck toward the aura of a deep blue sky. Other dinosaurs slowly fought and stalked their prey. Artie was mesmerized. He had decided he hated Walt Disney. Mary Poppins and cartoon animals dancing with actors, so what? But this was Disney and it was "audioanimatronics," and it was so much more than his Erector Set, his Remco Chemistry and Optical Illusion kits that spilled out in fuzzy-striped cards and powders and instructions, and his Electric Motor kit with its spew of axles, flywheels, and copper wire that Mom had patiently helped him spool on the armature. All that and one spark and the cheap thing worked five minutes. Here was photorealism that only happened to be gears and wires and machines. *Life* Magazine in motion.

After a trek past the Project Mercury capsules on the Space Walk—all the great astronaut stuff, heading for the moon—they paused at the Kodak Pavilion for more snapshots on its puckered lunar roof with the Johnson Wax golden rondelle and Coca-Cola tower just beyond them. Mom refused to buy two more rolls of film for Artie. He'd just have to decide what was really worth a picture.

For the rest of the morning they surrendered to motion and entertainment. The bleachers of the IBM Pavilion, surrounded by steel trees, that lifted them up into a giant egg-shaped Information Machine, where slides and movies flashing on a hundred screens were "just like the inside of a computer." At GM's Futurama pavilion Space Age easy chairs wafted them past tableaux of Cineramic sweep and gemlike precision, busy but reverently hushed, where families of the 21st century happily submarined through underwater resorts and glided over Antarctic harbors.

But after the Chrysler "autofare," three football fields' worth of blinding multicolored fluorescent gears and cams and bellowing "engine dragons" and "autofrogs," Becky announced a change in plan. She'd had it with people-movers and somberly lit dioramas of the Triumph of Man, usually at war. She was weary of limping down Avenues of Commerce, Enterprise, and Automation. Artie pointed out they still hadn't seen the Hall of Science and National Cash Register exhibits, but Nate glared him into silence.

As they visited the less crowded International pavilions they gazed at Chinese stone lions, Greek marble panels, French cafes and Danish glassware. Michelangelo's Pieta shone beneath a screen of blue lights, and Artie, while Becky rested her hand on his shoulder, thought back on his school group gazing at the Mona Lisa at the Metropolitan Museum. Becky playfully quizzed them on their Flags of Many Nations set; Karen actually remembered the colors of Greece and Italy. At the Indian exhibit they met two hostesses dressed in saris who were on their lunch break. The family joined them at the restaurant by the lotus pond. Music from strange plucked string instruments echoed behind Artie, and he couldn't take his eyes off the women until Nate, with a grin, whispered to him that it was impolite to stare. Lunch was tasty charcoal-roasted garlicky chicken and puffy bread, 7-Up and spiced tea. Nate and Becky wanted to know all about India, while Artie looked at the slim woman with dark almond skin, a dot on her forehead and her black hair swept back into a kerchief, who smiled at him as if they shared a secret.

In the evening Artie made a picturephone call to Karen at the Bell Telephone pavilion while Karen beamed at Artie's image on the videoscreen. Nate told them they'd had something like that at the 1939 World's Fair too, but no, he hadn't called Mom, they hadn't even know each other then. Their final exhibit was Pepsi Cola's "It's A Small World." Artie winced at the thought of a Disney boat ride through rooms of babbling automated dolls. But maybe Karen and Mom's sheer joy infected him. The sloshing of the boats was fun. Swiss children glided on the Alps, Mexican dolls danced on hats, the loopy song chattered over and over as the animated UNICEF of dolls, lit in pink, blue and gold, thronged the walls and ceilings in a perfectly choreographed jumble, radiating gleefulness on one last ride.

They ate clam chowder, beef pies and Johnny Cake at the New England exhibit in the Federal and State section. The Unisphere's world capitals turned on in points of silver, and one by one the Pavilions were illuminated: golden towers, red umbrella roofs, the Equitable Life population clock that signaled the world's new births minute by minute, and the billion-candlepower-spired Tower of Light. Fireworks flung themselves over the fountains to the sound of orchestras and pealing bells. The family leaned on each other and cheered for more until it was finally time for the subway home.

It was a smashing Fair, just like Life *had said. Becky sat on the wicker subway seat with Karen on her lap and Artie and Nate strap-hanging above them. Past the elevated tracks she saw the pavilions' grape cluster glow, the U.S. Rubber tire Ferris wheel, the star of the Chrysler Pavilion.*

The only time she'd gotten testy. That had been a little too much, the automated puppets looming over her that reminded her of doctors and nurses. And that giant domed movie, "To The Moon and Beyond," had unnerved her. Was it because she'd never see that day? Or was it that the spiraling arms of the formation of galaxies and planets and all those endless stars seemed to her like the explosion of her own rogue cells, the new dark universe within her bones? Osteoporosis, that's what they had told her, and she smiled when she thought it was so like Nate to play along with that, chivalry was not dead as long as there was Nate Kovacs. If only by some miracle he was right, that osteoporosis could explain it, a year after the mastectomy, the experimental adrenalectomy—she could think about the pattern of her expanding and disintegrating universe as if she could change it, almost as if she could reason with it, talk with it, but it was as unreachably deep within her as her babies had once been, and it would do what it would do.

A light year. The distance light travels in a year—how could you see past the barest sliver of such a night? Becky was glad she'd seen the International exhibits. Neither her family nor her husband had ever made the kind of money that could pay for world travel. Those two lovely women from India … if there was one thing she wanted Artie and Karen to remember from this, from her … lying next to Nate, the fear churning once again in her excavated body at four in the morning … she had known her life had not just been about the marriage and the family, but also these widening circles.

She inhaled the cinnamon shampoo scent of her daughter. Artie would have to be told. But sweet little Karen—did Nate really understand what it might mean for her future that there was no way to warn her?

Artie and Nate talked about the Yankees and the Mets. The subway accelerated. Becky suddenly wanted to pull in the receding Fair to her brain, she could almost feel the pupils of her eyeballs expand as she held Karen's waist and took Artie's hand and gathered the last aura of the pavilions' luminescence—she wanted them to see it all together for hours and hours, forever, but then came the motion of the cars and families all around her shouting and laughing and blocking the windows. A subway full of life, taking Rebecca Gail Kovacs into the darkness.

Chapter 2

THE MUSIC OF THE SPHERES

It had seemed especially impossible that November in the wake of the whole country's shock and sadness. The optometrist's store, the Italian deli, Tony the barber's shop all closing, the red-white-and-blue spiral of the barber pole frozen in midafternoon; the knots of children at Karen's school wandering across bare hopscotch courts that glittered with mica, let out in uncoordinated groups on an unexpected holiday into blinding silence; the glaring black-and-white bands of the flag on the slain President's cortege vibrating like the static of a frozen standby image that erased all normal reception, until the bright edges of the picture tube shrank your vision. In the bedroom you could hear all five television stations murmuring together past the courtyard window, as day and night, for the first time Nate could remember, the entire television dial circled the pit of the tragedy.

And then, just a few months after the mastectomy and the remission, Becky had complained of the deep ache in her bones....

It's probably just from being cooped up in a chair for a week like the rest of the country. But we'll just run some tests....

Now cabbies fighting through their normal day snarled at haulers in double-parked vans and at the Big Burns Oil truck just trying to do its job. The hearses absorbed the profane clamor as they inched toward the FDR Drive. The city was relentlessly routine, except for the two hundred people who had been at the service to say goodbye to Becky. Their consolations fell away like ashes amid the havoc in the street.

Couples' bridge games. Family picnics. Parents' Day at Camp

Saco. Two hundred kind faces reflected in the mirror of a future suddenly so senseless.…

The procession was at last swallowed up by the gullet of the FDR Drive and the snaking Triboro Bridge muscle of transit across the East River. Nate looked out at the shingled water and factories, the massive hospitals of Welfare Island, all the dark unknown monuments of power and industry that sat on the edge of their Upper East Side life. Born and raised in a house in Pelham with a garden and a backyard, he'd wanted to live in a leafy Long Island suburb, Mineola or Cold Spring Harbor, but Becky had persuaded him to move to Manhattan. To Yorkville, "Germantown," where the Bund had held its fascist rallies. They'd rented a two-bedroom around the corner from the rattling trestles of the Third Avenue El, in the midst of street violinists working the brownstones, horse-drawn ice carts, and the vague menace of the Jager House five blocks down, nucleus of all the orange-shadowed bars where workers from the milk-bottling plant and the subways and the Ruppert Brewery glowered at pedestrians from their Mitteleuropan lairs.

Nate had been repelled by the city in those years. He couldn't understand what in the world Becky had in mind until the children grew old enough to go to Central Park. They could stroll to the Metropolitan Museum with its esplanade of a driveway and magnificent wrought iron lampposts, and the Space Age Guggenheim Museum built just down the block. The "Silk Stocking District," Eleanor Roosevelt waving for a cab, the best public school in the City—all was theirs for the price of a bit of shtetl effrontery. Becky had seen how they all could grow.

Nate heard Artie asking questions about what would take place at the funeral, his painstaking, photographic curiosity alive even in the midst of his grief. Aunt Esther replied that their mother would always be with them. Remember that.

Nate fixed his eyes on the hearse ahead.

At the cemetery, holding his children's hands, Nate relinquished his emotions to the necessary chill of ritual, the words and prayers above the open grave. The trees were bare except for one golden branch that had hung on during the last storm, toward which the fallen leaves scurried, a coil knitted by the wind. As the coffin was lowered into the ground, the knot of mourners drew closer; beside Nate were Becky's sister Esther, as tough and dowdy as Becky had been supple and slim, and her pushy but now utterly quiet husband Harold, their little girls Amy and Sue, and Grandmother Miriam, severe as always, funerals and birthdays alike, in her long black coat. Nate's mother Corinne couldn't attend; her cumbersome wheelchair could barely fit in an elevator, let alone a hearse. So Nate, an only child, represented his family alone.

No of course he wasn't alone. He was holding Artie and Karen's hands. But when the shovel laid the earth down blow by blow, Nate was catapulted back into his solitary nightmare.

"Goodbye my darling!"

The words tore out from him like the terror *when Becky had gasped and clutched his hand, and then it was over and her fingers were cold as her wedding ring.*

The pale edge of the overcast sky pierced through his tears. He composed himself and touched his worried children's shoulders. Esther nodded to Artie, who tossed a tulip into the grave. Karen gave her flower a kiss before letting it drop in the dirt. She had never turned away from the coffin.

There was no ritual for the family's return trip to Manhattan, unless it was the motion of Nate's hands turning the edges of his homburg over and over until Esther warned him he might crease it. Soon would come deli food, pickled herring and kasha varnishkes, the upwelling of conversation and advice, and the eyes of the family on him wondering if Nate had what it took, with his heart murmur, myopia, two children to raise....

She's at peace now. Remember that. Remember her pain. Remember the spasms until the nerves of her spine went dead, the coruscating pain so deep it seemed death was a violator beneath the sheets....

Harsh metallic pops all around him. The sound of tiny bones cracking. What was it? Oh God don't start to crack up in the car...

He saw Karen's hand was on the button pad. She was playing with the hearse's mechanical locks.

"Sir, better tell your daughter not to — "

"HOW CAN YOU DO THAT AFTER YOUR MOTHER'S FUNERAL?"

Karen shrank from Nate. The tears were harsh, immediate.

"You mustn't play with the locks, honey. The doors could open and that wouldn't be very good, would it?"

Aunt Esther held his bitterly crying daughter and shot Nate an admonitory glance.

Nate sat back and turned away to the window. Blood beat in his head, tracing the pressure of Artie's stare upon him… mimicking the roar of the subway… he'd been taking Artie to meet Becky for lunch at his mother-in-law's apartment, everyone trying to muster normality, the old routine, in the face of the doctors' verdict, and the train was late. He'd wandered off to peer down the track and had been distracted by a magazine dropped on a bench, an ad for Schenley Whiskey. A model with a figure like Julie London. The glossy moue of that siren's lips was a spell, a refuge—and then he heard a boy crying.

Artie by the tracks, not knowing where his father was.

The silence was full of Karen's silence—and then her furtive singing.

"Horseman pass by… don't stop for my daughter… horseman pass by… Horseman pass by…"

She reached for the words like talismans just beyond her grasp and then let them drift away. Now Karen's silence was shared by all of them. Nate saw Artie's shoulder blades hunching, his lips pursed, and he knew his boy had a secret.

"Artie, where did you two learn that song?"

At the memorial sitting Grandma Miriam had laid a hand on Karen's shoulder and said: darling, you've lost your mother. But now she'd found her again. Not in the statue that lay in the grey coffin and didn't get up, shrouded in the blue dress Daddy chose for her and a veil of dotted lace. She'd let go of Daddy's hand, walked to a corner of the room, and found her again behind the lights of her closed eyes. There she was waist-deep in a Berkshires lake, in the park by the reservoir when the ducks appeared, hanging Christmas cards on long red strings around the living room. Not just memories. A secret, watchful communication that she hadn't realized at the time, between the remembered eyes and her beating heart. And she could make the images run thicker and faster if she ran herself. Just like Winkle did when he caromed across the wood floors and skidded around the hallway corner in a frenzy but didn't seem to be chasing anything. Mom would raise her eyebrows and say—kitty's chasing elves. So Karen chased the great absence in her heart as she ran down the hall of the funeral parlor past the varnished oak table with its urn of lilies and upstairs to the second floor where the others couldn't intrude on the life that still danced in her memory.

The crowd froze her. They were all Negro, with dark suits and glasses like the people she'd seen in a swarm on the tv one night. But here that somber mass wasn't just black and grey but a whole spectrum, a blend of beige and mahogany and coffee. In their midst was an enormous woman in a sky-blue gown, a chevron-shaped band of saw-toothed necklaces around her neck, the jewelry of an Egyptian queen. Her black hair had waves like Mom's, but a pair of ivory earrings gleamed against her skin. She gazed at Karen with tender curiosity.

"Are you lost, dear?"

"No. My mother is."

Artie had gone from annoyance to, as best as he could suppress it, crawling fear. Dad had asked him to play with Karen outside, just to be the focus of her jumpiness. So she'd started her ludicrous hide-and-seek, and now... could Karen really just *vanish*? He'd read about stuff like that happening, but not at funeral parlors. It's nothing. She was just playing, and I have to chase her, because dad was busy with the family, and *because I killed Mom for her. I had to tell her about Mom because Dad was at the bedside distraught and I heard the sobs and saw through the crack in the door Mom's face go grey like leaves under the ice, and then I had to see Karen's eyes and lips go cold too, with a whisper of "no … no …" and now I have to find her … be "the man of the house…"* look behind the pillars, in the curtained rooms with the stacked chairs …

He ran into a group that reminded him of a civil rights gathering. Karen had told them about him.

They had laid out the elderly Negro man in a blue workshirt and faded slacks and placed a harmonica beside him. Hiram Bonds, someone said. Artie gazed at Hiram Bonds as he clasped Karen's hand, pulled her close, and felt her calm down beside him. He stood between his sister and a kid about two years older and a few inches taller than he, even skinnier than Artie, with a full bell-shaped head of hair and a hawk nose in odd contrast to his softly lashed, gently probing eyes. Artie's first impression of Danny Geller was later echoed by Karen. He looked like a Beatle.

His father Bruce Geller, who seemed somehow tough and gentle at the same time, standing stiffly in a chalk-striped grey suit, had a glint of amusement in his eyes that even the most solemn occasion couldn't dim. Do you know who Hiram Bonds is? Hiram Bonds, Mr. Geller explained, had been writing and singing folk and blues since the 1930s. Many of his songs have been recorded by famous singers. Artie looked down at Bonds and asked which ones.

"Ever heard of 'Horseman Pass By'?"

As Artie drew a blank, Danny stepped forward. His eyes pierced into Artie's. He had a reedy voice riding on a whisper, which suited the song.

"Horseman pass by, don't stop at my chapel.
Horseman pass by.
Horseman pass by, don't stop for my daughter.
Horseman pass by.
Don't burn your cross under my good Lord's sky.
Horseman pass by."

He sang it softly enough not to intrude but with a subtle

audacity, making the space in front of Hiram Bonds and his coffin a stage. Artie glanced around to see if anyone disapproved, but instead he saw nods and smiles. He became aware that all around were little groups of men and women of both races humming tunes to each other.

Singing remembrance.

Past Dad's face the cables of the Triboro Bridge struck their rhythm of returning home. Dad held Karen's hand and explained that Hiram Bonds had been for many years a part of the battle of the Negro down south to be free of hate and prejudice and win equal rights. Negroes still couldn't vote, couldn't even share a restaurant with white people, and Hiram Bonds had made his music a part of the struggle to stop that injustice. Dad made it clear that they'd both seen something amazing, a glimpse of a country previously known only through images of Negroes bundled into paddy wagons, their "I AM A MAN" signs stomped into the streets by police to the staccato voices of the six o'clock news.

Artie loved to hear Dad comfort through explanation, his voice with a low reassurance easing them into their first comprehension of a world that somehow had leaped to a connection with another land, another race, another kind of music, but had left their mother behind. He found himself holding Karen's hand again, as if that could amplify the warmth of that teaching. Still Dad was so focused on Karen that Artie felt he was eavesdropping on a conversation that he himself had begun.

Karen nodded as if she were agreeing with Dad more than really listening to him. It struck Artie that Dad was trying, with the kindness in his voice, to apologize to her, and Karen didn't understand that at all.

Bright clouds billowed above Times Square, while Thunderbirds, Ford Futuras, and an occasional Rolls Royce joined an automotive regatta below. The women moved faster than the cars. Beneath the swing of wool coats, cashmere sweaters tugged at high bosoms, scarves whipped in the wind. Their bouffants and marcelled waves of hair shone in the wintry morning sun.

Bruce Geller loved his writing days. He'd leave the record store in the care of his assistant, usually an hour or two early, stroll Broadway, ogle the tail, then pop into Lindy's for some cheesecake, or Al and Dick's to shoot the breeze with the hustlers, gamblers, and pimps of the music industry. He'd started the writing sideline during a flat year at the record store and had found a niche. Under the pen name Bruce Sidney, after the great clarinetist Sidney Bechet who'd inspired Bruce to try his luck with the licorice stick many years ago, he'd written articles for *Downbeat* and program notes for concerts at Town Hall.

But the album liner notes were his favorite assignments. His latest back-of-the-vinyl gig had been for Cornelius Hill, an old bebopper hanging on in the midst of changes in jazz fashion and a serious heroin problem. So he appreciated the change of pace awaiting him now: an interview at the Brill Building with teen-hit producer Shadow Morton, part of Bruce's continuing experiment in whether a middle-aged writer could hold down a slot at *Hit Parader*. The subject was the Shangri-Las, three tough but tasty outerborough chicks who sang tunes of teenage love perishing in a burst of sound effects; "Walking In The Sand" had almost drowned in seagulls and waves. If it wasn't jazz, it was a living. And to make his descent into the charms of pubescent serenades more enjoyable, he'd taken Danny along for a special treat.

Bruce waved to the shoeshine guy in the porkpie hat that he knew and steered Danny into the building. Now it was working the room time in earnest. The Brill Building lobby's copper glow, its Art Deco architectural derring-do, like the tang of Scotch, chased away the heaviness of winter. A goddess of music caught in the wrought brass elevator door spread her arms to welcome him and his son. He could tell Danny was digging the Brill as much as he did.

Golden women and the backbeat of success. You could check out publishers on one floor, arrangers on another—in one series of elevator rides a musician could whip up a leadsheet, corral some hangers-on, go to the studio for a demo, and after clapping all that together, tour the building for record companies, artists' managers…. The Brill was a beehive of Top 20 music, and the finest honey was spun by a bunch of young, mostly Jewish composers, soulful, classy, and sweet, laced with accents of cha-cha and mambo and rhythm and blues in songs like "Be My Baby" and "Up On The Roof." Beneath them the older worker bees scribbled standards and pounded them out on aging pianos and wailed about the folkies. Bastards are killing Tin Pan Alley….

They knew what they were talking about: young guys with Brill smarts and folk in their veins were turning to pop. Jim McGuinn, told by Bobby Darin he should dig the new rock-and-rollers, was listening hard to the Beatles and Dylan. Danny, just fifteen, was making the turn from folk to something more electric. He'd already been the hit of summer campfire nights, and had kept up his hootenanny skills by playing for birthday parties around the neighborhood. For a year Bruce had heard spilling from Danny's room the choruses of Celtic minstrelsy, "fare thee wells" and "gone many a miles" and Woody Guthrie dustbowl ballads. Then had come "Blowin' In The Wind" and "Puff The Magic Dragon," which Danny could turn into angelic guitar singalongs for preteens who had no idea what the lyrics really meant. In his room by himself Danny relished the snarl of indignation of Bob Dylan's "Masters of War" and "With God On Our Side."

But last month Danny had heard the Animals' rock-and-roll version of "House of The Rising Sun" on the Sullivan show, and wanted a Gibson guitar and a Marshall amp.

In the dim hallway Bobby Haymes kidded Bruce about his clothes—he was wearing his plaid topcoat over a black velour with a tam 'o shanter—and Bruce struck back by asking him about his latest hit.

"I dunno. Hey Danny, kid, want to write me a hit? Share credit, swear to God."

Bruce laughed and clapped Danny's shoulder, amazed at

how his gangly beanpole of a son was already almost his height. A short, beefy bantamweight had mated with a petite PhD and produced a six-footer in the making.

Bruce took Danny to a cozy little studio smelling of old radiator pipes. From down the hall came the bang of kettledrums and tambourines: Phil Spector's sidemen buttressing another tune with his "Wall of Sound." Danny silently studied the empty control room shielded with glass, and paced between the soundproofed walls, checking out a set of drums, a Fender bass, and an ornate little box of a keyboard instrument. He struck some chords and a ripple of tiny sparkling bells washed through the space. The celeste fascinated him until an engineer strode into the room.

He didn't stand on ceremony as he handed Danny the old Gibson. Bruce told his startled son it was an early Christmas present. Danny hugged his dad warmly and then strapped on the guitar, sank to one knee, and plugged it into an amp. Gratitude done with, he was briskly on his private stage. He ran some scales, chopped at a couple of barre chords, tremoloed the E string and fired off a flurry of minor blues runs. Where had the kid learned to bend notes like that? Race music his dad had called it, Presley he'd called it … his son called it his own. As he toyed with the flatted chords a pall of sagacious world-weariness seemed to cross over Danny's face.

But after Bruce concluded his interview, introduced Danny to Shadow Morton, and walked back out of the Brill with him, Danny was carrying his guitar like it was just another school briefcase, goofily kicking at the pockmarked ridges of lurking curbside snow. He was his only boy again, for whom Bruce would do anything. With great pleasure he asked his boy what he'd been doing in school lately, and with even greater pleasure got the response that just yesterday Danny had won the part he wanted in the drama group's production of *Pirates of Penzance*. Danny held his guitar and cocked his free arm on his hip.

"I am the Pirate King!"

White knuckle flight. Bring it in right on the old bazoo. That's what Gordon Cooper had said, jauntiest of the astronauts, preflight thermometer riding high between his lips like a cigarette. Be like Gordo, Nate thought. Fire the retro-rockets and steer this day in manually when the autopilot fails.

Don't burn.

At Schomer, Fries and Associates they'd welcomed Nate back with open arms and easy duty. The bread-and-butter cases of white shoe defense law. Plead-outs and settlements. An embezzler ousted in a management consultant report. Gonifs, schnorrers, bad debtors.

Nate polished off the settlement papers so quickly he had moments during the day when he could relax among the oasis of mahogany desks and polished wood bookcases—and that's when the day shook him. Spasms, groans, plunges back into the mill of death. And the stigma of cancer and its aftermath was such that there was no way he could even talk to his colleagues about what he was going through.

All he could do was be careful. He shaved delicately with his badger-bristled brush and stainless steel razor, especially since Artie, feeling the first prickly growth of hair himself, was watching him. Any cut received a full minute's application with the styptic pencil. Sometimes he felt the whole morning was stanched blood.

His hand was unsteady. His insomniac boy crept into his bed almost every night. His daughter was a closed door.

But never go to the office disheveled. Put on your best tab collar shirt, Brooks Brothers suit, argyle socks, and Florsheims. For Nate knew that behind his boss Ted Schomer's solicitousness was a discreet evaluation of how Nate might or might not measure up. How he might no longer be tip-top, up to snuff, back in the saddle buckaroo. Becky and he had once gone to a costume party in cowboy-cowgirl outfits and their friends had half-kiddingly told Nate he could pass for Henry Fonda. From then on it was big buckaroo and little buckaroo, father and son.

Big buckaroo had a herd of doctor bills to confront, and so

he'd be trying to shoot them down not over a burger special and triple-layer German chocolate cake at Schrafft's, but a sandwich at Horn & Hardart's. He walked through gusts of sleet that threatened to leave a glaze of black ice on the pavement. At the Automat he got his change from the nickel-thrower matron behind the booth, pulled a chicken salad sandwich and apple turnover from the glass cases, and poured himself some fresh brewed coffee. The clean brushed-chrome surfaces encouraged him to eat quickly, as did the bustle of subway token collectors, maids, secretaries, and inevitably a man who fit no occupation, slouched at an empty lacquered table, his eyes a barely avoided snare.

Nate tried to tackle the bills, form some strategy that could navigate the thicket of medical surnames. Drs. Gabriel, Winograd, Wisham. Dr. Pascal was willing to postpone, Dr. Kim was preparing to sue. His friend Avery Lansing called him Dr. No. "How's fucking Dr. No?" Nate could see Artie's high school tuition in the balance. *Mastectomy, adrenalectomy*—a war fought for his wife's body beneath the flag of endless surgery, and he'd been sidelined in those terrible battles, unable to offer anything but solace and administrative help.

All the pills Becky took … he'd made light of it by bringing them to her bed with water and, once a week, a little flower in a carafe or a Whitman chocolate sampler. He knew the day the chocolates revolted her that the pills had become useless.

Treatment for decubitus. A word that mixed sleep and shadow and clinical precision to conjure up a furious brown sore on Becky's hips.

Easy, buckaroo.

He was so exhausted. Maybe he should have his prescription revised. But the Librium already soured his mouth and refitted his sleep cycle like a clumsy tailor. Or was it just the hideaway bed he slept on in the foyer that kept waking him up? What would putting a new bed in their old room cost? The bedroom's square of blank floor shocked him every morning he saw it, but he'd wanted to rid his home of the hospital bed that very week.

For a day Winkle had chased lint balls and iridescent dust motes through the space. He'd almost gotten rid of the cat too but the little smoky presence with the white paws had stolen Karen's heart. At eleven years old she was faithfully feeding it, cleaning its litter box, embracing the responsibility.

Nate lit up a Chesterfield. The Surgeon General was warning of a link between cigarettes and cancer. He felt a flush of exquisitely satisfying anger. To hell with your warning. Too late now for her, and as for me ... the sandwiches had already been invisibly replaced in their partitions, the man of no category was glancing Nate's way....

He rushed back into the street. Even in the face of a stinging wind he walked to 82nd Street and past P.S.6, the red brick fortress of a school that had launched Artie to Vandemeer High on a scholarship. Now behind those same window gratings was Karen. He wanted a glimpse of her, perhaps in the recess yard, but of course the rain would deny that. What he really wanted was to hover by her all day long and protect her from the memories....

Behind him was the Franklin Campbell Funeral Home. Here was a mystery that might be easy to solve, a courtesy no problem to perform, to relieve the pressure menacing his day. Nate asked to see the guestbook for the Hiram Bonds funeral. Not that he'd ever listened to Hiram Bonds—for Nate it was music more to be honored than enjoyed—but his children had been here, had been treated kindly, and then, of all things, taught a song.

He turned the pages of the guestbook until he found a Danny there, and two others with the same last name.

That night Bruce and Shari Geller stoked their apartment's pride and joy, its genuine fireplace, and relished together their son's latest progress in acting and music. When Bruce had taken Danny two weeks before to the free hootenanny at the Gaslight and Bob Dylan had walked in the door in a sailor's jacket and railroad cap, legs like pipettes in baggy corduroy pants, trailing amazement behind him, and then, with that foggy but needling voice, had launched into the waltzing cadences of "To Ramona,"

Danny hadn't just listened, he'd picked up the knee twitch, the lift of the brow trying to pluck some landmark off the horizon, every intonation of the strum, all the ways the former Bobby Zimmerman knitted together his coat of many colors. But not the singing style with its inflection of a backwoods holler. When Danny sang Dylan, it was in a New York voice with a seductive whisper, or a crisp sardonic bite that he could also bring to the patter of Gilbert and Sullivan. That was individuality.

Shari had a very individual predilection for making whisky sours, and while she exercised her cocktail skills in the kitchen, Bruce spun "Kind of Blue." He regretted that, as a critic, he'd never gotten the call to write up Miles. This was the exploration of the beautiful shore, right from Paul Chambers and Bill Evans' bass and piano charting the course with just two chords. This was discovering the musical Orient. Yet it was also the last flower of Miles before restlessness struck, Miles for falling in love, romance as a dish best served cool—and it swung with silken blues and sighs of flamenco in modal nautilus spirals, Miles somehow turning a trumpet peal into a whisper of longing and Trane with his spins and Cannonball with his trills building new layers of shining pearl on each volute of the songs. He'd played the record so often that it was covered by tiny scratches, but he was used to them. They were the felt on which the ball of the music glided.

He and his wife were soon pleasantly crocked. They caressed each other's aging zones, the flab on Bruce's belly the Vic Tanny exercises couldn't quite nick, the budding wrinkles under her eyes. She was still so thin, still could wear a maroon pullover and that dead straight new Sassoon cut like a twenty-two-year-old beatnik. Bruce felt it was time to take his shrewd, sarcastic, loving art teacher wife on the rug postgraduate style.

The phone rang and, cursing, he got up to answer it. He heard the deep, pleasant, but haunted voice of a fellow father of a Vandemeer High student, thanking him for showing such kindness to his children at the funeral.

Bruce assured him they hadn't been any trouble. He expressed his condolences. Nate Kovacs' voice had such a

masculine tenderness, a father trying to do what's right by—
Christ—an eleven-year-old girl and thirteen-year-old boy left
without a mother.
Nate expressed an interest in "Horseman Pass By." Bruce
offered to show him around the record store, pull down the
Schwann catalog and tell him a little about Hiram Bonds. He
looked over at Shari drawing her knees up by the fire. Her shadow
in the firelight played hide-and-seek with the glass surfaces of
the Dufy print on the wall and its Parisian racetrack scene. He
thought of how Shari was going to a seminar on Saturday, and
so her ticket to Miles Davis at Smokes would go unused…. *He
thought of her going away and never coming back….*
"So you like jazz, Nate?"

School and errands. A careful routine. An experimental
silence to every gesture between him and Dad as they tried to fill
the void with new rituals. Artie went to Liggets or Optima Cigars
to fetch packs of Chesterfields for Dad, or to the sawdust-laden
Atlantic Meat Market with its cuts and haunches suspended
on hooks to buy London broil for Sarah the new housemaid to
cook.
Between the errands and the return to a silence where Dad
was absorbed with his tasks and Karen was hidden away, and
sometimes the only sign of life was the mewing of a cat, there were
walks. His breaks from being the son he should be, responsible
and easily understood.
On 86th Street, he could cheer up at the lobbies of the RKO
Theater, where a column of lunettes posted on the mirrored wall
announced features and double bills to come, or even better,
the Loews Orpheum, which went more for panoramic displays
announcing movie spectacles like *The Colossus of Rhodes*
starring Rory Calhoun. Mom and Dad had strictly monitored
Artie's movies according to the reviews of Bosley Crowther of the
New York Times. As a result *The Guns of Navarone* had been
declared too violent for him to see and *Rhodes* had been branded
crap. Loews now proudly announced the coming of *Lawrence of*

Arabia, and Artie bristled with anticipation—no doubt he would be allowed to see a Best Picture of the Year.

But there were flares on the images from his walks. Double exposures. The walks would sometimes come out like negatives you extracted from the developer in the Camp Saco darkroom and you knew they'd be wrong. Maybe you could burn in one during the printing to darken shadows, or dodge another to brighten details, but some were just hopelessly blurred. Across the street from Loews the cozy little Grande where he'd seen his favorite movie, *West Side Story*, was being torn down. Next to it the displays of the Brandts Theater featured inky caricatures of mischievous Frenchmen named Bourvil or Fernandel chasing women whose dancer's legs seemed to sail in the wind, or black bars through which a haunted skull of a face peered in some Swedish adult horror movie. Artie couldn't take his eyes off the pictures; he sensed that behind them, for the price of a ticket, were discoveries that would further blur and erase all he knew.

He headed for 90th Street and 5th Avenue and shivered beneath the iron gates of the mansion of one of Manhattan's greatest millionaires, staring up the horsechestnut tree at icy drifts that had replaced the clusters of white flowers. Squirrels ran in the branches linked by traceries of falling snow.

Mom had taken him inside that garden. Or maybe not. He thought he had a memory, but he wasn't sure.

She had saved piles of *Life* Magazines for him. Those memories kept. They were arrayed in the far corner of his and Karen's room in a wooden open-framed cabinet. "Portrait of Our Planet," the earth sliced like an apple, its layers illumined by the discoveries of the International Geophysical Year. "The World We Live In." "The Wonders of Life On Earth." Huge turtles and brilliant flowers captured in their emerald lairs. "The Epic of Man." "The World's Great Religions." The Justice League of America. Every week when the issue of *Life* came Artie would also buy a comic book, and throw himself into organizing and reorganizing both sheafs of periodicals on the same day.

From the wonders of life on earth Artie turned to the alchemy of nuclear radiation, and its handmaiden, chemical accidents, which invested ordinary men, or even creatures from the sea, with extraordinary powers—and costumes to match. Green Lantern's bright red counterpart, the Flash, currently battling the Weather Wizard. Red-white-and-blue Atom, lordly Batman, and the old standbys, bland but inevitable, Superman and Wonder Woman. Would they and Green Arrow and Aquaman and Jonn Jonzz, Manhunter From Mars, and their pointless hot-rodder mascot Snapper Carr soon team up with Hawkman, a Thanagarian crimefighter disguised as museum curator Carter Hall, fighting crimes of the present with weapons of the past and future?

Artie loved riffling through his collection of superheroes. All that richly classifiable abundance.

But the blur and ghostly flare had invaded his room too. Not the side with Karen's mice puppets and stuffed dogs, *Charlotte's Web* and *Winnie The Pooh*. The shroud was over Artie's model planes and games and battery-powered toys, his books that narrated the exploits of once-shy-and-unathletic Chip Hilton, who began lettering in three sports after he'd had "a change in personality." It would soon be time to throw most of the toys away, except for the ones he would tithe to Karen as a way to preserve them. There was only one toy he still liked to pull out with her: a dome-headed creature with reptilian mitts who moved forward like a favorite pet if you rolled a ball right beneath his center, but hit him too far to the side, and he rolled backwards, stuck out his plastic tongue and laughed.

"Odd Ogg, Odd Ogg
Half turtle and half frog
He's the greatest toy of all
Odd Ogg plays ball!"
He'd toss the toys—but he'd keep the comedy records and the issues of *Mad* Magazine. He remembered how they'd all cracked up at Allen Sherman's *My Son The Folk Singer*. In Mom's words, he'd "slain" them together. She'd let him see *Dr. Strangelove*, saving that movie from Crowther, arguing this "sicknik" comedy wasn't much different from Artie's *Mad* Magazine. Artie bit

his lip as his eyes started to burn again. She'd loved watching him play bombardment in the schoolyard and shout war cries made up from Mad. "Oookabollakonga! Hoo hah! Here comes Veeblefetzer you ratfink clod!" Kids would actually slow down to get what he was saying and that's when he'd hit them with the dodge ball. The jokes he'd laughed at with Mom were a smart city's festival and smart people's secret. Mom and Artie had been a Conspiracy of the Brainy.

What was worse even than her not being able to hug him was when she barely had the strength to talk to him. That's when she became stiffness curled over the bedsore, the smell of powder, the eyes turning elsewhere, and he began to put away the hope …

A low guttural yowl filled the foyer, Winkle's reaction to footfalls by the door. Artie quickly wiped his eyes dry as he heard the bang of the entrance door, the creaking open of the hall closet, Karen's hurried footfall and quick kiss hello. Dad chatted with Sarah about dinner, and then peeked in to ask how Artie's day had gone.

"I went for a walk."

"You know I talked to the father of that young man you spoke to at the funeral, Danny Geller? It turns out he was friends with Hiram Bonds' manager. You know Danny goes to Vandemeer?"

"Yeah, I know that. I was going to tell you."

"Danny's father told me he's going to be in *The Pirates of Penzance.* "

"Oh yeah, the big Dramat play."

"Maybe you two can be friends."

"He's older though. He's two grades ahead of me."

"Well … are you feeling okay?"

"Yeah, dad. I'm fine."

Dad told him he was going to a jazz concert with Danny's father so Aunt Esther would be here to babysit and he would come home late. Artie promised he would be *the man of the house.*

"Artie, does Karen go in the closet often?"

"I dunno. She likes to follow Winkle in there."

Dad hesitated in the doorway. Sometimes it seemed as if

the pain and stiffness in his sacroiliac that he complained about afflicted his very speech.

"Could you keep an eye on her, Artie?"

"Sure, Dad."

After Nate left, Artie sat in the room, listening to the sounds of his dad's receding footsteps. He started to have one of those headaches that made his heart beat faster, and he stared at the plastic eyes of King Zor, the broken toy he simply couldn't toss, a crouched plastic dinosaur who had once roared and fired back little yellow balls at him when he hit him with a dart, but who now was a relic that guarded his bookshelf of secret identities, changes of personality, exploding reagents and government experiments gone wildly out of control.

This is where she lived now. If the closet was tightly closed this was where the red wool coat where Karen had hid her face in the sleetstorm still exhaled her Chanel.

A slit in the doorjamb was all she and Winkle needed to see by. His green eyes seemed a mile deep somewhere within. They magnified the glint from the door into pools of light that darted through the closet. Outside he was a grey wriggle of curiosity and frolic, but secretly he was a guide that saved light and vision and the scent of Mom's hand cream two days after they put her in the ground.

It's good to have glasses, Mom had assured her. They're cat's-eye glasses.

Karen reached into the crannies of Winkle's path as he caromed through the closet, and she followed the echoes of his flight. She turned up pictures of the founding of the U.N. Postcards from Miami. Love letters from Dad. Golf clubs. She let him burrow deep into the closet, reached for him to pet him, and the shadows purred.

Together we see in the dark.

Café Wha. Hip Bagel. Poindexter. Café Figaro. Names that could've popped up in that magazine Artie loved and Becky had taken a shine to, Mad or Cracked or whatever it was, crazy names that reminded him of the military in *Dr. Strangelove*. Down a stoop, past a sign halated in candlewax yellow, a guy in a peacoat gesticulated and roared in rhyme beneath a spotlight. His name could have been Bat Guano. In Nate's neighborhood night was divided by apartment house canopies, but here the route was transected by rose and umber and tallow auras that marked off sudden corners where the streetlights didn't poke far enough into the beds of shadow. He had never seen such constant coming and going, defying traffic lights and the expected silence of public squares at night. The crowd thinned out, then gathered before a shop window full of sandals and mandolins and guitar picks where a couple strummed and chorused on "Michael Row the Boat Ashore." A guitar and frantic harmonica squalled from another café. Wondering how he'd ever spot the jazz club, Nate kept moving, as if driving fast by headlight beams, into the careening carnival.

Not everyone was pleased at the proud hamlet of deviants. A day laborer in an ill-fitting raincoat charged out of a checked tablecloth trattoria and glared at three scraggly-haired young men hunched by a streetlight, two cigarettes and one conga drum between them. Territorial yeastiness at every corner, a tribe at every block, the derelict with his rotgut in a bag jostling the young man who hustled out of the liquor store with a bottle of Strega. Nate hugged his Burberry tighter to his chest, not because he felt cold on a forty-degree evening, but to hide the Brooks Brothers suit that seemed so out of place.

He practically ran off the street when he spotted Smokes at the next intersection. The cigar store converted into a jazz club occupied a sliver of the corner. The long mirrored bar was right behind the door where the tobacconist had once been, and the hallway led back to the tables and a blue-light bandstand, whose wall of jazz posters was gessoed yellow by the fumes of a thousand cocktail candles. When Nate gave Bruce's name the hostess grinned and pointed him out standing at the bar with a glass of Schenley Reserve and soda. His wry smile, acknowledging Nate's wariness in his new surroundings, made him feel more at home.

They shook hands, and Nate thanked him for the ticket.

"It's on the club. Music writing has its privileges. Welcome to the Village, Nate."

"Place lives up to its reputation. I feel like I'm from another planet."

"Nope. Just Yorkville."

Nate ordered a gin and tonic, and let his eyes roam the first jazz club he'd visited since Becky had told him she didn't like jazz clubs. He briefly met the bored glances of two kids in shabby cardigans wearing sunglasses indoors—they dressed like extras in a French film a friend had once coaxed him to see. A young woman accepted a light from one of them. She looked Swedish with her vaguely Oriental eyes and straight lustrous blonde hair. Her calves crossed beneath a tweed skirt, and her black silk hose was embellished with clock needlework. The puff from her cigarette joined the haloed clouds beneath the cage of spotlights.

"This is quite a place."

"You okay with it? Because we could try a bar at a steakhouse."

"No, don't trouble yourself. It's good to be out with a bunch of jazz fans. Good to be out, period."

Nate stopped himself. He hadn't meant for even that much of his feelings to slip through.

"Still, I bet you don't get very far here requesting a Sinatra tune."

"You'd be surprised. Cornelius Hill, the opening act—he totally digs Frank. Even the beatniks know you can't beat the Chairman on a ballad."

Bruce jovially ordered Nate another gin and tonic and tried to satisfy his curiosity about the new scene, although he could only drop tantalizing hints. There was so much happening now, so many crosscurrents. Folk music plugging in and playing electric blues. The son of a local composer strumming on an autoharp and leading a slap-happy modern jug band called the Lovin' Spoonful. Down at the Five Spot, Mingus thumped his jagged, defiant Caribbean Afro-swing while at the Village Vanguard Thelonious Monk took Ellington's bell-like left hand piano chords into territory so fierce and yet jubilant that his ring tore chunks from the piano sideboard.

After awhile Bruce could tell Nate wasn't getting it, just politely paying attention, and of course he had more important matters on his mind. But he could also read that Nate wasn't exactly immune to swing. He played some piano, knew Bix Beiderbecke's "In A Mist," and had fond memories of Eddie Condon's mammoth jazz orchestra jams at Town Hall. And Bruce liked Nate's modesty and decency, which carried through to his politics. It was perfect pitch that he was a staunch anti-Goldwater, pro-Rockefeller Republican doing volunteer work for John Lindsay, liberal Republican Congressman par excellence, a six-foot-four Yale grad who incarnated every one of those glittered-when-they-walked WASPS that busted bigots or negotiated treaties.

The conversation briefly stopped and Nate and Bruce were diverted by two women at a nearby table riding high on their Tom Collinses.

"Peter O'Toole said in *Vogue* he prepared for the role by sleeping with Bedouins."

"Lucky Bedouins."

They giggled hysterically, their necklaces slapping the rim of their glasses.

"Those women have one thing on their minds."

"Yeah. The right thing."

The men laughed quietly together until Nate's eyes dropped to his glass again.

"Thanks again, Bruce, for inviting me here. It's really … you know, my wife and I had been married since 1944? My eyes, a heart murmur … I was one of the few guys who wasn't overseas. I sometimes think that's the only reason I got to marry her."

"Hey, if she hadn't wanted to, if there was someone else, she would've waited. A lot of them did back then."

"But everyone's right—you have to go out. Be out and about again. Sometimes I wonder how much good I am at home with the kids. My contribution used to be check that Dr. Spock baby book then ask Becky for help."

"Yeah, know what you mean."

"Sorry, don't mean to be so much of a yakker—point is, you sit at home too much, worrying about the future—well, it starts to weigh on you, and you don't do miracles for them either. You could drive yourself nuts."

"Hey, at least you're in good company now. We're all nuts here."

Bruce cringed inwardly at how he'd said exactly the wrong thing, the kind of flip, sick humor bandied about by a community who swore by their psychiatrists, tossed off to a straight-arrow good egg who'd lost his beloved companion of almost twenty years. But Nate smiled as he drank the last of his gin, actually seeming to enjoy the remark. Still Bruce heard the tingling cymbals from the bandstand with relief.

Cornelius Hill eased onto the bandstand joking and palavering with his rhythm section. He wore baggy pants, loafers, and a herringbone jacket that was more like a tent, which he called his "Illinois Jac-quet" to the chuckles of the jazz fans. With a brisk little fanfare Cornelius swung into "Scrapple In The Apple." Bruce noted on his pad how Cornelius' set embraced standards like one of the anthems of bop, "How High The Moon," as well as a couple of Horace Silver tunes and Cornelius' own compositions. He was a Dex Gordon-style player, maybe a breath more behind the beat, etching his solos with held notes and pauses before letting any arpeggios fly. He switched to baritone sax for the ballad "Fur Lisa," the same horn he deployed to let loose a fusillade of honks on the giddily uptempo "Pittsburgher." At a time of jazz firebrands who lit up all the missing intervals, Cornelius Hill was content to swing hard and hone the changes.

Bruce, watching Nate, could tell he enjoyed Cornelius, and was pleased and relieved. He'd made a new friend and done his proverbial good deed for the day. And a guy who was such good company and tight with an up-and-coming politician might always be good for a connection or two.

After the set Cornelius worked the room and eventually

sidled over to the two men. Bruce told him Nate was from up past 82nd Street.

"Man, you from the lamb chop set? Well, for every music lover there's hope."

"Nate might have seen you, Cornelius. He got down to the Savoy once, he tells me."

"My gig with Fletch? They let you through the door in knee pants or something? Hope we didn't scare you to death."

"I was in my twenties, guys. I could take it."

"Man, then you is a young forties. Hang out with Brucie, though, he'll age you pretty quick! In a barrel, man! Uh-oh, time for the cat of the hour. Catch you later."

The trumpeter's quintet took the stage without warning and the bar's attention hurriedly caught up with them as Bruce took out his notepad. You could barely hear Miles' sepulchral croak of a voice as he chatted with the band, joked with Anthony Williams, the drummer, who looked too young to even be in the club, and punctuated each breathy aside with the popping of his heavy-lidded eyes and a stare that, even when good-humored, could cut like a switchblade.

They whipsawed into "E.S.P." and Bruce's reflections jammed right along with them…. Miles and Wayne Shorter's unison melody circled like a hungry hawk while Carter's bass loped, Herbie Hancock's piano stippled light and shadow in its path, and Williams' shivery high hat work snapped the quintet together. After the rhythm section locked up the beat, the cymbal's perturbations faded before crackling snares, and the sax and trumpet wove their solos in a space somewhere between ecstasy and scorn, a pickpocket racing down the starlit avenue with a calfskin wallet and five large in his hand. For their second tune they refused to ease up. They launched into "Agitation." Williams attacked the audience with a drum solo right at the start, then Miles and Shorter seemed to dither on their axes until Miles scurried away on the mute. Carter coyly refused to swing, then goaded by Hancock's chords, took off after him. The band accelerated, downshifted, sped up again. Bruce loved it, he could hear it, how Davis and his quintet wittily defied jazz conventions, foiling the expectation of tension and release with a top-speed dry martini meditation on the outer limits of the changes. Nate felt it was like a swarm of angry bees in his brain. A doctor had told him once that anxiety might be a function of the inner ear, a literal imbalance of perception. Maybe it was the aimless solos without any melody that had him breaking out in a cold sweat. Or the way Davis never smiled, and his burning stare, like the music, was an attack launched straight over the audience's heads. Some of the kids rocked in their seats, a woman grasped her slim arms and writhed, Bruce tapped his feet in the air to the beat—and Davis turned his back on them.

The man played to the wall. He turned his back to the audience.

Nate got up quickly, and made as polite an excuse as he could, mentioning the need to get back to Artie and Karen. Bruce seemed unsurprised by his reaction. Nate promised to make sure to see his son in *The Pirates of Penzance,* all the while staying pleasant and gracious; he'd learned over the past few weeks how to put on as suave and cordial an expression as possible in the moments before he found it difficult to breathe.

The cold ambushed him as he headed outside, turned the corner, and realized he'd forgotten where the subway was. A cab ride back would be way too costly. He saw a police car parked by the alley adjoining Smokes and decided ask the officers directions.

He found them in the alley. They were handcuffing a Negro in a crumpled fedora and a poplin raincoat. The Negro muttered something and they shoved him against the wall, and as he stumbled a splash of oil splattered the white coat. They dragged him toward Nate, and Nate recognized him at once.

"That can't be! I'm not holding, I haven't even copped today, man, you're ruining my new clean threads—"

Nate froze as Cornelius Hill stared desperately at him, even as the cop shoved the sax player into the front of the car, past the metal grating that blotted out his face. The second cop noticed Nate. He froze him with a look and came up to confront him.

The officer's football player's shoulders slouched and he sized up Nate like prey he could strike down without raising a sweat.

"What are you looking at, buddy?"

"Nothing."

"You know this man?"

"I—I'm from the club."

"You with the club?"

"No. I'm a lawyer."

From a chain of helplessly awkward responses Nate had stumbled onto a truly dangerous one, and he knew it. The cop's stare hardened. Nate felt his throat starting to close up and *he was a little kid with Buster Brown locks in a suburban garden, in the house his family bought in the Depression because when everything went bust they were teachers and lawyers and the family was still okay, and when WWII came his heart and bad eyes kept him off the troop ships and the battlefields, but now he was all alone with two hundred fifty pounds of beef with a baton and sidearm and that heart murmur was pounding. . . .*

The cop's partner clapped him on the shoulder.

"Loomis, he can't be this guy's lawyer. We can see him at night when he don't smile."

The cops laughed.

"Have a nice evening, Counselor."

Nate tipped his hat and walked away as fast he could. Only two blocks later did he remember he was lost. A stunted tree bowed down by icicles beneath a church steeple blocked the street sign from his view. Construction walls were pockmarked with scabby posters for a play that showed faces peering out of garbage cans.

A drunk was hectoring the news vendor from whom Nate got, almost as an aside, directions to Sheridan Square. He headed down a street lined with bars and heard some kind of dissonant Latin music. A leather-jacketed tough with a studded belt sauntered by him trailing a slim, grey-haired gentleman who took his elbow with mock noblesse oblige. The older man's houndstooth coat and fedora looked weirdly dandyish for a December night. The

THE MUSIC OF THE SPHERES | 43

muscle's surly gaze fell on Nate. Nate realized who they were and what they thought he was walking alone on the street at this hour. Nate veered away, found the widest thoroughfare he could, and then wondered: would Sixth Avenue even have a subway? Suddenly the street's illumination was down to a single silver light huddling beneath a giant brick fortress, whose cement cornices could have braced artillery.

"Hey, dearie."

The high-pitched voice, frail yet commanding, wasn't echoing from the street. It was coming from somewhere deep in the bowels of that building.

"Dee-rie."

Now it was playful, almost girlish. Mocking his fear. What was there to be afraid of? Nate involuntarily looked up, trying to match a face to the voice. It was then he saw the windows were barred, that he was looking up the wall of a prison.

"FUCK YOU!"

Nate hailed the first cab he could find.

When Artie woke up the next morning to make his cornflakes, bananas, and milk, and help with Karen's breakfast, he was startled by the sight of his dad slipping Oreos and Bartons' fruit sourballs into bags of wax paper. But he wasn't puzzled by it. Awakened suddenly late at night, he'd seen Dad in his coat stroking Karen's hair.

"I'm sorry. I didn't mean to wake you."

"You're cold."

"I've been out too long. Go back to sleep, darling."

Karen's nightlight cast a green firefly glow, like the reverse of a photo darkroom, on her four picture buttons of John, George, Paul, and Ringo. Having seen that Dad had noticed those buttons, and was now putting together the goodie bags Becky had once made up for them, he knew they were going to a movie, and he knew which one.

Artie hated teen movies, the *Beach Party* dum-daddle dum-daddle crap where the cry of "surf's up" sent the usual gang of idiots babbling into the streets—Artie had no concept of a natural phenomenon that could empty a suburb—after which they rode around in silly wood-paneled cars, smooched on blankets, and tried to outwit some "square daddy" out to spoil their fun. But this would be The Beatles, the joyously shotgunning piano of "Rock and Roll Music," that blend of guitar twang and bass throb and chugging drum so hard and on target it seemed like they tore a guitar string on "I Want To Hold Your Hand." *Bom-bom-bom-BAAYING!* When Artie had first heard a full Beatle record at Camp Saco, the music had such variety that they'd sounded like four groups, not four guys.

As Artie, Karen, and Nate arrived the refreshment stand of the Trans Lux theater was already thronged with herky-jerky teenage girls and mildly amused adults. Nate was only there for his kids, but still he felt the slight rush of anticipation that came with joining a phenomenon, and so as the lights dimmed before *A Hard Day's Night*, Nate shared the fans' curiosity, if not their ecstasy.

"You're not gonna be a screaming meemie too, are you Karen?"

"No, I want to hear the songs, Artie, I'm not stupid!"

"Kids, calm down."

After the movie started, Nate soon realized that between the girls' screams and the Liverpudlian accents he wasn't going to be able to make out much of it, but he was genuinely tickled by the onscreen antics. The Beatles were fairly pleasant-looking once you got used to that ridiculous hair. Shot almost like an old black-and-white newsreel, their movie hurtled along as the boys ran to the stage, ran to the studio, ran out into a park, always outrunning howling teenage banshees. It had goofy, silent movie kind of gags, and one haunting passage where Ringo briefly bid farewell to the band to pursue his own dreams; of course that little hitch was wrapped up by the final number, but as Ringo wandered a grim Thames river embankment trying to be his own man Nate looked over and saw Karen briefly shed tears at Ringo's loneliness.

Artie was transfixed by the tilt-a-whirl of music and photography. The handlers, reporters, and phoney hipsters trying to crash the nonstop party were left in the dust by the Beatles. The only energy that kept up was the camera. "We're out!" the boys cried, and the camera broke out with them. It flew beneath their feet on fire escapes, soared over them as they splayed themselves on a soccer field. It dashed along with them through the station and came up so tight on their faces on the final studio numbers that the movie became the biggest living room tv in town.

If only he could have a really great camera. ...

To Karen's credit, Artie thought, she giggled, she shouted, but never emitted endless screams. Instead she took the whole thing inside her. She ran from the theater yelling "we're out, we're out!" She clamped her hands by her hips, tilted her body stiffly, and jumped up and down like the Beatles on that soccer field, banging Artie on the hip until he banged her right back and Nate warned him to stop. But she laughed without a break and Artie enjoyed her hilarity.

Watching his kids, Nate suddenly felt there was an answering rhythm in the events of the day, even the whole awful year. Goldwater's right-wing rantings, Johnson's landslide. Three civil rights workers murdered, the Civil Rights Act moving through Congress. The North Vietnamese firing on an American ship, the measured response of American advisors. And for the awful pain of JFK's death, the balm of the Beatles. His daughter's exuberance delighted him. And to sustain that joy he realized that, despite everything, just as Becky had done and despite the gloom that this time of year would now bring him forever, he'd have to celebrate Christmas. As one of his friends had said, just tell yourself Christmas trees are Norse and give the kids a holiday.

The tree was tiny and decorated right after it was purchased. Winkle clambered happily through its branches, shaking down ornaments and batting the ones that didn't crack outright under the ottoman and the velvet easy chairs. Karen insisted on preserving as much of Becky's Christmas as possible, even hanging the cards they'd received on a red string over the old Spinet piano the way Becky had once festooned them high up on the wall. Sarah, the housekeeper, before leaving to be with her own family, had put together a turkey dinner to reheat that night.

Still, Artie thought, a half-sized Christmas tree, a few presents, in the glare of a frigid morning that crystallized streaks of dust on the unwashed windowpanes....

Winkle chattered and purred and watched the family threesome gather. Artie went for the gleaming red square package in the shape of a record album he thought was his, the gift he'd been hoping for.

"Give it to Karen, Artie."

Artie hadn't noticed the card was for his sister. Shocked, he handed the present to Karen. She tore it open, and the minute she saw the four mop tops on the cover she shouted with joy and ran over to kiss Dad. Winkle pounced on the wrapping with a glee that echoed Karen's.

Now Artie saw his present, a large heavy box in green. His heart pumped. Dad had heard him when he'd mentioned an article from *Popular Photography* about the new single-lens reflex cameras with the automatic light meters built in. As Artie ripped away the wrapping, he imagined new vistas of framing and composition, micro lens attachments, time exposures at night.

It was a Swinger. A black-and-white Polaroid Swinger.

"My friends tell me it's the latest thing, Artie."

"Thanks, Dad."

"I know you talked about the other camera, son. We'll get you that one day. Besides—this is instant snapshots!"

Artie assured him it was okay, and gave his dad a hug to ratify his gratitude. He didn't want to read the instructions or even try the thing; he'd seen the kind of pictures the camera took and he didn't look forward to creating more of them. What he really wanted to do was play the Beatles. He grabbed the record off the floor and headed for the stereo console.

"That's my record!"

"I know, Karen. I just want to play it."

"I get to play it!"

He handed her back the record. She parked it under the tree and crouched down to fondle Winkle's nose.

"Come on, Karen—"

"It's my record, I don't wanna play it!"

"What do you want to do, just look at the pictures and drool?"

Without warning, Nate's heart began to flutter. He quickly suggested that they have breakfast, and afterwards they could sit down and listen to the record together, as a family.

"It's my present!"

"Oh shit, she doesn't even care about the music. You should've gotten her some dumb fan magazine."

"Shit shit shit shit shit!"

"You two watch your mouth! Karen, I'd like to hear the music too."

"No. You both just want to take it from me."

"Karen, how can you say—"

"YOU WANNA TAKE IT FROM ME!"

"Oh forget it, sis, play it when you want."

"Darling, come on, it's Christmas. Let me have a hug."

"Why? You never talk to me, just Artie! You never tell me anything! Why'd you even give me this record?"

"What are you talking about, Karen? You're the one Dad's always fussing over!"

"I HATE THIS CHRISTMAS! I HATE IT!"

The pure, high timbre of her rage cornered them into the true space they inhabited, which had as little to do with Christmas trees and presents as the light sparkling on the ornaments had to do with the cold sunshine of the street.

"You hate this Christmas? You think I like it? I did this for you kids! I do every thing I can for you kids! I got you the Beatles, I got you the Polaroid Swinger, the latest thing!"

Artie flinched. Why was Dad linking him with Karen, when he was trying to be calm, responsible, *the man of the—*

"I didn't want the latest thing, Dad, I wanted A CAMERA!"

Karen sprang from beneath the branches. Ornaments crashed, and Winkle charged out of the living room and scuttled into the bedroom.

"Well you're not taking my Beatle record! You're not! MOM WOULDN'T LET YOU!"

She stomped away to cry on her bed.

Artie was scared at Dad's pallor as he mumbled he was going to the bathroom. Watching him hurry away he realized maybe he'd been a little … obnoxious about the camera. A Polaroid was after all pretty neat.

And he quailed with the fear that sent him to his dad's bed in the middle of the night, not the fear he couldn't go to sleep, but if he did go to sleep Dad might not still be there in the morning.

Nate closed the door to the room and paced the square left by the absent hospital bed. He couldn't breathe. Anxiety attack, heart failure, stroke? He tried his exercise. Supercalifragilisticexpialidocius. If he could say that his brain was still sound. He threw open the window and gulped the winter air. How much wood would a woodchuck chuck if a woodchuck could chuck wood?

Easy, buckaroo.

He closed his eyes, waited for the mercury of his panic to sink down, then headed back into the apartment foyer, eyeballed Artie in the stepdown living room, and shouted loud enough for Karen to hear him.

"I'm making English muffins! Anyone who doesn't come to the dining room doesn't get breakfast!"

That seemed to work where all his pleas had failed. His children soon joined him sullenly at the breakfast table in the kitchen's small dining room annex. Nate turned on the portable Philco and heard the smooth refrain of Bing Crosby's "Silver Bells." As he toasted the muffins and got the butter out of the fridge he knew that if they sat calmly for awhile he could coax them to apologize to each other and orchestrate some contrition of his own. He'd tell Artie he'd return the damn Swinger, then save some money and get Artie the camera he wanted as a double

Christmas-birthday present. There we go. Nate was nothing if not a builder of compromises.

"Dad, is the window open?"

Nate could see through the kitchen window that he had failed to close the window of his bedroom.

"Where's Winkle?"

Mumbling assurances, Nate rushed to look behind sofas and chairs. He and Karen checked the bathroom, the bedroom, Karen's room and all the closets. That left Artie to take the obvious look down into the courtyard, where bloody pawprints spattered a patch of snow.

There was no doorman on duty so Nate and Artie had to pull the super from his family Christmas morning to unlock the basement courtyard gate. Nate kept repeating to Artie the maxim that cats always land on their feet right up to the point the blood trail in the snow led them to their first sight of him.

When they turned Winkle over and saw the crushed paws and the gash in his side where he'd grazed the corner of an air conditioner in his fall, Artie saw that Nate was right. Winkle had indeed landed on his feet and taken a few brave steps with his broken body before collapsing and bleeding out into a snowdrift.

As the super waited in the corner respectfully, shaking his head, Nate cradled Winkle in his arms, rounding the corner as he knew he'd have to, as the shadow locked into place, as Karen's wails echoed from above the courtyard. He stroked the matted fur and stared into the black dilated pupils for some response, but the only signs of life were the blood trails in his path all along the ice.

Chapter 3

DISCOVERY

They looked like a *Life* Magazine photo out of Swinging London, the bass player in a slim-cut checked jacket, drummer in crew neck striped shirt and jeans, second guitarist in a double-breasted jacket that Artie figured made him really sweat. But Danny Geller looked the keenest in a tan Nehru jacket, tight pants and pointed shoes. His long hair and touch of bangs were perfect. Artie flinched as he remembered trying to arrange his own hair into a "James Bond comma" for Naomi Miller's birthday party. Naomi had exclaimed that Artie had a "kewpie curl," and the party had cracked up forever.

Audrey Mehlinger shouted to him about how cool the Phantastics looked. She was getting jumpy, ready to dance. When girls get excited, he'd been told, their tits rise. Audrey's were sailing up against her blouse. She had just the right soup bowl coif look, and her classy hair and semaphore tits raised the stakes. A couple of his older schoolmates shot him glances that both envied him and mocked him for being out of his depth.

The group's amps crackled as they plugged in their guitars. That was the part you never saw on tv, the first plangent note echoed with a bass drum stomp, the rattle of the snare as the knobs and struts gleamed. It was like watching the courtship behavior of animals you'd only seen pace their cages in the zoo. All of a sudden Danny stepped up to the mike with a mischievous smile and cooed to the girls around the bandstand that they were going to do a tune by "Them out of London." Artie misheard and until the Shadows of Knight single a year later would believe that his new friend had written "Gloria."

He shivered at the tensile edge of the guitars, like the extra burn around a light bulb filament, the sheer loudness of it. The girls flocked to the dance floor. Artie followed Audrey through the Frug, the Swim, the Monkey, her sequence that he knew from sixth grade parties, and that he'd chosen along with Audrey herself out of all those opportunities, each girl with her dancing style, her rapid whispers, her signals and Artie's responses, bouncing back and forth through Beatles and Supremes song titles, each dance a little drama of unspoken, teasing promises and demands that percolated from the songs—*STOP in the name of love. I'm happy just to dance with you, but talking to that boy again, you can't do that...* She was quick-hipped, shimmying, her moves now escaped from their school parties to the greedy stares of his classmates. Artie, trying not to think about that, kept his eye on Danny, how he pranced and pouted and lashed the sneering whisper of his voice into a roof-rocking cry of "Glo-ri-a!" The drummer kicked the song into double time. Audrey jumped against Artie at the final cymbal crash. Her breath was sugary until it decayed into a warm garlic smell. Danny stood amid the dancers' cheers in an aureole of light refracted by Artie's glasses.

Bruce Geller watched the band with pride, tempered by the idle thought that he wished he could wear a Nehru jacket like his son. That "Gloria" was a clever song, the normal downbeat note hit on the third beat instead to give the whole tune an extra thrust. Danny didn't have Van Morrison's street shout but he knew how to leap from a whisper to a wail, with a touch of Broadway and the Brill that was all his own. He launched into two other Them songs, "Don't Start Crying Now" and "Mystic Eyes." The tom-tom throb and wakka-wakka bass, the bite and the swagger of hard British rock accelerating into a climactic "rave up"... Danny was right on time.

Gone were the gentle folk rhythms of last week. Jim McGuinn had it right playing his folk songs to a sexy Beatle beat. Bruce had heard from a family friend that Tom and Jerry, two pischers who'd had a modest hit with "Hey Schoolgirl," were juicing up folky tunes with Everly Brothers backbeats and harmonies, and coming up with a sound so hip and seductive that they could even use their real Jewish names, Simon and Garfunkel, and it came off as wiggy and with it.

That's how the best popular artists worked. They combed the air for clues. Like the Beatles pushing Chuck Berry's "Roll Over Beethoven" harder for "A Hard Day's Night," sipping the honeysuckle of "And I Love Her" from the petals of "Till There Was You." They plucked new selves from the musical firmament. They thieved like magpies.

Danny raced through Kinks and Zombies tunes, and then the Rolling Stones' "Not Fade Away," before he slowed the band down for "Ferry Cross The Mersey." The kids sank into the embraces the song allowed, and Artie's chest quickened to Audrey's breathing, which only made his feet seem to drag even worse, his body a faltering accompaniment to their conjoined heartbeats. He was almost grateful when a ringing E minor chord signaled another rocker.

"Little tune I wrote, 'Holds Me Still,' based on what you do when you think a girl's the one. You hold onto her, you figure that'll all work out. But what really happens is… she holds you, man, she holds you."

Bruce grinned as his kid began to create his own sound in a high school cafeteria.

She… is always putting me down.
She… don't really want me around.
Why why why why why do I love her.
Why why why why why do I love her.
I should walk away but she holds me still.

The chords were "The House of the Rising Sun" turned inside-out. When Bruce had pointed that out to Danny, he got ticked off, his magic intruded on by his schleppy critic father. Good, that was the musician in him, protecting his musical packrat den. The band layered driving harmonies on the "Why's," the song was a little powerhouse. Bruce knew he could get The Phantastics a demo. As the band ended the set with a propulsively cheerful version of "Concrete and Clay," the kids applauded and shouted Danny's name. Teen fever was definitely happening at the Vandemeer Lower School Winter Dance.

On the ride home in Mr. Geller's car, Artie enjoyed how

Audrey was still all bubbly about the group, and excited to be riding in the car with the lead singer. The George Washington Bridge's steel shadows, the nocturnal skyline in a white tungsten mist drew closer past the bob of Audrey's bangs. Just out of sight of the doorman and beneath her canopy's red taxi light, Artie got from Audrey the thickest, wettest kiss he'd ever felt and his groin stiffened. When he returned to the car, Danny gave him a knowing grin, and he tingled with the wish he could follow Audrey into her Park Avenue apartment.

But the night was over except for the drive to Third Avenue, the moment when he watched Danny and Mr. Geller drive away, and the clamp on his heart as he kissed Aunt Esther good night, lay down on the bed across from Karen's, and thought of Dad resting, as his Aunt had called it, just taking a rest behind the locked doors of Mount Sinai Hospital.

Winkle was gone—no way to find him or anything else in the ambush of darkness. The scents, the souvenirs—all gone. Now what she found was from memory, and it was all she had...

Aunt Esther's frown sometimes seemed to Karen as wrinkled in place as a pie crust. But her face had brightened as Karen came out of the closet and shut the door firmly behind her.

Karen had in her hand one of the closet's albums, one of the records Mom had played while telling Karen the stories of the Broadway of *Guys and Dolls*, the movie puppet stage of *Lili*. Though she'd never seen the movies or the plays, she could almost throw a screen up in her brain, as if the shows had come back for what Mom had called a "revival" and they were watching them together.

She felt ripped apart inside and she couldn't help it and she threw Winkle's toys at Daddy and she screamed and screamed... When she'd looked at the cover of *My Fair Lady*, Mom had told her next year there would be a movie she would get to see. On the album Eliza was the puppet of Henry Higgins who was the puppet of a white-haired old man who, Mom had told her, could be the man who wrote the play, could be God, *or the strings went up to cabinets filled with nothing, shelves upon empty shelves behind a black wall that Winkle once pierced but that now held him too. And there would be no revival.*

And this time she could see the open window where the loss had come, and she'd screamed because she couldn't stand it anymore— and she'd fed the dark.

When she listened to *Lili*, she danced with the puppets. The puppeteer was so angry, but only because he was lame and suffered. It was the puppets that truly spoke, in their dance across the painted stage, of his true feelings for Lili. She wanted to dance across the room with the puppets to the music as she once had, but the apartment was frozen, the very ceiling bulbs held back their light.

How could she ever save the puppeteer?

Sitting in the solarium, next to two elderly patients parked in their wheelchairs, Nate watched the sunset trickle beneath a furze of trees in the Park, the white edges on their inkstroke branches barely rising above the iron struts of the windows. After a third day of "observation" the doctors had concluded, thank God, that Nate was not a candidate for electroshock therapy.

But when will you decide to put me in a cab and send me home?

Were they just mixing a new drug cocktail for him, Dalmane, Chlorohydrate, maybe a little Restoril?

A better remedy would've been no third martini—or was it a fourth? But when Toots Shor spreads his bearish arms and welcomes you to his world famous saloon… *"Hiya crumbum!"*… and clasps you with his paw and with a cannonade of a laugh ushers you to unlimited clams and oysters and an open bar to celebrate your boss's fiftieth birthday… no chance you'll let those opportunities for two parts gin and one part vermouth get away. Besides, Nate had figured he had enough ballast to hold the liquor. He'd parked himself at the oyster bar and made a lonely feast on shrimp cocktail and clams on the half shell, ordering one cocktail, then another.

On his third martini Nate had noticed the women. So many mink stoles, he'd told a colleague, you'd think the whole Canadian north woods was in the crowd. So you're a comedian tonight, his colleague had cracked.

Then one doffed her wrap to the hat check girl to reveal brilliant shoulders and a red velvet dress anchored by a bow beneath her plunging décolletage. She stood in front of the fireplace, glowing to beat the angular bronze hood, seeming to beckon Nate around the huge circular bar to lock eyes with her. Was she unescorted? Who knew?… the kind of women who came to a "men's joint"… but what was wrong with making conversation anyhow?

Nate lit her Pall Mall and conversation began. She asked him if he were at all related to Sandy Koufax.

Sandy or Ernie, they always asked about Sandy or Ernie, the lords of baseball and comedy, the heart of American sports and entertainment, and he always just grinned and shook his head—but this time his mind made what the psychiatrists called an associative leap. A weirdly liberating, unsprung moment. He drew himself up with drunken courtliness and did his best Cary Grant.

"My dear, I have no curveball, and I'm no screwball."

That got a big laugh from her. Her breasts shook like jelled aspic. His thoughts leapt wildly, a loosed spring rebounding on itself, Koufax, Kovacs, "Jewish kid" baseball hero refusing to pitch on Yom Kippur, Jewish comedy star upending reality with milk that poured to the ceiling, those three apes playing a tune that cued the whole nation to laugh their heads off. All that Nate was not, rising up from stadiums and studios to bend America's reality to their bidding in front of this va-va-voom number at Toots Shor.

"… so we went for an old-fashioned sleigh ride, in the country, really it was darling!"

"Do you like to ski, um… ?"

"Martha."

Nate had never skied in his life.

"No, Nate, I've never quite tried it."

"Nothing like the icy wind in your hair as you zoom down the slopes!"

What would Ernie do now? Grin and chomp his cigar as a whoosh of air made his hair stand on end?

"Oh a sleigh ride is adventurous enough for me!"

"Sounds like a perfect thing to do for Christmas."

"What did you do over the holiday? Were you at Stowe?"

"No, not at Stowe. What did I do for Christmas? I... I killed the family cat."

She shuddered so hard some of the Tom Collins sloshed over the lip of the glass.

"It was an accident. I just had to open a window, and sometimes... all you have to do is... is open a window.... I had what you call an anxiety attack."

"I'm so sorry. How did you get that?"

"Well.... I'm told it's a consequence of my wife's death."

A bunch of the fellas complaining about their wives—one had slavered over Edie Adams, the hot as a popover blonde wife of Ernie Kovacs—she could smoke my extra long Muriel cigar any time...

"Speaking of Ernie Kovacs, anyone ever tell you you look like Edie Adams?"

"Well, no, but... thank you, and.... I'm so sorry. I can just imagine what you've gone through. You know, I just have to go to the lady's room to powder my nose—"

"Of course. I'm sorry, I don't know how all that.... I apologize."

"Oh, really, that's quite all right."

"I just... I just wanted to open the window to get some air. Just open a window. Now my daughter won't talk to me. I'm trying to help her get over it, but I don't have any answers. I checked Dr. Spock, he doesn't know either. She loves Ernie Kovacs. Maybe sing that Ernie Kovacs song that the three apes do, you know? Ta ta ta, ta-tata ta!"

He made a little fluttering and rising motion of his hand, which caught the rim of the Tom Collins glass and sent her drink splashing into her face.

The rest was a blur of dashed sympathy and the bowels of

a swank bar disgorged into action. With just the slightest nod of the old shellcracker a slab of tweed muscle was up against Nate. The moment had its harsh watchspring, its meaty reality once again. Nate apologized as elegantly as he could, explaining he was the distant cousin of Ernie Kovacs and he was singing the song that could put his daughter in hysterics, and he sang the song of the those three apes again, louder this time, which attracted the second guy on Toots Shor's staff who was bigger than Toots, not to mention Nate's boss, the birthday boy—and Nate, staring at his boss from between the two musclemen, had to laugh at how this unpardonable situation was getting even worse, at which point the laughter interspersed itself with another off-key rendition of the three apes tune—ta-ta-TA, ta-tata-TA— didn't everybody love that music?—especially my kids—which prompted his boss's observation that perhaps he should go home to his kids, that he should accept his boss's generous offer of a cab ride, which, with one blast of cold air and the mighty whistle of a doorman, materialized, paid in full, whisking him across the Great White Way, beneath checkerboards in the night sky of hot red and yellow pulsing neon, past the Bond and Camel signs and giant smoke rings that shepherded thousands of good sober men in homburgs and their happy wives along Broadway to whorls of pixilated lights in a beat that syncopated off the jackhammer of his heart, and when the cabbie asked him where was home chief, Nate, as he choked in waves of terror, begged to be taken to Mount Sinai Hospital.

One part less gin, two parts less vermouth, and this trip would not have been necessary.

Unless this "rest" is the rest he's seeking.

Esther had cheered him a little with the news that Karen had abandoned the closet, but also told him Artie was darkly reticent about something that had happened in school…

Dalmane, Restoril…

Was it his decision to make alone?

Night seeped into the solarium, and Nate watched the orange sun dissolve into the forest.

Fuck that goddamn Mr. Shantz! Artie had studied so hard for the algebra test, and Shantz had taken off twenty points because his fraction bars on the rational expressions weren't long enough. Math is about being EXACT, the old fart would shout in every class, this isn't Beatlemania here! We have RULES. What kind of rules deducted twenty points and gave him a C- because his fraction lines weren't long enough?

Artie's grades were sliding, he couldn't sleep, he was sick to his stomach, all he could really concentrate on was parceling out his allowance to buy 45s at the record store. For his first four he'd selected The Beatles, "I Feel Fine," with that hovering buzz that shot off into George's hop-skip-and-jump of a strum, Ringo's eruption of cymbals, John's happy vocal, and then he'd gotten "I'm Henry VIII I Am" because Karen begged him—all right, he kind of liked it—then "Concrete and Clay" and the Zombies' "She's Not There," whose harmonies sent shivers up his back. From the console where Sinatra and Alice Faye had once warbled came the twang and boom of British pop, his own neighborhood of sound, the ultimate secret handshake club he shared—except for Herman's Hermits—with Danny Geller, leader of the Phantastics, the keenest kid in school.

He had tried so hard to get Karen to stop screaming at Dad, even though he understood, he always understood....

Artie shoved the damn test in his math notebook, shoved the damn notebook in his bookbag, and headed for midday assembly. Fuck your rules. Fuck school assembly, fuck wearing these dark slacks in the steam heat of the student commons that made his thighs gluey as postage stamps. As his classmates, in almost identical wool flannel slacks, jackets and ties, converged in the hall that led past the bookbag racks, Artie thought he heard all sorts of snickers aimed his way. Just a week ago was the first day he'd gotten his bookbag ranked again—the stomp, the handles torn from his grasp, the books scattered on the floor. Rank-out! The resumption of the picking on that had first begun on the spring day when he'd stupidly brought his Instamatic to school to film the hummingbird tulips in bloom. That act of photographing flowers had earned him a name that became an inescapable label, an irresistible put-down, a particularly nasty monicker that for the first time made him feel sympathy for all those guys on Christopher Street, a dual syllable shibboleth that within the week was erupting through the halls of Vandemeer High.

"KOFAG!"

Yes, as some class wit put it, not even a full-fledged fag, just a co-fag.

Artie knew the pranks had only broken off because of his mother's death. Classmates had, out of shock and decency, given him a reprieve, but he didn't want any longer to be handicapped with a private space of grief. So during an after-lunch boxball game, on sidewalks that had cleared in a break between snows, he had decided to be a real obnox. A quick theft of a shot from his own teammate and a hard smash over the boundaries lost the game for his side but proclaimed his reborn aggression. At "sockey" games on the field, played with a little rubber Spalding, he was better, his feet far quicker than his hands, and so he dribbled the Spalding with abandon past bigger klutzes and made sure to stomp ankles on the way to scoring a goal. Sure enough, the bookbag rankings and saluggi games with his ski hat resumed. Welcome back, Kofag.

Still, as he trudged up the stairs to the auditorium, a gale of laughter blew over him, and he was worried that today things would go out of control. A bizarre courtesy was being shown to Artie. His classmates practically escorted him to the high windows in the hallway that overlooked the snowbound football field. Artie stepped up to the glass and saw that a group of his schoolmates had gone to a great deal of trouble—about thirty feet worth of stamping, it appeared from this height—to carve out one word on that pristine expanse of snow.

KOFAG.

Their laughter was a sonic boom that cracked behind him as he raced down the stairs. The cold sliced into the collar beneath his tie as he burst outside, found a gap in the fence and hurtled onto the field. Snow clung to his shoes and caked his socks, and he realized he would leave a track to his name that would last equally as long in the snow as the insult itself.

In the whiteness that stretched from the stadium benches across the playing fields he didn't even know which letter to attack. Each seemed a mile long. A brilliant rank-out, he had to admit, a masterpiece of humiliation on a football-field sized canvas, and as he tried to stomp one of the letters away, he realized that the second phase was now kicking in with the sight of him whaling uselessly at his giant nickname. He glanced up and saw the kids packed against the windows. But still he kicked the pure, blinding, slippery snow, down to the dirt shot through with ghost grey fibers of ice where his nemeses' boots had stamped the hardest, until his shoe gave way and he collapsed into the frozen mud.

Spreadeagled on the ground, he looked up at the windows, at students doubled up with laughter even as teachers dispersed the crowd, and he didn't want to get up. Let the cold from the hard-packed ground seep through his jacket. All the way through him. He stared at the sky, he shut his eyes, he just wanted to stop looking at anything—but the crunch of footsteps forced his eyes open again, and through the flecks of slush on his glasses he saw that someone on the edge of the field was looking at him.

Artie sprang up when he realized who the tall, skinny figure in the deaconish black coat was. He turned away, hoping Danny Geller would simply walk off and leave him alone, but when he didn't, and when standing uncomfortably still made him feel colder than ever, he finally walked over to see what Danny wanted.

Danny had that smile on his face like he was sharing a joke with himself. He nodded up toward the auditorium windows.

"You gotta be less obvious, Artie."

"How can you be less obvious about something like this?"

"Keep it hid, y'know? So they don't know when you're gonna…"

"Gonna what?"

"Get back at 'em. Really fuck 'em, Artie."

Artie winced, not so much at the obscenity, but at the thought of any word that strong and harsh being applied to his response.

"I've watched you, and you always try to take it light, man, but this time, you really gotta fuck 'em now."

"Well, I can't fuck them now, I mean it's time for Assembly—you're really late, you know—and there's a hundred of them up there, and—"

"Yeah, I know. Look at 'em in their shitty blue blazers. I don't mean right now. I think I can help you. I think it's one of my fellow violinists in the orchestra who did this. I can find out."

"Really?"

"Then it's—like, then it's the "I Feel Fine" intro. Know that record?"

"I got that record. But what do you mean?"

"It starts with feedback, you know. When you like… let the electricity go crazy on the guitar… Eeyaaaaaaah… oh, it's all cranked up, it's painful… eeeeannnn… then bam, the tune kicks in!"

He smacked his fist into his palm, then rubbed his hands to warm them.

"What are you talking about, Danny?"

"It's like that intro. You wait, you wait, you get all ready… then at just the right moment… you annihilate the asshole!"

Dinner was roast lamb and mint jelly, mashed potatoes, and Birdseye string beans, Artie's favorite, and Sarah was now cooking the meals almost as well as Mom. Artie watched as Dad smiled and thanked Sarah for dinner as always.

Artie knew without glancing back at Karen that she was watching Dad as intently as he was.

When they'd waited for him beside Aunt Esther, Artie's hand gripping Karen's almost as hard as she was holding his, and Dad had emerged beneath the hospital canopy, Artie's first thought was gratitude that he hadn't been brought out in a wheelchair. He'd looked pale, almost as if one of those fluorescent lights from the hospital had settled behind his face, but still there he was, hat in hand, smiling, relaxed, as if he were just coming back from the office.

Karen had raced ahead to fling herself into Dad's embrace as his coat had spread like wings around her. Artie had waited until Dad had stretched out one arm to run and let himself be grasped to his side. Dad and Aunt Esther had hailed a cab out on Fifth Avenue. As they'd driven past Central Park beneath sycamores that had shrugged off the snow, and granite walls that no longer bared icy teeth to the passers-by, Dad had promised he would never go away again.

But now he seemed to float his fork above the lamb as if the food were a great distance from him, his movements so tentative, as if waiting for inner promptings to do once again what he'd always done.

Dad saw Artie watching, snapped back to alertness, and quizzed Artie and Karen about the past two days. The change was startling. Artie had never seen Dad so attentive, so curious about Karen's progress in fifth grade. He wanted to bare his own secrets to Dad, but he knew he'd have to hide the "Kofag" debacle, and then, only because he knew word would eventually get back to Dad, he confessed his math test grade over his fraction lines.

"That's ridiculous! I'm going to have a talk with the headmaster!"

"Really, Dad?"

"The other parents were complaining about this guy too. He's what you call a martinet, a guy who gets crazy about his rules and goes too far. No, that's enough, you're on a scholarship, working so hard, I'm going to call Dr. Fields."

Dad drew himself up in his chair, the offended gentleman, and Artie beamed. This is how he liked to see Dad, upright, even a bit starchy, on behalf of spoken and unspoken laws.

Whatever they'd done to him in the hospital had done him good.

"So you're gonna talk with the other parents?"

"Yes. I'll make some calls. Sometimes we have to stick up for ourselves, Artie."

Where are you?

On the album cover the braid of cigarette smoke was a flourish of despair from his upraised hand as he gazed into the middle distance. He crooned over a silken throb of violins that lingered on the memory of vanished love, while harps and woodwinds swirled like clouds sheltering the flame of twilight.

No one could rise up from a dying fall like Frank.

Seated once again in his easy chair, Nate drew familiar comfort from his Sinatra collection, after lifting his record out from under some smaller Beatles and Zombies 45s. He'd have to have a talk with Artie about wasting his allowance on that.

There were many tasks to be done. The doctors had warned him the pills might knock him for a loop occasionally until he got used to it—well, he'd just have to get used to it faster. His mother Corinne, as her nurse had served ice cream to Nate and Karen in the kitchen, had turned to him, and in one of the bursts of quiet asperity that had so often scared him growing up, had told him it was a terrible and tragic time, but there must be an end to it. Nate knew that invested in his mother's words was nothing less than her own crumpled body in a wheelchair.

He called Bruce to tell him he'd recuperated from his "bronchitis" and checked when Danny would perform in *The Pirates of Penzance*. Bruce was gung ho as ever about Danny's musical ability. He was also annoyed about Cornelius Hill's arrest for drugs; as a result this Saturday would be his final performance in the New York area. The man's cabaret card had been yanked pending his trial for drug possession.

Nate hadn't realized that all performers—in fact, as Bruce told him, any nightclub employee who had contact with the public—had to be fingerprinted and get a photo card every two years from the police to work anywhere with a liquor license. Cornelius' plight had helped renew some organizing within the arts community down in the Village. As a lawyer that might interest him, maybe?

The cop in his face. Cornelius' cries. The memory sent the winter cold back down his spine, but when thought of the new camaraderie between Danny and Artie, and his own new friendship with Bruce, he remembered what his mother had told him about making a definite border for the past.

While Dizzy Gillespie held forth at the Top of the Gate, Cornelius was playing the lower level Village Gate space, located down a narrow flight of stairs and packed with well-wishers and fans. The languid ritual of coats shed, drinks summoned, and table talk lit up with cigarettes was overlaid with another, more yeasty rhythm, as club owner Art D'Lugoff barreled between the tables and chummed the crowd. Nate heard wishes that echoed his own, that Congressman John Lindsay would make a run for Mayor, and throw out Mayor Wagner and his machine cronies.

"Looks like Bing and Bob have clocked in tonight."

Nate turned to the grin of a stocky man with a jowled red face, a rabbinical beard and bifocals, and the potato bulb nose of a peasant ancestor.

"Bing and Bob?"

"The heat. The plainclothes cops. White turtlenecks on parade. I'm Izzy Hamerow. Bruce woulda introduced me at some point."

Nate shook Izzy's hand, then eyed the two beefy men in the turtlenecks, one of whom, to his dread, was the bruiser cop who'd confronted him in the alley.

"Makes me sick. Racist cops. That's why we fought in segregated battalions, ya know. Crackers don't know better, it's the racist guys from our neck of the woods that backed the policy up."

"You were overseas?"

"Italy, mostly. You?"

"I was 4F. Myopia and a heart murmur. I served on the draft board."

"Hah! Rather be at Anzio!"

"I also ran a few bond drives over at the UJA."

"No kidding. You're a landsman? No shit!"

Bruce finally sat back down with them almost precisely when

Cornelius sauntered to the bandstand. His New York career about to be martyred to the cabaret laws, Cornelius had a new first-on-the-bill dignity, his playing less slick and more heartfelt, especially on the mournful high notes he threw into "Mood Indigo." Through the shafts of light in the spiderweb of cigarette smoke, Nate thought Cornelius picked him out of the crowd, or maybe it was flecks of the spotlight reflected in Cornelius' eyes.

The set concluded with a jubilant rendition of "How High The Moon" that brought the crowd, Nate included, to its feet. D'Lugoff took the stage. Caught in his own spotlight, with his tapered chin and hawk nose, he had the dignity of a Spanish grandee in his castle. But he was affably unpretentious as he reminded the crowd why they wouldn't be seeing Cornelius hopefully for a short while but awhile because a police committee that sits in judgment on musicians, without any court of law to back them up, has taken the piece of paper that lets him play for us... we all remember how Billie couldn't play the clubs and Lord Buckley died of a heart attack waiting to get his card reinstated... let's hope with the help of our Citizens' Emergency Committee—and he pointed to a table of sophisticates in the center—this whole *vercochte* system is junked in the near future.

He hugged Cornelius to the crowd's applause.

"We'll see you soon, my friend."

Nate sipped his Scotch and water and watched the jazzman surrounded by his fans until Bruce finally steered Cornelius toward their table.

"Yeah, well, I dig a New York crowd. I got eyes to come back real soon."

"You will, Cornelius. See, the strategy, Nate, is to use this case to fight the cabaret laws in court. The cops were harassing him, just waiting."

Nate nodded, while hearing in Bruce's phrase the obvious fact Bruce had skirted. The cops knew Cornelius was a dope addict.

"Can you play in other states?"

"Yeah. I'll do a tour, get by. Though no place like Art's, man.

These other places, the mobsters, they run it for the geetz and give you just enough to keep you coming back. Sometimes I think I should've stayed in Europe. You don't feel the draft there."

"The draft? Aren't you a little over forty?"

"Heh heh, no, not that draft. It's what we call the cold of the prejudice. They let cats be on the Continent, man, they let you be."

Bruce excused himself to go to the bathroom, and Cornelius lowered his face closer to Nate.

"Thank you for takin' an interest."

"What kind of interest?"

"Night I got busted."

"I didn't do anything."

"You didn't go away."

Nate almost shrank from the jazzman's conspiratorial gratitude.

"Miles told me I should charge police brutality. But man, that's part of the whole shebang."

"It shouldn't be."

"Well, you and Miles are gentlemen."

"Miles Davis a gentleman? The way he turns his back on the audience?"

"Yeah, well, maybe he don't like the audience enough. That cat don't like too many people at all, really. But hey—I see you're simpatico. And when I'm up on the stand it's good to make that connection."

Nate nervously sipped at his Scotch. The clientele in the room were starting to look his way. When would Bruce get back from the head?

"At least I got my coat fixed."

"What?"

"Coat I got cleaned right before the gig. The bulls, when they were dragging me to the car it got tore up. Maybe that's coat brutality."

"You picked up that coat right before you came to the club?"

Nate's brain sharpened out of the fog of Dewars and courtesy, synapses crackling that hadn't fired since law school, since his first professional years as a public defender.

"Well, yeah, then they got me sittin' in that dirty pokey room—"

"How close is the tailor to the club?"

"Right down the block."

Cornelius grinned. He was starting to catch Nate's drift, and then Bruce came by and caught on as well... the coat right back from the tailor's... what a crackup . . . and Bruce ordered a round of drinks, ice cubes clinked in whisky glasses, cigarette clouds hovered above the table as Nate spelled out the case for them.

Back before Nate's father had laid down the law that there would be no wasting Nate's classical piano talent on light jazz, he'd imagined clubs like this, face to face with suave Negro musicians who shook his hand and welcomed him to tickle the ivories, keep swinging. . . .

Blue sky over a beach, silver moonlight over a castle, all unveiling for Karen a lovely story where a man who has never seen a girl before believes that if you say you're beautiful, then you really are. Pirates who never prey on the orphaned and the innocent have the police at the points of their swords but it's all a misunderstanding, all forgiven at the end. And amid the costumes, the cast singing the Gilbert and Sullivan melodies Dad had once played on the piano, and the thwacking swordplay, there he is, magnetizing the spotlight as he swaggers across the stage.

Oh better far to live and die
Under the brave black flag I fly
Than play a sanctimonious part
With a pirate head and a pirate heart.

Danny's playful grin was crooked with healthy mischief, a blissful lack of dreariness and suffering.

But many a king on a first-class throne
If he wants to call his crown his own
Must somehow manage to get through
More dirty work than e'er I do

Artie watched Danny, and smiled as much at his own memories as at the Pirates' musical horseplay. Just before the school assembly's winter orchestra concert, Danny had given him the key to the backstage door.

"Look, Artie, you're gonna have to do it—I mean, something in me—I can't do this to a violin, man."

Danny had handed him the bottle of Elmer's Glue-All like a sacred trust.

"Hey, you can let the Stooge get away with having super-all-time ranked you forever...."

Danny hated Steubner, who was always toadying up to the music teacher, but "the Stooge" wanted Danny's approval above all things, and so had boasted of the Kofag stunt to him.

"It's okay to fuck up his bow, he has no talent and his old man has a fortune. But you better hurry, man, if you're gonna do it."

"I could get expelled."

"Then forget about it. Give me back the key."

Sometimes we have to stand up for ourselves, Artie...

For a few moments Artie had the school orchestra's instruments behind the curtain all to himself, cellos and trombones seemingly crouched before him in supplication. His heartbeat shooting up to his ears, he'd headed right for Steubner's violin. Stupe the Stooge (the one classmate with nicknames worse than Artie's) and his fellow suburban shitheads. He thought about them cackling about the show Kofag had put on for the school, and before he knew it he'd deftly smeared the violin bow with the same kind of squirt bottle he'd once used for color paper cutouts in third grade. *Your show now, Stooge.* A half hour later, when Steubner had stood up for his violin solo during the Vivaldi piece, he'd swept his gluey bow across the strings and it had sounded, as Danny put it, like Stravinsky played by a spaz. To howls of laughter the orchestra had cut the piece short and the Stooge had been hooted off the stage. A boring speech to the school in the next assembly that demanded all such pranks end right now was the only penalty Artie drew. The perfect revenge.

Away to the cheating world go you
Where pirates all are well-to-do
But I'll be true to the song I sing
And live and die a Pirate King,
For I am a Pirate King!
I am a Pirate King!

Why the hell was Karen putting up such a fuss in the apartment house lobby? It was really embarrassing, the car at idle, Danny and Mr. Geller waiting while Karen threw a really screechy tantrum until Grandma Miriam practically dragged her to the elevator. Danny, his lips still purple from his makeup, grinned.

"Your sister has some flash, man."

Dad returned wearily to the front seat, and Mr. Geller drove them all to an apartment owned by his taxi fleet owner friend. Danny, Artie, and their buddies, in honor of Danny's performance, were being allowed to join a party that Mr. Geller assured them would be one heck of a show.

When they finally arrived Artie felt he'd gone from watching a stage to joining one. Framed over wicker backed chairs and sofas and Ottomans were a giant painted American flag and, to Artie's astonishment, a framed comic book panel. You could see every printer's dot on the girl's face as she made a heartbroken phone call, screaming to the other end of the phone that the caller was a "BEAST!" A rug on the floor had concentric circles of eye-squinting primary colors brighter than Caran Dache crayons. God he wished he had his camera. Somebody was bellowing that if they had Cezannes and Van Goghs they'd sell them, old lady art, no pizazz.

Danny caught Artie's look, quickly sidled away from the crowd and motioned to him to follow him to the bathroom. The wall near the shower was painted with a blank nude that sprouted pink nipples. Artie felt a clutch in his stomach at her faceless, shameless glow.

Nate accepted a scotch and soda from the host and observed

the latest "Pop Art," as Bruce introduced him to his friends from the Citizens' Emergency Committee. The name struck Nate as an overblown response to the nuisance of cabaret cards, but he smiled and shook their hands and cautioned them that he couldn't really talk about Cornelius Hill's potential legal case. They were sprightly and gracious and welcomed him effusively. Nate couldn't figure them out; they had serious opinions, but they seemed walking New Yorker cartoons of jet setters determined to be *au courant* about the latest discotheques or foreign films for sophisticated audiences. They dressed in ascots instead of ties, the women doffing candy blue and white coats, wearing sweaters over tight Capri pants. Still, he found himself basking in their acceptance of him. Shari Geller passed Nate a cigarette case of Ritz crackers lined with pate. Nate helped himself to the crackers, some pigs in a blanket on a serving plate, and some startlingly tasty Roquefort cheese balls rolled in crushed walnuts.

"What's purple and hums?"

"An electric grape."

"Why does it hum?"

"It doesn't know the words!"

Gales of hysterics. What was so funny? So far Artie hadn't understood anything or anyone at this party, and was relieved when he saw his friend Russ Lansing head through the door. Russ, sandy-haired, athletically slim, a natural first baseman and tennis player, had a way of smoothing out any situation he was in, and suddenly the room of gibbering adults among comic strip panels had a congenial goofiness.

"Hi, group," Russ said breezily to Artie and Danny.

Nate was equally delighted to greet Russ's dad Avery and his wife Marian. Avery Lansing looked like Gregory Peck in his stern horn-rimmed mode but his limbs were all skewed angles, and his tapered fingers swirled as he made his outrageous comments. He was a humor columnist and essayist for various magazines, and he'd recently hit it big with a best-selling novel about a foreign correspondent and his bohemian wife, *Our Lady Of Paris*. Marian, with her warm hug and casual glamour, had always been a quiet foil for Becky at her most enthusiastic.

Avery instantly monopolized the conversation and declared he'd sworn off liberalism. He'd always hated Communists—I mean, really, believing an economic system provides everything you need and should rule your every move, what a bunch of suckers!—but now he was convinced that even your garden variety liberal was totally lame. He told Nate he'd just covered a panel discussion, a kind of teach-in, where playwright Leroi Jones had announced the only honorable black theater would be soaked in busted heads, called the whites in the audience cancers assuaging their lousy consciences, and then asked for contributions to the Black Arts Repertory Theater.

"Where's the Negro revolution going? These people were always so good-natured."

"Through gritted teeth, obviously—"

"It wasn't that bad, Avery! And I mean, he had a point when he said none of us would join the Negroes if it came to streetfighting and—"

"I would've walked out on his speech if I wasn't supposed to cover the damn thing! I only take that kind of abuse when Marian straps on a teddy!"

In the hallway, Artie, Russ, and Danny lounged, sipped Cokes, evaded the adults. Danny talked about the girls in the play. Allison, the one playing Mabel, had amazing legs—Danny had briefly seen her crouched down on the floor of the dressing room in her panties searching for a dropped earring. That was the thing about drama class, Danny told Artie, you got to hang out with the chicks, and at very close quarters. Artie threw in that he was thinking of dating, really next-step dating Audrey Mehlinger, and Russ gently kidded him that he hadn't looked enough. More to it than little Audrey, he kept repeating.

The room's music transitioned to strings, flutes, and sighing harmonies.

"This group the Mamas and the Papas sing about anything other than bed-hopping?"

"Have you seen that Sonny and Cher act?"

"I hear they both go to the same dressmaker. I schmatta you babe."

Nate kidded Bruce about his liner notes for teenagers' records. "Second childhood is where the bucks are Nate!"

While Russ opened the bathroom window, Artie watched Danny's fingers slide gracefully up and down a Zig Zag paper until it tapered into a cigarette. He and Russ talked about connections, college rooms in Columbia where deals could be made. Artie had introduced the two to magnify his coolness, and suddenly he didn't know what coolness was. The match was lit, cupped, the flame shot across the tip like lava from the marijuana's core. The scent clawed at the back of his throat, sweet, peppery, challenging. He nervously told his two friends he didn't smoke, even though he began to realize this wasn't anything like just smoking. His friends inhaling the ragged brown cigarette went far beyond the theater with the leggy French girls, the negatives totally blurred....

Back in the living room, inebriation had taken over. Bruce was showing Nate and some of his arts world friends an old review of his in *Spectrum*. The international sound. G.I.'s came back from Europe with Django Reinhardt records. Everyone gazing at photos in *Life* and *Look*. Ten years later Miles and Gil Evans are playing *corrida* motifs, Blakey and Silver playing mambo hard bop and mid-tempo Oriental riffs, all of jazz taking a boulevardier walk in new directions.

And here's the beauty, Bruce told him, of what he'd said back then. He showed Nate the liner notes of an album by the Byrds, *Mr. Tambourine Man*. Jim McGuinn, the group's leader, was talking about how he and the band wanted to put together "international folk rock music." Bruce's international theme had crossed over from one hip sound to another.

Of course the guests, more than three sheets to the wind, especially Avery, reading aloud the liner notes, weren't so kindly about the Byrds.

"Oh how absolutely, touchingly with it! The music is 'orange green yellow and near... the super hippies trip out to them!'"

Artie fled the bathroom coughing, but almost as raw as the rasp in his throat was the feeling of abandonment. Could a gate have already slammed on the friendship that had formed when Danny had high-fived him about the sabotaged violin? It was even worse when Danny talked about the great concerts he'd seen. The Animals playing "House of the Rising Sun" in a club. Russ could counter him with his memories of Stones and Byrds concerts, but for Artie, whose first rock and roll concert had been Danny's band, this web of music... he couldn't even carry a tune. How could he ever handle it? What could photography ever do to match it?

He lingered in the hallway, and picked out the sounds of the Byrds coming from the babble of the party. A cold blast of air leaked from the bathroom and Danny, having opened the window to clear the fumes, stood at Artie's side. They watched as Nate also seemed to listen to the song.

Nate had always thought that kind of guitar was hillbilly, but there was something so intimate about the boy's singing voice, that blanket of harmony... and then out of those sighing vocals came a refrain that was clearly the title... "Here Without You"...

And suddenly the boys with the Christopher Robin haircuts were touching Nate to his heart's core.

"Y'know, Artie," Danny mumbled, "Jim McGuinn's playing a Rickenbacker 12-string guitar, Rickenbacker, like he was the flying ace of World War I, shooting down Germans, like Snoopy and the Red Baron, and now we have all those silver missiles you see in the dumb films about atomic defense, remember they showed us that shit in school, Artie, that bright orange map that showed missile silos all over the country, and all the silver missiles on the map, they've become, like, the orange of Byrds records and the jet roar of electronic feedback and the jewels of the sounds of the guitars."

"What?"

"The words, the colors... it's all part of the sound. Man, when it really works, the Music carries everything . . . ."

Danny's ramblings suddenly coalesced with the ringing of the guitars into rhapsodic poetry, romance better than he could ever speak to Audrey Mehlinger. Or maybe it was the marijuana in him that talked like that. Or maybe it was the sight of his Dad listening to the Byrds, really listening to them, that made everything, even this stupid party, flow together and make sense.

"I think your dad's boss for helping that jazz guy."

"He is?"

"Yeah. You know, the Animals love jazz? Eric Burdon once shook Mingus' hand."

Dad noticed Artie and Danny. He made a mock courtly bow.

"The pirate king and his trusted adviser."

The partygoers looked their way. Artie wondered briefly if Dad had cracked a joke at his expense, but it wasn't a mean joke, and he liked seeing Dad get the attention of the guests. He turned to the crowd with the same grin.

"How about a little Gilbert and Sullivan to end the evening?"

Artie couldn't believe it. Dad hadn't played piano since Mom had lain down in bed and not gotten up again. He sat at the piano with a stiffness that could've been his sciatica, could've been reluctance, and for a moment Artie wondered if he was about to take it back, but then he spread his fingers on the keys. Bruce lifted the tonearm off the record. Danny headed over to the piano to Dad's side. He cleared his throat dramatically, then launched into an encore rendition of his character's signature tune just a beat before Dad jumped in and caught up with him. The room became a fractured campfire singalong, Dad pounding on the keys, Mr. Geller at one point taking a verse with Danny, everyone chorusing on "to be a Pirate King!"

Artie echoed the applause for Dad and Danny. Mr. Lansing sang "the shills are alive with the sound of music," Bruce guffawed, and amid the laughter Artie joined Dad and Danny by the piano.

They waited on the curb for the doorman to whistle them a cab.

"That was great, Dad, your playing the piano again."

"Thanks, Artie. It felt pretty good. Haven't lost it yet."

"Y'know, Danny said something about your helping a jazz guy?"

"Well, yes, I'm going to try and get his case thrown out of court."

"How come?"

"It's a little complicated, Artie. Let's just say he got a raw deal."

Dad grinned and rumpled Artie's hair, and Artie realized he was for the first time in weeks bare-headed with his father, not wearing a yarmulke or worst, an old fedora dug out of the closet, not fighting a headwind of sleet to get to the synagogue and a room of musty bookshelves and mustier old men called on to form a *minyan* and chant the prayers for the dead. As they gazed down the street together a breeze blew beneath the canopy that had the warmth of a pirate king's piano and the sway of the Byrds' guitars.

Nate's first legwork on a criminal defense case in fifteen years, and he was finding out that the Village really was a village. The tailor considered Cornelius' arrest a personal affront. He'd known him five years, good customer, nice man. Nate soon had a carbon copy of the ticket showing when Cornelius' suit was picked up as well as another employee swearing up and down that Cornelius ran in and grabbed his coat right before they closed, in fact they'd stayed open ten minutes later for him. I knew, the tailor pronounced, it was his Saturday gig, and he sorta has a strange sense of time. Manny Onofrio, owner of Smokes, insisted that Cornelius had come right to the club with his coat in a cellophane bag and had soup and sandwiches with the band, at which point Manny had the bartender keep an eye on the door so that Cornelius wouldn't slip out and, in Manny's words, get a little lost. Ironically the drug habit that put Cornelius outside the law was so obvious to everyone that there was plenty of evidence to set him free.

Still Nate had a dry-mouthed case of nerves as he shepherded

Cornelius into the Manhattan Criminal Courts Building. "Equal and Exact Justice to All Men of Whatever State and Persuasion." It had been quite a while since that statement had braced his first steps into the law. The weak dusty light ranging through the cavernous interior cast a grey pallor on Cornelius face; in his oversized suit he looked like some subterranean creature looking for a burrow to hide in and molt in peace.

The jazzman's fear provoked a definite queasiness in Nate, along with a memory of a whirlwind of paint. Black twisted lines, slashes of primary colors. The painting, if you could call it that, hung behind Ted Schomer's desk and had cost his boss God knew how much money. Nate's eyes had kept darting to it as he'd made his request to Schomer to take on Cornelius pro bono.

Schomer had inspected Nate from beneath his prize painting, steepled his fingers, and reminded Nate that the firm's pro bono cases were usually in the nature of a favor: little Tommy Fencik gets caught shoplifting at Ohrbach's. Nate knew exactly what Schomer meant, and in order to assure the boss that his buckaroo hadn't totally strayed from the trail, Nate laid out the reasons why Cornelius Hill's case could be quickly dispatched right at the arraignment stage. You could sum it up in one question: how could a heroin fix be in a coat just taken back from the cleaners?

Nate almost shuddered with relief when Schomer's lips pursed into the slightest bow of a smile. The case amused him. Typical paddy on the beat corruption, planted smack, undone by a cleaning ticket.

Schomer's only strict injunction to Nate: do it discreetly. No publicity. None. To keep it secret, Schomer had made a call to an ADA he knew, a fellow alumnus and art lover.

They stood before the judge and Nate laid a steadying touch on Cornelius' elbow. For a moment he thought he'd have to plead for him until the sax man croaked his not guilty. To stand before that bench was to feel a nakedness of soul no suit could hide.

But in the ADA's office, the rigor of legal judgment was gone, and Nate's plea went down as smoothly as a good rye whisky shared by old friends. The ADA chuckled at Nate's evidence, and Nate wondered how many Cornell Law graduates had those same English tailored suits and precisely doled-out smiles; his fellow Columbia Law alumni tended to be a little more on the browbeaten blue blazer side.

The ADA lit up a Dunhill pipe and let rip on the cabaret laws. An embarrassment, a throwback, a kangaroo court. Everyone knew the cabaret card had to go, but Mayor Wagner was dragging his feet on that like he did with everything else. The young man tamped down his pipe and gave it a good long suck, smiling tightly around the stem.

"We call this an Ex Lax case. Move the crap out of the system fast fast fast."

Cornelius loosened the buttons of his boxy suit and seemed to expand in the sunlight. He called Nate a miracle worker for getting the case dismissed, thanked the Good Lord he'd met him at the club. Nate relished such praise, so exotically different from the hail-fellow-well-met backslaps that greeted a successful conflict resolution in Schomer's office. He decided to share a ride with Cornelius, hailed a Checker cab, and the two men slid into the back. Cornelius lit up a Camel and propped his leg up on the stool.

Nate gave the driver directions to the Upper East Side and then to Harlem. The pudgy cabbie looked at them so peevishly that Nate made a mental note of his photo and hack number. The ride was almost too leisurely. Traffic moved in fits and starts flanked by the blaring of sirens that pointed at some incident uptown. Cornelius, basking in his deliverance, spun out a monologue like a breakneck solo.

"Man, poor Art gets bugged because he has a genuinely integrated scene at the Gate, so some black cats actually charge discrimination, and Art says yeah, I admit Herbie Mann gets a gig every once in awhile... "

Cornelius roared, and the cabbie bounced him a dirty look off the rearview.

"And then the white cops, they go after Art too. Man I've

been in the bathroom, seen one of those plainclothes guys drop a cigarette butt on the floor, ticket Art for that. Art's the man in the middle."

Nate smiled reflexively and wondered if the cabbie had a relative on the police force.

"Man, I can't thank you enough, Nate, I just—hey, are we near Fourth and Bleecker? Oh man, I gotta make a quick stop, just gotta say hello to somebody, you mind? Just an address at Fourth and Bleecker, only be a minute."

The cabbie took it in surly stride, double-parking in front of a row of walkups grey as the pavement beneath them, their doors surmounted with cornices whose layers of soot masked leonine faces wreathed in vines. Cornelius eased himself out of the cab and glanced at a pair of ground floor windows blocked by curtains and burglar gates.

"Be back in a few, Nate. And hey... thanks for watchin' my horn, man."

What in the world did he mean by that? His horn was back at his apartment.

Cornelius lumbered up the stairs, rang a buzzer on a mailbox, slipped inside. Nate heard another flurry of sirens. The wind blew a newspaper up against the wrought iron gate guarding the basement, and a burst of sunlight shivered in its wake, painting iron shadows against the lace curtains of the brownstones. Nate squinted through the taxi window as Cornelius came back out, hunched his shoulders, hustled down the stairs, and ran straight into two burly, fast-moving men who sprang from a parked car to waylay him by the curb.

"Right on time, Cornelius! Better than the A Train!"

One of the assailants yanked a small bag from Cornelius' coat. The other wrenched his hands behind his back and quickly handcuffed him. Now the first plainclothes cop was looming over the cab, the door flying open.

"Police! Out of the cab, now!"

The sleeve of Nate's coat was in the plainclothesman's fist. To his horror he was being manhandled faster than he could clear the cab. He barely grabbed his valise before the door slammed shut, the cabbie cursed and pulled away, and Nate stared into the face of the bruiser cop from Smokes.

"Whaddya know, Nate Kovacs, the hophead mouthpiece!"

"Officer, I had nothing to do with—"

"Case dismissed, huh? You must feel proud!"

Nate was spun around and slammed into a parked car. His valise dropped to the pavement. He gasped as much in horror as in pain as the cop yanked his arms onto the car roof, brute strength reducing him to a spastic puppet. The hands swatted him like clubs and tore through his pockets.

"Officer, I was sharing a cab with him!"

"You were gonna have a party? Little celebration?"

"I've just come from the Assistant District Attorney's office! I think you might want to be careful about how you proceed at this point."

Nate didn't know where the mettle in his voice came from, maybe sheer desperation, or the sight of a sidewalk's worth of people giving him a wide berth and disgusted stares. Out of his peripheral vision he could see his former client squashed down into the back seat of the unmarked Buick. At last his tormentor ordered him to turn around, and Nate peeled himself off the icy chassis of the car. The cop from the alley— no less frightening in a plaid shirt and London fog raincoat. He smoked his breath into Nate's face. He heard a train of police sirens, but they seemed to be receding away from him—if they could only pull this cop in their wake and leave him in peace.

"Concerned about procedure, Esquire? Lemme identify myself. I'm Detective Loomis Regan, and I'm conducting an arrest at the scene of a narcotics violation."

"Detective Regan, I was just giving him a lift home!"

"I see. We all make mistakes. Errors in judgment. How in the hell were you supposed to know what a stone junkie Cornelius was?"

Jesus, Regan was just toying with him, still believing Nate complicit in the narcotics sale. He was going to be arrested.

Loomis reached into his pocket, and showed Nate the bag of heroin.

"Ever see one of these? Take a good look. Kapeesh?"

Regan pressed up against him and practically shoved the bag against his face. It was translucent, like the sac of fluid attached to an IV tube, and its sheen over the powder crackled in Regan's grasp. Nate was glad he was backed up against the car because he felt otherwise his legs might give way.

"I got one big fucking reprimand from that snotnosed d.a. And look at this!"

Regan at last backed off with the bag and eyed the few remaining onlookers until they quickly dispersed. Nate found he could breathe again. He kneeled to pick up his valise.

"Just so you don't think I'm oppressing or discriminating against your client. Tell ya the truth, I like jazz. I really do. Charlie Parker. Always good for a great set Saturday night and a great bust afterwards."

He shot a baleful look at the unmarked car.

"So Cornelius is jonesin', happens to be in your cab... I'll keep you out of Dutch for now, Nate. Don't mind if I call you Nate, do you?"

Above the weave of drum, bass, and piano the sax keened, squawked, then soared in celebration of the Creator. Danny, who'd been in a jittery insomniac mood, now rocked his head with a kind of silent laughter, clearly digging it. Bruce waited on his observations.

Bruce just didn't get Coltrane. Miles' experimentation he understood. Solos on modal slices of the scale, orbits like those *Life* Magazine renderings of radiation belts, ignited by red and blue cosmic rays that expanded into lonely regions of deep space. But Coltrane was supposed to be the real musical astronaut and Bruce missed him entirely. ABC-Paramount-Impulse, riding a wave of music promotion in the wake of the Beatles, was sending freelance "hit men" to the various radio stations to promote jazz combos, part of their Big Drive in '65.

The John Coltrane Quartet's version of the *Sound of Music* ditty "My Favorite Things" had been a surprise chart climber. Bruce had written that it was a homage to Rodgers and Hammerstein laced with sly filigrees of hip intoxication. The swinger take on the tune, a whistling exotic Oriental soundtrack to an easy backbeat.

He'd then called Coltrane's solos a musical joke based on Swiss yodeling. That was when his music critic colleagues had made a joke out of him. One had finally suggested he check out some North Indian sitar ragas by Ravi Shankar, which Bruce had found interminable, but they did yield a clue. Coltrane was somehow trying to fuse raga and swing, African music and Eastern religion—okay, and Miles in *Sketches of Spain* was dipping into flamenco, part of music's new international plumage. But what the hell was going on in this record?

"Man, LISTEN to that! It's just four little notes. He keeps spinning out those four notes, just singing with them... Man, now it's... listen to what he's doing!"

"It's all over the place... "

"Exactly, Dad. Those four notes... they're searching for the key! Just floating, searching. Man, these guys are way out!"

At least Bruce knew, as Danny rapturously tracked the solo, that the restlessness his kid had shown lately was musical in nature. He knew from Danny's embrace of Coltrane that he was looking for other musical ideas, but where that would fit into the Phantastics he had no clue.

The four floating notes became a vocal chant of the title, "a love supreme," repeated over and over again. What the hell? Let Danny incubate more insights. Coltrane had recently placed near the top of a survey of most popular artists on college campuses. That meant he was filtering down to high schools as surely as marijuana and miniskirts.

"This at least sounds like real jazz."

"Sounds like blues to me, Dad. That weird up and down the neck sliding blues. And spirituals. Man does this bring it on home!"

Okay, spirituals, that's better, that was a lead he could use. Coltrane's new gospel. After all, the man had called a cut on one of his previous albums "Spiritual," and "Alabama," off the "Live at Birdland" album, had sounded like Mahalia Jackson singing a long sorrowful hymn. Now the music was cutting loose again… or maybe he could call this the album's Hallelujah chorus….

Bruce jotted some notes while Danny sat between the KLH speakers, entranced. At least while he was in the room with Bruce he wouldn't smoke a joint. Bruce was getting tired of cleaning up the weekend roaches so Shari wouldn't find them, trying to needle Danny into taking it elsewhere. You still have to obey the house rules, pirate king. So Bruce sat through music he found tiresome, runs of arpeggios that seemed to play hide-and-seek with the rhythm, and then a final eerie solo over a thunder of cymbals and tom toms, as Danny rested his head in his hands and exclaimed it was like Olatunji. Another useful blurb.

He hoped Danny would go to sleep now, but instead he rushed into his room and closed the door, and soon Bruce heard him weirdly sawing on his violin. Damned if it didn't sound like Coltrane.

Bruce decided to skip out to buy the *Daily News*, whose evening editions he enjoyed for the sports pages. He blanched with shock at the photo of Malcolm X's sheeted body. The stationery store's owner glowered at the headlines.

"Jigaboos are going crazy up there."

Later, devouring the news of the assassination page by page, he was stunned even further by the lead item on Page 8. The paper crowed that Cornelius Hill, acquitted of narcotics charges, whose ridiculous setup Bruce had thought would be a perfect opportunity to strike down the cabaret laws, had been arrested that very same day for the very same crime, in fact right while being given a lift home from the courthouse by his lawyer, Nathan Kovacs, of the firm of Schomer, Fries and Associates.

Two o'clock in the afternoon, but Nate was leaving his office. His attaché case was much heavier than normal, but it nonetheless accommodated all his remaining papers. Odd how little you actually keep at an office that's been your second home.

Nate took the same route back to the subway that he'd walked for fifteen years, past heaps of snow abraded with the morning's load of soot, the metal basket cheerfully warning "Every Litter Bit Hurts," and he thought about Skitch Henderson, a roomy new Thunderbird, golf in Mamaroneck. Not his tastes or possessions but those of his boss. That's how well he knew Ted Schomer.

If you knew your boss that well, how could you be fired?

He shoved in his token and pushed through the turnstile into the deserted station. The train announced itself, beam of light marking the tracks, headlights dilating as they blasted a path through the tunnels that underlay his vanished routine.

Before being summoned to Schomer's office for what seemed a regretful but relieved dismissal, Nate had fashioned some very stern words for a planned meeting with Karen after school. There had been disciplinary infractions culminating in a fight with her friend Nina Kempster, events so incomprehensible that they now seemed of a piece with his termination, the potential short circuit in the household you were always warned about, all the currents of comfort turned to one electric shock after another.

Now he saw Karen waiting in the principal's office. She was so petite, so fine-boned, with eyes so dark yet alive with mercurial inquisitiveness, eyes so like Becky's, that he couldn't put up a front for her, couldn't lord it over her and be the disciplinarian, especially when he himself had been laid so low.

But he had to muster some kind of parental indignity once he saw Karen's aggrieved little friend was also there. She had a tiny red scratch on her face, and her mother, Dorothy Kempster, a stylish woman in a fur coat with large, angry grey eyes, would clearly have some words about where that scratch came from. Thankfully Mrs. Kempster accepted his apology with good grace, although she felt there was no excuse for the scratching, her Nina might have gotten really hurt. The principal blustered his way through a speech warning next time might mean a suspension for Karen, but his heart didn't seem to be in it. Nate realized that leniency was on the table, for they knew he was a widower and Karen half an orphan.

Nate walked Karen back home down Park Avenue. The shrubbery of the traffic aisles glimmered a pale green, but Nate didn't feel like pointing out the first signs of spring to her as he might have done on another day, and instead let his silence speak for him. I bought the record, she finally muttered. The words exploded out of Nate. What did you think you were doing buying a Beatle record? Well, it's a single, I don't have enough money for the album! That's not the point, you're not supposed to be away from the yard during recess! And then you sneak away to play it in the Audiovisual room, and you get caught fighting with your friends? I get to put it on the turntable if I buy it! You shouldn't have even been there in the first place! And then you smack them and scratch them and spit at them?

"They cornered me!"

Nate stopped when he felt as ridiculous as he probably looked shouting down at this tiny girl, especially since he worried his anger would go out of control, for Karen sometimes seemed to contain all the luminous high spirits and feistiness of Becky at her best boiled down to resentfulness and spite. And Becky's most nagging flaw, her highhandedness, could be flowering behind Karen's wounded eyes into a disdain for Nate's words and everything he could ever be to her.

A leisurely catch with Artie on a sunny day like this. Karen, having just found her running legs, jumped to try and intercept the Spalding. She flew like a spark between them until he tossed her the ball. She dropped it, picked it up as if it were newly minted, and released it with a high ringing laugh in the first direction that struck her fancy. Any direction she chose.

He tried one last appeal.

"If you keep acting like this you'll never get into a good school!"

But how can I pay for a good school now?

He came into the foyer with Karen. Artie walked out of his room to greet him. He cringed as he remembered how Artie had

had to tell Karen her mother was dying. This time, as it should be, he alone would lower the next hammer blow on all of them. How he had taken a wrong turn in a Greenwich Village alley, tried to be a nice guy, a hipster kind of guy, and now the cold breath of the street was down their backs. *Hiya crumbum, curveball, screwball, ta-ta-ta, ta-tata-ta...*

Artie, pronouncing the name like a joke he couldn't get, gave Nate a message. He told him that an Izzy Hamerow had called, and wanted to meet with him.

"So Nate, anyone ever tell you you look like Henry Fonda?"

"I've heard it from time to time."

"That modesty, that bit of a stammer—it's perfect."

"Well, I doubt I could be his stand-in."

It wasn't too witty, but Nate was reaching for any words he could to make the conversation more appropriate.

Izzy sat at a big formica desk beneath a window that served as a frame for a brick wall. He munched an egg salad sandwich as he interviewed Nate. The room needed more light, the walls another coat of paint, and the office was chilly enough on this unseasonably cool day so that both men were still in their coats. Izzy's parka was open to a plaid shirt whose buttons couldn't hold back the flab that swelled over his pair of chinos. At last the radiator came on, hissing a leap between two octaves as the stream followed a trail of paint flakes up the wall.

"Actually, that could figure into my grand strategy, Nate. I need a jack Jew."

"Excuse me?"

"Like what some of the servicemen called a jack Mormon? A Mormon who isn't blonde, doesn't look fresh out of Utah?"

Nate folded his hands, smiled, and considered walking out on the interview quicker than that Miles Davis set.

"So this is why we're meeting? I'm Jewish and I look a little like Henry Fonda?"

Nate tried to avert his gaze as Izzy piled into the egg salad sandwich. On the opposite wall was a framed law degree from

Brooklyn College, and a photo of Bertrand Russell at a "Ban The Bomb" demonstration. He tried not to witness the inevitable conjunction of egg salad and beard, but with a quick chomp there it was, the chunks of egg adhering to Izzy's grey follicles. He pointed it out as delicately as possible, and Izzy nodded and napkined his beard with one practiced swipe.

"Well, that and you so effectively took Cornelius away from me."

"I didn't know he'd retained you. You could've told me and out of professional courtesy I—"

"Oh please, Cornelius couldn't 'retain' anybody. I volunteered to help him out. He's a good bebopper. That new jazz sounds like kittens thrown into a garbage truck. Anyway, once an uptown guy like you showed an interest, I figured, okay, better for him better for me because honestly, I was worried Cornelius was a little shaky. So once I learned he was in the shitter again, I called you up just to commiserate, and once I heard you were canned.... Look, lemme lay it out here. I'm overwhelmed with guys looking for the legal last resort. And judges are tired of seeing my pinko face, even if I do usually have a point about the First Amendment and all. I'm a polarizing kind of schmuck, let's face it, and I need someone like you. Handsome, oil on troubled waters, the whole David Susskind thing. Besides, I'm tired of being a one-man band. You'll have to study up a little, but we're not drowning in precedents here. Free expression law, with these new Supreme Court decisions, is kind of wide open. But it's never boring. Come on, Nate. Don't you miss the parry and thrust?"

Nate reached for any resistance he could offer to this latest swerve of his life.

"Do you have a profit-sharing plan?"

"What?"

"Ted Schomer had a pioneer profit-sharing plan."

"Yeah, he's a pioneer with his profit-sharing plan... he's gonna take it to California with him. Come on, Schomer's a sneaky prick. You're handling—well it wasn't just deficient employees and shortage and loss cases. I remember you guys repped a company that got sued for SEC fraud, right? Did a little Fifth Avenue estate practice? Was he paying you enough for that?"

Going into the office each morning after seeing Becky racked with pain, greeting the uptown chauffeured clients and trying to make his paycheck stretch between three doctors, two hospitals...

"Come on, you must've figured out he was screwing you blind. Anyway, I don't have a profit-sharing plan, Nate, because as of yet I don't have profits. But I think I can pay you close to what he was grinding you with even in the expectation of profits. That Citizens Committee at the Gate—you think they didn't notice what you tried to do with Cornelius? That "out of Vietnam" demonstration in your neighborhood, on Lexington Avenue? Think of how big the next one will be when Westmoreland gets 25,000 more troops. Johnson's bombing the North, doubling the Draft, plus I got Negro clients whose babies have rat bites and they're ready to have a sit-in on Mayor Wagner's lawn. This isn't only, to my way of thinking, the right side of the law to be in—it just might be what you call a growth business, Nate. And you've made a pretty good entry into it... and you did make a choice, Nate."

The radiator gurgled off with a loud clack.

"But hey... I understand if you've got other offers... "

Musical rooms. Artie into mom's old bedroom, Dad to the hideaway sofa bed in the foyer. Golden sprays of flowers on the forsythia bushes in the Park, and shimmering veils of leaves on the giant trees over Fifth Avenue. Two American astronauts orbiting the earth for the first time.

Artie was more than ready for the move. Karen's drawings had proliferated like a rash all over the bedroom walls. Women in Parisian white lace dresses like Audrey Hepburn in *My Fair Lady,* and endless *Pirates of Penzance* women in bell gowns and antique police and the swaggering Pirate King, who was Danny Geller right down to the hooked nose and drooping bangs. There was no room for his new Julie Christie poster or even his framed photographs.

Artie settled King Zor next to the turntable of his new birthday stereo player, which sat squarely in the center of the room, trailing wires to two small speakers on the chest of drawers and his new desk. Odd Ogg took up residence in the back of his closet. It was a relief to move down the hall from Karen. These days he couldn't get along with her at all. He'd gotten so tired of her arguments with Dad over school applications and interviews she was always late for. No matter how much Artie asked her not to upset Dad, not to bother him now that he was adjusting to a new job, the yelling never stopped. Finally she said she'd work on the school applications—just stop being *the man of the house* and let her alone.

You never knew what might set her off. He had picked up Mom's old My Sin by Lanvin perfume bottle on her dresser drawer and Karen had burst into tears. He'd had to place the perfume back in its exact same position and promise not to touch it again.

Artie escaped to the Park as the weather grew warmer and green moss coated the pitted stone abutments long since rubbed to the texture of an Arrowroot cookie until they had the mellowness of a face turned up to the sun. There was softball with his friends and walks along the reservoir where women now strolled under the cherry trees in the new T dresses that clung to their every curve. It seemed Manhattan was overflowing with Julie Christies.

He decided to take Audrey to the park on his upcoming date with her, their first unescorted walk. She wore a short-sleeved ribbed sweater and a knee-length skirt and looked classy without being flirty. First he took her to a movie, *Arabesque*, starring Gregory Peck and Sophia Loren, duly impressing her by paying for both tickets. The movie was a good choice, perky caper stuff, and she liked Peck almost as much as he liked Loren. Taking her to the Central Park Zoo, though, was a mistake. Despite all his fond childhood memories, why hadn't he remembered Mr. Lansing's comments about the place? It's an animal Alcatraz, he'd roared, you've got a lion in a cage the size of a camper van, for Chrissake! The big cats did look ready to be stuffed. The capuchin monkeys at least struck Audrey as cute, even if there were about a hundred of them in the stinking cage and they swarmed over each other's asses crying out for food. But as he and Audrey approached the elephant and hippopotamus house, the hippo in his exterior glass cage rotated torpidly and sprayed a ton of shit toward the spectators. Audrey said you wanted to just find the keys and let them all go free.

Wandering behind Belvedere Castle by the Great Lawn was much better. They snuck some kisses on the paths alongside the tulips, violets, and columbines of the Shakespeare Garden. She laughed and let him drape his arm around her as they watched ducks arrow their way across the ancient green pond. But when he tried to really make out with her she turned away and told him that she was going to spend summer with a London family and then spend the year as an exchange student in England. Gone for a whole year in London. She happily ran off a list of fashion stores she was going to see near Carnaby Street and up in Kensington.

God, not only would she be gone for a whole year, she'd be so far up on the hierarchy of in-crowd-ness when she got back that she might as well be dead.

Artie spent the first night in his new room with his mind orbiting back into the past, all those grade school parties, thinking about Audrey's tolerance of his makeout moves, her great Junior Miss clothes and the tits that floated beneath them. He said his farewell to her by playing "Yes It Is" by the Beatles and "Go Now" by the Moody Blues and "Little Miss Go Go" by Gary Lewis and the Playboys over and over until Dad ordered him to stop.

Karen wished Artie didn't close the door so much. She liked Gary Lewis and the Playboys, they were cute, they had an accordion in the band, which was funny, but probably if the door was open Dad would scream at him to turn it down anyway, and at least she didn't have to walk by and see his stupid comic books all over Mom's old furniture. Along with the high-heeled shoes and pumps she'd sequestered in the hall closet, she had at least also saved the perfume bottles and moved them to her room, the one with the prismed top that splintered light into motes of pink and green, the squat indigo spray bottle, the tiny Chanels, even if mom would never again open each fragrance for Karen to inhale like roses.

It still hurt her in the stomach so much, all that had been swept away by doctor's hands, mover's hands, masculine hands—even Dad's hands, with long pianist's fingers—and yet they claimed they knew what was good for her, and every school catalog Dad showed to her spoke the same way, made that same claim with lists of courses that marched in hard straight lines, stupid rows of students in matching skirts.

But Nina Kempster had shown her one that was full of paintings and sculpture, lines from poets, a flautist framed by a sunlit bay window. The Blakewell School for Music and Art. She was crying now for Dad to put it on the list of schools the same way she had cried for the perfume bottles. Nina loved the school too, they'd thoroughly made up, and together they'd escape.

Sometimes Nate wondered if he'd become the most déclassé possible legal practitioner, a Third Avenue chiropractor of the law. Three days after his arrival the beatnik bard Allen Ginsberg slouched into the office—an aging cherub with burgeoning hanks of hair, thick glasses, a sunken chest, and a wispy but needlingly insistent voice—for a chat with Izzy about one of his endless protest arrests. On the way out, Izzy introduced Nate to Ginsberg, who was astonished at the new partnership. He'd assumed Nate was an accountant there to do Izzy's taxes.

Nate hardly blamed the poet. He felt that every day he commuted not just to another neighborhood but another world. Past the gentility of the carriage houses of the Mews, and the gracious red brick Georgian walkups of Washington Square, was a political and cultural war zone. Coffeehouse owners, poets, filmmakers, and artists trooped to Izzy's door to make their complaints about what Nate had to admit was a bizarre array of penalties. Laws against putting on a play in a poetry space without a theater license, or showing a movie in a coffeehouse without a film license, or even against the founding puppeteer of the Bread and Puppet Theater showing his own puppets in his own home.

Behind the authorities' clampdown was the conviction that the Village was a den of sex and Communism, and for Izzy that all boiled down to the Lenny Bruce case. He followed the trial with the passion of a semipro ballplayer in the bleachers at the World Series.

"They were out to get him! His audiences were crawling with license inspectors trying to dress like beatniks!"

"He is a potty mouth, Izzy."

"Yeah right, potty mouth, sick comedian… Nate, you ever listened to him? Why is all his political and social commentary dismissed as claptrap while the dirty words are all that's emphasized? He's using them to unmask hypocrisy!"

"But when he uses so much obscenity, Izzy, that makes it a little difficult to defend him!"

"What makes him difficult to defend is that he's a paranoid loose cannon who won't listen to his lawyers. But the words? What's funnier, schtup or sexual intercourse? What's more real? And it doesn't arouse prurient interest! It's not like Lenny's trying to get you to jack off! They say he wielded the mike in a masturbatory fashion… it's too much!"

Gradually Nate accustomed himself to his new turf's witty carnality, it's cocktail of intellect and lust. He thumbed through the movie section of the *Village Voice* and its pages of high-contrast photos and ink sketch ads that juxtaposed severe announcements for Ingmar Bergman's *The Silence* with ads for films about orgies on Greek isles and Italian hideaways. Huge-busted Nordic blondes, Italians with gloriously blossoming thighs, and frisky Londoners starred in *Swedish Vacation*, *Seduced And Abandoned*, *The Young Lovers*, *The Knack*, *Banana Peel*, and *Marriage Italian Style*. Every month Izzy itchily awaited the arrival of *Evergreen* Magazine, and Nate had to admit he enjoyed his occasional peeks at "The Adventures of Barbarella, the Thrill-Loving French Sex Kitten."

Still there was always MacDougal Street to assail him on a late night, the barkers at coffee shops, one with the Salvation Army tag still on his raincoat, shouting their invitations to a poetry "show," the rumble of motorcycle packs, the pill buyers, transvestites, homosexual couples, a girl shrieking wheeee, I'm a beatnik, come arrest me, baby.

This was what Izzy called the shrink row, laughing academy part of the Village, which sometimes made Nate want to close Izzy's door behind him and never come back. But Karen had finally hunkered down to a high school application, charmed an interviewer, and, to her immense delight, gotten admitted to the Blakewell School. The family had celebrated with a burger and ice cream sundae dinner at Leo's, a coffee shop with comfortable red banquettes and brass chandeliers that had long welcomed Nate and the kids. Karen chattered about how she and Nina Kempster planned to take music lessons. Nate figured out the cost of tuition and the flute Karen so passionately wanted to learn, and he knew he was going to be joined at the hip with Izzy Hamerow for awhile.

He willed himself to learn how to apply the Supreme Court's new "redeeming cultural value" criteria to whatever the NYPD judged obscene. There wasn't much in the way of law books at the office—does this look like a library to you, Izzy would shout—and so Nate went to the public library, N.Y.U., the Lawyers' Guild, and the Columbia Center for Social Justice and Law. Young men who wore string ties over their white shirts, after initially surveying Nate as if he'd dropped in from Mars, would guide him to the right First Amendment cases, and after seeing what an iron butt he was about studying up, even refer him some clients.

One of them was Guy Ferren and his underground film import *Une Fausse Splendeur*. Ferren's troupe staged self-destroying "happenings"—pianos blowing up, wax mannequins burning to a crisp in a wrecked auto—before their coterie of fans and the bewildered residents of slum neighborhoods in the East Village. Ferren had also begun exhibiting *Une Fausse Splendeur* once a week at the Cinema Collective. Detectives had been so outraged by what they'd seen that they'd leaped out of the audience and wrenched Ferren and his film away from the projector. Nate had accepted the case on Izzy's behalf before they'd actually screened the film.

A bizarre series of mechanical constructions that a member of the troupe explained were "readymades" exploded in sequence. The camera tracked past them to a room where men chained in cages watched a pair of muscular naked women stalk each other. They pounced, grappled, appeared to have sex, and then, in a series of close-ups, ate each other until there were only two heads left. A troupe member explained to Izzy that the effects were achieved with parts of cadavers from a Parisian medical school. It was the first movie Nate had ever seen that had literally almost made him vomit. Nate argued vehemently that they ought to throw Ferren and his movie to the Vice Squad, but Izzy saw it as a test case of the principle, laid down by the Supreme Court, that a work must be judged in its entirety to arouse prurient interest. The sex in the film was surrounded by anti-capitalist, anti-materialist symbolism.

"Izzy, you've got to be kidding! Those women eat each other! How is any judge or lay person going to see cultural value in something like that? The guy's got bats in his belfry!"

"He's a French intellectual, Nate. His bedside reading was the Theater of Cruelty. Let's get back to the point of freedom of speech!"

"Freedom of speech? This film is… it makes you sick! It's anti-art, anti-sex, anti-everything!"

"That's great! That's it, Nate! It can't be obscene, it can't arouse prurient interest, because it's anti-sex!"

"No, wait a minute, Izzy—"

"No, Nate, you got it! *Une Fausse Splendeur* is a mordant satire on contemporary sexuality that's so disgusting it can't possibly arouse anyone! It might even cause people to give up fucking!"

To Nate's horror, the liberal judge they drew for Ferren's case bought the argument and even apologized to Ferren. Nate was thankful that Izzy took sole credit in the *Village Voice*. But the victory also convinced him to put Nate's name on the door. It would be Hamerow and Kovacs from now on.

Artie and Karen seemed proud that their dad now had his name on his business. If the transition filled Nate with a secret dread, if it sometimes bothered him that he owed his financial breathing room to his rescue of a lesbian cannibal film—well, he could at least afford to keep up Karen's flute lessons and take Artie to Met games at Shea Stadium. The lineup of once great stars who'd been cast off from National League teams, the Richie Ashburns, Gus Bells and Gil Hodgeses of yellowing baseball cards, posted an unbelievable series of losses. But Nate enjoyed watching the team, whom New Yorkers had embraced with a defeatist pride that one sportswriter had called "masochismo." The beloved losers were symbols for the troubles of the city, and a *Mad* Magazine parody of baseball, as surely as his job was a bizarre inversion of everything he'd ever thought about the law.

And on his few free nights he worked for his maverick Congressman friend John Lindsay, "The District's Pride, The Nation's Hope," who was trying to repeat Fiorello LaGuardia's feat of building a fusion reform candidacy and winning the mayoralty in a town where it was almost impossible for a Republican to win anything. Still Nate had seen in his own neighborhood the appeal of a six-foot-plus high-minded man with chiseled features who was so debonair in his embrace of the grit and grime of New York City. Bob Price, his campaign manager, opened hundreds of storefronts. He had Lindsay hike neighborhoods throughout not just Manhattan but all five boroughs. Sometimes, Lindsay exclaimed to Nate and the members of the Republican Club's inner circle, he had to carry file cards to remember what part of the city he was in. As Lindsay loosened up in the summer heat, he wore shirts with frayed collars and the sleeves rolled up, danced the Watusi at a disco, and took a much photographed swan dive into a pool in the Rockaways, and the voters seemed to come around to him.

And Nina Kempster's mother Dorothy joined the Lindsay

campaign. He'd never forgotten how she'd refrained from giving him a real tongue-lashing at the school. Now that Nina and Karen had regained their friendship, Dorothy was someone Nate could talk to about finding movies for the kids amidst all the sex films. No, *What's New Pussycat?* was definitely too risqué, but *Father Goose* was actually a family movie with Cary Grant. And Dorothy, who was divorced, told him that when there's grief or anger in the house a little girl will pull away and you reach out and they'll pull away again and sometimes, contrary to Dr. Spock, you have to drag them back by main force.

"They are small, you know."

After Artie went off to Camp Saco, Nate took a day off to spend a weekend with Karen at Harold and Esther's summer home, a little dove-grey house overlooking an estuary off the Long Island Sound. Karen, who embraced the country far more easily than Artie, loved the rosebushes and the Canada geese that visited the water. Nate walked with her down a path in the woods and taught her to listen for the bird calls: the gargled trill of a woodpecker, the cardinal's staccato triplets, the strenuous repertoire of cheeps and trills of the mockingbird. Redwings flashed across their path as a yellow wren in the tree above cantilevered from twig to twig. While Harold barbecued the burgers and buns with Cousin Amy and Cousin Sue, Nate sat with Karen on the front lawn and watched the fireflies. She laughed at the way they looked so clumsy at first, insect dirigibles wobbling over the bushes, until they abruptly rode the air on a serene path climbing to a swift green flame.

As he held his daughter's hand, all their spats when he entered her room at the wrong time, the issues of who was right and who was wrong in family arguments that seemed like anguished fittings of a jigsaw puzzle that could never be solved, all were forgotten as the volatile, exquisitely vanishing specks of light floated over the twilit lawn.

Nate returned from his getaway to learn that Izzy had put them on a team of lawyers defending Mobilization for Youth, a City-supported organization formed to combat juvenile delinquency with social programs A State Senate committee was investigating the "Mobe" for Communist leanings.

Why did Izzy always have to raise the stakes? Nate was suddenly caught in a city version of the McCarthy hearings, up against an old Commie-hunter from the HUAC days. What if he had to face off against men he might meet again at a "Lindsay for Mayor" function?

But he couldn't avoid confronting the Committee and their bank of microphones, and while he tried to be accommodating as possible, along with the quaver in his voice there was unexpected strength as he invoked cases like Slochower vs. Board of Education to argue that no one can be forced to brand their colleagues as suspected Communists or be dismissed for refusing to incriminate themselves. Nate, Izzy, and their fellow lawyers managed to stop the investigation and no one lost their jobs, but everyone knew that the Mobilization's days were numbered.

Some of the kids in the "Mobe" invited the lawyers to a meeting in Harlem. Taking the train up to 125th and 7th Nate could tell Izzy was nervous as he was. The Watts neighborhood in Los Angeles had just exploded. Thirty-four dead, nine hundred injured, whole city blocks burned to the ground.

They emerged near Harlem's biggest soapbox, flanked by a cluster of churches. Somberly dressed Black Muslims—Nate could never get over their rigorousness, how they seemed pressed into their black suits—lined the streets. One took the speakers' platform to address men and women who might have been the maids and mechanics, porters and dance band musicians of Nate's childhood—by day a great mass of humble laborers, polite, cheerful, patient, by night gathered in private, happy rituals they freely shared—who were now massing against all the indignities and blows they'd ever experienced, one great slow recoil of fury.

"Brother Malcolm said we were the same as the oppressed in Algeria, or in the Congo with Lumumba. Up here in the ghetto, just 'cause they don't kill you all at once doesn't mean they don't kill you one day at a time!"

The meeting Nate and Izzy attended was held in a nearby storefront by a group named the Militant Workers and Artists Forum, part of a teach-in on the lessons of the Watts riots and Malcolm X's assassination. The walls were lined with pictures of mourners at Malcolm X's funeral and his wife Betty Shabazz standing by the bronze coffin wrapped in white linen. The photos refracted so much anger it was as if a transcontinental ricochet of the bullets that had struck Malcolm had lit up Watts and then scattered right back to New York.

The Forum speakers decried having freedom to vote, but not freedom to live like human beings. One of the local antipoverty leaders had done his homework, and he knew that under the Economic Opportunity Act of 1964 the city poverty boards didn't have to include representatives of the poor, and that the housing bill would get poor people maybe 3500 units a year for next four years. LBJ is saying "We Shall Overcome," he roared, but what you gonna overcome with that? It seems all Whitey listens to is a brick through a window and burn, baby, burn.

An older man in a faded seersucker shirt and jeans got up to speak to the crowd.

"You're not sayin' all of what Brother Malcolm said. You use Brother Malcolm for your purpose. Malcolm wanted you to wake up to your humanity and heritage so you could leave the slave mentality behind, so you could act and think independently, not just riot in the streets. See, I heard Malcolm when he told the white reporter in Harlem that he understood our actions might have the seeds, the seeds of violence, but he wanted to use the attack to reach a positive goal. Don't just say yes to Mr. Charlie, let your anger out, make the whites see it will be costly to let us suffer. But then you have to give the man a chance."

"No, man, those guys should've blown up the Statue of Liberty the way Malcolm wanted!"

"Malcolm had nothin' to do with that! Malcolm never would have done that! Malcolm saw in Mecca that you could reach out to the white man as a human being as long as he treated you with respect!"

"Hey, old man, Malcolm wasn't nonviolent!"

"You make fun of nonviolence? We got the vote with nonviolence! I saw nonviolence beat down Jim Crow at the worst in Mississippi. I saw Martin Luther King lead those people and shout we're on the move now! We're on the move! The violent man doesn't think of the race, he thinks of himself alone, his own revenge, to prove himself a man. But you think nonviolence is unmanly? You think it's weak? I heard Martin when he said that true peace is not weakness, no, Martin gave us Jesus' words, I come not to bring peace but a sword."

Nate looked at the room. A crowd alien to him right to the pores of their skin, denied human rights that he had always taken for granted. Next to him a fat, grubby partner he never would have chosen in a million years, who had led him to one of the fault lines where the city could crack apart. His hair stood on end as he realized he was in one of the strangest and most frightening places he'd ever been... and yet it was just two miles from his own neighborhood and the cadences of the old man's words reached straight to the essence of his purpose and profession. Nate's mind and heart were newly anchored.

"You see nonviolence is a signal, it's a signal that the oppressed are rising up and moving toward Justice, which is the only real peace, and you can ignore the signal, hell you can even stand in the way, but then you're opposed to the sword of Justice, you're opposed to all that's righteous. We're not yet at the point where all we do is burn our homes down like a bunch of fools. We can still raise up, we can still work toward Justice!"

It was weird being in Camp Saco when Audrey was in London. To lie on the same wool blankets and blue sheets that he'd brought up to Maine for the past six years, to watch dusk seep through the pine trees outside the screen windows and louvered shutters, and then read a letter from her with cheery tidbits like English guys are so funny and they can get away with

ANYTHING (just what he wanted to hear). Now he would send her a letter that was like a pathetic little tug on an ocean-length cord, about how he was old enough now to help the counselors take the kids on excursions like the Kezar Lakes Canoe trip, and how he pretty much had the run of the photography hut, and WHAT COULD THAT POSSIBLY MEAN TO HER?

Artie knew that, as sleepaway camps went, "Camp Sicko" was insane. Without knowing anything about camp budgets, he sensed it was run on a shoestring from the way that, during a "raid" on Bunk 3, kids from Bunk 4 had thrown a broom right through the cabin walls.

But Artie and his family had gotten used to his summers at this down-at-heels haven, where seventy or so hypereducated kids from New York City were shepherded by a bunch of collegiate city counselors—along with a rawboned, vaguely military contingent from the South—through a summer of sports, canoe trips, hiking, arts and crafts, and, thankfully, photography.

Hank, the photography counselor, a pretty neat guy who managed to be both an art school student and a track star, trusted Artie with the Camp Saco darkroom. Most importantly, he allowed Artie to use his Nikon SRL camera with its wheel of lenses. Artie became the official camp photographer, securing definite coolness and a kind of proprietary detachment from a routine where one kid still screamed for the counselors and wet his bed when mosquitoes bothered him; where an older counselor who had pissed off a couple of the southerners found a huge dead snapping turtle in his sheets; and where those same good-old-boy counselors once washed a kid's mouth out with soap for a dirty word, only to have to clean up his Cedarhurst puke for ten minutes afterwards. Now the camp was also a place where Artie could take a canoe out solo to a bend of the pond shrouded with glimmering reeds and dragonflies, and snap close-ups of hummingbirds over the water without feeling he had to explain himself to the more rugged elements in the camp, who'd once called him "farty Arty."

But he got more and more nervous about Audrey Mehlinger

being adrift in a Swinging London full of blonde, freckled Carnaby Streeters, and so took more and more long walks alone down the camp's forest trails. One morning when photography was unexpectedly canceled because of a leak that had sprung in the Quonset hut darkroom roof, Artie took off for the Badham House. Deserted long ago, it was shown off by the town as a little time capsule of Maine history. The old woman who watched over it loved to hint to the kids it was haunted. For Artie it was a treasure trove of light playing dramatically on rusted stoves, old bookshelves, dusty windows and piles of newspapers. Artie walked through the old House with its Civil War pictures, World War I German flag, and shriveled books. He took some carefully underexposed shots by the windows, and emerged by the cove that brushed up against the property.

At first he thought it really was a ghost, the gleaming white back, the loose blonde hair, but then he realized it was Michelle. The gorgeous camp dining hall waitress, the one that looked like the Swedish woman on the Noxzema commercial, "take eet all uff" Michelle as they called her, and there she was, lying on her stomach by the cove, the strands of a bikini tossed carelessly off her shoulders, a towel draped on her... bare ass? He was alone with take it all off Michelle! Not that anyone would ever believe that, unless... Artie crouched behind the screen of the bushes. The camera trembled in his hands like it had its own heartbeat, and he fought to keep it steady. He focused on Michelle, blurring out the leaves, and slowly, breathlessly pushed the button. The click seemed deafening, but she didn't budge. She lay there endlessly, with her towel and tube of Coppertone, and Artie couldn't leave. It was like when he'd taken a picture of a fawn on the Kezar Lakes trip; he tiptoed, slowly, trying to get a better angle, framed her beneath the gentle dip of a birch branch, and took another shot.

Now she stirred, and Artie, terrified, fascinated, wondered if he would be discovered right at the point where she rose naked. No, she hadn't noticed him, which was good, but she was tying on the bikini, which wasn't what he'd hoped, but maybe that was best, given how the blood vessels in his skull were exploding. He needed to steady the camera again as she walked into the water and her buttocks rolled and flexed on the longest legs he'd ever seen. She took a swim. He spun the lens wheel with trembling fingers, took two more shots, then she was getting up and walking back out and he spun the wheel again, oh God this was an Ursula Andress shot, the breasts dangling almost out of the leopard skin bikini. She lay back on the towel, fumbled with her cigarette pack, drew one out and smoked with total pleasure, craning her head to watch a duck swim across the cove, which allowed Artie two more shots outlined by the curve of a sumac branch and its pale white flowers.

Holding his breath, he crept, then ran back to camp. Words thumped to his heaving breaths... okay, she didn't get naked, maybe if I'd hung around, no that's good, that's good, it wasn't sick, it was like *Life* Magazine, maybe if I'd waited, maybe if I'd said something, no, are you crazy, you've got the pictures!... maybe....

As he crested a small hill and came to the wood bridge that led up to the camp's flagpole, the sunlight of the afternoon struck the hillock and the stream at the same time and he heard, from a counselor's portable radio, the Song that had been topping the WABC "Cousin Bruuucie!" Top 20 survey an unprecedented month. Guitars like steel files rasping into your brain, drums a fist banging on a door, three minutes and forty five seconds of relentlessness without a bridge or a break. He had seen the record but no one was allowed to play it on the camp p.a. system, it was too dirty, so you had to sneak into a counselor's meeting to hear it. But you couldn't escape it out in the sun wherever anyone had a transistor radio... the Song emblazoned with the blue logo of the capital city of rock and roll where Audrey frolicked and maybe he'd get to go one day... the photos in the camera juiced up every hope... an electric guitar like a laughing foghorn... NAA NAA, naa naa NAA, na-nah nah nah NAA NAA... he had to get to the darkroom... to the bedroom... and that beat pounding, pounding, let me in

because I'm so sharp, driving round the world... to make some
girl... and ah cain't GET NO!... no no YES!

They broke out the jay in the shelter of some trees at the
edge of the parking lot, quickly toking up between cupped hands,
eyes over their shoulders. Danny inhaled not just the reefer but
a whiff of Jimmy Hinton's fingers before the smoke hit his lungs.
Weird having a black pal, the bursts of orneriness, the distance,
the pungency of the skin. Weird and really great though, when
Jimmy told him about his job delivering snack food on a cart to
jazz studios. Being at Rudy Van Gelder's studio in New Jersey
when Coltrane's new record *Ascension* was cut. Six other horn
players as hunkered down and quiet as Musical Mission Control
listening to Trane before he led them in a full-out orchestral blast
of horns somehow freeform but also in unison that had everyone
in the studio screaming. Solos that danced with the bass and
drums, utterly loose and free; Trane called it "playing the big
room" and "cleaning the mirror."

Now, sharing joints and his parents' red wine from under his
jacket, it was Danny's turn to show Jimmy what he knew.

The crowd was insane. Plenty of fellow dopers, as he could tell
from the fugitive orange sparks everywhere. But also a constant
rush of teenyboppers who skittered by in their little tweed skirts
and ruffled blouses, followed by, sometimes leeringly followed
by, professorial types dressed in sports jackets with turtlenecks
draped over their paunches, who probably had hidden hip flasks
in their goody baskets.

How do you read an audience like this?

Forest Hills stadium on a summer Saturday night. First comes
an announcer straight out of Kingston Trio world, the honey deep
voice perfect for introing ballads about trains and highwaymen.
The older folk fans smile patiently to his patter. A breeze rustles
by and lifts the heat of the stadium, and in the breaking of that
spell the little girls scream to the anticipations that have them in a
tizzy. You get the feeling this old boy, for all his geniality, is there
to pass a torch, and yes, the next guy he introduces is the WINS

jock with the slicked back hair, straw fedora and mod jacket who calls himself the Fifth Beatle.

"Hey, it's Murray the K, and I got just one question... what's happening baby?"

What's happening is that Jimmy Hinton's in a fit of stoned hysterics, and the folkies have frowns on their faces like they need a Bromo Seltzer and the girls are going crazy for the man with the microphone to leave the fucking stage. But he riffs on about how he first discovered this guy's music in the clubs of Greenwich Village, and how it's grown, it's hit the airwaves, it's busting the charts, it's the wildest, the grooviest thing going....

"There's a new swinging mood in the country and Bobby baby is definitely what's happening! It's not rock, it's not folk, it's a new thing called Dylan!"

Out in the burrow of the spotlight, as the squeals and cheers die away, he looks so skinny in dugarees, a flowered shirt that caves in over his chest—in the clubs you don't realize how small he is, like the breath of the crowd could blow him away. From where Danny sits Dylan seems all guitar and frazzled dark hair and eyes that are pained, agile, curious, sometimes flicking skyward as if intercepting a joke and tossing it to the stars. He seems to be whispering to the guitar, and the guitar slowly answers with a strum.

"She Belongs to Me." Yeah, sure, this woman who takes the dark out of the nighttime, that you're proud to steal for and then leaves you on your knees. Danny heard it instantly. Two trains running. The "you" and the "I". The sneer and the harmonica's lonesome howl, the love and disdain, stereo reality. Already he can feel a part of his mind alchemized, a new way of seeing in the shadow corner where his visions of women and music are laid down. Already he's alert like never before, and then comes the real head feast. Words like the dope he just smoked, launching pads for the brain. The songs pour out of the tiny figure bent like a bow toward the mike and Danny surrenders, he's filled up with their images, the Cowboy Angel on forest clouds, a gypsy queen black Madonna, both outside the Gates of Eden, but proud and on fire, and then...

something so simple and pure… seasick sailors, empty-handed armies going… going… classic folk song doubling pattern expanding and deepening the meaning of abandonment and loss… and then… after awhile Danny, who thought he had Dylan down pat a long time ago, is just riding the rails of the music, just trying to hang on.

If he doesn't get it all it doesn't matter, the songs are veining themselves in him like fluorescent streaks in stone to be ignited below the spectrum later in the night.

Dylan's eyelashes beat like a second heart, a dandy flirting with his destiny, or a supplicant before the altar of whatever has shed its words upon him. The collegiates lean forward straining to piece it out, the chicks are awed into silence, you can hear the rumble of subways and crickets in the trees beyond the pinpoint guitar. Strike another match, yeah, the matches light up in the crowd, then the applause and the cheers.

Dylan drawls that some friends have dropped by to keep me company. The amps, the electric organ and the drums that have all along had the folkies fuming in their little territory now receive their players. Danny cheers as Al Kooper takes his place behind the organ. They rock into the first chords and Jimmy shouts it's a blues, he's playin' a down home blues. With his snarl and wheedle and a roar that seems too deep for his meager frame Danny knows that now Bobby baby's throwing down the challenge because he knows and Danny knows exactly what he's going to get.

Clap, boo, clap, boo, and the snake hiss… Authentic? Nothing more authentic than the cry of the organ and crunch of the bass hewn right off the kick beat.… the Marshalls buzz and the slander fades away… when they pound their fists just sync the drumbeat to it… face to face with the other man with the guitar…

The folkies snarl, the dopers and the teenyboppers rush the stage, the cops shove them back, and Danny and Jimmy are laughing because it's such a perfect union of poetry and mockery, of passion and comedy, of church and circus, and it's a total rush to hear and see and be one with all of it all at once…

*... the music is a temple and the voice rises to try to fill it...
pleading to all the sirens in the stained glass... I'd do anything in
this godalmighty world...*

The hisses and catcalls grow louder. He tunes and strums
like a matador baiting the bull. Then the piano tolls, the drum
slams down with a whomp of bass right in the stomach.

*... .I'm here and on the move now... I nod and Koop brings
the organ rushing in louder, Robbie makes the guitar scream, this
is my Rock on the granite of the folk and blues... yeah, here we
are all "electric," all popping in the lab as the coils shoot up and
Frankenstein rises in Hollywood and the beakers blow and they yell
"sell-out, clown, asshole!"...*

He plays a very muted "It Ain't Me Babe," just a little bass
and drums, a good sport gesture, but it doesn't soften the hostility,
so he turns to the band and they turn it all the way up. The drum
smashes down to a wail of organ and Dylan, frail but wire tight,
breaks out with a cry that mocks himself, the "I" and the "you" all
at once, and flays himself open to the music. He scales the notes
like an alley cat in heat, a clown taunting the children, a cowboy
on a fence sneering at the range boss, a carny barker summoning
the freaks, all the tramps and vagabonds at his command infused
by the bitterest kind of honesty and owning up, of love and anger
and pride.

*Turn every recoil of fear into a shot across the harp... this is
the real spirit of the highwayman... beyond the spotlight there's the
dark and no one can help you but yourself... and HOW DOES IT
FEEL, CHILDREN, HOW DOES IT FEEEEL....*

Some cheer, some scream, some boo their lungs out. Danny,
followed by Jimmy, takes off. He knows there won't be an encore
for a crowd like this, or if there will be, he doesn't care. He makes
it to a guard in the wings, yanks out his school bus pass, yells he's
from the press, and he and Jimmy rocket right by the guard up
the stairs to the stage. When he first sees Dylan in the wings he's
surprised that he's casually grinning and flanked by motorcycle
toughs, a cadre of bodyguards, who shoulder aside reporters
trying to grab an interview. Now there's a leather-jacketed thug in

Danny's face, backing him away, but he jumps above his upraised arm. He has to voice his thanks somehow, be part of the chorus of the night.

"Hey, Bob. Bob! Fuck 'em if they don't believe you! Fuck 'em, Bob!"

Dylan looks around, arrows in on Danny's fervor, catches his eye. He thinks he collects a cool flash of pristine shared anger from Dylan just before it tails off into a sleepy smile and an offhand wave. Now some guard shoulders Danny and Jimmy toward the stairs and gives them the choice of walking or rolling back to the pavement. Danny flares up at the guard with all the borrowed lightning that now pulses through his body, like someone who should be there, the leader of a band even thought the band hasn't happened yet, but Jimmy tugs at his sleeve and says, hey man, it's cool, he saw you, you talked to him.

What the hell? Artie had hastened to respond to the letter from Danny in the dull waning August days of Camp Sicko and take the advice practically shouted through his slashing penmanship. Buy this record when you get into town, warning, the longest single ever made, on two sides of the record, but the coolest. Now he had played it and thought it was a gyp, or maybe some weird novelty song, the next "Wooly Bully." As his bunkmate Ronnie Gaston had said, the guy sounded like a cowboy with brain damage.

But those crazy words had a way of sticking with him, and later, back in the city, in Russ Lansing's apartment, they really listened to *Highway '61 Revisited*. Somehow if you didn't have to turn a 45 over and could let the words of "Like A Rolling Stone" tease and challenge you it started to sound better. He could hear poetry in the album, and siren whistle satires of national politics that even Alan Shermaned the Bible. Or maybe at the Lansing apartment, with its blend of adult playground egg and sling chairs and sleek striped furniture right next to a grand piano, anything sounded fun and hip. He once more tried smoking marijuana, since Russ assured him not only would the lyrics make more sense on dope but the guitars on "Queen Jane" would sound less out of tune, but of course it didn't work. It really seemed that Artie, in Russell's words, had a cast iron head.

Dylan would have been at home in Coney Island, Artie thought, standing by the beach a week later as he glanced at the Wild Mouse and the silent Steeplechase over his shoulder and waited for John Lindsay to mount the platform truck. A stiff autumn breeze carved whitecaps on the ocean behind him as the whole crowd shivered and bundled closer. Artie hugged his jacket to himself tightly; on it was his volunteer campaign button, "If I Were 21, I'd Vote For Lindsay". It had been a terrific day. Hot dogs and Cokes at Nathan's—and then shaking hands with Lindsay, getting a personal acknowledgment behind the movie star smile. Ah yes, Nate's son, thanks for all the fine work.

The crowd swelled up past the street and up onto the Boardwalk. Sammy Davis Jr., all pumping arms and fluid motion as a five piece band set up, jumped on the platform to cheers and applause and shook hands with people in the front as if he were running for office himself. He wore knife-edged black pants and a blue blazer and a white shirt just like on the Ed Sullivan show. Sammy crouched and spun his arm like he was about to bowl the candidate onto the stage: here he is, the next Mayor of the City of New York, Mr. Supercalifragilisticexpialidocius himself, JOHN LINDSAY!

Artie knew from Dad's phone calls that he'd overheard that the campaign was in trouble. Lindsay and the Conservative candidate William F. Buckley, fellow gentlemen and Yale graduates, had refrained from personal attacks on each other—and so by the time Lindsay had finally struck back not at Buckley but at Buckley's followers, calling them right-wing extremists with a politics of hate, it had come too late and Buckley had gained on him in the polls. Meanwhile Democratic candidate Abe Beame was so earnest and pleasant it was tough to attack him, and behind Beame's decency and Buckley's jibes the race was getting away from Lindsay.

The man who'd so thrilled Artie as he loomed over him with

his gracious, patrician smile looked gaunt and embattled as he reached out to his supporters on the windswept beach.

"Cities are for people and for living and yet under its present tired management New York City has become a place that's no longer for people or for living...."

He spoke of how he would enlist the city's minorities and make them part of the team, to make them "insiders" with a share of the American dream, instead of isolated resentful outsiders. He talked about the decaying neighborhoods he'd walked through. He promised his election would be about reform: clean government, decency and dignity. He mentioned that the future of the country lay in diverse, dynamic cities, and he would never let New York fall into the "backwash of history."

"If New York is ungovernable, we're all through. I say to New York rise up. Let's go to work, let's go, let's build a new city!"

Nate knew Dorothy well enough by now to know she wasn't crazy about alcohol. Her ex-husband had apparently had his problems with it. Out walking with Nate one night, she'd pointed out a shabby corner of 86th Street near the German oompah bars.

"This was Lou's favorite hangout. His 'my wife doesn't understand me' retreat. Luck of the draw, I suppose. I got the Jew who drinks."

But under the influence of the Moulin Rouge décor of the Café Au Go Go, with its walls of papier-mache Folies Bergere masks, and swayed by the exhilaration of the John V. Lindsay victory party, Dorothy began to sip martinis at the open bar until she was practically leaning on Nate's arm. Is Lindsay gonna be a no-show, you think? Am I getting tipsy for nothing?

Nate told her the story of how he'd learned Lindsay was the sure winner at a time when the television networks were calling the race a Beame victory. Having helped count the votes in his district, unsurprisingly carried by Lindsay, he'd happened to call a friend of his who was a district captain in Riverdale, a Bronx Jewish neighborhood, heavily Democratic, a sure bet for Beame.

Lindsay beat him, his friend whispered in disbelief into the phone, Lindsay took Riverdale.

When Nate got home he found Artie on the edge of the sofa watching in wretched disbelief as CBS called Beame the probable winner. Don't worry, he'd told Artie, as he sat on the couch and put a hand on his shoulder, Lindsay's going to win.

"Wow, Nate, that's terrific. You probably convinced your kid you were some kind of magician!"

There was a commotion in the front of the room and Dorothy, after peering toward the door, leaned against Nate as if a gust of air had rocked her on her high heels.

"My god, he's STUNNING!"

Nate hardly minded. Most women had that reaction to John Lindsay. The Mayor-elect steered through the room of happily babbling fusion Democrat supporters like a human clipper ship. Nate gradually escorted Dorothy closer and closer until Lindsay caught sight of Nate and immediately excused himself to talk to him. When Nate introduced Dorothy and Lindsay turned the full wattage of his smile on her she seemed as starstruck as Karen had been watching the Beatles. Lindsay mentioned he'd heard about Nate's successful defense of a family that had been threatened with eviction from a housing project because one of their kids had allegedly used drugs.

"It must be fascinating to shuttle between the Village and Harlem on a case."

"Oh, there's never a dull moment, John."

The Mayor elect headed over to the next circle of well-wishers, but not before a warm handshake with Nate and Dorothy that left her duly impressed. They watched Lindsay, trailing the hopes and a good deal of the sexual heat of the assembled supporters, make his way out the door to his limo, after which Dorothy insisted playfully on just one more martini before they headed home. As they headed for the bar the lights flickered and went out. Laughter at once hearty and anxious arose as the bartender, rimmed in a half moon of flashlight glow, hustled by them.

"Sorry folks, looks like we blew a fuse!"

A departing guest pushed open the door, and they saw that

a matching darkness blanketed the street. There was silence as passing headlights briefly swept the club and vanished.

"My God, I think the city blew a fuse."

While some of the guests at the Café Au Go Go gathered around candles and a transistor radio for a different, stranger kind of party, Dorothy and Nate and the other parents were the first out the door. Nate fortunately managed to flag down a cab. He and the cabbie agreed they'd pull over and take on other passengers on what was becoming an unprecedented citywide emergency. Mayor Wagner's last disaster, the cabbie muttered. His radio's news became a litany of services ended, advice on how to get home, reassurances that everything was still under control.

The cab seemed to move through hovering apses of light, the buildings now dark spires against a moonlit sky. Every intersection was a shadowy frontier, a dance of approaching and receding highbeams as white-sheeted figures waved flashlights to direct traffic. From a candlelit bar came the pounding of a piano, the customers riotously singing "Do You Believe In Magic?"

Dorothy saw them first, two women in fur coats making their way down the street, one staggering against the other. As Nate got out to open the door, the dizzy one, raven-haired, almost six feet tall, gestured with her cigarette like a wand, and thanked him profusely before tripping on her heels and crumpling against the cab. Dorothy shifted into the front seat, and Nate and the woman's companion practically had to fold her into the back.

The driver continued down Fifth Avenue and Nate, sandwiched between the women, was concerned at just how blotto the first one was. The second one fortunately seemed clearheaded. What seemed a drunken flush on her skin was revealed by passing headlights to be her normal hue. She was as tanned as if she'd just walked off a beach, her eyes, etched with fine wrinkles, good-humored despite her concern. She spoke with some kind of Latin accent.

"I am trying to tell you, the lights really are not on"

"You mean I'm not seeing things anymore? Oh my gosh, the streets look like rivers… "

Nate inquired gently if she was okay. She leaned on him, and the scent of Chanel tumbled out of her coat. Her curves rippled against her mink stole and her bright lips glimmered with moisture when the headlights swam past the cab.

"I'm sorry. I'm Greta Morgenstern, and this is my friend Marcela."

Greta Morgenstern. A statuesque woman like her, and a name like Nate's cousins in Bensonhurst.

"This is my friend Marcela, and we've just come from a… ridiculous party! He spiked the punch, I know it."

"Greta, I think we should just think about how we get you home."

"This government guy, he was very well-educated, but… the way he kept looking at us, and he never even tried to engage us in conversation, just talked to the other guys and kept gawking at us… so rude… It's not easy to be a working woman on your own, um… "

"Nate."

She sagged against him. Nate shot a glance over to Dorothy, who looked amused by the whole encounter.

"I thought I could just walk home, but the streets are—it hasn't rained, right? I thought he was watching me, the government guy, but then it seemed everyone's eyes were popping out, like Don Knotts on Steve Allen? And vodka punch doesn't normally do this to me. I mean… I've been… schnockered before, but… "

"Greta, it can sneak up on us. But he was weird that guy. He kept talking about your C.I.A."

"He put something in the punch, I know it."

"Ladies, it's a strange night and it's giving all of us some strange thoughts."

But Nate, even as he tried to put them at ease, had to admit that a woman whose best of Bendel's fashions and fur coats screamed Fifth Avenue propriety, who had such an educated accent—it didn't make sense she was drunk to the point of seeing things. Maybe someone had slipped her a Mickey Finn. He wondered if she was a party girl or really quite responsible and shocked at what was happening to her. He wondered how old she was. He wondered if there was a civilized way to see her again. The cab pulled over to a five-story walkup chambered with candles.

"Oh Marcela, your face... it's so beautiful now. It has all these... colors."

"Thank you so much, I think I'll put Greta to bed now."

"You two are so nice. And Nate, you are such a knight in shining armor. You really are. Marcela, invite them to your show. Marcela sings Bossa Nova, you know, in a cute little supper club. Come on, tell them your... schedule or something!"

"Okay, okay, if you'd like to come... I can call you?"

Jesus, this was awkward, with Dorothy in the cab.

"Just look me up in the phone book. Hamerow and Kovacs, we're a law firm."

"Oh my god, he's a lawyer! I'm gonna be needing you when I find out what the government put in the punch!"

"Dad, when are the lights gonna be back on?"

"Soon, honey, I hope very soon."

Karen's face seemed so tender, her skin almost like a baby's in the candlelight.

"Don't you know?"

"Karey, how would I know that?"

"You knew Lindsay would win before anybody."

"That's because I work with the Republican Party. I don't work with the power company."

Artie turned around in his bed. "Karen's hair got burned in the candle."

"What?"

"When we were playing Parcheesi. She smelled like a burnt chicken."

"Don't joke about that, Artie! Are you okay?"

"Yeah, Dad, I'm okay."

He kissed Karen's forehead, and remembered something he could tell her that might distract her from fear of the night-long blackout.

"Do you know Mrs. Kempster's friend has a seal point Siamese cat? Well, I found out it's due to have kittens, and I was thinking—"

She propped herself up on her elbows, her face already beaming.

"Would you like a Siamese? Dorothy tells me they're real chatterboxes!"

"When are the kittens coming?"

"I think just in time for Christmas."

Karen, as she hugged Dad and the bubble of her gratitude happily burst, remembered an intimation of shadows that she'd half-comprehended. Mom had looked wearily up from her bed and told her that even though she's a very little girl, we all watch over each other in this family, so occasionally even you need to watch over Daddy a little.

"Dad? I know you didn't mean to open the window."

"Of course not, darling. I still feel terrible about that. And we'll take good care of this cat. All of us."

Later, in his bed in the foyer, watching the faint wisps of candle flames in the windows across the way through the blinds of the living room windows—men in shirts half-opened, grandmothers seated by dead tvs waiting for them to go on again, a whole world of intimate glimpses of people he'd never known who lived just across the street—seeing the outlines of the furniture he and Becky had assembled over fifteen years dimly flicker as passing cars lit up the building walls, he thought of the unveiling of her footstone coming up, felt again the weight of all his responsibilities, and wondered if he had paid enough attention to Artie. His son had so much wanted to show he was stoically in charge of things. That had given him the luxury of devoting all his attention to Karen, and maybe in the process he'd neglected Artie a little—but Karen was so much harder to connect with.

He decided he'd finally buy that camera Artie wanted for

the holidays. Somehow he'd find the money and the time. He wondered if there was ever any way to be a complete parent, especially standing alone. Dorothy had given him a quick but very affectionate kiss before heading beneath her canopy. When he'd locked eyes with the cabbie, and told him this was the first night he ever put three women to bed, the guy had roared and dubbed Nate the good Samaritan of the evening.

Yes, that Greta was something... a knight in shining armor... yeah, sure.

Nate thought of the candle in Karen's room. It was the tallest from the kitchen cupboard. But Nate resigned himself to a night of very little sleep, to hours of constant vigilance against anything burning.

Meanwhile, in his bedroom, Artie stared at the pitch black courtyard, where ripples of laughter and the echoes of transistor radios defined a space larger than he could imagine.

Danny stood on his roof, hugged his coat to himself, and gazed at a skyline without a single lamp but the moon and stars. He could almost hear the moment when all the radios would turn on again and the canyons would wake up and be filled with music.

Karen drew comfort from the lone candle that so worried her father.

And as Nate finally fell asleep, he remembered the perfumed smile in the midst of the harmony of all those random collisions of light. *Let's build a new city...* a nocturnal world expanding into his life with chance encounters, the hilarity and fantasies of strangers—while other lights answered at his back, candles, flashlights, the resilient lights of New York, soon to be captained by his chosen Mayor and friend, guiding him through traffic home to his children, even while reminding him that, after all, he too had fantasies, he had freedom, he had choices.

What had the government put in the punch?

My God, what a night! Shepeard's and Rendezvous had been happening more than usual, but it had been a rare treat when the lights had suddenly died and the Rolling Stones record smooshed to a slow crawl and then stopped—well, you couldn't dance after that, but this was some kind of evening, especially with the cameras. Norman had grabbed her by the hand as soon as he saw the bloody enormity of what was happening, and they'd rushed home to get his Leica. He'd given her his Yashica with the Zeiss lens bag and said, try your luck, luv, if you can get any images tonight they should be fantastic.

P.J. Clarke's was raucous as all bloody hell, looked like they were setting up for a gangbang, and it would be one strange photo by candlelight. Have a drink and relax, baby, if we were under attack you'd know it by now.

It was fun to be behind the camera for a change. Out in the street, experimenting with the kind of time exposures Norman told her about, not knowing what you'd get, a truck heading with emergency food to the subways as a streak of light, people as blurry ghosts in the midst of a strangely thrilling calamity… I mean it's not as if bombs were falling on London.

Pamela was still jazzed when Norman and she finally made it back, four warm but very potent drinks later, to his apartment in Tudor City. They had an exhausting Lucifer-match lit trek up the stairwell, but she wound up letting him sleep it off while she donned her Mary Quant black plastic mackintosh over a sweater and jeans and headed out to greet the dawn in U.N. Plaza. The sky's eggshell blue looked all the more brilliant with no city lights in the way. She wondered what in the world all the diplomats would do today, probably gather in the park and chase after the secretaries. Maybe she could meet up with that simultaneous translator she'd boffed after that silly night at L'Interdit.

A cold breeze crept under her mac as the sun sent its first light over the East River. Piers and bread factories peeled out of the rust-colored dawn. The sea green rampart of the U.N. seemed to give birth to the reflected skyline of York Avenue. Pamela, transfixed, took photos of the great glass wall, then wheeled around and, close up, snapped the brushed steel of the peace pillar catching the first light, before she crossed the street heading for the plaza and its retinue of flags. She loved the U.N. It was a true place of hope, a pilgrimage spot for her, and she still felt a catch in her throat at the sight of the Union Jack — although she was thankful that modeling had given her a way to shuttle between her two glorious cities, a ticket out from her father and his beastly drinking and rattling on about his MI5 connections, and a future that might just be free of British tax laws as she accumulated a fortune from the modeling business. Jeannie Shrimpton, Pamela Huntington, why the hell not?

There seemed to be a young man making a speech in the wide avenue in front of the Dag Hammarskjold Memorial Library, even though there was no one but a couple of bored guards to watch him. He was hardly the usual street corner loony, tall, slender and very blonde, quite all-American. She'd later learn his name was Roger LaPorte, and that he was a member of the Catholic Workers movement founded by Dorothy Day. A little tired of playing with her new camera, Pamela paused to listen to the speech. The young man explained that the United States' current actions in Vietnam were illegal and immoral. Pamela thought they were simply stupid, definitely an aspect of her new country she didn't adore. This domino theory about how they had to fight the Communists there or they might have to fight them in Hawaii or something. The young man's eyes swept the empty Plaza with what seemed to be desperate longing, and he shouted out that he was against war, and all wars, and that he did this as a religious action.

He sat down next to his satchel on the pavement and crossed his legs, and something about the pose reminded her of Buddhist monks and what she'd seen in *Life* Magazine, but the associations simply didn't knit fast enough for her to prevent what happened next. The boy took a large can out of his satchel and poured clear fluid over himself. Pamela felt what seemed like an electric shock freeze her to the spot as she smelled the gasoline, an animal paralysis in the face of danger, and she tried to cry out but there was nothing she could do as he lit a match and tissues of blue and yellow fire replaced his clothes and then his face. As he howled and writhed but somehow stayed upright Pamela's knees gave way and she fell to the pavement. She was dimly aware that at least the guards and two city patrolmen were moving, that they were trained to help, and they beat with their garments at the flames engulfing him. Out of shock from the sheer killing storm of fire, his motions ceased, he was a charred statue beneath the coats that flailed above him, and as the wind whipped the flames Pamela had the awful sense of a pair of shadow eyes fixing her alone amidst all the objects in the universe.

Pamela's hands trembled but found the camera. She raised it in the direction of those prayerful eyes she would always swear had looked directly into hers. She clicked the 85 millimeter lens into place, and took the picture.

MIXED MEDIA

*"You know what this one fucker did? When we were all packed
together in the holding tank?"
Danny Geller from Vandemeer High School. His son's friend.
Those words, that memory.
"He followed me around the cell. 'What's a freak?' Sniffing at
me like a dog. 'Are you a freak? What's a freak, freak?' The other
guys in the pen are laughing, they know there's no way I can get
away from this asshole, they're bumping into me, trapping me, they
know what's going to happen if I'm ever stuck in the same cell with
any of them."
"You think I'm one of those guys, Mr. Kovacs? Could you ever
be one of them? Could Artie or Karen?"*

On 86th Street the subway stop barricaded with parade
sawhorses; masses of people walking across the Brooklyn
Bridge into Lower Manhattan; Washington Square a parking lot,
cars radiating like the spokes of a cracked wheel onto the grass.

Everyone took the transit strike light at first—grin-and-bear-it
New York. Then the jitters set in, the nasty cracks in the papers
and on the airwaves. Lindsay solved the problem of subway crime
his first day in office. Mayor Wagner left for Mexico and took
the trains with him. One joke going around from the hip young
Negro comedian Lucas Oxley: *Bad week for white people, sayin'
man, the buses and subways are on strike. How do we get to work?
That's the question Negroes ask every day.*

The sheer grind of it... after three days Nate really started
to feel the meanness, the endless nuisances... walking Karen to
school, rain or shine, arranging car rides for Artie, waiting for
multi-passenger cab rides downtown and haggling over the fares...

But for Artie the transit strike was a surprise gift: a ride to school each morning in Mr. Geller's Ford station wagon and a tight space in the back seat from where, as if invisible, Artie could eavesdrop on Danny and his crowd and follow like a trail of breadcrumbs the older kids' boasts of their exploits downtown at the Night Owl Café, Lugano's, the Bitter End, the glistening haunts of all the new groups. At Steve Paul's Scene, Danny had noshed on cheeseburgers, knocked back some wine, and caught a fantastic electric band, the Blues Project, jamming with Zal Yanovsky—Zal riffing a lot harder than he ever did with the Spoonful—while under silver-blue spotlights the chicks in miniskirts and kid boots jumped on tables and go-go danced for hours. Artie loved the stories, and lacking any connections to Danny's world of rock—not rock and roll anymore, just that one word, heavy with the night, packed with fire as a vein of coal—he wanted them to be true.

He and Danny's friends snuck with Danny into a Vandemeer music room with a reel-to-reel tape recorder, and Danny played for them some of the "riffs" he'd been jamming on with Jimmy Hinton. The music was like an aural manifestation of the smell of pot that night Danny had lit a joint in the bathroom: a haze of coarse-grained, billowing sounds, jagged melodies Danny played on the violin, the muddy reverb of Jimmy Hinton's bass. When they switched to electric guitars, heavy dueling fuzz-toned notes echoed through the tape. Artie didn't understand it. Was this the reason Danny had broken up the Phantastics right after his dad had secured for him a chance to get four songs on an acetate— this was why Danny had said a band like the Phantastics wouldn't be worth cutting? So he could experiment with what he said was some mix of Dylan and raga and Chicago blues and that weird sax player Coltrane?

But since Danny shared his music with him Artie decided to share take-it-all-off-Michelle. They huddled in a rehearsal room during lunch break and Artie showed Danny the black-and-white photos he'd so furtively developed and printed at Camp Saco, as he relished the memory of how Michelle's back and white eyes had lit the printer paper when he'd framed the negative in the enlarger's beam, how her languidly overlapping thighs had peeked slowly from the chemical bath of fixer, supine beneath him in the red darkroom light, until he finally had had to unzip his shorts and use the Camp Saco darkroom for an activity not included in the camp directory.

Danny ogled the snapshots.

"M'man, let me tell you, you show a woman you can do this camera shit for her, make her look like this... that is their bag, man, they will dig you the most."

Artie thrilled to it all—the trains and buses not running and the stories in the car and now this...

"Just ask any fashion photographer. They will lick you up and eat you with a spoon."

From the day Lindsay had been elected, Nate had heard about the planned reorganization of city government into ten new superagencies, including an urban task force with a civil rights beat. He knew they were bound to need legal counsel, and Nate saw the chance to bring his new knowledge of civil rights and poverty cases to city government—not to mention collect city benefits and a pension for himself and the kids. Nate liked the Lindsay aides he'd met: the new Finance Commissioner, courtly Roy Goodman; Sid Davidoff, the mod-dressing former college wrestler advance man, the human Swiss Army knife for prying apart the daily tangle of crises; Barry Gottehrer, former *Herald Tribune* editor and special Executive Assistant, kind and already road-weary in his thirties—he liked them all, and he itched to make the leap from his Village free speech detour to be, as the kids said, where the action is.

But the transit strike had put the kibosh on his plans for an interview. No one in city government had time for Nate now, though Nate's friends constantly pestered him for details, as if by knowing the Mayor he somehow he had his ear to the ground beneath every office in City Hall. Big John had hit the ground sinking; the largest municipal union, angry at losing its cozy relationship with Mayor Wagner, was out for his blood his first week in office. Lindsay had so pissed off TWU chief "Iron Mike" Quill that Quill would've yanked his men from the buses and trains right on the day of Lindsay's inauguration had not Deputy Mayor Bob Price convinced him to hold off until, for Chrissake, after New Year's Eve. When Quill told Lindsay he wouldn't take *bubkes* from a schmuck like him, Price had to translate the insults. The Mayor, with his Congressional patrician rectitude, was not exactly a skilled horse-trader at this point. As Nate confessed to Dorothy, that damn Mike Quill seemed to have the city on the ropes.

She took another puff on her cigarette.

"I just wish this *mishegoss* was over."

Dorothy could calm even Nate's most exasperated moments, and when he next voiced his worries and second thoughts about Karen's new school, she just laughed.

"Half-Bakedwell, my ex called it. But if he felt that way about it, I figured it must be okay."

And just like that, over a seafood lunch at Oscar's, Nate's worries about the secrets of Karen's new life—for she was coolly reticent about her days at Blakewell—could take a rest. Artie, who was getting B+'s and A's again, was much more forthcoming about his schoolwork, and especially his World Peace and Disarmament elective course. The kids seemed to have found inspiration in the course's red-haired, pipe-chuffing teacher Clark Thomas, coach of the school's Debating Society, who told them that being into modern issues could make them truly able to appreciate Shakespeare or Ibsen. The old Artie was back, the precocious kid who'd loved to impress Becky with his broadsides against the stupidity all around him. Nate told Dorothy how Artie had shown him an aging copy of a "Homemaker's Manual For Atomic Defense" that he'd found in one of the closets and now wanted to share with the World Peace class.

"Hey Dad, if the Bomb hits before we make it to the basement fallout shelter, do we put a newspaper over our heads or just crouch under the table?"

Compared with Artie's loquaciousness, Karen jealously

guarded her silence. There was the flute, of course, a breathy trilling presence that nicked at whatever quiet remained after the clamor of Artie's rock-and-roll records behind his shut door and the chitters and yowls of Aisha, the Siamese kitten. She carried a book of Emily Dickinson poems and Edith Hamilton's *Mythology*, and dropped hints of a history class taught by a dotty Socialist Englishwoman, who, Dorothy assured Nate, was harmless. Blakewell was a tad "advanced" but when all was said and done got its students into excellent colleges.

"Nate, you're the father. You may be the only parent, but you're still the dad."

"But if I don't know what she's doing?"

"Just cherish her, show her you love her. Fuel her, she'll run."

There was time on that bright Saturday afternoon, during the enforced doldrums of the city's transit breakdown, for Nate to begin to feel at home with Dorothy.

The next day Mike Quill collapsed with a heart attack, and a woman recognized him carried out on the stretcher and screamed that she hoped he'd die.

As the strike continued another four days, and the city, racked with commuter traffic jams, bled time and money, Bob Price checked in with his friend Dr. Zuckerman to see Quill at Bellevue. As Price leaned over the oxygen tent, Quill, his features blurred through the stiff, ice-colored plastic, recognized the Mayor's fixer, gasped, and held up four fingers. Four dollars a man. Court-ordered injunctions and tossing Quill in jail hadn't worked. Now the hammer of critical illness began to drive a deal.

Back in Nate's office, it was the usual round of battles over what you could show and tell in a movie, a play, or a book of modern "Sapphic" poetry sold by a bookseller who'd somewhat damaged his legal case by advertising the poems as "sexational." Nate wearily read the legal complaint of a professor suing his college to let him become a "doctor of sensuality," then sieved through court transcripts for review and filing, part of his chores as a forty-six-year-old junior partner.

From beneath the court papers he retrieved a handwritten envelope in a delicate script, and a card engraved with a tropical bird, which invited him to join "his friends" at Cafe Curacao Saturday night and enjoy Brazilian cuisine in an elegant setting.

The golf course had been a little jewel in the heart of Mamaroneck. Quick, come meet us there before the hoi polloi discover it and the lines stretch into the damn parking lot. And there she was, part of the group welcoming him for a round on Charlie Kantrow's birthday. That's the way it was done. You met a girl because Charlie met a girl.

Nate shifted uncomfortably as his cab inched his way down Fifth Avenue, past the splendid neon enfilade of 52nd Street flashing its invitation to the world's capital of jazz. Fifty-two blocks to go. The strike had been settled, nightlife was exploding back, and Nate was stuck.

She drove one straight down the fairway, then hooked one into a sandtrap on the green. In golf as in life, coming on so strong, needing a little help in the twists and turns. Slowly gravitating to his side on the back nine. Rebecca Gail, soon to be his beloved Becky, soon to be mother of Artie and Karen.

The cab approached the Washington Square arch caught in a backwash of tail lights. Nate paid the fare and walked the rest of the way. He needed to shake off more than anxiety over the traffic jam. He wondered if he could retrace his steps eighteen years back to social reflexes almost forgotten.

He could remember, almost on his skin, Greta Morgenstern's perfume.

Café Curacao was a respite from the coffeehouses and the discotheques' relentless pursuit of the Now. Bent over deep red cocktail candles, couples in jackets and evening dresses enjoyed steaks and some kind of Brazilian goulash in a hushed, epicurean swoon. At the bandstand a pianist and guitarist in tailored suits plucked at a delicate melody, the lovelorn slipstream of a serenade.

The woman Nate remembered as Marcela, dressed in a startling low cut gown, greeted him cheerfully, took his coat, and led him to Greta's table. He instantly registered the presence of Greta's prosperous boyfriend, about Nate's age, a good deal bulkier, dressed in a pale blue jacket and what Becky used to call a "sporty" tie. He realized that the invitation had come from the club, that Greta was probably a habitué who was there regularly on Saturdays and had just asked Marcela to remind Nate to drop by.

Well, what had he expected? He had indulged in a fantasy for a little while and now it was over. Nate masked his disappointment as best he could as Greta introduced Dr. Steven Weiss, a Madison Avenue psychologist. He remained the picture of congeniality as, realizing what Greta must've thought when she'd seen Nate with Dorothy, he awaited the inevitable question.

"But Nate, isn't your wife joining us?"

Nate explained efficiently that Dorothy was his friend and that in fact he was a widower. He acknowledged gratefully the gestures of compassion. He wished he were back on the living room couch with Karen once again trying to win him over to Soupy Sales and the Monkees.

Once they all got used to the fact that the evening would be a little awkward—but, Nate decided, brief—Dr. Weiss chugged into conversational high gear by explaining that the Club Curacao was a home away from home for Brazilians who'd fled the country's military coup in 1964.

"But you can't tell from the music. It's all about romance and sun and sand. What I love about Brazilian music, Nate, is that the saddest it gets is 'I have made love to you... and I cannot make love to you again... for another twenty minutes!'"

Greta whooped at his mock Portuguese-accented joke, her breasts riding the laughter under her aquamarine dress.

"So what kind of law do you practice, Nate?"

The duo on the bandstand launched into a tune and a playful female chant of "*vai vai vai vai vai*" echoed over the clink of wineglasses.

"You defend rioters and demonstrators? Don't get me wrong, I'm with you all the way. I can't believe Johnson is bombing North Vietnam. I mean, is this why I didn't vote for Goldwater?"

Greta eagerly interrupted Weiss and told him to show Nate the newspaper cutout he had in his jacket pocket. Nate unfolded it and skimmed it in the candlelight. It was a *Village Voice* ad for a book called "The Psychedelic Experience," something about a Dr. Timothy Leary and a Richard Alpert engaged in "legitimate experimentation with psychedelics" at Harvard until "sensational national publicity" led to a suspension of their work, which they were trying to continue "without academic auspices." It was a combination rallying cry, plea for help, and sales pitch.

"That's what the guy slipped in the punch, Nate! I know it! Steve, Nate was such a gentleman, I went on and on in that cab like a crazy woman and he just patiently listened to me, even though he was probably worried sick about his kids during the blackout, but I wasn't crazy, Nate, I was on a bender because that guy from the government put this psychedelic stuff in the punch!"

"I'd be interested in pursuing this further, Nate."

"I'm not involved in torts law. If you want to sue this guy, I can recommend—"

"I'm not talking about a lawsuit. See, what I've heard is that the government has been testing people a long time with this stuff—students, soldiers, the works—to see if it could drive the Russians crazy. Now it's gotten out of the lab and guys like Leary, psychiatrists like me, we want to use it for therapy. But we may need lawyers to defend our rights to do that."

"To use this as… therapy?"

"I've heard LSD has been used in Europe to treat frigidity, alcoholism, depression in cancer patients… and these visions can be intensely therapeutic. Could lead to incredible breakthroughs. Aldous Huxley spoke of being able to perceive the *mysterium tremendum*, the unity and beauty of all life forms."

A female voice was insinuating itself into the back of the conversation, like an open window freeing the room from stale air. Greta clutched his hand.

"See, according to this ad, Nate, maybe all that was wrong with me was that I wasn't prepared. I should've been reading

from the Tibetan Book of the Dead or something."
The song ended with a wave of applause. Nate saw that Marcela, the coat check woman, was holding the microphone and acknowledging the crowd with a bashful droop of her head. The guitarist said Marcela Carvalho would be singing one more song for them.

She sang the tune about quiet nights and the window that looked out on Corcovado. An empty silver beach lit by a sky of powder bright stars chased the babble from his brain. Marcela sang with a voice too wispy to be professional, even Astrud Gilberto had more oomph, but the breathy sibilance, the "L"s that rippled like flecks of the current of a stream, brought a world of yearning into the room. For a cocktail hostess she was very good.

The guitarist trickled notes over lightly brushed piano chords, and it was as if a tropic breeze had blown onstage. Marcela's legs were reeds that swayed to its warm drifting. Her body rocked from deep within her hips to the cadence of the song, a motion, a friend of Nate's had once told him, that Latin women were born with.

She smiled at the cordial applause of the crowd and sauntered over to their table. Her eyes were half-closed with the pleasure of the moment, and Nate sensed it was a squint the sun had conferred on her, along with the bronze of her skin. There were sun wrinkles around her eyes and the cleft between her breasts. Nate imagined a girlhood of the Copacabana beach and its endless sambas.

"Marcela, that was divine!"

She basked in Greta and Steve's compliments, and Nate felt the need to draw her attention.

"Did you ever sing before? I mean, professionally."

"A little, in Rio before we left, but here… sometimes they let me come out and play."

Who was "we"? How did she make her way through New York life?

"You should come out and play more often."

"Well, that's an invitation I wouldn't turn down!"

Greta drunkenly parlayed Nate's compliment into more than he'd intended. Marcela gave Nate a softly teasing smile.

"Saturday night I'm always here. And if someone comes to hear me sing, I sing."

Over the coming weeks, the invitation kept pecking away at Nate's memory. He shrugged it off as the pleasantry of a bar person trying to encourage a repeat customer. But it crept up on him as the winter relented for a few days in February, an inconvenient but welcome distraction, a false spring.

Nate sensed all sorts of opportunity in the air, especially in the "Camelot in New York" confidence the Lindsay administration exuded now that the transit strike was finally over. After the transit workers had burned Lindsay in effigy (which, as some writer had joked, was "a small town in New Jersey") Lindsay had responded by furiously denouncing special interests and proclaiming that the old "power brokers" would never dictate the destiny of the greatest city in the world. That speech and the image of the Mayor walking to Gracie Mansion during the strike, passing dazzled pedestrians with his long strides, had eased the pain of a settlement that had basically been brokered by Bob Price and had given the transit workers almost everything they wanted.

The *Times* supported Lindsay, the people rallied behind him. Nate had a feeling that, after some initial missteps, the Lindsay administration could at last start moving against those power brokers the way that LaGuardia had moved against the grafters and gangsters when Nate was young.

Nate knew to call Bob Price first. Price cordially handed him off to Sid Davidoff, who told him to meet with Barry Gottehrer in the Tweed courthouse, several blocks away from City Hall. Gottehrer ushered Nate into the dim corridor of the beautiful old building. Balding but with a benevolent youthful energy, he seemed like a doctor on the urban scene, with a soothing bedside manner for every problem on the street. He had that hint of sportiveness all the Lindsay aides had now, like kids suddenly given free reign in an old teacher's classroom. Gotteherer told

Nate that Lindsay was going to get rid of payroll-padding jobs like pothole inspectors, ban cars from Central Park on weekends, and oh yeah, end all that damn fingerprinting of performers in the nightclubs.

"I know you'll be especially pleased, Nate, to hear the cabaret card is good as dead."

They finally reached Gottehrer's office, a cluster of cabinets and Formica-topped desks in suspended animation. There are rumors, Gottehrer bantered, that somewhere in this building we're walking over a hoard of old Boss Tweed's buried money. Nate remarked that he'd certainly inherited some prime real estate, and Gottehrer replied that it was because he'd be meeting the kind of people Bob Price didn't want near City Hall.

"I'm the guy looking for troublemakers, Nate. New urban leaders, that is. We're gonna form a special Mayor's Urban Task Force and part of our job will be to spot these guys before they're out in the street trying to start a riot. Show them City Hall cares about their neighborhoods. Invite them into the process, hear out their demands."

It seemed a perfect setup for Nate, and he jumped right in. He and Izzy had been representing distressed Negro and Puerto Rican families in the ghettos for months. He was confident he could provide valuable counsel to the new urban task force, and whatever superagency was set up to oversee it.

"You're looking at him, Nate, I'm the new superagency. I've got a crisis calendar filling up, I've started meeting with people at this seedy bar in Harlem, the Glamour Inn? You get everything in that hole-in-the-wall but glamour. Being the man in the middle gets pretty strange sometimes."

"I know, believe me—and I can help."

"You already are helping right where you are, Nate."

Nate instantly knew he didn't have a chance.

"We want to find out what's going on out there. The Mayor wants us to break down the isolation, really be involved in the streets. It's a key part of how we want to get in front of what's happening! Make every neighborhood a part of this city, and make New York the most open, the most involved, the most forward-thinking city in the country. Everyone can help us do that. And your legal expertise, your knowledge of your clients, their grievances… priceless."

Nate gracefully offered whatever services he could provide for the city in his current capacity.

"John likes you, you know. Man doesn't exactly suffer fools, he's not the friendliest guy in the world, but he always asks about you, Nate."

Gottehrer finally got to what turned out to be the point of the meeting: to pick Nate's brain about some of the groups he'd rubbed shoulders with down in Harlem. The Militant Workers' and Artists' Forum, the Harlem Action Front, groups that resorted to inflamed rhetoric, but you could still work with them. Nate told Gottehrer that the H.A.F. had leaders who'd been trained in Martin Luther King's Southern Christian Leadership Conference. He remembered one community activist in particular: a former high school track star and CCNY student named Roy Hicks. Roy had already been one of the leaders of a well-organized and peaceful antidiscrimination sit-in at a Housing Authority office. And as a character witness in one of Nate's cases, he'd helped keep a family from being thrown out of a city housing project after one of the sons had been caught with drugs.

But Gottehrer had a puzzling reaction.

"Roy Hicks? Are you sure? It's on my calendar—your Harlem Action Front is complaining to us about his arrest."

Nate was stunned to hear that an old buddy of Roy's, a junkie, had fingered him to the cops as an accomplice in a bodega holdup. The well-spoken and studious young man who'd helped in a Hamerow and Kovacs legal case was suddenly, in the eyes of the NYPD, a street thug charged with armed robbery.

They sat in a semicircle on soft blue couches, Jim McGuinn in a teal-colored turtleneck and suede jacket, David Crosby in some kind of medieval smock with drawstrings in the front and a broad fur collar, Gene and Mike Clark and Chris Hillman flanking them like acolytes of a serene, smiling priesthood. They were gathered around a musical instrument built from the finest hardwoods of India, with a gourd on the bottom and a column of strings. At the side of the stage a public relations flack rhapsodized to Bruce Geller and the rest of the musical press horde.

"We think these boys are innovators and people who are onto something. That was a wonderful new thing The Byrds did with 'Mr. Tambourine Man' and this time they're doing music even more exciting! I give you Jim McGuinn!"

Danny sat fascinated and occasionally chuckling to himself as McGuinn, like a kid explaining his Mr. Wizard science project, gave the reporters a brief description of the Indian sitar. He played a tape that revealed how the sitar's tone could be bent to sob or even snicker, and how its sympathetic strings, like the current beneath the plashing of a brook, amplified the melody into a borealis of sound. Crosby mentioned there were seventy-two raga scales.

Danny studied Crosby's serene, moonfaced smile. He looked like the amorous swain of a madrigal. The troubadour look. Man he must get laid over and over. Danny had heard rumors of his house in Hollywood, with lovely blonde girls bearing bowls of fruit to the guests.

McGuinn mentioned that their new record would have a raga chorus on two guitars, but also be influenced by John Coltrane. They played samples of the jazzman's amazing soprano sax from the cut "India." It was a tape they said had been their constant touring companion. McGuinn told them he'd been inspired to try to make the notes on his guitar sound like the valves on Coltrane's sax.

Popping flashbulbs, scratching pens, scratching heads—hey Jim, which would be the Coltrane tunes and which the raga tunes? At least his Dad scribbled his notes and kept silent. Danny knew the old press hacks, these music establishment clowns in their quasi-Mod patterned shirts would never get it, this special knowledge, this gorgeous musical amalgam The Byrds were composing in their California enclave.

At last a reporter asked if they ever got mobbed by teenyboppers. David Crosby smiled and replied, yeah, all the time. There was relief in the room; the press conference had at last landed on ground that everyone could relate to.

Danny left the conference with only one thought: they had to get a sitar in the band.

Lately he'd become a musical sponge, knowing that the hit songs and the influential albums would be made by whoever could cook up sounds that were extraordinary and untraceable. He sensed that the music scene in 1966 was a totally unique evolutionary convergence: dinosaurs and Ice Age mammals and lions and dolphins and all the birds from Archaeopteryx to the quetzal walking, swimming, and flying the earth together. He could spin Dylan and The Beatles, but then he could listen to the plink of banjos and jug band guitars of the Lovin' Spoonful, then the Stones' *Got Live If You Want It*, crackling with blues riffs, Bill Wyman's rope trick bass lines, and Charlie Watts' mighty kick beat under the wet panty wave of screams. Then Donovan, and "Sunshine Superman"'s mewing guitar and bluesy harpsichord, its deliciously spooky, funny cabaret licks, and then right over to the plangent guitars and sweet campfire harmonies of the Beach Boys' "Sloop John B" off *Pet Sounds*, a tune and an album he just couldn't get out of his head.

Then Coltrane. Danny journeyed with Jimmy Hinton down to the Half Note, a small Italian restaurant and bar on Hudson Street. Jimmy held tight to a kind of loneliness all the time, the practiced isolation of the Negro kid with glasses posing in a sea of white faces for his New Jersey prep school photo. But he opened up and became a gangly dervish when listening to Coltrane, the true son of his music teacher father, whipping his hands in the air as he shouted about how Trane's sheets of sound explored every aspect of a scale or set of intervals. Coltrane played even in simple ballads the dialogue of the self of the melody and its soul—mirror shimmers, scalar runs, trills and echoes of bird song. Elvin Jones laid down the bedrock of volcanically compressed drumbeats, McCoy Tyner let loose his thick, free-swinging rhythms over the lope of Jim Garrison's bass, and over it all was that lovelorn spirit of a sax calling like a bird split from the flock by a storm, beating back against the wind.

Trane shut his eyes and for two hours enclosed his instrument, a monolith of sound that got larger and larger, beyond song, beyond chord progressions, while some of the hipsters ducked in and out of the bathroom to wolf down Dexamyl to stay with him, and others just tranced out on his night flying. Sometimes Danny thought, as the torrents of music crashed through the tiny club, *what was Trane doing with this?* Was it what Ken Kesey said before he'd taken off with the Pranksters on his schoolbus Furthur? *What we hoped was that we could stop the coming of the end of the world...*

It was religious, heavy, heavy as could be—but when Danny went back in his room and played some Ravi Shankar, inhaling deep from his water pipe, he knew where Indian music and Coltrane's "India" met: on the nightlong dreaming and dancing ground of surrender. And not just religious surrender, but what you really wanted to do under the night stars.

Danny was, after all, forming a band.

He and Jimmy began to compose together, starting off a tune with a melody, chord progression, or bass line, or simply laying down riffs in jams that went on for hours. Jimmy practiced harder, and he knew chords and harmony better—sometimes he'd cackle that Danny didn't know shit, hey, white boy, this is the blues, hey, you messin' with jazz now, and Danny felt the sting of Jimmy's words. Was he far enough away from being the cute kid answering "need a folksinger for our parties" ads in the *Village Voice?* How many walls would he hit, how many light years away was he still from the real heavies?

But, as he would say to Jimmy when his friend pulled his blues chops on him, hey, we don't copy Muddy Waters either. We don't just get into the blues bag, we develop our own sound. Jimmy was so much the better guitarist that Danny shifted more and more to the violin, and he bent the music his way. Danny knew how to take their music forward, how to make it, as he said with a chuckle, "sicker," more raga-rock, more unpredictable. Danny cultivated unpredictability. He loved to introduce himself to girls at parties with a bow, a quote from a line of poetry or a song, and then walk away. They knew he was teasing them or testing them, and either way it worked almost every time; Danny had long since left behind in about fifteen different bedrooms the virginity so troublesome to his friends. It was the strangeness people loved, having something go bump in the night but then become their own special vision in the dark.

And when the joke was on him Danny could go with that too, like the way they met their bass player Rick Hastings at a crash pad somewhere near the Jersey shore. Danny and Jimmy and drummer Perry Donatello were taken by Rick's friend down a crazy road in a dump truck, until there was no way they could make it back without the guy's help—and then they were persuaded to buy some hash oil from the guy's connection as the price for meeting Rick and at some point getting safely back to New York. They wound up digging Rick's music, breaking out the hash oil, and sleeping in a room with three other musicians in a broken-down house with a fireplace in the middle and a hole in the ceiling that the wind came through. It didn't feel strange, it felt like Danny's life was bouncing and jarring and skidding the way it should: it felt right at home.

While Jimmy burrowed deep into the blues, Danny browsed the textures of the music he heard off the radio as if they were the cloths of an Andalusian bazaar. He culled jazz chords from the Zombies and Baroque harmonies from "Walk Away Renee." Above all he embraced the sheer theatrical élan of the Yardbirds and Jeff Beck's quick-change rhythms and snarling guitar. With double stops and slurred bowing he could cop almost all their best music on his violin, like "Over Under Sideways Down"'s Russian raveup. And when the Stones came out with a gypsy sound on "Paint It Black," Danny played the grooves off the single for hours, soloing madly.

As Danny became the unofficial band leader, he had free reign to court multi-instrumentalist Johnathan La Grange, a late-twenties recluse who taught music to the underprivileged and otherwise lived off an inheritance. He met Danny in his gloomy railroad car apartment, broken up by shafts of lights from open doorways that refracted in tiny spectra off his collection of instruments: an oud, balalaika, bassoon, Renaissance sackbut, an English horn, and, almost astonishingly ordinary in that gathering, an electric piano. Yeah sure he was weird with his yellow pallor and granny glasses and dressing in black like a monk but visually he could be the band's eerie still center. Danny could imagine him sitting upstage right, near the drums, in the midst of his antiquarian musical trove.

What clinched it was when Danny saw, resting by a fringed ottoman in Johnathan's bedroom, an electric sitar.

That weekend Danny bought a bag of dope that was nothing but manicured seeds and stems, and, in the way he loved to listen to music—getting high and plucking apart the harmonies into separate tone-colored bands—he let his imagination run. He could hear his violin riding a bed of sound thickened by Johnathan's drones and Asian twangs; Nell Friedlander, a singer Rick had introduced to him, doing the high harmony; Jimmy laying down his spade blues licks to Rick's crunchy bass as the music resonated with Chicago sounds, gypsy sounds, raga rock, sounds from all over the world.

The last element of the band was supplied to him by a gorgeous British photographer, an ex-model wearing a Union Jack miniskirt who'd come to a concert by the Peregrines on the arm of the lead singer and started shooting pictures of everyone backstage. Pamela Huntington, lean and blonde and perfectly coiffed, also turned out to be something of a poetry fan, and she added to the drunken and stoned-out conversation that Dylan was incredibly influenced by the French surrealist poet Arthur Rimbaud. Damn, Danny thought, staring at her long-legged stride as she sliced through the crowd, she knows about French symbolist poetry, or at least enough about it to make it seem as foxy as she was.

A little skeptically, he purchased a paperback collection of Rimbaud's poems at Bookmasters. He devoured it for two weeks.

He wrote in his diary a quote from the introduction, Andre Breton's "Beauty will be convulsive or it will not be at all." He immersed himself in Rimbaud's hashish-infused images. Riotous savages, phantoms of Aphrodite and drowned Ophelia, a black-robed Caesar smoking a cigar—very Dylanesque, that one. He thrilled to the revelations of a sage proclaiming he sat Beauty on his knees and wounded her, the necessary clear-eyed arrogance to give personality, bodies, even human masks to the demon elements that besieged him. How else do you conquer in the name of art? When he came to the little poem "Voyelles," the top of Danny's head came off. Letters, the very basics of language, were for Rimbaud the bands of the rainbow, perceptions infused by all the senses: A as black corruption, E the luminous white delicacy of morning, I the red of beauty and blood, U the green of the sea and O as Omega, the last color of the world and time, the violet eyes of the beloved.

Danny wanted to call the band Voyelles, and fought hard for it, but everyone hated the idea, and Rick pointed out it sounded like a greaser doo-wop group from the fifties. Nell suggested the Volz, but how would people pronounce it. Vahls? Or Voles, like backyard rodents? Johnathan, with a sly pursing of his lips, suggested the Voyeurs, but Nell thought it was too creepy.

That night the dope was so strong that they all fell asleep on Johnathan's floor. Before Danny sacked out he picked up a well-thumbed copy of *On The Road* lying on Johnathan's cocktail table. In the faded yellow light of an old Tiffany lamp hung from the ceiling Danny read about how somewhere along the line, the girls, the visions, the pearl would be handed to him, somewhere along the line.

Danny lay back, smiled, and as he fell asleep, he imagined Johnathan in the back next to the drummer in his nest of exotic instruments; the rest of the band ranged in front, Nell on vocals, Danny on violin. Ladies and gentlemen… The Voyage.

Izzy pitted himself against New York's Finest. Calling a series of cops to the stand, he hammered away at why the police neglected to investigate the possible participation of suspects other than Roy Hicks, and why they leaned so heavily on the word of Elmore Woods. But the Irish and Italian line held like granite, backing their junkie witness. That pushed Nate into doing his brief share of the dirty work: shaking up the eyewitnesses. How were they sure it was Hicks? A quick glimpse of features and a telltale red jacket in the dark?

Nate sensed he'd better soften the edge in his voice, not come down quite so hard on what were, after all, ordinary citizens trying to do their civic duty. But Izzy had been right. The Hicks matter got Nate "right in the kishkas." In walkups where bathtubs were scabbed with trails of raw sewage, the windows popped like blisters, and the alleys were choked with garbage that smelled even in the cold, Nate had sought the best possible witnesses to Roy Hicks's volunteer work on the antipoverty front. They'd once called the Negro families coming up from the South into the big cities "migrants," like the Okies from the dust bowl or the Mexican grape-pickers. Okay then, they're another group of migrants, refugees from historical crime and devastation, like the ashen-eyed European Jews he'd helped resettle along Second Avenue. He could truly assist these people. He need not feel discouraged or disoriented or overwhelmed handing out his firm's cards, at Izzy's insistence, while he witnessed poverty which, tenement by tenement, seemed so invasive that no one could contend against it without careening into despair and crime. He needn't worry that the violence in the black men's talk... *cops were waiting for Elijah Muhammad and Malcolm's followers to have a war that would pile the street with bodies, but no man, they'll just bring in the guns, they'll be plenty of guns...* or that the acrid distrust that seethed in the Negro men's eyes would incite one of them to aim a pistol right between his own.

To counter the eyewitness testimony, Nate piled on the character witnesses that Tom Hayden had helped him corral. Hayden, a leader of Students for a Democratic Society, had the bravado of a born provocateur and the canniness of a seasoned politician. He'd been beaten during civil rights work in Georgia, he'd spent a year building the Newark Community Union Project for a salary of ten dollars a week, helping ghetto tenants fight for better garbage collection and stop an urban renewal plan that would have evicted thousands of families. And he'd been Nate's walking, talking credential at the Harlem Action Front's storefront headquarters. Now he and the local minister and Hicks's teacher told the jury how Hicks dutifully came to Newark to learn community service.

But the prosecutor had a trump card: an old woman who insisted she'd seen Roy meet with the gang beneath her stoop an hour before the robbery. There was no question Roy had been with the gang at that meeting, but Roy had insisted he was just trying to get his junkie friend Elmore out of there. The woman had an earful of opinions about "rabble rousers" coming into her neighborhood and trying to make trouble for "peaceful, working colored people." Nate managed to cut her off with objections, but he could tell her remarks resonated with the elderly black jurors that had slipped through as a quick racial balance compromise in the *voir dire*.

When Roy Hicks himself took the stand, he strode into the room with a pride beyond his years, slightly built but with the stern demeanor that suggested the stiff-backed posture of his soldier father. Roy's dad had died from a training accident at Fort Hood where he'd had words with some Southern soldiers, so that Roy could never be sure it was only blind fate that had killed his dad, never snuff out a slow fuse of unreasoning anger.

Under Nate's careful questioning, he told jury that the police had picked up Elmore Woods for possession before, and given him what they call the treatment. You punch a junkie in the stomach even lightly, that's twice as bad as with anyone else. Nate secretly shuddered even as he got the testimony he wanted. He knew he was injecting yet more bile into the new tensions between the ghetto and the Mayor and the police. Harlem residents had agitated for a Civilian Complaint Review Board to regulate the cops. Lindsay was pushing for the Board, Police Chief Michael Murphy had called the Board a threat to law and order. When the cops cruised the streets, they glared dismissively at the Negro men gathered on the stoops as if they were already prisoners in a pen. Roy did exactly as he had been coached and calmly recounted his every move that night, from working at the Harlem Action Front center, to taking a detour to try to persuade Elmore and his pals to abandon their plans, to heading back home to watch tv with his mother.

"Those other kids, yeah, they're criminals. I looked right in their dumbass faces and told them. Man, Elmore should've seen I was looking out for him, but... hell anyone you know ever gets into drugs, you'll know what I'm saying."

Nate had warned Roy the prosecutor would denigrate his relationship with Elmore, and he couldn't wait to beat that drum. Well, how did you try to persuade Elmore and his gang to go back home? Oh, you tried to just talk them out of it? Three kids already packing guns? Well, if what you said had that kind of weight with them, couldn't you have literally dragged Elmore away from the gang if you wanted to? Said you had some dope for him? Nate objected to the leading questions but couldn't cut off Roy's anger. I don't work like that, he replied, I don't treat my friends like they're treated on the street every day. Treated by who? By their teachers, by those cops. Man, they think just because I protest discrimination and police brutality, I'm a criminal. Oh, so given how you feel about the cops, obviously you never threatened to turn the gang in? Nate objected and got that question tossed but Roy blurted out his answer anyway. Why would I do that to my friends? Then can we take it from your disrespect for authority that you might not be that sincere in stopping an armed robbery? Perhaps you even decided to join in, as Elmore Woods testifies? Roy shouted back that a brother on drugs was a brother that could be used against his own people. Izzy roared his objection right at the prosecutor and it was ceremonially struck from the record. But Roy's haughtiness could not be erased, and it flashed at the prosecutor, at the defense, the stonefaced half-black jury.

That Saturday Dad took Karen for what he still called, as Mom had done, "a fresh air stroll" through the park. Almost apologetically he talked about how big a case this was becoming, and how perhaps there would be even more late nights than before.

Karen listened quietly and watched as he nodded and occasionally tipped his hat at a procession of old German and Irish nannies passing by with baby carriages. The Park, in the crisp interval between winter silence and playgroups shouting on the Great Lawn, ambled beneath the awakening sun, and Karen felt her father's melancholy and his kindness like a warm breeze. She found she could talk to him just to see him smile, shout the praises of Davy Jones, her favorite Monkee, and even sing one of the Yardley girl Slicker commercials from the show, and without Artie to make fun of her, there was just Dad to praise her singing voice.

She told Nate happily about the dance performance the school would put on in a couple of months, in which they would—she used her teacher's words—embody nature in interpretive dancing, choosing classical music for each sequence. Soon she'd be playing Bach pieces and a Handel bourrée on the flute, she breathlessly exclaimed, and she told him about a "student exchange" day she'd spent in the U.N. School, where everyone's a diplomat or an interpreter's child and the classes are held in colorful cubicles connected by ramps, halls, and little partitions.

And then, knowing she had the advantage of a moment where Dad truly yearned to help and please her, felt badly about his late nights at the office, and was clearly very, very tired, she told him about Gyre and Gimble, the new London-style boutique that had opened just down the block from Blakewell. It had mirrors and colored spotlights, polished wood paneling, and a discotheque's load of records for the background music. Nina Kempster was helping out on Saturday's there just for the fun of it and they needed another girl to pitch in. Just to help out, to learn a little about fashion with her friend, please please please?

He was taken aback, and he said something about how you're much too young to work at a store. She told him she wouldn't get paid, it would all be for fun and occasional treats. When Dad said he'd have to talk to Mrs. Kempster first Karen nodded agreeably. She knew Mrs. Kempster approved, and that would be enough to sway Dad.

Of course she didn't tell him everything. As Dad had told Artie and she had overheard, even in a court of law you don't learn everything in what he called discoveries. Everyone had secrets. The nude drawings of a man she'd made when she and Nina slipped into the older kids' life drawing class, now torn out of the sketch pad and hidden away in her souvenir chest. The really cute boy she'd met at the U.N. school with a face like John Sebastian.

Nina had said that once they were working in the back rooms of Gyre and Gimble, she could smoke a clove Gauloise, a gift from a friend of a friend, a guitarist working in London, while they listened to Donovan records, all those twinkling triangles and woodwinds, Karen imagining that she was the girl child Linda circled with doves, the queen Guinevere that the troubadour gazes on from the groves of Camelot.

All those soft, beautifully embroidered clothes the music seemed to incarnate—they were acquired secondhand from the trunks and attics of elderly people. Satin and velvet, gowns and lace blouses. She'd already snuck in with Nina and tried some of them on. Nina had told her that Eleanor might take them for a whole day to help her on "raids" of estate sales to gather up clothes from people who died with no one to give them to. If that meant cutting a day or two of classes, she thought they could manage it.

She knew Eleanor also planned to be a costumer and seamstress to rock stars, male and female. Karen imagined herself in the front room, guiding one of those luminaries through the smart wool suits. Narrow bell bottoms. Hip huggers. She could feel the intimacy of tailoring clothes for someone as a current that traveled through her fingers. A singer in a band. Karen lay in her bed with only the reading lamp on and bunched the sheets between her legs. Across from her Aisha crouched, studying her, her eyes capturing the light in a green glow like twin telescopes, and Karen fell back into their trail of dreams.

Back for Easter vacation from England, Audrey seemed to be another artifact in the Mehlinger living room, whose up-to-the-minute Danish modern furniture, slim ceramic vases and photos of Coca-Cola ad visuals had given such a racy zing to her parties. Her bare knee rocked from beneath a pinafore that made her look thin, severe and utterly stylish, and her hair was cut in a bob, bangs swept over one eye. Once the hi-fi throbbed with the British *Rubber Soul*, which had five songs not included in the American album, and singles by The Who, "Substitute" and "I Can't Explain," that the WABC Top 20 survey hadn't even detected, the living room had the vinyl spoor of impossible coolness.

"Oh I LOVE 'Drive My Car.' It's not even ON your album?"

The strut of that song, its little evasions and playing hard-to-get, Artie now read in Audrey, all delivered in a crisp new British accent that she'd apparently picked up on Kings Road with the dress. He stared at the cover of the British *Rubber Soul*, the boys' faces wafting like smoke, peering sleepy eyed from their private forest pleasure garden. Through the mysterious scorn of "Norwegian Wood" and the world-weary sighs of "Girl" came oldest Beatle and leader of the group John Lennon's message that women were impossibly, transcontinentally elusive. The album's folk-tinged sophistication threw a barrier between him and his affection for Audrey as surely as the British pound symbol on the album sleeve.

He suggested they take one of their old favorite walks in the park.

"You know, Artie, you need some new clothes."

"For the Park?"

"For ANYTHING!"

As they entered the Park at 86th Street, Artie reflected on the smallness of his allowance and the wretchedness of his plaid shirt and jeans. Fortunately she soon changed the subject to her own clothes.

"It's the latest Twiggy look. Or Lesley, as my friends call her. Did you know Lesley Hornby is her name? The British can't get enough of her and Justin de Villeneuve, her squire. He's one of the most famous hairdressers there."

"We hear a lot about Liz and Dick."

"Oh, of course, they're always good for a bit of a giggle. And Sybil Burton too! It's news when Sybil catches a cold."

"So this is Twiggy sort of hair?"

"No, it's more wavy. Like Cilla Black. You know the day I was in the salon she dropped by?"

In the back of the Metropolitan Museum, the dogwoods had fanned out in crimson and white sprays of flowers, and magnolia scent drifted down the paths. The fountains had been turned on and Audrey, then Artie sipped at the water trickling from one of the old stone cisterns. They headed for the Great Lawn, where there were benches Audrey could sit on without damaging her new dress. Finally she chose one near the flowering trees that surrounded Cleopatra's Needle, across from the old pond beneath the castle where they'd had their Park date almost a year ago.

Artie's heart began to thump mercilessly. He reached into his jacket pocket.

"Audrey, I don't know if I told you this, but I've started experimenting with a different sort of photography. Kind of like ad or fashion photography."

"Oh, that's a fabulous idea! It's all the rage now, even in art."

"It's my first time trying this."

He handed her the photos of take-it-all-off Michelle.

Audrey slowly flipped through them, seemingly puzzled, then burst out in a high-pitched laugh.

"That's very… attractively framed, Artie. Yes, it looks like it could be in a magazine, except… she's so gross!"

Looking at the photos over her shoulder, Artie had to admit that Michelle did have a ridge of baby fat, and her nose was a little blunt. Audrey slapped the pictures back in his hand.

"Was this your dreamgirl out in the country? Did she like your James Bond comma?"

"She's not my girlfriend! It was just in Camp Saco last summer."

"Well what did you both do, stage this as some sort of audition for her? Like an acting photo or something?"

"No, I hardly even knew her! She didn't know I was taking the pictures!"

"My god, you were SPYING on her? That's disgusting!"

Artie knew he had made a cascade of mistakes. In desperation he remembered some advice Russell had shared with him about girls. If you go too far, or do something wrong, he'd told him, girls naturally get upset, even angry—but they love having their minds changed.

"Audrey, I'm sorry, I just wanted to show you… I mean I had to practice somewhere and I just thought this would be… a bit of a giggle, you know? She's nothing compared to you, in your new fashions and all…"

He saw the softening in her downcast eyes.

"You are so beautiful right now."

He threw his arms around her and gave her the hardest kiss he'd ever tried. Suddenly he wanted to pierce through the English accent, graft himself onto her shiny flip British adultness. Her hands flew up against his chest, and the pictures scattered all over the pavement. She yanked her face away and gave him a hard shove. It didn't seem like her mind was changing. He tried to maneuver for another embrace, then crumpled from a blow to his ribs.

"God, Audrey, you haven't elbowed me since third grade!"

He tried to laugh off the shortness of breath. She turned away slightly and grinned, and he had a sense it was okay, that she knew this had gone on far enough.

"I mean, we're not in the P.S.6 schoolyard anymore."

He had a flutter of hope for the afternoon, until she froze her grin into a grimace of disdain and wouldn't even look back at him.

"That's for sure. Spy photos and this stupid bloody groping!"

"Oh cut with the bloody English accent! You sound like bloody Julie Andrews!"

She bit at her lip and primly drew herself erect from the

bench. It seemed a mock-tragic performance, until Artie saw a genuine tear welling beneath her eye.

"I was wrong about you, Artie. To come back after all this time, and see you as you really are. You've changed, Artie."

"What are you talking about? These? It's just snapshots!"

The breeze stirred the photos and flipped them toward the grass. Artie rushed to gather them.

"I haven't changed at all, Audrey!"

"I think I'll walk myself home if you don't mind!"

He watched her trot a few steps in her high heels, shouted one last apology that seemed to fall in brittle fragments at his feet, and thought about running after her until, to his amazement, she yanked off her shoes to get away even faster. Audrey was actually fleeing him across the grassy hill, and the stares of every guy in her path welcomed her into the distance.

"You turkey!"

"Danny, you told me that—"

"No, man, the idea is you take Audrey's photos. You show Audrey how you can make her look great. Not another chick in a bikini, man!"

A bunch of Danny's friends hung close by and picked up on the tail end of the conversation.

"I told her it was a photography exercise!"

"She's not gonna see that as exercise. Maybe extracurricular activity!"

By now the chain reaction was unstoppable as a saluggi game at Vandemeer High.

"What a turkey!"

"Turk, Turk, Turk!"

"Showing hot photos of one girl to another? That is so Turkish, it's the Ottoman Empire rising again!"

"Gobble, gobble!"

By the time Danny started singing "Istanbul Was Constantinople" the hard little bolus of misery Artie had carried in his gut all day exploded. He had been completely frazzled since

Audrey left him. He'd rushed home and feverishly written three apology letters, only to tear each one apart. But now he decisively charged toward the front door of Johnathan La Grange's candlelit corridor of an apartment, through the hive of guests costumed in Little Lord Fauntleroy shirts and bowties, paisley muu-muus, and brightly colored miniskirts, whose flamboyance seemed to mock his loss. He wanted to just fling himself down the subway line and into his room where no one but the cat would see his misery.

"Hey, hey, don't get uptight, Arturo! Come on, man, we're celebrating my new band!"

Artie allowed Danny to lead him back through the crowd to a table laid with a potluck assortment of potato chips, pretzels, croissants, prosciutto and melon, and a bin of fried chicken.

"We got a feast here. Besides, you want her back, you'll get her back, but I think you should keep moving, y'know? Like, I think you should meet a chick that really digs photography."

Artie couldn't even understand the concept.

"Just don't get hung up, Artie. Never get hung up."

Artie lingered at the table and was trying some bologna slices wrapped in cream cheese that were pretty tasty when a musky aroma of woodsmoke with a tang of burning mint found him. Danny passed him a small metal pipe with a black gummy residue in its bowl.

"What's this?"

"Try it."

Artie stared at the pipe, then clamped it to its lips and inhaled as tightly as possible. The stuff scored his throat and he coughed out the fumes.

"This some new kind of pot?"

"It's hash. As in hashish."

He felt as if he'd just been touched by a portion of the *Arabian Nights* or *Alice In Wonderland* and the party got better. He enjoyed meeting Nell Friedlander, who described herself as the Voyage's vocalist and requisite tambourine girl, then rumpled his hair and invited him to photograph the band anytime. Jimmy Hinton smiled at him as he noodled some blues guitar in a corner. Artie felt he needed some Coke to cool his throat. He passed an old elegant mirror, noticed how the glass melted to suck down his reflection like a waterdrop, poured the Coke, drank it, and realized that was a strange thing for a mirror to have done. Suddenly his throat burned with the taste of the black tar, his tongue grew spicy, and his teeth shivered like reeds. Danny came over and looked into his eyes.

"Houston, we have ignition…"

"We have liftoff!"

Artie chimed right in, Danny laughed, and Artie seemed to finish the laugh. For the rest of the night he had an extraordinary ability to flow in and out of other people's conversation. Danny's buddy Larry Ryan had a huge brow that almost glowed in the dark, and Artie shouted he had a big head. Yeah, Ryan laughed as he took a hit of the hash, and Russ and his friends picked up the cry of big head, big head, big head. So many people, so many conversations where his thoughts could dart in and reframe the others' experiences—he zoomed and close-upped, his saunter through the party guests a flickering jump-cut film strip.…

Another blood-beating rush… the party shimmered… Artie retreated to a corner to his own thoughts and words. Childish and heavy on labials… hyennnngurrr, mmmuuuuu, hhhthwhellllhmmm… a trail of happy mouth vibrations. Everyone smiled his way, let him alone, not bothering him as he stood aside and babbled to himself and unleashed different-creatured memories with a frondbrush grasp on reality, with Artie, good old Artie, pre-stoned Artie lining up the images any way he chose. A silky cricket trill memory of Audrey… no no, not that… he opened his eyes to a blur of candlelit faces and his own flaring afterimages… stay out in this, vibrate, float through… and music tugged gently at him, a strange Indian-sounding guitar over another thicker, darker guitar that melted to a drone, and a sizzle of harmonica, and he could feel the passing tones do their dance, the timbres of the guitars and bass and drums braid and twist… until the guitar lead amazed him, so phosphorescent, a high voltage wire torn down to a guitar neck, blues and raga, earthbound and celestial, one the bud and the herb itself, one the smoke. Danny was ecstatic, talking about how he and Jimmy were working out violin and guitar lines like Butter and Elvin and Bloomfield, and it was the weirdest music Artie ever heard, but he understood it, tone-deaf as he was Artie suddenly understood.

The effort made him hungry. He tried the prosciutto and a slice of melon, decided it would go well with a fried chicken wing and a piece of chocolate cake, then topped that off with pretzels, potato chips, bologna, and more cake. The cake was exceptionally good, and so he took a fistful of it in one hand, another prosciutto and melon in the other, and relished the harmonious congelation of flavors. Words, music, tastes, all oscillated on the edge of hummingbird wingbeats of time… and only after awhile did he notice Danny watching him.

"Don't mean to intrude on your munchies, Arturo, but …"

He extended a finger which seemed to elongate toward the door. Artie gaped at the leopard skin dress cut in half moons to reveal luminous hips over bare legs. The ultimate Yardley girl. Her blonde hair vibrated in thick invisible waves crackling like guitar feedback. Her eyes cut through the room, sizing up everyone like—he just sensed it—camera eyes. Danny filled it in—unbelievably, a chick who not only digs but does photography. Someone next to him exclaimed "oh wow, there's the shutterbird…"

Artie let his high move him forward, as if he were a balloon knocked by Danny's pointing finger right into her path. Her eyes… the pupils were so sea green, but had the force of eyes much darker. He suddenly felt he needed his old self, some trail through the scrambled connections back to sanity, but there was an appreciative smile on her lips as she spotted him, she seemed to understand and accept him and where he was at a glance. His hand floated out to hers.

"Hi, I'm Artie."

"I'm Pamela Huntington. I hope you don't mind if I don't shake your hand."

He looked down at his fingers, which were coated with gravy and chocolate.

"I see you've been enjoying the cake."

Yes, he acknowledged the cake was really good, but this was not where he wanted this to go, just control your other self, come on...

"Danny said you were a photographer?"

"Oh yes, Artie, in fact I'm photographing a lot of the local bands."

"That's a great idea, with all their instruments... well, they're not a band without the instruments, yeah, and... I'm a photographer."

"Well, that's marvelous! You're starting young! Have you seen 'The Photographer's Eye?'"

The question made absolutely no sense to Artie, but he answered it as best he could.

"No, but I have one."

Pamela whooped and laid a hand on his shoulder.

"Well, my pet, that's a bloody good start then!"

"You sound like you're really English..."

"You're kind of cheeky, aren't you? Artie, I have to get myself a drink, and find whatever it is you've found, but we'll catch each other up again."

It took Artie two days to lose the high, wearing sunglasses whenever he went out, wondering if he'd slipped across some fault line of experience and would never be able to retrace his steps. When he got back to what, to his intense relief, felt like normal, he cast his mind back to Pamela Huntington. He finally realized that she was probably at least four years older than him, and that she had never "caught him up" again at that party, but apportioned her time carefully among various men present, one of whom she'd brought with her. He also remembered a woman saying in a huff that a certain kind of blonde could wear anything, and their bizarre scarecrow of a host, Johnathan La Grange, whispering dryly that that was one you caught with a golden net.

Aisha tore after the spool on the string, added a curlicue or two on the thread as she batted it with her paws, and then, in a jump-cut, mewed in Artie's face. Artie had dozed off, just like that, right while the cat was spinning herself around her toy.

These nights, he couldn't sleep much, beckoned from dreams by a woman stalking the jungle of his memory in a leopard-skin miniskirt. Royal danger he couldn't measure up to, that had tempted him, played with him, spun him around, then vanished.

And when he couldn't sleep, alert to every sound from the street to the kitchen, he heard that his dad couldn't sleep as well. He glanced at his dad's desk, usually so neat, with piles of memo pads and pencils in precise rows. Now it was heaped with loose paper, the disorderly footprint of the Hicks case, like a subway when it was just an eye down a tunnel but felt all the way through the platform. Dad was always working on the case with his partner; he was always late coming home. He seemed to care about it too much. Artie could hear his more frequent trips to the bathroom at night. He wondered if he was taking more pills, if all of it might somehow get him sick again.

He clipped his 45 spindle disk into the center of "Along Comes Mary" and spun it on the turntable. The hit single shot off in-crowd drug codes like sparks. Harmonies that sighed to catch up with Pamela and a flute like a trace of her perfume… he thought of her again and his hands sweated, he shivered, dreams gathered.

There was a carbon copy in the middle of the desk, clearly typed by dad's secretary. Back in the foyer, Karen, taking a break from her homework, stood and watched Artie walk over to it.

"I think this is dad's writing for court."

Karen stood by his side and turned the paper back around so she could read it from the beginning. Artie read again the passage about complaints that activists had broken the peace of their community.

"The fact of the matter is that the Harlem Action Front is a part of this community, that Roy Hicks was born there, and that both he and his friends are trying to tackle problems that have festered there for years. So today, ladies and gentlemen of the jury, you judge a son of this community committed totally to that community's welfare, and the only criterion for your judgment must be the following: did Roy Hicks commit the crime of which he was accused?"

"What crime?"

"I don't know. Guess it's really serious."

How did Izzy do it, Nate wondered, how did he flick off the case back at the office, gabbing away with Allen Ginsberg about a recipe for a pot seed cookie "groovy breakfast high" in the latest issue of Ed Sanders' *Fuck You* Magazine? Nate, waiting day after day for the verdict, drained by a post-trial depression he hadn't experienced in years, knew he had to grab a Scotch and soda's worth of consolation before heading home to his kids.

Early on a Friday night at Café Curacao, dusk still trickling through the windows, the guests looked like waxen refugees from the light, and there was another hostess this evening. Marcela, in a plain, slightly wrinkled white blouse and sans culottes, was at the hat check stand. The allure Nate remembered was now tightly contained, part of the glad-handing routine. Still she smiled warmly at him as she took his coat, then leaned out of her booth and directed some remarks in Portuguese to the bartender. It turned out his first drink was free as long as he tried a Brazilian potion called a *caipirinha*. The drink was like a Margarita with a minty tartness and he sipped it gratefully.

He was going to walk over, thank Marcela, and make a quick exit, when she slipped onto the barstool right next to his. The bartender slid her a glass of soda water and lime. She pulled out a cigarette and Nate reflexively lit it. Leaning toward her he could see the shadows under her eyes in the updraft of the lighter and the freckles on the skin drawn tight over the collarbone. His eyes darted down to her legs, too long and muscular to coil easily under the rim of the bar.

A gruff, bellowing laugh startled both of them, and a mountain of a guy who looked like the wrestler Bruno Sammartino strode across the café, talking to the manager.

"Is that the bouncer?"

"Yes, I guess that's what you call it."

"You ever have trouble in a place like this?"

"Yes, you would be surprised. Many people are careless. A nice businessman has a couple of glasses of wine, a *caipirinha* or two…"

She fluttered her fingers toward the sky.

"I notice you're not drinking."

"I guess I see too much of… but sometimes we all can use the drink."

"You can tell that about me?"

"I think you're having a tough day."

He told her about the case he had just tried, and that seemed to genuinely fascinate her, spark the fatigue right out of her eyes.

"You know it's really great that you can defend people like that, against the police."

"Believe me, I'm not crazy about it, but that's part of my job."

"In Brazil they don't have that job anymore."

Marcela spoke with a kind of confessional urgency about the Brazilian military, and the coup that had driven away Marcela and so many of her compatriots, including an old boyfriend, a businessman that had paid for her ticket out. She perched on the edge of her stool, hands gesturing ardently, as if somehow she could still defend the land she'd fled.

"I didn't want to go. I was manager of a nice restaurant there, near the Copa. But of course Carlo was right."

"You two came to New York together?"

"No, he's in the country now. Saratoga Springs."

She added so much froth to the s's that Nate laughed in spite of himself, and Marcela shrugged and chuckled with him.

"I'm sorry. My English…"

"I should apologize. Your English is excellent. It's just that Saratoga Springs reminds me of stodgy old battle axes and then when you say it, it's almost like it was Paris."

"To Carlo it is Paris. Old ladies with old money. Big houses. He wanted us to go to France. The Riviera."

"So why did you come here?"

"I didn't know anything about France. But America... oh, that for me was the 1961 tour. The Good Neighbor program? Gerry Mulligan came, Charlie Byrd, and they loved Gilberto and Jobim, and we saw all these concerts, with jazz and with *bossa nova* together, not this 'Blame It On The Bossa Nova,' but the really beautiful stuff Gilberto and Astrud still do, and I'm thinking, America is the center of this music."

The lights hidden in the ceiling softs brightened in the dusk. The *caipirinha* settled warmly in Nate's blood and tugged him free of the silence.

"It's really a pleasure to talk to you, Marcela."

"Yes... Greta said I should get to know you."

"Did she tell you I'm a widower?"

"Yes, I'm very sorry."

She slid herself off the barstool, and favored him with one last smile.

"I have to go. But stay longer."

"Maybe a little longer... Marcela? Don't forget you once ran a place like this."

"Maybe one day I have my own restaurant, and you're a famous lawyer, and we will sit and talk at the head table."

"First I have to win a couple of cases."

"Well... good luck... I think you will win this case."

"I don't know. There's a saying... from your mouth to God's ear."

"Maybe he's listening, maybe not... but I feel, somehow... you will win."

Nate and Izzy, audibly wheezing the whole rushed subway trip down to the court, took their positions besides Roy Hicks as the jury filed in. Nate was once again both unnerved and amazed by the ritual at the core of his occupation. The course of justice of the United States of America, the most powerful country in the world, devolved upon twelve ordinary men and women who filed in like a crowd at church or at a temple, shuffled into their seats, and, at the summons of a civil servant, deputized their leader, in this case a schoolteacher and mother of three, to stand up and read a few simple words that struck the courtroom like an earthquake.

"We the jury find the defendant, Roy Hicks, guilty of the crime of armed robbery..."

The bleating sighs of Roy's family and friends also seemed part of the ritual, an ancient call and response. Izzy spat out a curse under his breath. Nate felt a cold silence anneal him to the chair. Just take it, watch a bright, courageous young Negro man get led off to jail.

"You watch your step now!"

"You take care of our boy!"

That was not part of the ritual. Those cries threw into relief a whole new landscape.

"You be careful, Officers!"

"Yeah, we know where that Civilian Review Board is!"

"Disgrace! Outrage!"

"No more police brutality! No more!"

"You not takin' any of our kids no more!"

"We got eyes on you now!"

It seemed that all the character witnesses Nate had amassed were spontaneously erupting at once. The minister joined the judge in appealing for order. The police slowly moved out of the courtroom, never taking their eyes off the crowd. Nate saw the demonstration as one more facet of a disastrous loss. He believed his speech had not been hard-hitting enough—God, if he'd mentioned the word "community" one more time—and his words had been tainted by doubt in his case and in himself.

Without even waiting for Izzy to take the lead out of the courtroom he packed his portfolio and headed for the center aisle to pay his sad respects. There the first comradely hand was thrust his way, by a Negro man he didn't even know. Nate stopped and shook his hand, and suddenly there was a crowd around him. They were grim, they were not his friends, but they thanked him and acknowledged his service. Nate shook one hand after another, Izzy right behind him, far more demonstrative, actually hugging one of the women, tears in his eyes. Nate felt a tumult of emotions as he tried to make his way outside. He didn't belong here, he didn't deserve the gratitude of these people, and he needed to get home to his family. With the blast of sunlight outside the courtroom came a pair of microphones. Nate made out a face he knew, a cross between a cynical rake and a boxer, and recognized Gabe Pressman just as the ace newshound was in his face asking what he thought of the verdict. Behind Nate black voices were rising up in one long discordant complaint. The minister was no longer crying for order but letting them loose, and their energy crackled through to the tv cameras bearing down on Nate. He managed to tell Pressman that the verdict was unfortunate—he respected this was a tough case for the jury, he understood the difficulty of keeping the peace, but still... and that's when Izzy shouldered through to the mike and made sure all the cameras were on them as he told Pressman that they were going to immediately appeal this travesty.

The minister, Dale Jenkins, stepped up to the microphone, and proclaimed that the community stood as one behind Roy Hicks, and by community, he insisted, he meant a community that believed in justice. He clamped a hand on Nate's shoulder.

"This may be a loss in this court, but we've won a moral victory today! We have come together to say: we no longer sit in the back of the bus, and we no longer stand in the front of the jail. We will all have our day in court again, and next time, the verdict will be far different!"

"All right, Dad!"

Together Nate and the kids sat on the old living room couch and watched the Pressman report. With Gabe in his urban war correspondent mode, the piece told the story of a neighborhood at the boiling point—and right there in the cauldron was a careworn but staunch defender of his wrongly accused client. Nate noticed for the first time how heavier and more haggard the camera could make its subject. But his voice was firm and clear and Artie grinned with family pride. Karen was uncontrollable. She clapped her hands and bounced on the cushions until the springs groaned and Nate had to tell her to stop.

"Daddy's on television!"

It didn't matter the third-personing of it, as if some presence other than him had earned the ratification of the universe of the Monkees and Leonard Bernstein's Young People's Concerts. He was flooded with pleasure at her outburst, pleasure at having stood up for a principle in a gentlemanly way, without knocking the jury, but strongly enough so that his children could hear him on the eleven o'clock news.

"That's great! It sounds like your speech."

"I left a copy here, didn't I? It's called a closing statement."

"It was great, Dad."

"Maybe not that great, Artie. We didn't win."

"You'll win next time, Daddy!"

And as Nate, like his Mets, soon learned, the right kind of loss could pay some dividends in New York. A moral victory wasn't a bad thing to have when you could pay your dues defending the poor and oppressed and earn the cases of the rich and infamous. Hamerow and Kovacs freed clients who'd been grabbed up by police for disorderly conduct during a rent strike demonstration but hadn't been properly read their rights according to the new Miranda decision. Meanwhile Izzy realized that drug beefs would be easy pickings for defense lawyers until the cops got used to the Miranda rules, especially as already forbidden marijuana use skyrocketed and LSD made its way up the controlled substance hierarchy. He took the cases of famous denizens of the Village and their connections caught in the pot rap and got many of them thrown out of court.

"Look, Nate, it's victimless crime, and if it's gonna pay, it might as well pay us."

Nate, as the moderate, or, as his friend Avery Lansing put it, the Abbott to Izzy's Costello, earned a raft of job discrimination complainants along with the occasional big money client like the producer who wanted the firm to vet his script, where some total

nudity was planned, for the most legally troublesome portions—
and incidentally talk it up on the q.t. to potential backers.
The city coasted into summer on a giddy current of sports
and good times. The AFL and NFL agree to merge and play the
Super Bowl in 1967. Lindsay's Cabinet of Commissioners met in
shirtsleeves under an oak tree by the East River rather than in
the Susan Wagner wing of Gracie Mansion. There was a bikini
contest in Central Park.

And Hamerow and Kovacs' new status yielded, besides
the occasional Yankee and Met box seats, press screenings and
show tickets, just in time for Artie, who needed a diet of more
intelligent entertainment. Artie was ecstatic at the chance to
see *The Mad Show*, the theatrical incarnation of his beloved
magazine. Superman in a Broadway musical, Batman on tv.
Camp, they called it, converting the serious to the frivolous and
sublimating the frivolous—self-consciously silly movies like *Help!*
or tv shows like *Laugh-In*—into art. A loony evasion of a confusing
and threatening world. Shrink row on theater row, prosperous
battiness, the goggle-eyed hoot of JoAnn Worley.

On a week when the heat of the sidewalks seemed to waft the
petals off the trees in the Park, Nate, Artie, and Dorothy Kempster
took their seats in midst of an auditorium built into a salon. The
walls sprouted cherubim and putti that frolicked within vineyards
and puffy clouds. Within this setting, which, except for the p.a.
system, could've sprung from turn-of-the-century Paris, the
Blakewell dance class performed Saint-Saens' *Carnival of the
Animals*. Nate appreciated the students' topical inventiveness: an
elephant who waddled up to the front and showed a belly scar LBJ-
style to the laughter of the audience, another boy as a tremulously
adventurous kangaroo, with a recognizably adolescent mix of
swagger and fear.

The lights shrank to a few blue and silver spots and Karen,
Nina and a third young girl, all in white dancers' leotards and
gauzy dresses, danced "The Aquarium." They traced balletic
circles around each other, their hands fluttered like fins. They
backed toward the center, roamed the perimeter of the stage,

skittered toward the corners with eyes upturned to the light. Dorothy sighed and her hand drifted to Nate's shoulder. Artie saw a flash of Pamela's blonde hair drifting through a stoned haze. Nate, despite the gentle pressure on his arm, couldn't avoid thinking of Marcela's face in the glow of his lighter. Artie watched the look on Karen's face, the eyes locked open, trying to glean every last glimmer on the stage.

The fish parted to make one more sally against the invisible aquarium glass, then glided back together, and Karen, the last one to head off into the wings, gave a little dorsal wriggle of her hips to go with the wave of her arms. The crowd laughed, Artie shouted with surprise, and the three girls got the most applause of the show.

She'd imagined him out there, even though she knew that was impossible, now that he rehearsed every night with his new band. And when she'd wriggled her hips, a gesture that just seemed to waft into her from the music, and heard the cheers, it seemed proof that if he had been there...

At the sleepover with Suzanne, Karen and Nina were still practicing their dance moves until they became bumpcar slams. They opened the window, passed around a Gauloise cigarette, and tried to keep the acrid burning clove in their lungs so that whatever the kick was could sweep through them. Suzanne fell asleep on the cot and in the bed Nina and Karen shared they talked about boys they knew and if they would ever be as cool as the boys in their head. In their closeness and their mention of Nina's upcoming trip to the Berkshires, on which Karen was invited to come along, Nina wondered aloud if they'd ever be half-sisters. Karen told her she'd have to stop snoring first. You'd need more perfume trumped Nina, and they relished the friction of their mockery and mutual delight.

"That's what Lindsay gets for his great white pasha act!"

Nate flinched from the comment—he hadn't expected, pouring Chianti for Dorothy and her friends at Manny's Chop

House, to get hit with some of the backlash bubbling up from Brooklyn and Queens. Lindsay's presumed support of the ghettos above all other neighborhoods was fueling prejudice in working-class whites of the outer boroughs. If you took the temperature of the city, it was spiking a fever.

"Bernie! Enough with the backtalk! Go on, Nate."

As Dorothy admonished her cousin, Nate conceded it was a nightmare scenario: East New York going to hell at light speed, the Italian toughs and their group S.P.O.N.G.E., Society for the Prevention of Niggers Getting Everything, setting up picket lines at the intersection of Ashford St. and New Lots and Livonia Avenues, the dividing lines between the black and white communities, harassing people on their way to work, yelling "Go back to Africa!" Lindsay had gone down there personally to try to calm the situation but soon after his visit an eleven-year-old Negro boy had been shot by an unknown sniper. Two hundred cops had had to move in to calm the streets. Gotterher had called a special meeting in the City Hall Blue Room.

"They've got a truce now. The meeting was a madhouse, the Italian kids and Negro kids and families all yelling at each other. Lindsay got the help of a Mob leader of all people and promised both sides a neighborhood city hall and duplicate services. It's working."

"For now Nate, maybe. For now. But you stick in their corner long enough… they're always threatening to riot. The schwarzes love to burn their own neighborhoods down."

"Like there weren't fires in our old neighborhoods?"

Dorothy, a little drunk, dipped her shoulder against Nate's arm.

"Dot, we didn't riot all over the Bronx."

"Oh, but come on, all the store fires for the insurance? Dad used to call them 'Jewish lightning'."

Nate was still chuckling at her remark as he walked Dorothy home. He enjoyed how she shared his gift for mediation—even if secretly she agreed with her cousin that, at the very least, Nate might not be totally prepared for what he was getting into.

"What was the line from the show, Nate? There's a million stories in the Naked City? Just don't you be one of the bad ones."

He grinned and put his arm around Dorothy and savored the bob and dip of her waist, a tennis player's body, still lithe and quick. But with all their flickers of affection, they couldn't quite behave like teenagers. It was obvious she was leery of the territory outside of marriage. As they headed home, she came around to a story about a secretary in Lou's office, and Nate wondered if she was going to reveal an affair of her husband's. Instead she told Nate how the poor girl had gotten an abortion in Puerto Rico, and had bled her life out in the bathroom on the plane back from San Juan. Nate realized that the story was Dorothy's confession of sexual reticence—she had once compared the Pill to Russian roulette—and by the time they reached her apartment, their delicate physical byplay was over.

Beneath her canopy they snuggled together and abruptly she rubbed her hands up and down his back, repeating his name, saying what a good guy he was. A plea for understanding, and he granted it. She gave him a gentle peck on the cheek, a girlish wave, and, sailing along on his reassurance, headed down the lobby.

He had to admit he also was relieved. He knew that, without ever losing the stamp Becky still had on all his affections, he could go out with Dorothy and experiment safely with some of the lively temptations that were now being thrown his way.

Just that past night, at Elaine's, a converted Yorkville goosegrease restaurant that had become a writer's haven, Nate had joined a gripes-and-cocktails session of Bruce and his friends. Bruce had wondered aloud how long he could service teenyboppers, watch *Hullabaloo* and *Shindig*, track *Billboard* and *Record World* for trends. The act was wearing thin. The freshness of the British invasion was over; The Animals had played the Wolvettes in an awful mod tv version of "Little Red Riding Hood," singing "We're Gonna Howl Howl Howl Tonight!" The writers all lamented the winding down of the sort of life where you could combine ad writing for Bloomingdale's, pieces for magazines, and a few published short stories into a freelance living, the bibbity-bobbity-boo writer's life—put 'em together and whaddya got. And there was downward pressure on the whole food chain now that the merger of three of New York's biggest newspapers was going to create the *World Journal Tribune*. As the drinks settled in and the men's gazes hovered over the packed tables, they agreed that just about the only healthy signs of life on the scene were the tightly miniskirted ones on the arms of aspiring writers who, on track one day to join the circle grousing at the back of Elaine's, were enjoying their brief hopeful years piloting go-go babes to the bar.

It was Bruce who finally dispelled the general surliness by handing out leaflets for the debut of his son's band, The Voyage, and asking everyone to pass them on to their kids. Unlike his tiresome friends, Nate reflected, Bruce had, thanks to his son and his music, some enthusiasm for the present day. It all seemed to have a pleasant symmetry for Bruce now; while, as he put it, he flogged the merch at the record store, his son was starting to make the new music his own. And Bruce crowed about how one of his record producer buddies hung out with Mike Nichols, Lenny Bernstein, and the other co-owners of Arthur, the hot new discotheque started by Sibyl Burton. Bruce told Nate his connections could get him and a date in on a Saturday night.

The Manhattan scene du jour. A Kennedy clan, Peter Sellers stalking a Playboy blonde kind of place. Nate realized that he could use a break from seeing the tensions of the city flayed open before his eyes, and that he and Dorothy could definitely enjoy the tinselly glamour over cocktails.

The ritual of the name as password, one or two couples allowed inside at a time, reminded Nate of how his father had described speakeasies; all that was missing was the sliding panel on the door. Once inside he was surrounded by dandies in full "youthquake" mode in Victorian waistcoats, striped double-breasted suits, candy-colored shirts, and loud ties. The women shimmied like burlesque dancers in dresses that could've been petticoats, but slick and silvery clean. The club's design had traces of the old El Morocco where he and Becky had once had drinks on New Year's Eve, but the perspectives were juggled by blasts of light, the metal edges of go-go girl cages and music that knifed into his brain at four times the volume of Artie's stereo. The shiny new world chased all his memories away.

Marcela breezed confidently through it all and drew the stares of all the swingers in the room. Tawny, tall, rangy—what a figure in that azure wraparound dress. She walked gracefully arm-in-arm by Nate's side, thanked him for pulling out her chair, did everything right.

Nate knew that he'd been the one who'd felt and acted clumsily from the moment that he'd abruptly decided that he wouldn't bring Dorothy but Marcela to the discotheque. With a stuttering heartbeat he hadn't felt since his college years he'd called the Café Curacao, and when that wrestler-necked bouncer at the Café had barked he'd have to look for Marcela, Nate had almost hung up the phone. Then Marcela had told him the boss would have to okay her absence and she'd call back, and Nate had nervously insisted that he call her. As if the kids could overhear his office phone calls from miles away. As if he didn't have the right to call.

Two gin and tonics later the scene took on a merry cabaret quality. Nate was even thinking of trying a couple of the dances, which looked like stylized thrashing. Marcela abruptly seized his hand and steered his attention across the room. Nate recognized him immediately, the brilliantine black hair, face like lined walnut, a music star's macho reserve and courtly smile. The Sound himself. Stan Getz exchanged some pleasantries with Marcela, and then, when she introduced Nate, shook his hand.

"Nice to meet you. You guys do good work. And thank Izzy again for all his help."

The great sax man's acknowledgment left Nate with enough bravado to take Marcela out on the dance floor. As the Beatlesque blur of music enveloped him Nate rocked his knees, swung his shoulders. Marcela laughed and gave him hand gestures to mimic.

They were frugging. Some jerk took flash pictures and it broke Nate's mood until he saw the photographer was Andy Warhol. The flashes sizzled in the grinning faces of Kirk Douglas and Robert Redford. The tunes ran on, Pink Floyd, the Easybeats, the Knickerbockers, and he liked the twang of "Secret Agent Man" and the skipping jazzy beat of "Along Comes Mary." Out of the blue he tried some jitterbug style spins and twirls with Marcela, and the young couple nearby shouted with approval. Nate felt like Alan Bates in *Zorba the Greek* caught up in the embrace of the *taverna.*

The music slowed to a booming heartbeat of guitars on some lovelorn tune by the Kinks. Marcela embraced him, billowed around him with sheer fabric, the pulse of her back, the musk of falling hair. Nate moved in a careful box step, reached for a joke to steady himself against a whole new drunkenness that ambushed him.

"If my kid dances like this… call the chaperone…"

On the way out, Nate saw Marcela pocket an ashtray. Once they were outside, she handed it to him. He looked down at the white base, the "Arthur" in block letters.

"For your son."

"I don't know, might encourage him to smoke."

"It's a souvenir!"

The hazy air was charged with the shouts of partygoers and the tracks of headlights. Marcela's dress clung tighter to her hips. How mischievous but also thoughtful, he decided, pocketing the ashtray. What fun.

Her apartment was the same way: brooding niches devoted to candles and small clay figurines, totems of her homeland, but also a mix of globular furniture, round and soft, covered with tropically incandescent mats and throw rugs.

"You must miss Rio."

"Yes, so much sometimes… you know, while the military was in the streets, and we were driving as fast as we can to get to the harbor… a samba school was doing a morning practice for Carnival. You can need so little."

Nate reached over and clasped her hand. She gazed at him, and stroked his palm in a way he felt in his groin.

"Marcela, do you ever regret that you came here?"

"It's very lonely. I hope it will be better over time. I like the Café, I'm a good hostess."

"You'll be a very good restaurateur. And—actually, I could help you with some of the more annoying permit laws. Do you... you basically like New York?"

"Oh yes. And I liked this night. I really liked this night."

He was astonished at how flexible his back became as he quickly glided next to her on the couch. Their lips touched, hers a supple petal blossoming in his mouth, tongue melting forward. Nate drew back.

"Boy, you are some kisser."

Was her smile gentle or mocking?

"Marcela, this is a little difficult for me. Also... maybe a little quick."

The clutch in his chest, the hand still stroking her arm belied his words.

"I guess we're different, where I come from... about how we feel... how we can show it, maybe."

"Where you come from is very nice. God, Marcela... I would've liked to see the way you walked on the beach in Rio."

He made his excuses, backed away from her, but allowed himself one more long kiss right up to the point he cursed at the back twinge that finally announced itself.

"I'd be no good anymore in the front seat of a LaSalle. Guess it's time to call it a night."

He stroked her cheek and she took his hand and gloved one of his fingers with her lips. The pleasure was excruciating.

She looked at him, laughed, laid a hand on his shoulder, and bounded toward her bathroom. Nate thought of a deer racing through the grass. His head pounded. He looked at the finger she'd sucked, the ring right nearby.

The switch clicked and the room darkened. She moved through streaks of extinguished light. He was stunned by the ripple of her long tanned legs and the black pelt at their center, the elongated, falling breasts of a woman only a few years younger than him, but nipples erect and hard as youth.

"You wanted to see how I walked on the beach in Rio."

As he leaped up, the pain in his back shivered away and he raced after her, but a moment later, as she lay on the bed, her bronzed half-moon buttocks beside him, his legs pulling free of his bunched up slacks, his fingers fumbling at the shirt buttons felt almost like they weren't his own.

She gave him a searching look, then reached under his briefs and drew her fingernail across the base of his scrotum. A molten wire inside him shocked him on top of her. Her lips clung and another mouth greedily welcomed him—and at last all he had to do was hold on tight and concentrate on each writhe of her hips until his body was contained and braced and trembled and he let loose a strangled cry of surprise that melted into the groan of trying to stay and stay.

She understood when he had to leave soon after. She understood everything.

He crept back through the living room quietly at two in the morning and headed for the bathroom in the hallway connecting Artie and Karen's bedrooms. He hoped the shower wouldn't wake the kids, but he had no choice, he had to wash the scents off him. The warm water spattered down his back, and he drove the back of his hand into his mouth to muffle his sobs. Tears of mourning fell to the shower floor as bitter and hard as he'd felt in years.

After he donned his pajamas and stretched out on his sofa bed he realized sleep would probably not come. But it wasn't until almost dawn that he walked to the living room window. The streetlight had shut off, the moon floated in the slot of sky above the facing apartment house and its water tower, and it seemed to Nate that for one brief hour of Manhattan's life, moonlight lay on the cornices and mouldings, trickled through the slats of the blinds, and fell across the vibrant flush of his skin.

The leaflet in Artie's hand promised that Murray the K's World would be "the most revolutionary thing that ever happened in the world of entertainment.

"The lights change, the scenes change, the entertainers change, and YOU will change! You are the center and everything is happening around YOU!"

Music from the most thunderous stereo he'd ever heard sparked twenty-one screens into a fusillade of slides and peacock-fan light patterns along with giant tv images of the dance floor itself, which occupied most of the space of an old airport hangar at Roosevelt Field. There were hundreds of kids dancing on the floor, rocking in place on chairs in the back as they sipped Cokes, scrambling everywhere.

Mr. Geller cracked that it was like a combination of the World's Fair and the light screen torture sequence from *The Ipcress File.*

What would it be like, Artie thought, to play all the music he'd been hearing this summer on those speakers? Instead of Camp Saco, this "Summer In The City"—and he loved the jackhammered keyboards of that tune—had been nothing but music. On his friend's stereos, and sometimes, unfortunately, on his own, with its little speakers that now seemed so insufficient, their bass barely able to make a tabletop quiver, he'd picked up on a code, a new world given in fragments, songs not "battling" for Number One but joining in a rush of all sorts of colors and sounds and elusive meanings. The Butterfield Blues Band howling gutbucket music out of a manhole, as Mike Bloomfield tortured lightning out of his guitar, or soared into the raga drones of "East/West" that Artie remembered from when he first got high. John Mayall's harmonica yowl and scat, tongue and lips clicking out a dervish tap dance, while Eric Clapton dove far below the bouncy jug band blues of the Lovin' Spoonful to fetch up peeled back high notes of raw passion.

Freak Out by the Mothers of Invention, a band with armpit hair on their faces and crazy music to match, mad king triumphal marches with pinging xylophones, and all over the inside sleeve was a *Mad* Magazine-type diatribe, in comic book balloons and street mimeo typeface, about how disgusting and antisocial the music was. Later in the summer came the Doors, where the organ and bass, played by the same wizard of a musician, and the singer's laments both seemed to emanate from a haunted cave. But Artie didn't get Morrison that summer. He didn't get the Byrds' new stuff. "Eight Miles High," banned from the airwaves, all about drugs... the bass growled, cymbal flickers erupted, then the guitar took off like a jet's afterburner into... what? It didn't seem about drugs... maybe it really was about airplanes? Even the Beatles' *Revolver* and its magic toy chest of orchestras, sitars, ocean waves, music hall brass and dance bands—the Beatles had utterly changed, turning away from the camera, sharing private jokes behind mirror glasses and strange collages, a few breaks for the "Yellow Submarine" funny stuff or the sweet ballads but always throwing you off balance right up to the last song with its lunatic crows cawing on a mystic hill. Artie and Russ had tried to smoke their way into that one, but in the end Russ had turned to Artie and just shrugged.

But there was one thing Artie did get in Morrison's priapic roars, in the wrenching lyrical turns of "She Said She Said," in all the invitations to flights where you might find bliss, or come in for a rough landing, images going in and out of the blaze of guitars—he could almost feel on his skin the presence of Pamela Huntington. She was nowhere to be found and seizing his mind every day. She would know what "Eight Miles High" was about, she could even talk to the Beatles behind their shades. So many songs became Pamela arias, the propulsively lovelorn or angry ones. "19th Nervous Breakdown," the rich bitch you sneer at it but want to save, "It Won't Be Wrong," if only he could say that to her, "And Your Bird Can Sing," no you can't have me, and when I shout how free I am you'll take me in your arms... though you make me feel like I've never been born...

The World boomed out "These Boots Are Made For Walking" and the screens came alive with images of kid boots, leather boots, pink and blue, rhinestoned and shiny, blurred and pixilated and double-exposed so that they seemed to dance along with the beat. A cameraman hefting a giant camera and fishbowl of a lens paced by Artie. Artie briefly saw himself as a bright blur on one of the screens.

Yes, it all revolves around You.

The lights suddenly darkened to raucous cheers. A p.a. voice roared "All right all you young ladies and gentlemen, are you ready?... are you ready for?... The Voyage!"

The band's equipment was moored above Artie on a suspended stage. Compared to Danny's crisply gotten-up Phantastics, this new band was a harlequinade straggling into place as they hiked up the ramps to their gear. As they started to tune up it was all immediately a little strange, off-kilter, blithely indolent. Nell sauntered back and forth in her kimono and rattled her tambourine, and La Grange, a scarecrow in black, took his place in a little cockpit of stringed instruments. Danny in a silk jacket and ruffled shirt that could've come out of a Gilbert and Sullivan play, guitar slung over his shoulder, hair longer than ever, picked up a violin and drew the bow in a howl that had the audience bristling to attention. Their tuneup became one long drone fueled by La Grange's sitar sound, and Danny stepped to the mike and chanted vowel sounds... a, e, i, o, u, o, uuuu.

Trippy, whispered the kid next to Artie.

The drum and bass hit the beat of Bo Diddley's "I Can Tell" and it all worked in a flash. Drum and bass r & b heavy, the sitar rising like smoke to give the tune an Asiatic tinge, Nell and Danny trading off on the blues vocals and shouting defiantly, harmonically at each other on "I can tell you don't love me no more!" The crowd loved Danny's switching from rhythm guitar to violin and double-barrel soloing with Jimmy Hinton in notes that writhed and slid over each other. It was all the new strange stuff but with New York City heat—sinuous, dusky, exotic, hard-hitting, and raga blue.

The crowd cheered, Mr. Geller hollering louder than anyone. Artie briefly wondered if his own father would ever come out to applaud anything he did, but that couldn't dampen his excitement at the great band Danny had put together.

"This is a little one by yours truly, oh so truly…" crooned Danny, "kind of a gypsy hoedown"—and the next song slammed into a "Tombstone Blues" beat as Danny attacked the violin with some kind of Near Eastern rhythm backed by Johnathan on the oud—Danny had told Artie there would be an "Over Under Sideways Down" kind of tune. He sang about the traffic and pollution and television assaults on his brain as the screens flashed frenzied Op Art patterns around the stage. Suddenly he brought the tune to a halt, a plinking of the oud and a few walking bass notes, a darkly fuzztoned shriek from the guitar, while he whispered "I don't want this life I want the other…," Jimmy echoing him softly like on the Yardbirds tune.

The band shuttled the song between the craziness that had kids dancing on the tables and the pauses that dropped the crowd like stringless marionettes, right up to the final raveup. Danny launched a long howl of a solo part gypsy, part raga. He jackknifed to the thunder of the drum and bass, hair whipping up and down, and a photographer ran up the ramps onto the stage. Artie recognized immediately Pamela's flash of blonde hair as she bounded across the platform in paisley blouse and miniskirt, chasing angles on the band like a greyhound. She crouched at Danny's feet and the crowd went batshit. Artie shoved his way toward them as she kneeled for one final shot by the edge of the stage—and the club went black. The strobes erupted and swung their blades of light over the dance mob, now a herky-jerky flash barrage of leaps and flails and gaping faces. Pam flickered off the stage. Artie burst through the crowd into the wings just as the song's climax crashed around his ears, but she was gone.

The Voyage eased into their next tune, Jimmy Hinton's "Down In The Darkness," a shuffling lope of a blues rumba stretched like taffy and backed by simmering organ from La Grange. Artie blinked away the dazzle of the strobes and wandered in the leftover space between the fans and the song.

Down in the darkness, where we wind up with nothing, baby I have you…

Danny's violin crooned seductively behind Jimmy's guitar lines that rose like fumes from a burning joint. Artie gave the wings one last look, and suddenly there she was, seated over her camera and absorbed in the humdrum task of changing her film.

She looked up, made him out and gave him a slightly baffled smile. Everything he'd planned to say for months evaporated.

"Great band, huh?"

"Yes, I really fancy them. Very colorful."

Her fingers deftly slotted in the film.

"Are you photographing them for a magazine?"

"Just for my own portfolio, for the moment… do I know you?"

Artie stammered out how they met and she flashed him a bright little smile of recognition.

"Oh yes! You're the young photographer! Aren't you taking pictures of the band?"

"I really don't know how. I only know daylight photography."

"It's all in the shutter speed, Artie, the film stock—you just have to experiment."

The camera back slammed shut.

"Well, have to run. I'm working."

"I thought you said you—"

"Oh, I've done some of the screens here. The art, you know. Have to see how they work, the exposure, the framing. I rather liked the boots. Did you like my boots?"

"You work with the disco?"

"Yes I suppose I do. You're quite the purist, aren't you?"

He didn't hear the tease in her voice; every drop of mock-reproach scalded him. Seeing how dismayed he was, she playfully, theatrically blazed her eyes into his.

"You should read some McLuhan. Mixed media, breaking down the barriers—that's what's happening, pet. Anyway, cheers."

She flipped the camera over her shoulder, a Leica, top of the line, and headed for the door.

"Pamela! Could I see you again… I mean… your photos?"

She smiled tenderly, he thought, but in an instant it hardened into professional briskness.

"Well, if you don't mind seeing me with a bunch of other photographers, I'm in a group show. Kent MacIlwaine Gallery. October 10 is the opening. You can remember that, can't you?"

She strode away and Artie, suddenly feeling disloyal to Danny's band, shouldered his way into the crowd just as their final tune, Danny's sprightly, Zombies-ish "The Journey," was winding down. *Through the hoops of jewels and fire… in the ring or on the wire* he sang, the violin riffs anchored tightly to the changes, La Grange playing an electric piano; this was a tune, Danny had told him, where they hoped for some radio play. The crowd roared, and Danny held up his violin in a final salute. Afterwards, the night blurred into The Rascals' set, the first famous rock band Artie had ever seen, but not before he once again went behind the stage to shake Danny's hand, and took in the hub of the World's dazzling kaleidoscope, with the echoes of the Voyage and Pamela's invitation burning in his brain.

Step One in the flow of frequency modulation—was it before or after or did it matter—the Steve Paul Scene, one dimly lit cellar lazaretto after another, up to the bandstand where tonight Al Kooper and the Blues Project rule the roost.

The band kick-starts the rhythm of "Wake Me Shake Me" with Danny Kalb smokin' on the guitar. Suddenly with a playful nod Koop himself summons Danny out of the audience. Danny plays behind them, *respetto* and all that, firing off two-note accents with his violin, legato lines beneath Kalb's guitar. Then in the long instrumental break he steps up, and suddenly the bass and drum and even Koop are laying back into the rock-solid sustains that encourage him to solo, and so he does, faster and faster as the bass, MOTHERFUCK, tremolos to the rave up, and the violin bow is a darting bee as Danny feels the band launch into a great pile-driving build behind HIM before they blast into the final chorus. More applause, a great blanket of it from Roosevelt Field to the Village, and Kooper cracks that there are too many Jewboys in this group already, before telling the club Danny Geller has a new band, the Voyage, catch 'em when you can.

Danny keeps flashing back to it, hearing the organ, the guitar that leaped into the fray with him, the slash of the cymbals, this has been going on for some time now, ever since the 250 mikes of white lightning from 'Frisco came out and Danny sucked on the tab. The lead singer of the Voyage has to know what a real trip is like, said Rick. Sound reasoning. It's so imperceptible at first, the way all Danny's senses befriend the lightbulb, the rainbow veils... and then tiny sprites laboring within to produce its flame... and he might have burned his retinas out had Nell not slapped his shades on. Acid is like *The Outer Limits*, do not attempt to adjust your tv set, we are controlling transmission. We are in your past with Kalb and Koop and the crowd at the World, we are in every moment that blossoms now in a chair whose frame has a million tiny tendrils, a lamp wire creeping through the carpet, a pesky light switch that blinks away and then pops out in the shape of one of Nell's nipples. The whole room is an undersea garden and we're scuba explorers, the shimmer of our progress casting new wave patterns on the coral at every moment.

Outside the streetlights pulse, expand into a hierarchy of window light, star light, rising tiers of starfire amid the cobalt crackle and swirl, all in tune to Rhasaan Roland Kirk. LaGrange took off the Appalachian folk dobro and now has "Domino" on and the flute and sax are crisp silver and deep crimson, the bass oozes like delicious chocolate icing, the piano is warm blood and cool streams. *Life* Magazine called it dermo-optical perception. Charlie Parker called it hearing with your eyes, seeing with your ears.

Danny bathes in the music on every level, A, E, I, O, U. La Grange, the maestro, is also shape-shifting, flinty Scotch Irish and Cherokee redman and Indo-European Cro Magnon, the faces subtly changing with every pulse of the beat. Yeah, he's slippery, that LaGrange, but maybe because he contains so many selves within his ancestry. Why didn't I see that before, why didn't I see every man in myself, a hundred selves in every one?

An intermission, pause between movements, flicker of the

old frames of reference, recognizable walls, furniture, bandmates, and then the apple in his hand shimmers, pulses, breathes, its juices flow to his tongue, he can't even feel his own teeth bite it, it's honey, it's manna from heaven. The tonearm settles on the scherzo from Beethoven's Ninth and Danny can see-feel-hear an arc of moonlight shooting through the Village, and everyone in a hundred windows is dancing, dancing to the kettledrum and the lunar French horn, all the crazies of New York dancing together in glory, and then suddenly Danny's back down 2000 miles to that apple in his hand. His whole consciousness is a kite, way up in the high winds then coasting toward the ground again, and the best way to hold onto it is the gentle tug that never even aims for control.

He winds up in the chill of dawn in Washington Square, beneath one splintery bent note of fire above MacDougal, with Nell Friedlander, who's been his foundation the whole trip, his hug of silk and musky flesh, sweet, sweet Nell whose old man is in town, I gotta get my own apartment. The other wanderers nod and smile, the kite pirouetting down to earth, but there are a few more spasms in the wind. Danny hears the clop of horse's hooves following him. Damn, he never liked horses, and likes them less with cops attached. He fights a gagging wave of paranoia, but no way, how could they know what he was doing... colorless odorless tasteless... and so he dares to turn back, and now he's laughing.

The mounted police he fears are bare-chested bearded men of the forests, melded right into their brutes, centaurs in the morning light. They smile and bid him welcome.

On a basement wall on West 43rd street screens blast pictures of road signs intercut with flashes of a woman's body. Speakers roar with motorcycle engines. At the Whitney Museum Artie stares at an Op Art weft of lines with a vertiginous swipe in the middle. On Hudson Street, diffraction gratings serenely turn, a signboard bombarding him with flashes of "No," "Ow," "Now." "Turn, turn, turn... we are all one."

Overload and meditation environments. *Mixed media, breaking down the barriers...*

Vaporize your linear mind, bomb your senses, project yourself into the "low-definition field" and make the experience your own. He tried until the sense of urban dislocation and bludgeoned awareness gave him a headache. Later he compounded that painful incomprehension by reading *Understanding Media*. McLuhan's ideas pelted him like hail. How could infinitesimal holes in the matrix of the tv image lead to some kind of depth perception that would end his desire to have a specialist job in the future? How could automation lead to artistic autonomy and nonuniformity?

In the new age, when private nervous systems would go intensely public, when an electronic media nutrient broth would have us wearing our nerves out in the ether, influential men and women, the musicians, the politicians, the Pamela Huntingtons, would have a deep commitment to society. But the "medium cool" that would lead to this was… television? "Bewitched" and "Hullabaloo," a show with rock groups sandwiched between Gleem and Clearasil commercials and introduced by folksinger Barry McGuire in a tight-fitting tuxedo jacket snapping his fingers like Dean Martin? And the "hot media"—old-fashioned, linear, fragmented, stale, reductive—that was books, that was the movies that drew Artie deeper into reality, society, and politics. *Cool Hand Luke* gunned down, but the hope and defiance he fills the beaten-down prisoners with survives; Sir Thomas More amid fogbound green English hills giving up his life for his conscience; a family's murder in an actual suburban house, made all the more real by tv black-and-white with a stain of extra darkness, and the same grim contrast in *Who's Afraid of Virginia Woolf?*, as the couples, after years of living their lies, finally explode with nocturnal knowledge.

Russ Lansing assured him don't sweat it, just be into what she's into. I mean, you're both photographers. Russ always seemed to guess when there were leaps Artie couldn't make, and so when they went to the Riverside Museum of NYC to see a giant multimedia exhibit by a group called USCO, which included a light garden, meditation environment, and something called the Tabernacle,

Russ insisted they toke up even though Artie never smoked in the daytime. They disappeared into the park and smoked a quick, fugitive jay in one of the tunnels. Pot had never seemed more the whiff of the illicit, the tinder of sex and rebellion, than when you were worried the cops might see you at any moment.

The high and the blurring of Artie's day and night worlds gave a whole new edge to the exhibit. The boys activated flowers made of lights when they walked by. They sat in an artificial hexagonal cave on a rotating couch, and sprawled beneath paintings of demons and gods. Multichannel speakers rained down music as a glowing eye shed beams on a fountain, and a shadow painting of a Hindu deity shot out a blinding red pulse. A loin chakra, one girl helpfully pointed out.

Artie heard, in the hum of engines and clicks of switches, the hard work and technical ability of the commune that created this, and that scientific brio bridged the gap for him. In his playfully rejuvenated thoughts he understood new media: the West's technology embraces the East's mythology, and we receive through our electronic arts a seamless web of tribal kinship and union within an oral and auditory culture that takes in all our senses. What matters now, in "Eight Miles High," in "The End," in exhibits like this, is not nuggets of meaning but the experiences of the songs and the art. All the information, not a single level of information movement.

Art is a ceremonial union, it creates the possibility of coming together. How will you become retribalized and depth-involved? Just what will you do with all of this?

On the night of Pamela's gallery opening an October cold snap forced Artie to pull over his red turtleneck the junky old blue worsted wool coat he very much wanted to outgrow. The Kent McIlwaine Gallery was a space large enough to hold three segments of framed photos and a video installation on the back wall. The video, a series of faces deliquescing into colorful amoebas, was described as an impression of an acid trip—which, Artie decided, remembering his first experience on hash, would be like putting a cherry bomb in your head.

Metal slabs embossed with titles like "Vivo," "Blackout" and "Oral and Tribal" showcased the photos anonymously. He hung up his coat and studied them as if preparing for a homework assignment. Some were snapped askew at tilted angles, with a frozen movie feeling of subjects caught in the run. Some were of shreds of torn posters or wall scratchings. He'd read somewhere, maybe "The Photographer's Eye," that Cartier-Bresson felt that even cropping tainted an image. Was that an aspect of mixed media, photography that was totally tainted? On the opposite wall were photographs of ghostly cityscapes that he recognized as the '65 blackout. Artie enjoyed these time exposures of mantled figures carrying silver candlesticks, white-sheeted traffic cops, people asleep in a church or filing up from the subway. Not so successful was a murky double exposure of stragglers in a nightclub and a passing taxi. But in the glass above the photo a twist of blonde hair glimmered—he turned and he didn't quite recognize her in a dark coat, but his racing heart knew her in a second.

"Pamela?"

"Artie! How are you, sweetie!"

She gave him a quick hug, and he felt like the Coca Cola in his cup had magically turned into burgundy going straight to his head. He rushed to trot out his one well-formed opinion of the event.

"These are great, but—this one's weird though. I mean, I would've just shot the light of the taxi streaking off the window."

"I see."

"But I guess the double exposure makes it more 'mixed media.'"

"No, actually I just was in the mood for one little fucking experiment."

Artie shriveled into his shoes.

"I'm sorry, I didn't know these—it's just an opinion."

"Please! At least you have an opinion! Mostly it's just, oh it's gorgeous Pam, fantastic Pam."

Artie laughed with amazement. Even her clowning dazzled him.

"I wonder if Sarah Moon goes through this... another ex-model behind the camera... oh never mind... so, you feel it doesn't work?"

"No, just maybe..."

"I agree, it was just a tossoff. Anyway, Artie, I have to mingle, there's an awful lot of people to chat up here, but I'll be back, I promise."

She was good as her word, appearing ten minutes later to mischievously grab his arm and tour him through the "Vivo" pictures, which Pam explained were Japanese. The blur of a car negotiating a corner in a parking lot. Grainy snapshots of atomic ruins.

"Now perhaps you prefer 'The Family Of Man' kind of thing, but these are the styles of the moment."

"Pamela, I want to learn all this. I mean, all I've done mostly is just take shots of camp."

"Oh you mean like chronicling pop culture, that sort of thing?"

"No. Summer camp. Baseball games and canoe trips?"

"Oh bloody hell!"

Her laughter lanced into him, but the minute she threw an arm around him it took the sting away. She took him to the "Oral and Tribal" corner. He stared at a series of low-angle, steeply tilted compositions of doo wop street corner groups lit by trashcan fires, Jim Morrison in black leather enveloping a mike stand like a sleeping bat, and there was Danny Geller, the slash of his violin bow catching a stream of light as his body jackknifed down and his hair flew above him.

"These are yours, right? These are terrific!"

He was thrilled to be able to praise her music photographs without reservation. He drank in her words as she told him how she captured the night shots by incident light rather than reflected light.

"You have to read the light on the scene along with the

darkness. So I knew I could overexpose this man's face, and it would come out a little ghostly, but the rest would be perfect. Now… what do you think of this one?"

She seemed a little cautious as she led him to one last giant picture on the back wall. Entitled "Burned Man" it was the most low-definition, ambiguous shot in her collection, a negative image of two blurred figures, one hurling a smear of a cape or jacket down on the other, whose image was filtered by an aureole of white licking tongues of light.

"I'm not even sure what it is."

"It's a man burning himself in front of the United Nations. He's protesting the war in Vietnam, but also all wars, everywhere."

Artie tried to scratch some phrases out.

"You were there… when that guy… did you have a picture in a magazine?"

"No, they were all hopelessly shaky, just like this one. I couldn't keep my hands steady."

"It's amazing you didn't run."

"Well, I did after, after I smelled the flames, I ran away to be sick, it was… horrible… but at the moment before that, something took me over. I was… brave because… I knew this had to be remembered. I was so sorry I couldn't properly photograph it, so I worked on it a long time, to give the impression of the courage of it, the horror—and how it affected me. I was meant to be there, to see this, to change. He was sacrificing his life to stop a war, and I was there, and… I think of photography, real photography, as something passed on from this man to me."

Artie was in awe of how she could measure herself against such an event to recognize the beginning of her vocation.

"When you see someone die, Artie, it changes you."

"I saw that once…"

Artie immediately wished he hadn't said that, and turned away, but Pam's curiosity was unstoppable.

"What did you see, Artie?"

"My… my mother."

A look of pure anguish streaked Pam's face.

"Oh God, Artie, you poor thing. I'm so sorry."

Art is a ceremonial union, it creates the opportunity of coming together.

"She was at home. I just… saw it."

"You're so young to go through life without a mum."

He wanted to get back his lousy old coat and bury his face in it before any tears got out. He was grateful when Pam glanced away from him as a potential patron cheerfully summoned her.

"Oh shit. Artie, come with me a moment."

She took him to a quiet corner of the space and took her wooden medallion off her neck. Artie recognized the peace sign, but not the strange ellipse and crossbar at the symbol's vertex. She handed to him.

"It's by a very fine craftsman in London. See, it blends peace and the Egyptian ankh, a symbol for life. I find it very comforting."

"This looks handmade. I can't just take this."

"Don't worry, luv, it's not one of a kind. When I go back to England, I'll get another."

"You're going back to England?"

"Just for the holidays. Piccadilly at Christmas, not to be missed. Try it on!"

He placed it around his turtleneck. She adjusted it with a flick of her fingers, then laid a hand on his chest.

"It looks lovely. Please keep it."

Then she was gone, rejoining her other friends.

Her gentleness was as abrupt a change as if the blur of that car in the "Vivo" garage had downshifted to a parking space by a sunlit meadow. And as she disappeared into the gallery crowd the medallion's wood seemed to still burn with the ray of sympathy that had seared into him. He didn't know if it would comfort him, but he wasn't about to take it off his chest.

August 3 was the day of Lenny Bruce's death, and Izzy took it as hard as a death in the family. The snapshots of his corpse, cold and pale as a gutted fish on his bathroom floor, the syringe still in his right arm, surfaced all across the country. The cops had allowed a horde of photographers to snap their fill, a hideous insult to the man's humanity.

Izzy turned the next few days into a Lenny wake, playing recordings of his choicest bits at the office. New York's lord of the Church, Cardinal Spellman, confronted with a visit by Christ and a train of lepers—"I'm up to my ass in crutches and wheelchairs here!" But after every fit of laughter, Izzy would frown at the floor and shake his head.

The law killed him, he muttered, the law killed Lenny.

Izzy resolved that the profile of Hamerow and Kovacs would toughen and become more radical. He actively sought out the new wave of draft resisters. Nate quailed at the thought of representing them. He had seen too many young men sign up for duty in North Africa, Guadalcanal, and Omaha Beach for him to side with the extreme fringe of war protest. He didn't buy that Ho Chi Minh was some Jefferson-spouting neutralist. No matter how many superficial variations it assumed, Communism was Communism and a threat to America.

Izzy could smell his reluctance. At first he bearishly kidded him that he must be distracted by the sex in his new life. I know you're getting your brains fucked out by Miss Tapioca, buddy, but what's left I need here in the office. But soon he cracked the whip with nastier remarks and Nate had to remind himself he was thirty years removed from the schoolyard.

"Nobody cares about whether you still get your fucking Christmas card from Gracie Mansion!"

"Izzy, you know I don't play politics in this office."

"Aah, c'mon, you're always looking over your shoulder at City Hall. But even your bubbalah Lindsay is starting to sniff where the wind's blowing on this war."

"These clients are so confrontational, some of them don't even care if they win or lose!"

"Like the song says, boy, whose side are you—"

"Izzy, for God's sake! How far are we going to get if they're clearly breaking the law?"

"There's Mr. Draft Board talking. Remember, I was on the

battlefield, Nate, I was a fuckin' grunt, and as far as I'm concerned, this war is breaking the law! International law! The Geneva accords that stated the partition of Vietnam was temporary until elections could be held! Constitutional law! Congress never declared war! We just wrote LBJ a blank check and he and the Joint Chiefs invaded the country on the basis of total bullshit! Him and his miserable Harvard fucking so-called brain trust! You oughta think about whether you want your kid serving in this war, Nate, then maybe you'll get the picture!"

That hit home. There was no guarantee Artie's relatively mild astigmatism would get him classified 4F. But how do you justify burning draft cards?

Nate dredged up whatever case law he could on symbolic speech vs. lawbreaking conduct, taking still more time away from nights with his children and the last vestiges of his restaurant dates with Dorothy. When it came to the rights of free speech, where did burning a draft card fall? Was speech that counseled a young man to follow his conscience and resist the draft necessarily an incitement to lawbreaking, creating a clear and present danger, or was it protected? Nate researched the Tinker vs. Des Moines School District decision and other precedents safeguarding nonviolent protest. One of Hamerow and Kovacs' clients had merely sat in front of a draft board wearing a placard pasted with photos of dead G.I.'s and burned villages and gotten himself arrested on trespass and obstructing passage charges.

This was not the time to move farther left. The mood against the Lindsay administration had hardened so much it was difficult even to negotiate with the city a route for the next planned peace march. The House UnAmerican Activities Committee was investigating the antiwar movement. Lindsay was getting so slammed over the Civilian Complaint Review Board that at the wake for Traffic Commissioner Henry Barnes, the top officer at the police guard wouldn't even shake his hand. Lindsay fumed about it at the Republican Club—don't they realize Commissioner Leary's techniques for clearing the streets have been praised all over the country? Damn it, I am the Mayor, and I don't have to tolerate that kind of offensive behavior. Then again, Nate thought, what would you label the words of a Lindsay aide comparing the Police Benevolent Association to John Birchers and Nazis?

Battle lines. A song Nate had heard coming from Artie's room that reminded him of a slow boiling hot day, the guitar like the buzz and sting of a mosquito that drives you nuts. Nate got the draft-protesting human signboard off on a suspended sentence. And he won Roy Hicks's case on appeal. He argued there had been an improper charging of the jury by the judge, who had failed to mention that Elmore Woods had been held incommunicado in police custody for hours before he confessed. Nate was there at the Harlem Action Front office when Roy reunited with his brother. They now each had the close-cropped hair, the denim and jeans mufti of the new Black Power leaders. Their fists slowly torqued together in a ritual that cast Nate far into the background. East New York. Harlem. Stokely Carmichael expelling the white membership of the Student Non-Violent Coordinating Committee…

Look at what's going down...

After one of his endless nights at the office, an unmarked police car passed him on the corner and, waving hello with a perfunctory grin that left a tremor in Nate's chest, Detective Loomis Regan patrolled his territory.

Wednesdays and Thursdays with Marcela were his reprieve— late afternoons only, thanks to his children and her schedule, but he almost couldn't believe his good fortune that these luscious interludes were waiting for him. He always got a sardonic glance from the super, but at least these days he wouldn't have to buy him off. Marcela would check carefully her wheel of Enovid pills, a mandala of permissions, then draw the shade, cast the bedroom in a tallow-hued light, and invite him to the long, alluvial waves of pleasure he found in the current of her body. She guided him to suck her nipples, glide his hand between her legs until she slickly rode his fingers to when she was ready for all of him.

She would kid him about his rush to climax, saying that being with an American man made her feel like a teenager again. She taught him to be considerate in other ways. On the day he mentioned Becky's birthday over and over, she touched his hand firmly and mentioned she too had lost someone, an old fiancée who'd died in a construction accident in Brasilia. Nate realized Marcela had after all also lost a job, a beloved dog, a whole country as surely as if they were dead.

"I'll never get away from that and you'll never get away from your Becky, and that's what should be. You're a part of the dead and the living."

Nate knew he could never lose her over jealousness of Becky. But her agitation over events in the news unnerved him. Richard Speck's murder of nine student nurses had her spooked. What kind of country is this, she muttered, striding back and forth with that wide country gait of hers. She calmed herself by playing *Parsley, Sage, Rosemary and Thyme*. Songs that floated freely between caring about the state of the world and dreaming within the state of oneself, a balance Marcela seemed to share with the very young. She adored Garfunkel on "For Emily."

"Did a boy ever have this kind of voice? God he has the gift of pretty."

Later the silvery harmonies of the Mamas and Papas rose above the beat of a ticking clock. He realized that however familiar Marcela was starting to feel, he'd now entered the territory of this song; no husband, no wife, everybody's "baby." Are you playing some game with me, baby? Tick tock tick tock.

She combed her black hair in the yellow light and he could hear a chickadee whistle softly in the alley.

One week she surprised him by saying she wanted to visit him at home. They waited for a night both kids were away on sleepovers. To see her come to him grinning in one of his borrowed robes fired him up to a lust he could barely believe, and he made love to her with a passion of new freedom and a race against the last shadows of remorse. Those tawny velvet limbs would now blend with pale skin that freckled in the sun, would

184 | CATS' EYES

stand between him and an image of woman forever precious but more and more faint and spectral.

He lay in bed with Marcela's hair falling around his face, and it suddenly came to twitching life. Marcela giggled as Aisha burrowed in beside them. She stroked the Siamese, who purred and bared her belly avidly to this new friend of the household. Nate stroked her too, and their hands found each other, then their loins – just to want Marcela and take her and fire up strong and eager and happy as a boy, these were the moments that carried Nate beyond anxiety, beyond memory...

Karen's friends seemed to think EVERYONE showed up and bought clothes at Gyre and Gimbel. Oh God, the Doors are in town, maybe you'll get to measure Jim's inseam, Karen. You can tell us if he really is the Lizard King. Ha ha. But Pamela Huntington, before she left for London, did indeed show up to buy a muslin scarf, and when Karen mentioned that to Artie he wouldn't shut up. What did she talk about? Did she come in with a guy? Was it, like, a hairdresser kind of guy?

"I don't know if it was a hairdresser kind of guy. She always has people with her. She's a scenemaker!"

"How can you say that?"

"That's what my boss calls them. They show up everywhere trying to be cool. They come in all the time for the latest clothes."

"She's better than that. She gave me this medallion!"

"That was very nice of her."

"Then how can you call her a scenemaker?"

"Because both are true."

"What do you know? Shut up!"

"Anyway, she sounds too old!"

"Why am I even talking about this with a fourteen-year-old?"

"Why are you asking me?"

She began to wonder if Artie ever really understood anything. Always shutting his door, insisting he's working, listening to music, leave me alone. Always doing things through a camera or a book. But if you touch, smell, feel—she knew Artie smoked marijuana just from the inside of his coat in the closet, where she uncovered that same scent of charcoal and clove that wafted from Eleanor's office.

And when little Aisha had purred and wriggled and squashed her face against her cheek, Karen had inhaled a musky tropical perfume, an exotic scent that no woman Karen knew would ever wear.

Cats told the secrets you had to know.

Not that Nina hadn't mentioned it that night she slept over, with all the coolness she could manage, but still nursing her lower lip under her front teeth in a way that held back tears, saying their parents had probably "dropped" each other. But here was proof that Dad had left her in the dark once again, abandoned both her and a lady she'd welcomed into her life, who could make her laugh, who'd quieted her fears when the blood had rushed out of her, forcing them to miss *Georgy Girl*, womanhood shaking Karen like leaves in the wind.

That Saturday after closing time at Gyre and Gimbel she and Nina put Donovan on the stereo. Nina had the papers and she'd learned how to roll them. They'd rifled a pinch of leaves from Eleanor's bag. Karen inhaled deep and practically coughed her lungs out, and when she finally quelled the burning in her throat it was like the wonderful moment that had happened with the flute, when the teacher had warned her learning the embouchure and sounding a note would take a lot of time, but she played G the very first lesson.

In no time at all she was there.

She loved Donovan's curly hair, his way of taking a woman's point of view, the sigh of flutes and cellos, raindrop soft guitars. *She ran her hand through the antique dresses and underclothes, rich and soft as the webs the fairies spun in the midsummer night. She sat among shelves overflowing with ribbons and brocades, stuffed with silver brooches and turquoise amulets and bracelets.*

The Magician's name is Love....

In his world she and a friend smoke and dream together, and their dreams are present before them, and in the dreams there are no dropped people, no oblivious brothers and uncaring fathers. There can be no betrayals in a world made new.

Chapter 5

FUN CITY

Washington Square in late winter, the clouds like tarnished mirrors above the Park—how, Nate would later wonder, could you expect the demonstration not to go wrong? Only the hard-core ideologues assembled while it was still this cold. None were more fanatic than the Progressive Labor Party, who made the old Communist Workers look like Republicans. The PLP had organized trips to Cuba in defiance of the State Department. They tempted arrest whenever they could.

Nate was making time in his work day for a phone conversation with one of Karen's teachers. The holiday season had brought the usual pit of sadness for him, but even Karen had displayed less enthusiasm for Christmas than in years past; by January, it had all emptied out. Her grades had plummeted, and any warning from Nate seemed to drive her deeper into new hobbies like the easel that had been Nate's gift to her, where she spent hours painting young girls whose dresses melted into tulips and lilies. It wasn't her usual defiance either. She would promise to keep up her grades, but then take refuge behind her activities and rituals, shielded in secretive detachment and an inviolate new femininity, and slip away from him.

Now while Nate was trying to persuade the headmistress at Blakewell to be a little more patient with Karen during a season that always troubled her, barely a mile away Washington Square Park echoed with denunciations of the Vietnam war, the draft, the racist Congress. Lucas Oxley took the podium. The slim, light-skinned Negro, whose dapper suits and topical humor had once won him spots on the Ed Sullivan show, dressed these days in an Army jacket, jeans, and Ray-Bans. His even-featured Caribbean good looks were offset by a full beard, and with that facial hair had grown entirely new material.

"*Ever play Black Monopoly? You go to jail… game over, motherfucker! No Get Out Of Jail Free cards… ever! And that's a bitch, because in Black Monopoly, landing on Boardwalk or Park Place and goin' to jail are the same move!*"

Everybody who'd been at the demo told Nate the same thing: as soon as Lucas Oxley hit the stage, the crowd eased up, enjoyed themselves. Hey, the man was funny, and he was breaking it down like they wanted to hear.

"*See, both the U.S.A. and North Vietnam claim to be fighting for Vietnam. Thing is, North Vietnam is already Vietnam. Know who lives there? VI-ET-NA-MESE! They own the pink slip. This country rents Vietnamese. The U.S.A. is like that guy who comes floating down in the Hertz commercial, Whitey in the seersucker suit, and he comes floating down to Vietnam into the driver's seat, grabs the wheel, and says, 'This is my Vietnam! My drugs, my dinky dao, I paid good money for the motherfucker!'*"

No one could say why he dropped the word "black" and got into the hate words. Maybe it was the rhythm of the jokes and the pain, in that weather and with that crowd.

"*But when the road gets a little rough, guess who Mr. Honkie wants right there in the front seat? Niggers! Lotta bumps, man, lotta land mines, I need a nigger up here for awhile. You watch my ride, boy, and make sure it doesn't get shot up—oh shit, incoming, I need more niggers here!*"

"Only nigger I see around here is you!"

Everyone was sure the shout wasn't from a black man. Lucas apparently spotted the heckler.

"Actually, there's lots of niggers here, but you're the only cracker I can see."

A fight erupted, but even in the closely packed crowd, even in a crowd full of the Progressive Labor Party, it didn't spread. Spectators tried to break it up. But it only took a minute before the cop cars on the rim of the square sounded their sirens. Police waded into the crowd, the few foolish citizens who resisted were quickly hauled away, and three officers bounded onto the platform to arrest Lucas Oxley.

"Man, you got to be kidding! You want to explain to these people what the charges are?"

Lucas pointed his microphone at one of the officers, who swatted it down and muscled him off the stage. The crowd snapped back with shouts of police brutality. The cops charged into the front ranks, drove them back, and arrested the loudest catcallers as an officer stepped to the microphone and gave the crowd ten minutes to disperse. They baited the cops with boos and insults but finally cleared the square.

Nate was just about ready to head home and order, cajole, or beg Karen to tackle her homework when Izzy told him they were going down to the precinct to talk to Lucas Oxley. Nate found himself confronted with the kind of inflammatory, potentially notorious case that Izzy most coveted and that Nate had most wished would show up at Kunstler or Lefcourt's door, anywhere but Hamerow and Kovacs.

At the precinct house, Lucas raged about this asshole in the crowd out to get him, the one who really incited the riot, and how the cops were gonna pay, they pulled their fucking game on the wrong brother this time. Izzy launched into his plans for the case, how he'd challenge the "heckler's veto" with Supreme Court precedents, subpoena crowd witnesses, when Lucas interrupted him.

"So Izzy, hold it, when you take my case, do you have, like, lead attorney and backup, that whole scene?"

"Yeah, sure."

Lucas nodded toward Nate.

"I want the Brooks Brothers brother."

Sometimes it seemed to Danny that the act of recording might kill the music. He knew they were damn lucky his dad had been able to set up free studio time to lay four songs on a demo. Plus they got to be guinea pigs for a new state of the art RCA 16-track board. The Voyage had no management yet, but Don Russert, a talent booker, had gotten them some club appearances.

At Ondine's, a weird waterfront club built around the disembodied hull of a yacht, they'd backed up Curtis Knight and the Squires, featuring Jimmy James, an amazing frizzy-haired black guitarist who played his guitar behind his back and with his teeth, making Danny feel better about shifting to violin. They'd picked up some good notices in *Crawdaddy* and *New Beats*. "The Voyage's hippy, trippy gypsy sound promises laughing days and howling nights."

But now, between Danny and Jimmy attending college classes at CCNY, Jimmy commuting from Newark where he lived with his mother, and La Grange's teaching jobs—a club paycheck split six ways couldn't support any of them—the gigs were minimal and now the recording hours had just about shut them down.

Danny lived for the stage. His wardrobe, like the velvet pants and puffy-sleeved embroidered kulak shirt he'd gotten, with a coyly sweet smile, from Karen Kovacs at Gyre and Gimbel. The amps pulsating through him until he felt the violin strings in his spine. He wanted to yank the drags right out of people and sweep them up into his high, his Pied Piper power. In the audience at the Doors' gig, he'd really felt it: a long dark undercurrent of matadorial enticement from Jim Morrison to the hypnotized audience, swelled by the suspense in the music, the purling guitar and organ's long sarabande, Morrison wrapping the silence around him like a cloak, until with a drumroll and cymbal crash came the howl of release and the crowd flipping out, willing to go anywhere with him, be anything, a drunkard in a Brechtian march, a dervish, a courtier in a Renaissance Fair or a celebrant in a witches Sabbath in dazed, stoned, predatory L.A. Danny had told Morrison it was amazing how he led the crowd.

"I don't lead any of it. I just kind of extend… an invitation."

Jimmy had kidded Danny about Morrison, because he could tell this West Coast prince of rock with a definite Rimbaudesque penchant for nightmare was a threat to Danny.

"Fuck it, Jimmy, he's on top for now. But don't worry, we're gonna be up there too. We're gonna throw the feast. Lots of ways to make it, man, long as we don't o.d. on the blues."

"Danny, you don't know shit about that. The blues is the

heart and soul. The Doors are always working with the blues."

"Yeah the blues is the blues is the blues, it's a great starting point, Jimmy, but we gotta have our own sound! Be our own sound!"

If the sound ever survives the studio, he thought, where his skin crawled with impatience as the drum was miked six different ways. La Grange especially liked to hang out with the engineers and tease out their secrets, watching a hand draw a fader up the mixer board, messing with decay and reverb, and that's when Danny felt his sway on the band's sound begin to dissipate. He tried to freak out the process whenever he could. Fascinated by feedback, he played ten different variations of the main violin riff of "I Don't Want This Life" at varying distances from the amp until he got a screaming double-tracked intro to the tune that made his hair stand on end.

The band bitched about it, wanted him to cut down his intros and his solos, but Christ, even Clapton, Mr. Blues Purist, was now saying forget the chords, just play.

"Son, just so you understand, when you move on to a full album, your studio expenses will be deducted for your royalties, so the time you take is—"

"I'm trying to put into this demo some of what makes us burn onstage!"

"The engineer didn't even know what you were doing. Maybe if you'd hipped him to what you had in mind."

"I was exploring! It's up to the board to follow the band! La Grange is hanging 'em up being so technical about every fucking note."

"Well, you've got about ten instruments going and he plays six of them."

Bruce gave Danny a gently conspiratorial smile.

"Look, son, I'll never stop you from doing your own thing. But just… this isn't the final album, the point is to get four tunes down without, you know, wearing out your welcome."

Danny didn't want to argue with his old man and the other old men paying the tab. They all needed a break anyhow. He and

Rick and Pete took a night off to catch The Mothers of Invention's "Pigs and Repugnant" show at the sweaty little Garrick Theater on Bleecker Street, Maestro Frank Zappa resplendent in ruffled shirt, purple pants, and stovepipe hat, a mad scientist mixing instruments together to see what combusted, scatterings of chimes, licks that darted from the sax players to the keyboards, all bound with the golden thread of Zappa's guitar that could crack the audience up on a silly tune like "Bacon Fat," playing one stupid note over and over on the break, or cut loose at white heat on the Watts riot number "Trouble Coming Every Day." Danny knew it was nowhere near as crazy as it looked. How Zappa kept his circus so tightly ringmastered, yet so loose and free, syncopating intricate charts and onstage insanity, was a marvel to Danny. Zappa even pulled the audience into it, let them yell at the band members or had them sing "Louie Louie." Then he brought up the soldiers.

Everyone froze. A serviceman had just been killed in the Village, and these three guys with buzz cuts and full dress uniforms looked wire-tight. Zappa was known to serenade audiences with "Plastic People," or tell them if their children knew how lame they were, they'd murder them in their sleep. But what the hell was he up to now?

"Ladies and gentlemen, we have some guests from our ARMED FORCES here this evening, just returned from OVER THERE in Vietnam. They happened to be at the last show."

Two of the band members dragged from behind the amps a bloated four-foot-high plastic doll.

"Now we have here a gook baby, and we'd like to invite these young soldiers to mutilate it before your very eyes. Kill it!"

The saxes blatted over the audience's dead silence. Zappa calmly handed the men a pair of billy clubs. They pummeled and smashed away at the thing as Zappa's band played dissonant fanfares, and the audience skittishly laughed until, to the horns and keyboards' chromatic churn, the Marines pulled the arms off the doll and tore at its legs. The doll bled gouts of stuffing and finally fell apart.

There were a few cheers but most of the audience just sat and stared at the mangled doll and tried to get its bearings back. A male voice quietly sobbed. Zappa and the band tore off a fast instrumental break and ended the show.

The stunned crowd lingered in the back of the theater, coming to terms with what they'd just seen and heard, but only Danny was so attuned to Zappa's curiosity and risk-taking that he wanted part of it for himself. He asked two of the soldiers to come to the park and smoke a jay with him and Pete and Rick.

They clustered on a bench near the floodlit Washington Square arch. Dave, knife-thin under his military jacket, was so cranked up that Danny, handing him the joint, hoped the grass was the mellow kind. His friend Lenny seemed calmer, or maybe it was just his reassuring aviator glasses. When Rick bent low and cupped the flame of the joint in his hand, Dave chuckled.

"Hey don't worry about cops, we'll protect you from the cops, man, we'll FUCK 'EM UP!"

For the next half hour, Danny, Pete and Rick hunkered down in the smoke trail of the weed and listened to the soldiers riff about the war. Con Thien, the demilitarized zone, yeah, right, the worst duty you could get, the free-fire zones, if it moves, feel free to fire on it, the old women, kids, dogs, and take some ears or penises so any survivors spread the word. Kill to break Charlie's will. Danny opened his mind to the nightmare, vibrated to it like a tuning fork. Take satchel charges in the rear supply line from people who do your laundry. Then watch Bob Hope while you're fucked up on Chinese opium laced with black tar heroin flown out by the CIA to keep their Montagnard allies happy. Or maybe you want a taste of a Saigon whore run by your sergeant-major in the khaki mafia. Then say goodbye to the Rear Echelon Motherfuckers and it's back up to the front line, the fishhook, the Delta, the whole humming sun-pounded patrol through palms and creepers and blockhouse roots that you just hope will stay this boring, broiling slog your whole time before you're back in the World, because when it doesn't it's bullets everywhere and booby trap step and bomb-blasted arms and legs and guts flying in one long scream.

Lenny took a meditative hit on the jay.

"Fuck Charlie. And fuck the guys with the eagles and stripes, it's always about the body count. Any civilians killed are VC trying to escape. Green light to do what's right."

Thank god for the drugs. Dexies for fighting all night, a fifth of J.D. to come down, and of course plenty of grass, patrols wearing marijuana plants on their backs "for camouflage." The radio played whenever their lives didn't depend on silence. Dave almost sobbed with gratitude when he heard Danny and his friends were musicians. He wanted them to thank the Doors for them. He hugged them and promised to come to their concerts. Then he took his lighter to another jay. Zippo inspection, Lenny shouted, and Dave laughed, then sank back into his turbid darkness.

"Hey, man, I hope you never have to go. I hope you guys never, never, never have to go out and try and survive that shit."

Lenny, itching to cool out his friend, turned the subject back to Danny.

"You wouldn't believe the shit that's going on out there, we shouldn't be there, man, it's just all wrong. You guys look like you're coming on draft age."

"We're all in college now."

"Not forever. They got musicians in the infantry."

"Oh yeah, Uncle Sam wants you."

"Not that we'd advocate any actions that are disloyal or anything."

"General Waste-more-land needs more meat!"

Dave laughed and pointed at Danny.

"He's got your number. He wants YOU!"

That stoned guffaw rang in his head all through the subway ride. Yeah, funny, the war machine could gobble him up, Danny Geller, New York musician in the middle of a fucking free fire jungle. What could he do to try to stop it? Zappa at the Garrick, Morrison shouting they got guns, we got numbers, Danny had to absorb their fury, he had to write a song with the blood trail and ravines full of napalm fire and then that awful mist Lenny talked about that came down and wiped out every last bird and bug and leaf that survived. The Voyage would expand its music yet again to take on the War, and create, along with realms of pleasure, a theatrical and musical and political realm for all the lost soldiers.

"So it's like we overthrew a Vietnamese government? That's how it started?"

Artie was thrilled to share with Danny his knowledge about Vietnam.

"Oh yeah, Danny. We killed Diem and put the generals we wanted in power. Not that we admit it."

"So South Vietnam is just a bunch of puppets. Those elections mean nothing."

"Well, I dunno about that, but the point is we're involved in their civil war. I mean we say we want self-determination and democracy for Vietnam but we're sending our soldiers to fight for the government we want. It's bullshit."

"You're the wise man, Artie."

Wise man. One of Danny's cracks, but... Artie grinned at the confirmation of the value behind what he'd secretly been preparing, his whole new sphere of activity. He'd joined the Debating Club, and found he was good at it. Now that Danny and his music and the mixed media world abutted his own, there seemed to be no more linear, segmented, old media activity than this: one affirmative, one negative, marshaling facts and building arguments through four rounds of debate—but he was good at it.

And when Mr. Thomas, the debate team coach, gave them news that would not be officially announced until that Friday—he would be replacing the departing Headmaster of their school— Artie thrilled to the implications. Mr. Thomas, the man who'd taught the World Peace and Disarmament Class, an enthusiastic Lindsay supporter, was now going to be in charge of their lives as students. There had been talk of submitting Vandemeer's hopelessly uptight dress and haircut rules to a vote on the Student-Faculty Council. Mr. Thomas would be sure to support that kind of measure, and Artie had begun writing nuggets of speeches in his notebook that he could store up for next year, tokens that beckoned him to winning debates to come before the entire student body.

"Thanks, man, It's unbelievable, Artie, how fucked up this whole thing is. I talked to two G.I.'s—you wouldn't believe the shit that goes on there—I'm writing a song. A song to help stop the war. And you're inspiring me, little bro."

Artie was stunned. That wasn't a crack, and Danny had never said that to him before. Maybe he and Karen were the nearest thing to a brother and sister Danny would ever know. Could he really be that close to this strange, demanding, and thrilling presence in his life?

"Oh, and by the way, Artie?"

"Yeah?"

"She's back."

The dim light from Odalisque's open door spilled onto the wax paper bag in Danny's hand. Funny, Artie thought, that was the way he'd once carried treats of sourballs and Hershey kisses to the movies. Only the cellophane-wrapped tabs and sugar cubes in Danny's bag were hardly for the children's section of the RKO. According to what Danny had told him, these party favors could blow the minds of at least a hundred guests, and so Danny and Artie were welcomed eagerly to the packed dance floor.

There was cheese, wine—and no one cared about Artie's age—salad, bread, chips, and plenty of Brownies. It was a party to celebrate not just Pam's return, but the debut of her new partnership in Huntington-Branch Studios. He spotted him immediately in an unbelievable minidress of white plastic circular scales linked by some invisible mesh across her skin. McLuhan's description of a tv screen: a matrix of dots where your perception craved depth involvement. . . .

She was working the party with her portfolio under her arm. She seemed to put on the airs of a proud schoolgirl to keep the conversations with men from veering toward the hunger she knew she sucked out from them, and she kept close to Nigel

Branch, a flamboyantly dressed Brit in a gold shirt, maroon pants, and matching Ascot, who had that popular aging Oliver Twist street urchin look and the barely contained pugnacity of a street brawler.

But when Pam saw Artie she seemed delighted and ran over to embrace him. Her eyes were ringed by some dark makeup that made her look sulky and amorous. He inhaled her warm breeze of perfume and performance sweat, leaned against the plastic mosaic of a dress, and held her tight. He saw that she too now wore a peace symbol crossed with an ankh. She fingered his charm and laughed.

"Aren't we a pair? So good to see you, luv! I'll be right back."

She wouldn't, of course, there was entirely too large a crowd to work, and so Artie settled into a slow, gradual orbit of her march through the guests. He passed the time sipping his white wine, noshing, and taking hits of passing joints until the luminous pink and green zebra stripes and fractal swirls on the disco walls throbbed and hummed beneath his gaze.

At last Pam summoned him with the barest glance, laying her portfolio on a table. One look at her pictures and his lust was sharpened by envy. Pam had been to Expo 67! She had glorious pictures of the silver-honeycombed Buckminster Fuller dome of the U.S. Pavilion, the slim British pyramid crowned with a peaked Union Jack, and the Cubistic angles and planes of Habitat '67. Above all she had managed, through ingenious time exposures and depth-of-field and f-stop settings, to capture Expo's film experiments. She was as good as *Life* Magazine, with her pictures of the eight-balcony high Labyrinth screen, mirrored by another screen in the floor; the Czech pavilion, where images were blasted onto spinning hoops, triangles, a hundred shuttling and rotating cubes; a steep low angle shot that captured an audience entranced by the auroral dazzle of "Kaleidoscope."

"The multiple screen, total immersion films were just mind-blitzing, right to your sensations, your emotions! And the use of non-linear time—I mean in the Kino Automat film they actually stop the movie and you get to choose what happens next—our profession is going to be revolutionized, Artie, in our lifetime! Think about it, film and photography actually employed to really involve us, open up our senses—we're throwing off the old programming and looking at even the most ordinary things in a whole new way!"

Then she showed him some pictures she'd taken in the East Village. A man pounded a tom tom, the shutter slowed down to give a blur to his frenzy, while a woman in a sari undulated half out of the frame. Another musician Pam had shot from above—I love it when I get to climb a tree, she laughed—bent toward the pavement and played the recorder, his tangled hair blending with soft-focus maple leaves,

"Music in the streets, it's so evanescent, Artie. It's never performed again. You get one chance to find it and pounce on it at the perfect moment, and then it's gone forever."

For a moment there was no party, no blather of guests, no wine, no drugs, and the music blasting through the speakers was far in the background, a curtain drawn to let in the cool night air of Artie and Pam's attention to each other. But the gathering soon jostled for her attention and swept her back up. Artie took another hit of a passing joint and the music filtered back with the high—at first it was like any folk rock with its chiming, madrigal harmonies, until it suddenly took off with the bass thundering ahead, a white-hot arabesque of a guitar riff, and over it all, a female voice that caressed and howled at the same time. Artie loved it. He rushed over to Danny, who had his arm around a girl's waist, their foreheads almost touching. When he saw Artie, he plucked a wax paper bag from his companion's hand and offered it to him.

"No, no thanks. Do you know who that band is?"

"Jefferson Airplane. Folk modal quintet. Man, listen to that break at the end of the tune, and that guitar... aah, I don't think Jimmy'll ever be able to play that kind of solo. San Francisco sound. You ever heard the Grateful Dead?"

The girl cooed in response to the band's name.

"They are so cosmic."

"The Grateful Dead? Seems like a very paradoxical state of mind."

"Not if you're on acid, Arturo."

The dancing had begun. Artie was stunned as Pam suddenly tossed off a balletic leap, drew her leg up to the side of her head, then lowered it and doubled over laughing.

"Was she ever a ballet dancer?"

"Yeah. Dancer… model… "

Artie's voice drained with helpless fascination.

"God, she can do anything."

"Sure. For the right lucky guy."

Danny handed him a tweezered roach.

"Hey Arturo, you should talk up one of these girls. This is a golden opportunity to… need I say more?"

"I'm just waiting to talk to Pam."

"I dunno, man, I think she's with Nigel."

"Well, yeah, but not for the whole night."

"Yeah, but for the night afterwards, if you know what I mean."

Artie had suspected as such, but he still felt his high puddle out onto the dance floor.

"Artie, even if they're getting it on… she's a free woman, y'know? The problem is for right now, if she has to report, you want to stay out of that guy's way."

"I probably don't have a chance with her anyhow."

"No, no, of course you've got a chance man, she's not uptight, she likes you. You have to believe, you have to remember that anything can happen. Pam's a turned-on girl. It's just that tonight, Artie, I mean, if you could forget Pam a moment—do you realize how much fucking is going on out there?"

"A Whiter Shade of Pale" pounded through the disco's speakers. Danny seemed to cock his ears toward the ceiling.

"Baroque music in rock. Great idea… and to get a hit single out of it… y'know, it's like a whole other state of mind, Baroque music… it's like… I'm really crazy about Madamoiselle DeBoeuf but she's promised to the Duke and I'm just a Count so I'll enjoy the order of the stars spinning in the universe… "

Danny's meditations on music always made sense in a sidewise sort of way. Artie much preferred him to talk like that than to point out all the girls in their tiny skirts and black-belted minidresses, gathering on the club's bandstand like waterfowl in some wing-shaking private ritual just before they flew away through the ceiling.

Time slowed and swept up other music in its wake, "Psychotic Reaction"'s cackle of harmonica and bass, a sinister chorus of "I Had Too Much To Dream." He heard a rattling ruckus behind the disco walls and some party guests in T-shirts and jeans leaped out with huge rolls of construction paper and began to heave them across the floor. Pam and the other dancers leaped back and everyone else retreated to the walls so that the paper could be laid down across the club. The refreshments had been replaced by pots and palettes of oil paint. Danny threw his arm around him and whispered in his ear.

"Artie, you gotta get into this."

The music changed to Donovan, a harder-edged Donovan than he'd ever heard, a bluesy harmonica lead and fierce guitar strum punctuated by whipcrack percussion. He could barely hear it above the shouts and laughter… no Cadillac, no Chevrolet, just some of your love…. The women peeled out of their blouses and dresses. Artie gaped at the fluted dancer's muscles that rippled across Pam's back and torso, the jut of her bikini-topped breasts. She and her friends began to thrash to the music as the men grinned, doffed their shirts, and reached for the palettes. Artie watched as they smeared paint on each other, or simply poured cans of it on the floor, where some of the girls lay down and rolled in the paint. The men slapped daubs on their chest and dived down to join them, torso to torso. It looked to Artie like a bizarre game of Twister, and then, as they slammed and grunted into each other, the mating ritual that it was. As Pam kneeled voraciously down into the tangle of bodies, Artie suddenly lost his taste for the wine, the brownies, the grass, all of it. He turned to Danny to say goodbye, but Danny was bare-chested, arms entwined around his new girlfriend, weaving latitudes of color around her bare belly. Artie turned away from him.

The sound echoed, smeared… just want some of your love…

Pam caught his eye. He nodded, tried to smile, and froze with fear and anticipation. She grinned, picked up a palette, and headed over to him. It was almost as if she were a waitress offering him a drink. Her hips swayed, but the hand that held the body paint toward him was steady.

"I don't know how to do this."

"There's nothing to know, baby. Just do what you feel."

Her voice was low, hazy, incredibly stoned. He dipped his shaky fingers in the paint and stroked them across her chest. She leaned back and as she did her belly grew taut and his hand dipped toward her belt. She didn't push it away. A guy held out one of Danny's tabs toward her face. She turned away and her tongue snaked out to lick it, even as her pelvis rotated toward Artie. Artie's heart slammed against his chest as he drew his hands back, wiped his fingers in the paint and traced curves and circles along her skin. He tried to use the patterns on the walls. He glanced over at guy who was painting an eye radiating starry beams on a girl's back. That seemed way too challenging at this point.

Pam smiled greedily and drew closer to him, and he bent closer, maybe to kiss her—and the lights went off and left behind only buzzing auras of ultraviolet. He involuntarily jumped back from Pam's new face, teeth and eyes gleaming a moony whitish-purple. All around were surprising objects of fluorescence, pearl necklaces and buttons that bobbed like fish between zones of paint, the designs on the women's skin a coralline flame, their limbs a dark nimbus beneath them. Pam took off her bra. Artie could see her breasts set off by his paint swirls. Her nipples were outlined in violet glitter. Eyes half-shut, she danced ever closer to Artie.

Some line provoked knowing laughter from Pamela and most of the other dancers across the room. About the trip, of course… the trip… Artie suddenly felt lost again, his design a stupid lather

202 | CATS' EYES

of paint against her body, a badge of his helplessness, but she didn't care, she laid her hands on his shoulder, pressed against him, her thighs rocking against his groin... gimme some of your love... He called her name, wanting her to acknowledge him, wondering if she even knew who was painting her.

"Ooh, we fit nicely, luv."

It was no use now. Not only was his heart beating, his blood vessels palpating, not only did he throb... he pulsed. Her hips rocked and suddenly her belly was tracing the shape of his, over and over. Artie tried to transfer the increasingly out of control pulse to his fingers, and now he was tracing figure-eights all along the side of her ribs and back, not willing to touch her breasts, but massaging her with the thick viscous paint as hard as he could. She sighed and told him again, yes, just do what you feel, and that was too much, the pulse spasmed and he shook with the pulse, swam with the pulse, he felt it leap long and burning from his loins and he shut his eyes and was bombarded by a blast of his own phosphenes in the dark as he immersed himself in the unbearably sweet shock of the moment.

He opened his eyes. She shimmied and drew back from him. Artie blinked away the fog of his trance and saw the handiwork of his violent shudders on Pam's skin in waves of black light.

Nigel came up, threw his arm around her, rocked his hip against her side and sized Artie up with a nasty grin.

"I don't believe we've met."

"That's Artie. He's a gooooood body painting partner."

"Well, not a fuckin' Picasso, but creative, eh?"

Pam leaned toward him, her eyes purple and avid, her nipples erect and glowing.

"And such enthusiasm."

She tenderly drew her fingers across his face.

"Later, luv."

They were gone. Artie's arms quivered with fatigue. His underwear caked, and along his inseam was a faint purple sparkle. He went to wipe the sweat from his face and saw his hands burn with vortices of brilliant color.

Sometimes Nate seemed to be stuck with three refractory children.

Artie, back two hours late from his party, and outraged at Nate's objections. I'm a junior in high school, I'm with my college age friend, I took a cab home, what's wrong? I could have stayed all night but I didn't! Unbelievably insolent—and what was that colored crap on his hands and pants?

Karen, who had yelled at him that night that she was sick of reading books, history was just someone's stupid opinion of what happened, and what if it's all lies? Maybe that ex-Socialist teacher wasn't as harmless as Dorothy thought. What's wrong, Karen shouted, with just making pretty things for other people to see and hear and wear?

When Nate had finally told her that if she wanted to keep up her art and music, let alone Saturdays at Gyre and Gimbel, she'd have to do her homework two hours a night, pass her courses, and that was that, she'd answered him with a slammed door, just as Artie now angrily slammed his door behind him. The master of the house and he slept outside his kids' slammed doors on the convertible sofa. Perhaps with the income from the new caseload he should consider a three-bedroom apartment on the West Side, as Dorothy had suggested. That is if his third tantrum-throwing big kid, Lucas Oxley, didn't destroy his livelihood.

Oxley talked a good game, but in his ignorance of the nuances of the law he seemed determined to bypass an actual acquittal and go straight for legal martyrdom. He constantly forgot that his case would be tried not before a jury but by a three-judge panel who would pay more attention to specifics of disorderly conduct and inciting to riot laws than Lucas Oxley's opinions on civil rights.

"See, Phase 1 man is, hey, we actually got the right to sit in the front of a bus. We can actually vote in this so-called democracy. We can say we're 4/5 of a human being now. Phase 2 is—hey, how do we pay the rent, get jobs, apartments, how do we get somethin' to eat? What, you want something to eat, boy? Don't you got your malt liquor?"

The rudeness, changing a comic monologue into an

attack… it seemed to Nate a standup version of Miles Davis turning away from the audience. He could believe Oxley might arrogantly set out to start a riot—but he held his tongue, as always with the most truculent clients, and tried to explain that while Oxley could no longer be prosecuted for his words alone, if the context was a situation where those words could lead to violence—

"I was just there to do my act as a favor to some people, then get back to my lady friend uptown!"

Lucas fidgeted in his seat, plucking at the sleeve of his Army-Navy coat, and Nate could feel a bout of unruliness coming on.

"Do you know Harry Belafonte's willing to help me out if my legal expenses get too great? Man advised JFK to ally with Dr. King and he's willing to help me out!"

Nate could tell Lucas wasn't so much testifying to the greatness of Belafonte as his own exasperation that, though a friend of Belafonte, he was still trapped in a picayune legal case in the Village.

"If I had Bobby's ear, man, I'd tell him to ally with Stokely Carmichael if he don't want to wind up like Jack."

"Lucas, that's a perfect example of the kind of inflammatory remark that can really rile people up, in your words, and that's what this whole trial's about! Did you intend to do that to that crowd?"

"You saying did I intend to rile the crowd up? What do you mean rile the crowd up? They're already riled up, man, either 'cause they're black in white America or they're gonna be shipped to Vietnam. Or maybe just 'cause they don't like what they see out there, which is their goddamn right as an American! I was trying to cool these people down in my own way! I'm heading up to the rally, I see a brother sitting on the subway up here, just sitting there in his ragged ass coat, out of his head, screaming you're killing us, you white motherfuckers, you're killing us! I'm not gonna insult people's intelligence and not face the racist bullshit, but if I can get 'em to laugh a little, maybe I can help them get through it, man!"

"That's fine then. You're trying to get the crowd to vent their anger, let off steam."

They stumbled their way into a decent lawyer-client relationship, playing off each other; just as Nate could prompt Oxley into articulating his pain and how he dealt with it, Oxley could goad Nate into doing his best for him. At the trial, Nate led Oxley through a recounting of what his intentions were that day, to show that he didn't have the requisite "scienter," or mental state, to cause a disturbance according to the law. And Oxley unexpectedly helped his own case when he dropped his bravado and confessed his true feelings about his act. He told the judge he couldn't go to work with hate in his heart. To make fun of someone you have to recognize his humanity.

"Under the full moon I can hate like anybody but not under the spotlight, man."

In his closing statement, Nate was surprised at the ring of his own voice. Check the record—what did he ever say that was a provocative as what that heckler said? And did a comedy professional like Oxley, with a burgeoning career at stake, really decide to incite a riot at a small rally surrounded by police? Doing a routine he'd already done at colleges without incident? Nate cited the Supreme Court's decision in Terminello vs. Chicago. To engender strong feelings and invite dispute was a function of free speech, which sometimes serves its best purpose when it gets people angry with conditions as they are.

"And comedy and satire, as we all know, even as it makes us angry, can give us pleasure. The police who arrested Lucas Oxley because of the unfortunate actions of one heckler in the crowd apparently took the phrase 'laugh riot' literally!"

The judges smiled, even Lucas chuckled at that one, and an hour later, as they walked out of court, with Lucas totally exonerated, he proved with one question (and one that previously had tended to go to the senior partner) that Nate was now a man he liked and trusted.

"Hey, Nate, know where I can score some weed?"

Karen, Nina and their new friend Josie had such fun with the new Donovan album. Karen had found a flapper dress and turquoise armband in the back room of Gyre and Gimbel. She'd pretended a stray quill feather was a cigarette holder, gotten herself up like the vamp on the cover of "Mellow Yellow" and flounced around to the song to the giggles of her friends. They sang along on the electrical banana line—Josie knew all about how to fry the inside of a banana's fibers, although she said the high wasn't that great, just legal—and they tried to pick out the Beatles' rumored voices in the bunch of partygoers yelling in the song's background. Then they broke out a jay from Josie's stash and got totally high before playing the rest of the album.

Karen adored how Donovan evoked all her favorite worlds, from castles to Caribbean sunsets. Then he could write something right out of her own world, "Young Girl Blues," its slow hung-over bare strum of the guitar stroking her somewhere deep inside—so much a sweeter caress than from the boy from the U.N. School who groped her as if she were some toy with concealed buttons for lights and buzzers. She sensed there were whole realms of experience waiting to be savored and her would-be boyfriend turned out to have the touch of Archie and Jughead.

She loved floating on the eddies of her high to Donovan, or to the Doors and "Strange Days," and her heart quickened at the thought that in a couple of hours she'd be seeing Danny's group perform at Hunter College for the first time… even if she couldn't be lost… in the right way… because, Dad had insisted, Artie would be with her to take her and bring her quickly home.

Danny, uncharacteristically, also planned to be straight during the Hunter College show. He worried that if he even smoked, let alone dropped, that he might collapse onstage. They'd been rehearsing old and new tunes for days in an unused church rectory, and meanwhile the recording had galloped ahead. After reading in *Life* about the Beatles new album, and its planned use of French horns, oboes, bassoons, a harmonium, steam calliope, tamboura, sitar, and harpsichord, Danny had realized he'd been wrong in slighting the resources of the studio. The future stretches out beyond our imaginations, the Boys had said, and they believed in musical infinity as well. Danny was into it now. The band sometimes took a song through one mix after another until janitors came in at 5 a.m with the vacuum cleaners. Danny learned how echoes and reverb could make theater out of musical space. They could get muddy thunder out of the bass and a bone-deep throb out of the rhythm guitar for Jimmy's "Down In The Darkness." Then, on Danny's songs, after building the bottom, they could layer the band's sonic iridescence, bleeding in the violin, La Grange's oud and balalaika and electric sitar, or jazzy electric piano and an eerie English horn. La Grange beamed and said it sounded positively symphonic. The studio's magic was a whole other plane of harmony that could wed Jimmy and Danny and LaGrange in textures and undertones while keeping their differences intact.

Danny brought them two new tunes, his anti-Vietnam protest song, "Agent Orange," and a song that had just seemed to bubble up out of the same energy but a whole different well, a serenade called "Eden Is Here." Jimmy didn't think much of "Agent Orange"—he groaned "another level, Danny?" and called it more paranoia than protest—but after hearing "Eden Is Here" he said all was forgiven. The band whipped together that one at light speed, sensing airplay, maybe even, within the alternative universe of FM radio, something like a hit. They released the cut to WOR and WBAI. Scott Muni played "Eden" on his show and in his coffee-soaked growl intoned "Let's keep our eyes and ears on this band." A writer from *Creem* heard the new songs and described the Voyage with a term Danny loved. Black light music.

The program for the concert featured on its cover Pam's shot of Danny, his hair whipping above him as he attacked his violin. Karen gazed at it while Artie tried to relax and get into the right mood for the show. With Karen by his side, he felt silly, unable to join the audience on its happy expectant wavelength, forbidden to smoke his way into that—never imagining Karen felt exactly the same way.

Suddenly the lights darkened. A screen behind the band came alive with an intermingled throb of brightly colored ferns and amoebas. Danny, in a flowered sorcerer's robe, played the violin in shrieking chromatic patterns, then turned to the amp until the banshee howls doubled themselves. Glowing eye shapes burst into ectoplasmic, multilayered embraces.

They crashed into "I Don't Want This Life." Karen's mouth hung open as she tried to take it all in. The band played a breakneck ninety minutes looser and happier than Artie had ever seen them, or would ever see them again.

The only disappointment was Karen's coiled little presence bringing him down. She so clearly couldn't assimilate what they were playing. She looked almost ready to weep in the middle of "Agent Orange," Danny's antiwar song, which had a foot-stomping rhythm, spooky balalaika, a razor-thin violin screech and lyrics that bled over-your-shoulder menace.

In the black market of your sleep.
Down all the hidden paths he creeps.
He's a cop, he's a cop, it's a cop, so you drop
Agent Orange swooping down to make some death,
with each breath.
If you're not a friend of the U.S.A., Agent Orange is on the way.
What will you do, when they come after you, think for yourself
or you won't get through…

The song chorused over and over on that line, Danny and Jimmy vamping on violin and guitar back and forth right through to the finale. When the song ended Karen at last jumped up and applauded with the rest of them. Funny, he'd thought that song was losing her.

Danny stepped up to the microphone.

"This song is for all the lovers out there… or those who wished they were… or once were… or never were… but should be… sometime… "

The Voyage segued into "Eden Is Here", with its gentle lullaby rhythm laced with violin and English horn solos.

Eyes on the flame
The match in my hand
This place we know
The place where we stand
Let's say we are lost, let's make that our promise now
The light is high and the light is far
It comes back to be the place where you are
The time it is gone, the time it returns...

The chorus was a simple repetition of "Eden is here" and by the end of the song Danny had the crowd singing along with it. Artie could see Karen was truly into it now, spellbound by the band's every gesture and entering so deeply into the family that the song created that for a moment he felt out of place. But as the band instantly changed the mood and cut loose on "The Journey," the last tune of the show, everyone got up to dance together. Artie felt weird dancing alone next to his sister, but this wasn't a dance dance, he realized, this kind of dancing in the aisles, from now on, would be about responding to The Music. For the first time, along with Karen, of all people, Artie joined a concert crowd in shouting "More!", and the band sent them home with two Jimmy Hinton blues numbers.

They went backstage and congratulated Danny. Though his eyes darted back and forth among his well-wishers, he slammed Artie on the back and gave a great big hug to Karen. And on the way back home, still fired up by the music, Artie admitted to himself the night had been fun, kind of like when the family had seen *A Hard Day's Night*, although Karen wasn't joking or playful about what she'd seen. Except for praising Danny and the band, she didn't seem to want to talk much about it at all.

"Danny's gonna be a rock star, you really have that feeling."

"Well, Artie, now you can see a budding tv star. More of a flash in the pan, I hope."

"You won the Oxley case?"

On the late night news Dad, flanked by microphones, praised the judges' verdict as a just and fair application of free speech law. Oxley took the mike and struck a different note.

"I'm gonna be suing those cops for false arrest!"

Dad's smile petered out, and he shook his head slightly.

"Are you going to do that case too?"

"I think I've finally convinced Izzy to hire an associate."

As Dad listened to Lucas' brief tirade, he mentioned that tomorrow an interview would appear in the *World Journal Tribune*. *Newsweek* was also coming to the office to talk to him and Izzy. This case was going to make some waves.

Artie, puzzled, finally figured out what so worried Dad: he actually could become famous.

The tv went to a commercial. Karen sprang up from the chair, and peered through the slats of the Venetian blinds, amazed.

"It's snowing!"

Down in the Village, Danny and the band watched the surprise late March storm lay its silver dust on the Bleecker Street pavement. La Grange broke out the latest tabs of Owsley reputed to be mellow. Somehow the night spun out into the park and a snowball fight. Where angry speeches had recently echoed, the gentle missiles of ice left luminous contrails. Their footprints as they raced across whitened lawns glowed like fireflies. The moon doubled and within its binocular gaze seemed to judge Danny kindly. Shadows were whiskers, the snow nuzzled and embraced him as he rolled in it with Nell and Pete and they laughed in the lunar and lamppost weave of the night.

It was the start of a two-day acid bacchanal. They didn't start coming down until early Sunday evening, settled in before the tv. Nell doled out some canned artichoke hearts but they had a tender, lifelike warmth and Danny couldn't eat them. He wolfed down three slices of less endearing pepperoni pizza as the group watched *Mr. Ed*.

"Jeez, what the hell?"

A blonde hula dancer claimed the grey screen, coconut shells on her breasts, tawny and golden and savage.

"It's Wilbur's wife. She's trying to get him to buy the Hawaiian furniture set."

She grinned lasciviously at Wilbur and writhed against him. The dance bore into Danny's loins. Her breasts overflowed from the shells.

"If I were Wilbur, I'd be buying the lawn chairs."

"If I were Wilbur, I'd throw her down right now."

"NO, GO BACK!... bummer... "

To a chorus of disappointed male shouts, the show had cut to Mr. Ed, who'd decided to join in on the fun, dialing a phone number with a pencil to order up the Hawaiian furniture himself.

"Man, Mr. Ed's always goin' behind Wilbur's back, man, he's a devious motherfucker."

Yes, he was, Danny thought, with those sly, almost Asian eyes he had, that trickster's confidence in his basso profundo voice. The palomino was the force behind the scenes, and as Danny's attention vibrated in and out of the show, it was Mr. Ed's manipulations that stitched the action together. Danny realized he must have blanked out, for suddenly everyone was chorusing to the closing theme...

"A horse is a horse, a horse is a horse, of course, of course, a horse is a horse is a horse."

They all cracked up as Danny's repetitions reduced the chorus to nonsense, until he suddenly stopped.

"A horse is not a horse."

"What?"

Danny saw the face of the grinning Chinaman, and the palomino ghost whiteness like a cloud around his eyes.

"A horse is not a horse."

"Danny, what the fuck are you talking about?"

"A horse is not a horse, man."

"What the fuck do you know about horses? You don't even like to ride them."

"A horse is not a horse."

"Danny, don't freak me out, okay?"

"Maybe he's goin' white light on Mr. Ed."

Danny heard Nell asking if he wanted to walk her home. His reply was an instant yes. He couldn't bid goodnight to the rest of the band fast enough. Ed's face had taken on a beard. He was shafting off the framed photos, the mirror, every reflective surface of the room.

Within minutes Danny and Nell were bounding across snow hillocks that seemed like icebergs, too hugely pure for that kind of intrusion. They were floating on deep indecipherable currents; above them was the indifference of stars playing hide-and-seek in city lights and trees, but here was Nell's body to guide and entice him until his feet sensed the pulse of the coming April earth, the roots conserving the warmth beneath the ground that soon, in Nell's bedroom, were the skin and the arteries of her welcoming body. Yes, yes, he thought as he rode her, Eden is here, we'll have a hit with that one, Eden is here, Ed isn't here, Eden...

The snow melted to ragged patches the next morning, but still, as it always did, reminded Artie of that awful day "Kofag" had loomed before the eyes of the whole school—an unwelcome counterpoint to his discussion of Dad's victory in court, which had actually made the front page of the *World Journal Tribune* and page four of the *Times*. In the corner of his eye he saw Steubner lope up to him.

"So did you ever ask your dad how he feels defending Commies?"

"Hey, Stooge, lawyers are supposed to defend people regardless of their beliefs. You'll learn that when you fail law school."

Artie appreciated his friend Stoltzman's speaking up for him, but it wasn't nearly harsh enough for his taste. He turned around and walked right up to Steubner.

"Oxley's a comic, Stooge, not a communist, which makes you an asshole."

Steubner cursed and swatted Artie on the arm. It was the wrong day to do that. Artie was astonished at his own reaction, as he punched Steubner over and over until his target was scrunched against the wall yelling at him all right, all right, just stop it, cut it fucking out, please!

Artie almost felt contrite to see the Stooge cowering before him, but not so remorseful that he didn't yell in his ear to leave his dad out of his Neanderthal political views. He strode away to the grins of his friends, and while he never knew if the rumors of the fight that circulated around the school helped him, a week later he won the election to represent his student government homeroom next year.

In the subway was a poster advertising Murray the K: Music in the Fifth Dimension. A tour featuring some of the latest, hottest bands, including Cream and The Who, "Direct from England." As soon as Artie got home, riding his last wave of winner's confidence, fighting down the quaver in his voice, he called Pam at the Huntington-Branch Studios, and as neutrally as possible suggested it might be a really good idea to take photos of this show, conveying that after all it wasn't a "date," just two photographers meeting to chronicle the event. Yes, that would be fantastic, and would you pick up a ticket for me? You're a doll, Artie!

Artie raced down to the RKO 58th Street. The next three days were a constant cresting and ebbing of anticipation, sparks to the brain, catches in his breath, a cycle that only petered out on the day of the concert when Pam showed up with Nigel.

But despite the presence of Pamela's "partner," it was great to have her by his side. Even dressed in jeans and a T-shirt, ready to race the length of the proscenium to snap her pictures, Pam was irresistible. Artie pulled out his new Nikon, but before he started snapping pictures, Pam laid a hand on Artie's shoulder, and tweaked the shutter speed on his camera. Sometimes the gap between them seemed so enormous—she was in Provincetown for the weekend, or visiting Montreal—and then she was no more than the width of her hand away, and he felt that if only… with just one little synapse of a spark jumping between them…

Pam sprinted to the stage for shots from the low side angles she favored, while Artie simply snapped pictures from his seat. Yeah, bird works too hard, doesn't she mate, cracked Nigel, as Artie smiled, nodded, and maintained a polite distance from this prettified thug who he sensed knew a little too much about him already. Mitch Ryder and the Detroit Wheels banged out their hits on a rickety castle set that Pam managed to get onstage to photograph. The Cream did two songs that sounded to Artie like an endless growling blues-raga drone—but then the Who took the stage. The gleaming diamond-hard Mod machine of guitar chords that rang with piston precision, the explosions of snares and crashing cymbals, the radiant singer in Union Jack colors who seemed ready to take the whole world on in a pub brawl, left Artie's camera hanging forgotten from his neck—and then, as the stutter and slam of "My Generation" burst into its climax, the lead guitarist, unbelievably, took off his guitar and whirled it smack into the amp. As he drove it over and over into the floor and smashed it apart the rows of fans emptied out and rushed the stage. Artie jumped into the crowd, instinctively shielding his camera but otherwise yielding blindly to the race toward the flame of a rock-and-roll rage so pure it could even sacrifice the instruments themselves. Amps moaned and cried out with feedback as the drummer kicked over his set and pieces of guitar flew in front of the crowd.

Artie was so dazzled by the act's auto-destructive finale that he didn't even notice that Pam and Nigel had vanished.

He kept looking for her, during an April that was one long burst of exhilaration. Artie found in Central Park a thrilling wanderlust for him and his camera, as if *Life* Magazine had hired him to chart the city "Portrait of Our Planet"-style, and the cobalt blue ionospheres and golden magnetic fields were revealed not by genial scientists in button-down suits, but capering mods in Napoleonic waistcoats. "Fun City" permitted kite parties, go-go dancing contests, giant freeform capture-the-flag games, even psychedelic sidewalk painting. New bicycle paths were created and traffic barred from the main routes on Sundays.

The Park was for people, not cars.

He would look for Pam even in the midst of thousands. For weeks the word had spread, through meetings in rented halls and conclaves at the New School and the Free School; through announcements on WBAI listener-supported radio; through street tables manned by volunteers from the National Mobilization to End the War, buttons sold for nickel contributions, mimeos handed out in colleges and coffee shops and the new illegal but flourishing head shops in the Village—with their water pipes, zig-zag papers, and other paraphernalia on sale right on the counter—that there would be the biggest march ever to the U.N. to protest the war in Vietnam.

Artie couldn't believe all the kids his age all around him, the first time he'd seen that since the World's Fair, all united in their belief that their *Dr. Strangelove's* absurdities had latched onto the military's actual Vietnam program like RNA to a double helix, and had, through reverse transcription, built a war. Pacification zones of sheer annihilation. Destroying a village in order to save it. Gentlemen, you can't fight here, this is the war room. They attacked the demented conflict, the Draft, the constant threat of nuclear holocaust, with absurd appeals to sanity, with the gentle *Alice in Wonderland* "White Rabbit" fairy tale warp of slogans like "War Is Unhealthy For Children and Other Living Things," and with twisted, raucous echoes of the ra ra cheers they'd been taught in countless color wars and high school rallies. "Hey, hey, LBJ, how many kids did you kill today?" "Stop the war in Vietnam, bring the troops home!"

Banners hemmed Artie in until not only couldn't he see if Pam had somehow shown up but he could barely see where he was going past the signs for SANE, Women's Strike for Peace, American Friends Service Committee, churches, lawyers' guilds, black organizations, National Mobilization to End the War. Still he kept taking pictures, and his camera became a magnet for the counterdemonstrators on the sidewalks who shrieked "Kill the commies!," "Reds, reds, reds!" and "Support the police!," and for the kids yelling back at them "Join us, join us, join us!," and cheering as new cohorts broke through the hecklers to merge into the crowd.

"Bring the troops home! BRING THE TROOPS HOME!"

At the U.N. Plaza he borrowed a pair of binoculars, and stared with wonder at Dr. Benjamin Spock, whose beak-nosed visage had beamed from *Baby and Child Care*, the book Mom had brought him up by, and who now stood behind a brace of microphones, a gaunt, towering tribune of war protest, and thundered that the only option in the face of the injustice of this war would be civil disobedience against the United States' Selective Service laws. Stokely Carmichael followed, and then Dr. Martin Luther King, Jr., whose message of nonviolence and integration, the hip high school seniors said, Stokely had rendered obsolete. Through the binoculars, with his slick, closely-cropped hair, mustache, and dark coat, King almost looked like a headwaiter, and his accent was almost shockingly southern. But when he began to speak, in an incredibly sonorous baritone, Artie put down his camera. It was not wrong, King thundered, to mix opposition to the war and civil rights. The war was destroying the promise of hope for the poor that had briefly loomed with the antipoverty program. The war machine was sending both poor white and black men to die in disproportionate numbers. The war was destroying the land of Vietnam and the soul of America, and in order to atone for our sins and errors it was necessary for the community of all men and women of goodwill to boycott this war, to refuse to serve, to join together to bring the war to a halt.

King presented a petition for peace to the U.N. undersecretary Ralph Bunche, and Artie joined the cheers and chants that volleyed off the facades of the U.N. building and the ramparts of Tudor City and rolled in waves along the East River.

And then on Easter weekend, bicycling with Russ toward Bethesda Fountain and the bandshell, Artie was slowed and ultimately forced off his bike by a growing procession of flamboyantly dressed mountebanks. Who'd called this costume party? On each forehead was a headband with a different talisman, a hexagram, a peacock's feather, a third eye. Revelers were handing out leaflets and blowing bubbles. Women in tight jeans and shepherdess dresses lazily sprawled on the grass.

Sheep's Meadow was filled with thousands more massed in the finery of Arab djellabas, Indian saris, capes in luminous rose and purple, silk top hats ringed with violets, and Chinese mandarin robes. With so much to photograph he paused, hunted, waited for Cartier-Bresson's decisive moment. A ring-around-a-rosy dance became an opportunity to isolate the raised handclasps in a long lens that turned the background to spring-colored haze. He halved the shutter speed to blur their motion. He shot a couple whose scarves flowed together with their embrace. Click. "The Flamenco: The Passion of Spain." Click-click. Ruffles from "Medieval Madrigals" bangles from "Gypsies: Mysterious Tradition." Walking and singing passports.

A young woman came up to Russ and Artie and handed them flowers.

"Welcome. Join us in the sunshine."

"What is it?"

"It's a be-in. The rest is... us."

She smiled and drifted away. Artie looked down at the daffodil, and remembered how he'd earned his hated "Kofag" nickname photographing flowers. He felt as if he'd been shrived of those days forever.

For the rest of the afternoon they sat transfixed next to their parked bicycles, sharing the joints that made their way through the crowd, Russ with his face painted by a devotee of Flower Power, Artie snapping pictures until he finally stopped to just lay in the sun, and and let his unhindered glances float across a human ocean of new life forms, scuba-sighted golden dolphin and parrotfish and blue whale colors. Artie swigged some circulating Ripple wine. He felt protected by his skepticism and his Nikon from the frivolousness of the crowd, yet utterly united with its hazy warmth and friendliness, the freedom of some group to hoist a banana balloon above the crowd, of some guy to say something as silly as "you're all so beautiful, man... " in front of a microphone, no notes, no preparation, to dismantle your ego and, as the brittle scaffolding falls away, to be bathed with the backwash of loving attention. Good old Ginsberg, perched on the platform of a flatbed truck, recited William Blake, "the eye altering alters all," before he led the crowd in meditational prayer and chants of "Ommmmm… " that faded slowly in the breeze.

Just as he took his picture, a hand pushed his lens down.

"Hey, camera boy."

The wistful blonde kissed him on the lips, smiled, and drifted away. He sat down and took that in for a few minutes.

She had to be here, Artie thought. He didn't want to leave Russ or his bicycle, so he used the long lens as a telescope, looking for her… maybe if he stayed a little longer… still it was all okay… all meshed together… Work and Love in effortless exchange, The Who, war protest, and this lovely, mild garden of peace. That day it seemed that such a balance and rhythm would prevail for the rest of his life, and soon Pamela would swim into view at the edge of his longest lens, in bright focus against the sumptuous mist.

"Really? That's what they called it, a Be-In?"

"Yeah. Not a bad pun. And it worked, no incidents, nothing. Can you imagine if thousands of us got together in one place and got drunk?"

"I think that's a great idea, actually. A PUKE-IN! I haven't had a good session of vomiting in a long time, and I think the public would FUCKING appreciate it!"

As always when the three men got together, Avery played the conservative jester while Bruce, always mindful of his son, defended the counterculture. Nate nursed his drink and listened to the argument.

"Avery, the way you frown on all this, I'm surprised you don't make Russ get a crewcut."

"Well, I think it would be a little silly for me to force Russ to adhere to my generation's conventions when I've made a tidy sum making fun of them."

"Guys, isn't it just that maybe the kids want a little more choice and less regimentation in their lives? I mean aren't we all a little sick of Levittown and Ozzie and Harriet and the Cold War and the whole rat race? Is it really so hard to understand their alienation from—"

"So they embrace Communism? My god, that's the Church without a virgin."

"Maybe it's that we can't protect them."

Bruce and Avery stared at Nate, who realized that this remark, which had just leaped out of him, begged for clarification.

"I mean there's still the nuclear threat, the racial situation's still bad down South and getting worse here… "

Avery twirled the swizzle stick in his martini glass.

"We did deliver a certain degree of prosperity, though, as I realize whenever I pay the tuition bill. And if they want to change the world, they're not going to do it sitting in Central Park."

The waiter brought him a second martini.

"You know I listened to one of Russell's groups. The Jefferson Airplane, I believe. And do you know what I kept hearing? Madison Avenue, for Chrissake!"

"Madison Avenue? Avery, that's nuts. You should hear the protest stuff Danny's writing about the war."

"Listen to the album! Surrealistic Bedsheet or whatever! It's all about how drugs are great for your brain! Don't take your mother's pills, take our pills! It's plastic but it's fantastic! The joke is, these kids are going to grow up as hooked on mind-control and pills and technology as they accuse us of being. They're going to be just like us with stronger drugs!"

"Little more to it than that, Avery, as I'm sure my son could tell you."

Bruce seemed awfully cavalier about his son's drug-taking, Nate thought, as if he viewed it as a distasteful but necessary facet of their recent success. He joked to Nate and Avery that Danny was becoming the best business partner he ever had. He cheerfully quoted the Voyage's latest reviews, including one critic who wrote "I'm not comparing Danny Geller to Jascha Heifetz, but I have a feeling if the Maestro were young today, he'd be part of a pop group."

The Voyage had been signed by Associated Booking Corporation, who had scheduled them to play a gig at the Westbury Music Fair that summer. They'd locked in several gigs at the Bitter End, and their demo had led to a year-long contract from Silver Records, with an option for two more years and a $2500 advance against future royalties of 5%. Not much, but the kid was getting his own apartment.

Nate wondered if Bruce was nervous about Danny striking out on his own at such an early age. As Avery had told him, *my son Russ runs with the pack, but he does come home every night.* But Bruce was clearly enamored of his family's tenuous link with the youth culture, and still itching to write more about their music, although the death of the *World Journal Tribune* had just about wiped out his writing sideline. In the wake of the "super-paper"'s death and the fall-off of writing assignments, Bruce was left with just his record stores and the Voyage.

"All right, guys, I'll grant you, it is getting a little weirder. I used to enjoy all that stuff, the Spoonful, the Byrds. But now all this druggy, gloomy, weird… just another phase, I hope."

Bruce clearly didn't want to linger on the topic, and so he shifted to the subject that never failed to intrigue him and Avery.

"So, Nate, you're looking a little tired. Guess there's been some catching up now that Marcela's back…. "

Walking back home up the hill between First and Second Avenue, Nate thought about how tough it was getting to play along with his part of the table talk.

Lately their lovemaking had seemed to taper down to the mechanics of Nate's eagerness and Marcela's compliance. Artie went every day to his summer job filing documents for the Housing Department, Karen disappeared into Central Park or a laziness and inertia that her vacation only seemed to amplify, and while that left more time with Marcela, her attention seemed so tenuous Nate didn't dare to push it. She was kind and playful under the sheets as ever. She groaned along with his clenched cries—at least he thought she did—but he could sense how briskly she rolled out of the bed, sought a glass of wine, a nap, music.

Tick tock tick tock.

They reserved for themselves a Saturday when Karen and Artie both planned to join their friends in the Park. That afternoon, when he kissed her navel, she took a long, heavy breath, slid her hands below him and, just as he quickened at that motion, she brought her fingers back up to his face wet with the pungence of her own sex. He could barely stop from gagging. Up went his kisses back to her rib cage and her breasts, and she sighed once again, but with a very different inflection.

He and Becky had been married fifteen years and they'd never...

He was aware, as never before, of the twitters of a bird. Marcela had purchased a finch whose cage hung near the foot of their bed. As he kneaded her breasts the finch launched into a cockeyed song, tweets and whistles that were anything but musical. Finally, as Nate kissed her nipples, she burst out laughing. Nate lifted up his head.

"I'm sorry, I can't help it, it's so funny the way he's trying to sing! He learned nothing from the canaries... "

She put her hand to her mouth and finally stopped.

They talked for a while about her new pet, how she'd found it in Woolworth's and taken a fancy to it. The bird fired up again, and Marcela turned away from Nate, propped her head on her elbow, and stared at the finch's cage.

Nate got up for a drink of water, and looked back at Marcela, who was contemplating the bird as if Nate had vanished from the room. He jumped back into bed, reached over and turned Marcela around. He slid down the bed and buried his face between her legs, darting his tongue down her inner thigh. She breathed deeply, and stroked his temples with her hands. Yes, she moaned, there, yes. Nate forced his tongue toward the acrid scent. He opened his eyes and the wattle of flesh inside her peeked at him. His tongue was a rod, he tried to make it taste nothing, just a salty brackishness that he could tolerate; he kept licking, kissing, to the rhythm of her moans, and despite his best effort, the scent got down to his throat. But he didn't choke, he wasn't repelled, he slowed down and let her sighs call to him, and gradually there seeped down to his belly a kind of harmony with the muskiness that had a warmth of its own. Nate flashed on his friend Jerry, just back from the Army, sharing a discovery, the Greek wine *retsina*. So thick and resinous that Nate at first couldn't drink it. But he kept sipping until got hold of him. *Retsina*, he thought, *retsina*, as he licked and kissed and opened his senses, *retsina*, until she cried out, pulled his head away, and kissed him full on his mouth still wet with her lubrication. He grew so hard he plunged into her and shook and burned way too quickly, but she was ready, she shouted and cried along with him.

She stroked his hair and thanked him, and he rolled over and gazed at her with a smile.

"Not too bad, Nate?"

"Well if a lawyer can't manage oral persuasion, what good is he?"

Marcela laughed and whacked him with a pillow, and they lay in the bed warmed by their skin and the sunlight, the finch sharing in their blissful silence, until Marcela rubbed his groin and whispered to him that, in this case, she was a pretty good lawyer herself.

Nate instantly grew erect, and for the next several minutes tried not to writhe off the bed as Marcela wetly unsheathed her lips and, with her tongue deftly abetting the motion, played her mouth over and over the length of his cock until he thought he couldn't take it, and when he finally came the orgasm wasn't just a pillowed space of shut-eyed bliss in one half of a bed, it was wide open, with rooms of pulsations, and a ceiling so high it stunned him.

After checking that he was all right, she snuggled next to him.

"You deserved that today."

Nate nodded weakly and stroked her hair over and over. Now he felt only like lying beside her and melting into the drowsiness of the afternoon. She turned on the radio. . . . an eerie song they'd never heard before, with a train of harpsichord music, but the high plaintive voice seemed strangely familiar. Bursts of marching orchestra and guitar. When the d.j. identified the band they were astonished, and kept the radio on to hear more.

WOR played it throughout the afternoon. Whole sections of the city sank into a meditative trance. Artie and Russ stopped their handball game when they heard it on a car radio and then went upstairs to listen, and Artie forgot about the Milky Way he was carrying in his jeans. By the time the songs cycled through a second time, he was plucking gooey fingerfuls of melted chocolate and caramel off his pocket lining. Karen and her friends ended their walk in the Park to sprawl in the grass next to another girl's portable radio.

Days later, after Artie bought the album, Nate played it on the console while Artie was at the movies with Russ. It was, after all, as Bruce had told him, way beyond hits and Number One, the event of the year. Over the next week Nate secretly went back to it when the kids weren't around, as if it were a medium through which he could decipher their culture. It seemed to reveal a welcoming place. Great vaulted rococo theater arches with echoes of applause creating room for comedy and fantasy, and for everyone to sing along. It started with French horns in a regal fanfare punctuated by electric guitar, went on to a nursery rhyme song with booming drums and a hint of playful secrets when you turn out the light, blossomed into a lilting tune that reminded you a mind should wander where it will go, and wound down to bizarre songs with scratchy trumpets, heavy breathing, and barnyard animals that serenaded a prim meter maid and her silly lover and satirized a rush hour so frantic that a pack of dogs seemed to be hustling to make the train. Then it sounded like the band launched off into outer space, boosted by waves of applause.

Moments of revelation and ridiculousness and harmony that always caught you off-guard. Retsina moments.

Sgt. Pepper's seemed to Nate like the humor of his pretend-cousin Ernie Kovacs. Or a lighthearted British musical version of *The Twilight Zone*, where ordinary people were ambushed by extraordinary events every day, and, in the words of *Hamlet* that he remembered from his oratory classes, if it's strange, then as a stranger give it welcome.

Only sometimes it wasn't so lighthearted and welcome after all—the dread that seeped through a chamber music song in which, to the numb chorus of parents, a girl vanishes from her home. And Nate wondered why the Beatles chose to end the album with a song that intoned a ghostly invitation to drugs, tore itself apart with orchestral shrieks that mimicked a hundred air raid sirens, and ended with a piano chord interminably crumbling into nothingness. After all the smiles and dreams, and after putting so many people, both famous and unknown, on the album's stage, the Beatles had commanded all the trapdoors to open.

"Let's see your place, Danny, and I happen to have some primo weed to christen it with." Danny's first invitation to his new apartment was to his dealer.

As they smoked some sinsemilla together, Danny looked over his studio and grinned: crates for furniture, an old bridge table discarded on the street, a Zappa poster, a faded couch whose once-splashy colors could have adorned a holiday hotel in Wildwood, New Jersey—some décor. What the hell, to choose an East Village residence in Alphabet City, you had to have a taste for accents like cigarette burns and water stains ingrained in the walls and floors. But if out west Ken Kesey was looking for ghost towns to move to, here you could buy a police lock and a window grate and colonize a bit of Avenue A. And if you could stand doing clothes in a scabby sink and cooking burgers over a tiny electric stove you could live for $85 a month.

Danny fell into a rhythm that so perfectly suited his floating musician's sense of time that he wondered if he'd ever be able to return to CCNY and take the requisite number of courses to keep him out of the draft and Vietnam. In the morning he'd grab a pirogi at a Uke place or split pea and challah bread at B &H

Dairy. He'd do some work as a sort of ambling old clothes service for the Diggers free store, helping those ragged crusaders, named after an English peasant rebellion, who believed in free stores and free money, looking up people he knew in the West Village and convincing them to donate.

While the West Village was getting way too spiffy with its galleries and even fur stores, in the East Village, as Abbie Hoffman put the word out, "everyone is on a neverending TRIP!" Danny could hobnob with the activist clown prince and other loiterers at Ed Sanders' Peace Eye bookstore, recently ruled not obscene; he could read Camus, Beckett, Norman Mailer, or simply hang out by the two portraits of Ginsberg and Peter Orlovsky in drag and samples of hip celebrities' pubic hair.

Then he'd head to Tompkins Square Park, where the April Be-In had left a permanent floating encampment. Each lawn was a charmed circle with its own wrought-iron boundary, one for the Puerto Ricans, one for the nodding junkies, another for Slavic families and a fourth for hippies, and there Danny was grounded as he'd never been before in a scene that was, in a swath of parkland, acid made flesh. No more secrecy in the beatnik coffeehouses and bars of the other half of the Village, not when you could turn on and walk out into the sky with your cohorts. No more hiding in your room when there was the collective grace of a community of pacifists and artists and freaks and missionary outlaws all around you.

As evening wafted in he might talk to some of the more intriguing arrivals, like a Berber mulatto who told him that the flutes that he sold from his stand on St. Mark's were used to train hawks in Morocco. Along Danny's sauntering walk the scent of the Orange Julius store sugared the air, and a little girl played naked in Washington Square Park, the tribal time dying away peacefully with no regrets.

Then would come a busy night, as he made his place ready as a crash pad for whomever the Diggers would send his way. At the store he would receive his guest, sometimes cognoscenti like the Canadian Mushroom Mel, en route to New Orleans, with whom he could talk about the political scene, but more often than not a female companion for the evening. Danny was always courteous, never crude, never ever wanting to deny anyone his or her right to be or not to be free in any way. But generally women who made their way to the Diggers to look for a crash pad or just meet people from the scene were off on an adventure, and Danny knew how to make himself part of the safari. He could adapt to whatever class of chick appeared: an artist with belled anklets; a student from uptown or Scarsdale looking to broaden her mind while foraging through the boxes to pick up the latest clothing cheaper than at In-Different Boutique or Tra La La; or the runaways from down south and the midwest, four hundred of whom would crash in Tompkins Square Park that summer. Now that Danny didn't have to report back to his parents, he rarely missed. What a lover, like a writer or musician, truly needed, was his own time.

It was so musical with women, playing the chords and rhythms of their curiosity, knowing what tones to sound. For the scene-hopping intellectual like Teri, Danny still loved the poetic angle, and she'd be happy to talk Rimbaud or T.S. Eliot with an up-and-coming rock star reviewed favorably in *Crawdaddy*. Two movie dates—*Persona* to acknowledge her intellectual and physical daring, *Blow-Up* to disorient and entice her—then, after feverish conversation and a fat doobie, it was as easy as slipping into a warm bath.

The runaways were more straightforward, almost seeing it as a trade in services, like Martha from West Virginia, in her plaid shirt and jeans and blanket around her shoulder, a farm girl who, once she cleaned up, was a Jane Fonda in the rough. Six feet tall, rangy, long blonde hair coursing down a broad back, legs from Mars—god did she like to be pinned and do the heavy pinning herself, butter-churning the orgasms out of him. He so wanted to keep her with him for awhile that he gave her head with long, slow oscillations of control that she surrendered to with barely muffled screams.

He had to admit, though, that his new life clashed with the demands of professional performing and recording. Jimmy ragged him mercilessly about being late for rehearsals. Danny showed up promptly for the four or five concert nights a week, and he knew enough not to blur his brain too much with alternate realities before the gigs. But yes, rehearsals were suffering, his songwriting was drying up, and Ed kept popping in to complicate stuff further. First he did his centaur in the mirror thing. Danny freaked, thinking, deep into his trip, there was a cop in the room in disguise, until he heard that low, gravelly mocking voice. Hey hey Wilbur. A real trickster. Ed popped up in the midst of the most pleasant visions, and ignored Danny's perfectly reasonable demands that he not bogart his trip.

Finally he realized he had to give up acid, a decision made easier by his discovery of peyote. The less demanding mescaline helped Danny settle into the rehearsals and the songwriting, up until the day the phrases he plucked out on his guitar were nicked one time too many by the echoes of police sirens coming through his window. Danny followed one of the threads of a crowd that swelled through the East Village toward Tompkins Square Park.

Amid the lawn's charmed circles a border had been violated. The musicians he liked to jam with had been joined by about two hundred chanting protesters with arms locked together. Someone had made a noise complaint and this time the precinct foreman, confronted with hippies refusing to leave, had called the riot squad. Some were trying to get the crowd to disperse—let's just go home and come back tomorrow, peace, stay cool—it all seemed to be winding down to the usual chants of love and solidarity and unity, a last joint, a final ritual shout of "the park is for the people" before the party split to the Digger store for free rice and beans, right up to the point the cops attacked.

Danny watched the nightsticks dive on the crowd's heads like a swarm of hungry birds. It was so weirdly quiet, like branches snapping, when arms and hands were cracked apart. Danny's friends were dragged like mannequins to the paddy wagons, still not believing they'd been targets of police billy clubs even while they gagged on their own blood.

Danny joined hundreds that marched to the 9th Precinct House shouting fascists, murderers, but even enmeshed in the communal revolt he spotted a watch on a man pumping his fist in the air and remembered he was a professional musician with a band soon to be gigging five nights a week at The Scene. His bandmates were forgiving when he described the police violence he'd been caught up in, but Jimmy spoke for them all when he reminded Danny now was the time to take care of business, put the music first.

Still the police batons coming down and the blood spray...

Danny lent spare hours to stuffing envelopes for the East Village Defense Committee. The task smoothed out the fractured rhythms in his life while not encroaching on his music, and for a couple of weeks he prided himself on the new balance he'd achieved between the neighborhood and the Voyage.

Then one July night Jimmy didn't show up. It was incomprehensible that he, of all of them, would miss the night's expensive studio time without even calling. The session crumbled, the engineers walked away. Everyone knew that while Danny was the ostensible frontman and leader, it was Jimmy who cracked the whip.

Danny, for the first time since their relationship had been redefined by the business ties of the band, called Jimmy's home. His mother, a teacher who spoke in the clipped tones of a woman who put her education at the forefront of the dialect she'd grown up with, was so bone-tired she'd reverted to her old southern accent. He could hardly recognize her. She sounded like a maid.

"Mrs. Hinton, is Jimmy there?"

"He is but he's asleep, he can't speak to you now."

"Is he all right?"

"He's recovering."

Her voice was taut with blame, as if somehow Danny were responsible for whatever had waylaid Jimmy.

"What happened?"

"He got caught out there in the street. He was lucky he didn't get arrested or shot."

"What did he do?"

"He didn't do anything! He was just out there! He was driving to see me and he… he was a Negro boy out in the street! Don't you know the police are shooting Negro young men on sight down here? Turn on the damn radio or television! Don't you have any idea what's going on?"

They tell me, "Lucas, Mr. Oxley, you should use your comedy, lend your talents to help maintain law and order in the city this summer." I say after hundreds of years of keeping black people as slaves and sharecroppers and ghetto-dwellers—you want me to follow an act like that?"

The Hicks brothers were polite to Nate only out of a sliver of gratitude. The firebrands out by 125th Street had pulled them away. Nate figured Lindsay and Barry Gottehrer were recruiting plenty of potential troublemakers for his Youth Councils. The ghettos had become nothing but trouble.

Hamerow and Kovacs' office rang with the mallet blows of workers knocking out one of the old coach house inn walls to add space for an office for their new associate. Nate couldn't wait for the racket to end and the new kid to start pulling his weight. Milt Davis was the son of a Southern hardware store owner and a nurse, a former high school basketball star, and a graduate of Howard University: the kind of young black man that had once been called a credit to his race, outwardly calm and polite but with the height and adventurous hipster streak to engage the firm's more militant clients. And he could go in a flash from articulating a point of law to quoting one of Lucas Oxley's latest tirades.

No, man, there's no discrimination up north. No slums. Just preferred Negro housing. N double-A R C P. National Association for the Advancement of Rattraps for Colored People. And that thing in Watts? Just a remodel, baby.

Milt welcomed the chance to go down and meet clients in the Brooklyn ghettos, a sheer hell Nate was only too happy to avoid, and, in the wake of the City's school decentralization plans, likely to get worse. The Mayor had called on MacGeorge Bundy of the Ford Foundation to come up with a decentralization plan for New York's schools. Two of the designated experimental schools were in East Harlem and Ocean Hill-Brownsville in Brooklyn. Nate couldn't begin to understand it: one of the worst and most violent poverty pockets of the city would get the chance to take on responsibilities held by the Board of Education, hire and fire principals and teachers, and set up their own curriculum.

Hey, I want to try and help cool things out. So when I go to Harlem, I say—at least you're not livin' in Bed-Stuy. When I go to Bed-Stuy, I say—at least you're not livin' in Brownsville. When I go to Brownsville, I say—at least you're livin'.

Milt had respectfully reminded Nate that Lindsay was right when he said that if you wanted even a shred of racial harmony and integration, you had to give black people the power to solve their own problems, no matter how difficult that appeared. Then Malik Brown, boss of a local antipoverty center and brother of an ex-client, had clapped Milt on the shoulder and invited him to the Moorish Science Temple. You want to get eyes for what's happening, a detective just shot a black kid and Sonny Carson's threatening to torch the borough.

Sonny Carson, head of the Brooklyn chapter of CORE, former street tough, frequent entry on Gottehrer's crisis calendar, near the top of the police list of the fourteen worst agitators in New York, harangued the reporters and the police and inflamed the crowd to the point where one of his followers, a hulking bodyguard, walked up to a *Daily News* photographer, seized his camera and smashed it to the floor. Fragments of the lens and flash attachment rolled under the chairs. The photographer trembled in his seat. Even Carson seemed nonplussed by the broken glass, the scat of violence in the Temple.

"Got to admit, Izzy, the brother's tactics were pointlessly polarizing."

"Hey, Nate, get a load of this. Our young friend Milt has just had his cherry busted in urban law."

Lindsay volunteers came down to the ghetto and killed a lot of rats last election year. Well guess what? The other rats had kids! So did we! In the same room! That's what we in the ghetto call urban renewal.

By July Lindsay had walked up and down 125th Street more than any other Mayor. Nate helped all he could, tipping Gottehrer off when one of his clients let slip a hint of agitation brewing in some corner of Harlem. But Brooklyn still smoldered, Fifth Avenue stores had their windows smashed by a crowd leaving a Smokey Robinson concert. And in East Harlem, a Puerto Rican mob spilled into the streets after an off-duty police officer intervened in a street brawl and killed an unarmed assailant. On a night of steaming humidity and the smoke of trashbasket fires a line of kids faced a platoon of cops across police barricades on Third Avenue. Then some crazy jumped into the no man's land in the middle of the street for an insane whooping war dance, a shrieking cataplexy of song. He transfixed the crowd for twenty minutes until the night was split by a summer downpour. Everyone headed home.

But whatever relief the City felt vanished the night Newark exploded.

Nate wondered if New York had just been lucky up to this time. He could feel it whenever he met anyone from the Administration, the war to keep the peace, everyone thinking *have we cooled it out or is it just building up a bigger explosion down the line.*

Whitey's kinda funny that way, man. He worries when we riot. He worries more when we don't...

Two days later, Jimmy came back to work. He wouldn't talk about Newark, and explained the bandage on his face by saying he'd fallen on some broken glass, but he'd gotten a tetanus shot and everything was all right. The band let his seething silence into the music. Jimmy reworked his signature tune, "Down In The Darkness." There was now a crunchy four-note riff with a bent note snarl where a simple strum used to be. Jimmy punched up the song, took out the languor, gave it a nasty edge.

The next day Jimmy went missing again. But Danny had heard the news on the radio and he knew where Jimmy was likely to be.

The crowd at St. Peter's Lutheran Church was formally dressed and overwhelmingly black. It was strange to Danny to see jazz musicians dressed in a way he associated with black Muslims, but then again, the Quartet had always performed in suits. But some men wore fezzes or daishikis, and one man a billowing dishdasha. Down the pew was Jimmy, small and solemn, oblivious to all but the casket heaped with yellow and white flowers, and, perched on an easel, a portrait of John Coltrane.

Danny knew better than to break into whatever reverie Jimmy was lost in, or to inject himself into the largely black crowd in the pews. He stood in the back near the church entrance as the last of the mourners filed past the casket. Albert Ayler and his quartet played "Truth Is Marching" from the balcony, snake lines of horns with the passion of a funeral organ. A friend of Coltrane's recited the poem from *A Love Supreme*… thank you God, in the shadow of Coltrane's death, over and over. The Reverend John Gensel concluded his benediction with all praise to God, and thank you John Coltrane.

As the mourners, white and black, filed out of the church, Danny let Jimmy share his thoughts with other people on the stairs, and then, as he made it to the pavement, he slowly approached him. Jimmy smiled warily, as if expecting him all along but not welcoming the moment.

"That was beautiful, man."

"Yeah, it was a beautiful service."

Jimmy had never sounded so tired, or looked so small and huddled within himself.

"Tell everybody I'm sorry. I should have told them I'd be splitting today."

"It's okay, man. Everyone knows your mind's been blown by all the shit goin' down at that—"

"Danny, it's not okay. Can you dig that? It's not okay!"

Danny was stunned by the sheer rancor in Jimmy's voice.

He'd been trying to let him off the hook. Jimmy looked nervously over his shoulder at the church.

"I gotta get back to Newark. My mom's worried sick about me these days."

They headed over to the Port Authority. The men seated on milk cans, fat Puerto Rican women squawking on the stoops, all the humid squalor of Eight Avenue seemed to harden Jimmy into his silence.

"I can't take this shit anymore, Danny. I don't mean to hassle you, it's just—the commute, all the bullshit with the Voyage."

"What bullshit? We're doin' great."

"Uh huh. Look, I'm gonna lay down a couple more tracks and then I gotta—I gotta go, I gotta leave. What the hell, your whole rap lately is changing the band's sound."

"With you. With you, Jimmy. What are you talking about? You want to leave the band?"

"Maybe you just haven't been listening much."

The conversation had totally blindsided Danny, as if one of those parked buses had gone into gear and backed up into his path.

"Look, Jimmy, if this is about what happened in Newark."

"You think I want to leave the band because of Newark?"

"Hey, that can bring you down. I mean, what happened in Tompkins Square—I couldn't do anything for a day after that but think about it, try and do something about it. So I've become a part of the committee working together to restore the community peace with the Puerto Ricans, the Serenos, even the cops, and the vibes are totally better. It's really a people's park now."

The more he spoke, the more Jimmy stared straight ahead with a bemused contempt he barely shielded from Danny.

"So you think that's what we should do in Newark? Work with the white storeowners and the cops and the National Guard for peace and good vibrations?"

"Well, you have to rebuild, right?"

"You're so fulla shit, Danny. You're always comparing. A few freaks get their heads busted and you think it's the same as an urban insurrection? Do you have any idea what goes on in

Newark every day?"

"Jimmy, we're about to put out a record and hold some steady gigs. This is not the time to quit because you're totally understandably angry that the pigs came in and—"

"It's not that, okay? It's about the Voyage! I just don't feel it's my music anymore, and I want to get out!"

"You never seemed to mind that I fronted the band!"

"Damn right, because I didn't want to front any French poet ego trip psychedelic white boy bullshit! It's all out of your head, man, and it means nothing to people who aren't on the same head trip you're on!"

"That's bullshit, Jimmy. Our music, and it is ours, man, yours, LaGrange's, mine, it's personal, it's political, it's trying to expand awareness in every direction!"

"I don't know what that means, Danny. I know what it meant with Trane, but with us—I gotta get back to my music. The heart, the soul, the funk. And the hell with awareness, I want action! Look, I dig it, okay, you can't understand, how could you ever understand what just went down… "

They drew near the grey institutional clamor of the Port Authority Bus Terminal. Jimmy looked down at the ground.

"It's just how it is. I don't want to be angry with you, Danny. Not on this day."

He looked behind him at the milling crowd of seedy panhandlers and hurrying tourists, and quickly ducked into their midst.

"Jimmy, you can't make this decision while you're in a bad head space. All I'm asking you to do is think about it! Jimmy!"

Leaving the station, Jimmy finds the rust-streaked and bondoed junker car his uncle gave him. He drives to his mother's apartment. His usual route, now an artery through a ten-square-mile riot zone in the center of the city. His usual drive, now stuck in his memory like a skip so deep in the groove of a record album that the stylus will never leap out.

Near Bergen Street and South Orange Avenue, he swerves

to avoid hopped-up, drunken ghetto kids cruising three or four to a car. He barely skirts the rubble from looted stores and the starbursts of broken glass near the curb. He passes the familiar geography of the Branford Theater, the blue row houses beneath high voltage lines, Four Tops concert posters plastered on a construction site wall—only now the darkened windows in the abandoned buildings you long ago stopped noticing sprout greedy orange flames. Burglar alarms cry out through the smoke from gutted storefronts. A thin flaming comet arcs from a roof; a crash of glass and the fire races through a parked car and lights up the stripped metal gates.

Bystanders up ahead pelt the street with stones and bricks. Jesus, thinks Jimmy, oh Jesus, keep driving, but he knows he has to keep his eyes not just on the road but on the crowd, somehow he has to look both ahead and to the black faces alongside the street because he's seen how the stores that remain untouched are the ones painted over with "Negro Owned Business" and "Soul Brother." Catch their eyes when you can, be as black as you can, show that face and they won't throw the brick.

Now he's heading toward the corner of Avon and Livingston, the Mack Liquors store, and he's ready for more looters and brick throwers so he doesn't see the guy in front of him until he has to slam on the brakes. Whafuckyoudoin'nigger? A black guy in his undershirt, flying off the red wine in his hand, and Jimmy pleads sorry, and the fool slams on the trunk cursing him as he drives away. Jimmy figures that's the end of it, eyes on the road, never seeing the guy pick up the iron pipe and hurl it at the driver side door.

It just grazes the glass, but the window smash jolts him forward and he humps the car over the curb.

He almost faints from the blood beating in his head but he knows enough to race out and check for damage. The hubcap's gouged but the car's okay. The lights ahead are stuck on red and blinking mindlessly. It's okay, could be worse, he turns around to get back to the car and slams into the running kid with the beer box. When he falls to the pavement his cheek is raked by the teeth of some tiny animal. He scrambles up from what he thinks is a rat and through the blur of the concrete he makes out his crushed glasses.

Now the street is a fog of sodium lights and flame through which race shadows looking back at him, phantoms sprinting with crates of beer, other black ghosts on the stoops of the walkup, where one shouts get down, boy, get down! The cry to play harder, but now it's a shout to fall and flatten himself on the pavement. A male voice roars "Freeze!" Jimmy hugs the sidewalk, can see ahead of him the dim shape of a boy running, and behind him the yellow helmet of a cop sighting down a shotgun. The blasts hammer his brain, but he's all right, he feels the pavement, he feels his legs, he hears the spent shell casings fall at his feet.

The bootfall, the cops' shouts, the women's cries over the fallen boy—all a spidery mass of shadows and screams and Jimmy scuttles into an entryway, where a skinny black man wearing a bandana beckons him up the stairs.

Coltrane is on the bandstand, it's like he's charming a colossal viper with his soprano sax, and Elvin tom toms and smashes and fills up all that space with a river torrent of Mother Africa, caught on a rock that splashes diagonally in a cymbal shower. Now Trane plays "Alabama", sparse notes circle mournfully over a bass melody, a piano headwind that gives the dirge direction but no place to land… and you feel the South, like this beating heart, can be broken…

Some of the men have shaved heads in mourning for the millions of slaves and the black living dead who followed them. They pass the bourbon around. Guns lean against the wall. They tell Jimmy they've shot into the street a few times, but only to divert the pigs, protect the blood with the color tv in his arms, the mom with half a cow from the supermarket. Sorry your car got hit, man. Get a bandage for the brother…

In the studio recording "Ascension," Coltrane had stood amidst all those young players… John Tchichai, Marion Brown, Pharaoah Sanders… in their acrid sweaty T-shirts, it smelled like horses in there. The fever of the streets, "burn baby burn," but the fire's seeped up in the music's wake, a cry for some angry faith. The trills, yodeling, honks, howls, suddenly anchored with a legato note, always those long held notes calling the music back, regathering the music, stringing pearls in longer sequences, geometries, arabesques, constellations… and all the young men were with him…

"Cops drivin' in with sirens silent. That's NOT so they can keep the peace, that's so they can sneak in and take a brother down. Or you think they doin' what they have to do. Hate the deed, not the man, right? You nonviolent? Still think that's where it's at?"

When he hits the higher register Trane's speaking in tongues. He says he wants to give the listener a picture of the wonderful things he senses in the universe. So often it sounds like shattering but there's a story he tells about the vessels of creation shattered with the breath of life. All can feel that. Mother Africa. Mother India. All the listeners. The Byrds, the Beatles. All can join in the purification of new feelings, new sounds, the clarity of seeing what we all are. One thought, Trane had written, can produce millions of vibrations.

"They try to divide and conquer us! Liberals are the worse, got you comin' and goin'. That your bag? Be a middle class nee-gro, one of the Toms, the whip-me's, the sellouts, the house boys?"

We are a tribe at last… in all our different sounds and colors… now McCoy's piano is down to chimes, the bass behind him… we repair the vessels all together in celebration… thank you God…

"Turn on to your own people and fuck the ofays! Be what you are, brother, what you have to be! Are you ready for that? If you don't know what you are, better find out!"

The little VW Beetle with the bright lemon yellow and green two-toned design first appeared on 89th Street in the middle of July. Artie watched as Mrs. Shulman from the eighth floor eyed it balefully. It popped up and down the street all that week evoking derision or delight. But Artie was there when its occupant slid into the driver's seat. A beautiful brunette in a minidress splashed with cubist colors. When the car radio came on it was playing "Somebody to Love."

Sgt. Pepper's was Number One, and *Surrealistic Pillow* was right behind it. You could hear Grace Slick on WMCA, where Dandy Dan Daniels shouted "Listen to the pipes on that chick!" Listen to every kind of music. Jazzmobiles on city plazas, "rug concerts" at Alice Tully Hall where kids sprawled together on the floor beneath sometimes amused, sometimes infuriated conductors to hear Mozart or Stravinsky. Bongos over the rooftops, violinists practicing in distant apartments, free jazz sax runs flaring like Bunsen burner flames out of the laboratories of city hallways, and the songs on the radio that crossed all boundaries. Artie no longer felt yanked between straights and heads, between culture and counterculture. Like the subway map that took him between neighborhoods, the music led him through every territory.

Music and the promise of sex were, like the blues song said, the two trains running everywhere, the IRT and the Broadway local. Brigitte Bardot, Verushka, and Elsa Martinelli all wore the latest waistless dresses in pale chiffon, shawls and serapes crisscrossing their breasts, flowered shirts open to the navel and beyond—and they actually wore them in *Life* Magazine, next to an ad for Caribbean travel that showed a bare-assed woman walking into the sunset and a slogan for a VW van that read "You'll never lose it in a parking lot." And whenever Artie saw advertisements for dance clubs like Cheetah, "Come dance like you never danced before…", or the invocation of the new Electric Circus to "darling daughters and sweet mothers"; whenever he took out his camera to add to his photographic diary of all that was happening; whenever he thought of black light or body paint, or whenever he saw a certain shimmer of long blonde hair or a touch of avid wildness in a woman's eyes, he felt Pamela's embrace, he thought he could smell her scent on a New York City street, he made yet another call to her gallery and hung up without leaving a message.

At Bethesda Fountain, the angel's serpentine green robe, every fold highlighted by the summer sun, stretched over the water pouring down the basins beneath her, while a breeze whipped a fine spray into the air that cooled the rim of the lower basin. Boys and girls let the current fan their tresses, fingered beads they just bought from the vendors, and played guitars. Hundreds of others shuffled around the basin to the rhythms of bongos and maracas, the smell of incense and the caterwaul of blues harps.

The Fountain was the Park's locus for heads and wannabe heads, and attracted hundreds of young women every day. Artie and hundreds of guys would walk the circle and eye them as casually as possible. Their denims were patched with cloths and ornaments of every kind of pattern; all along the firmed rumps and thighs on the stone rim were latigo crescents, beadwork, stars and rainbows. If only, he thought, like Danny could, like Russ could, if only I could *pick a girl up*. The more highly charged that phrase became the farther he drew from acting on it, especially if a girl reminded him of Grace Slick or Pamela Huntington.

But at the Fountain, despite his fixation on the unattainable, Artie found a girlfriend, or rather she found him. While he was snapping pictures he framed a girl with black hair tossed in ringlets and a soft baby face who gave him a shy offhand smile. It turned out she lived in one of the old walkups across the street from Artie, and had frequently watched him heading out of his building.

Lisette Baldacci turned out to be a far more intriguing and vivacious date than he expected. She was surprisingly hip to the Lower East Side. She had a friend who lived with the Diggers, and steered Artie to the store when the Diggers handed out the free meals at four o'clock. They could simply drink some soda, leave the food to the impoverished, and Artie could talk to some of the locals while Lisette picked out a blouse or a denim jacket she knew she could fix up.

Artie asked almost all the people he met if they'd seen Danny. He'd called Danny several times and gotten no answer. The last time he'd seen him was when he'd showed Danny a photo collage he'd made up to advertise The Voyage. Artie had put together swipe-and-slash fragments of photos of the Voyage members in a collage, like the cover of the Byrds' *Younger Than Yesterday* album, and interspersed it with jackstraw patterns of

Manhattan buildings, lampposts, and signboards. Danny had praised it to the skies and the group had mimeographed it and wild-posted it on blank walls to advertise their second-on-the-bill slot at the Westbury Music Fair.

Danny had given him four free tickets to the show. After Russ, Artie and their friends had broken out a joint, and the Voyage was introduced by none other than the husky-voiced Allison Steele, the Night Bird, Artie was shocked to see that Jimmy Hinton had been replaced by another guitarist. He was crestfallen when the new lineup came up ragged and the blues-rock-hungry crowd sloughed them off, especially Russ and his friends, who made fun of the band. Hey, Artie, is love a flame? I thought it was a flashlight. Does he ever get his hair caught in the violin? Does it fucking matter? Artie's friends were there to cheer on the headliner, Canned Heat. Bob Hyte, the Mole, Blind Owl and Henry Sunflower Vestine. They were there to jump up and down with the crowd to the fat man's roar of the Refried Boogie. Artie couldn't even break away to try to get backstage and assure Danny everything was all right, and when he kept failing to meet him in his neighborhood he worried about him.

Briefly he made the Lower East Side his new stomping grounds. Stunned by a display on Avenue B by *Ramparts* Magazine, photos of devastation in Vietnam and the anguish of napalmed children, Artie did some table work for the Lower East Side Mobilization for Peace Action. He explained and handed out leaflets steering poor kids of draft age to advice on medical and other deferments. In return Puerto Rican families barely off welfare left LEMPA donations.

He and Lisette joined a Digger ceremony when the group tried to plant a small fir in a mound of dirt on St. Mark's Place. The Group Image played on a flatbed truck while Abbie Hoffman held up a sign that read "Only God Can Make A Tree." Finally the ceremony came to a harmonious end when Captain Fink confiscated the tree, but only to have it replanted in Tompkins Square. Artie, on a cushion of a high, swept up in a crowd getting off on itself and the warmth of the day, graduated to tonguing with Lisette.

For awhile summer alternated between Artie's job in a Dickensian file room in the Municipal Building and the ever more strenuous makeout sessions on Lisette's stoop. But soon he realized that, even while he was tracing his tongue along Lisette's, he was imagining Pam's, until he knew he was being unfair to Lisette—he was double-exposing her. Toward the end of the summer when Lisette landed a job at a diner on Third Street, and said, without too much conviction, he could drop by any time, Artie wasn't too disappointed.

When Dad said he'd allow him to come to a fundraising party for the upcoming October anti-Vietnam demonstrations in Washington, Artie felt the political and intellectual energy of the event chase off the lassitude of the summer and hone his wits for the school year to come. He called the Huntington-Branch studios and this time left a message. He wanted to make sure Pam knew about this convocation of antiwar leaders, writers, musicians, and a movie star or two, for he couldn't imagine her not making that scene—his scene, not that Nigel asshole. And if she came with him, he didn't care. All he needed was to steal a few moments with her.

When he arrived at the unexpectedly ornate surroundings of the International Press Club, he almost walked into a strikingly good-looking man with Beatle length hair and bushy sideburns. Paul Newman. Cool Hand Luke himself. Artie only stopped gaping long enough to check himself out in a gilt-edged mirror. This was the first time he'd worn both his ruffled white shirt and bell-bottom pants at the same time. He could almost chew his hair now, and its length seemed to complement the fineness of his features and the "poodle teeth" Mom used to tease him about while assuring him his bone structure would make him a handsome man. Lisette had said he had a "dreamchild" look.

Around the banquet room waiters circled with asparagus tips with mayonnaise dabs, Swedish meatballs on toothpicks, and ham

242 | CATS' EYES

and turkey canapés. He plumped a couple of the juicy meatballs down. Now Paul Newman was talking with a powerfully built, bald political operative, with glasses much like Artie's, whom Artie would later learn was Allard Lowenstein of the Coalition for a Democratic Alternative. He overheard them discussing attempts to find a Democratic challenger for Johnson who would take the issue of the War to the people.

He took his eye off them one moment to survey the crowd— and was astounded to see Dad with a woman who looked almost like Melina Mercouri with black hair. He waited for her to wave goodbye to Dad, but instead she laughed sweetly and leaned on his arm. That was Dad's "lady friend"? Artie went over to Dad to thank him for letting him come to this party, met the disturbing Marcela, who cheerfully coaxed out of him some information about his school life—then he turned around to see Grace Slick just across the room. An evening he'd fantasized as an event where he would show Pam the breadth of his knowledge, connections to the political scene, and surprisingly adult insights had suddenly become another demonstration of how women could reduce him to dumbstruck idiocy.

Nate was relieved that Artie seemed charmed by Marcela, although he realized that could perhaps become complicated. But that in turn convinced him that introducing Artie and Karen to Marcela at an event they all could share, so that the kids wouldn't concentrate exclusively on Marcela and their unpredictable feelings about her, had been the right idea.

"Hey, Dad, that's Grace Slick over there. Know who she is?"

"Yes, Artie, believe it or not, I've heard of the Jefferson Airplane. Why don't you get her autograph? You have something to write with?"

"No… I mean… no, it's okay, Dad… getting an autograph is so… corny… it's not like she's Whitey Ford and I'm eight years old at Yankee Stadium."

Nate took his eyes off Artie and scanned the room for Karen's arrival. To invite Karen here—well, a couple of his friends had told him that perhaps Karen felt her home was a two-against-one situation, and that it was terribly important that she stop feeling so isolated within her family.

She was probably old enough for an event like this, probably older than he thought. Nate could see it in the way she now tied her hair back a touch severely in emulation of that marvelous young singer, Janis Ian, whom Leonard Bernstein had introduced on one of his Young People's Concerts. He'd watched Karen try piano chords for the first time, trying to sing "Society's Child," and he'd helped her discover the fingering, with a fierce tremor of love that had almost paralyzed him.

His eyes roamed the guests. Lucas Oxley circulated through the crowd, still treating Nate as if he were on retainer, still quoting the laugh riot speech. He wondered how anyone could make a coalition out of black militants like Oxley, Paul Newman, the Harvard-Brooklyn duo of the leonine Norman Mailer and swaggering Jimmy Breslin, doe-eyed hippies led by a siren like Grace Slick, and the white radicals now mouthing off for newsmen at the back of the room.

Nate reminded himself that he was there to meet potential clients and reinforce his growing belief that Vietnam had become another Korea, an Asian war out of control, but this time with a President unable or unwilling to fire his General. The escalation had to stop, as Lindsay had asserted in a wisely moderate statement. Still he was glad there were no Lindsay aides here tonight. His Honor didn't need any more controversy, and Nate was tired of it himself. He no longer mixed with men and women of a certain reasonableness and college attainment, but instead was stuck in a chain of verbal donnybrooks, the drunken parleys of some odd kind of Third Avenue bar, men with scraggly locks and beards full of boisterous aggression just short of chaos.

But these clients were his modus operandi now, and the whole city, maybe even the country, knew it. People recognized him on the street. He was a supporting actor in a cast that included Kunstler, Lefcourt, Weinglass, "The New Defenders," "The Counter-Legals." And because he was civilized and accommodating with the press, *Look* and *Life* left messages for him, seeking more quotes about egregious behavior by some of his clients. One writer from *Look* had even insisted on interviewing him at his home. The rude bastard had crunched one of his photographer's popped flashbulbs on the living room floor, and lit up a Tareyton, whose smell had bothered Karen when she returned from school.

Nate's life was dizzy with possibilities: negotiations for a summer house, glamorous new friends and possible connections. But underneath the hectic allure was a spark of mania, like the shouts of wayward panhandlers on MacDougal Street that had him always watching his back.

Karen entered the room. She had Danny Geller with her; she'd later tell Nate he'd shown up at Gyre and Gimbel and she'd invited him. She had on a short wool knit dress adorned with peace symbols. The men around her noticed, grinned, approved. Perhaps Nate hadn't thought through the consequences of her working at a Village fashion store. Danny was dressed in some sort of black poncho outfit that emphasized his unshaven sallow complexion. He looked shaky. But he had a ready smile as he also attracted some greetings, probably from fans of his band.

As Nate headed over to Karen her eyes shot away from his, frantic with adulation.

"Oh no, I don't believe it! It's Grace Slick! Oh God, Daddy, do you have a pen, I have to get her autograph!"

Nate gave her his pocket pen and she scuttled away. He glanced back at Marcela, who'd managed to entrance a record producer. They were discussing the charms of Miami just as the President of the International Press Club archly rang a small ornamental dinner bell and summoned the group to the meeting.

Artie and Danny took their seats amid the rows of plastic folding chairs slotted into the club's banquet room. Plush divans and settees were shoved against the walls beneath a collection of framed maps and big game trophies: lion, antelope, even warthog. An oddly imperialist setting for David Dellinger, director of the National Mobilization to End the War in Vietnam, to announce an October demonstration to close down the Pentagon and the U.S. war machine.

Artie had the handbill with the list of speakers and he whispered footnotes of information to Danny whenever he could. Danny seemed to be still bummed out by Jimmy Hinton's decision to quit the band, but he thanked Artie repeatedly for filling him in, rising above his weariness with courteous, even devoted attention to the men at the podium. A reverend from the Episcopal Peace Fellowship proclaimed that they would bring the sounds of the joy and affirmation of man to the Pentagon, whose only business was wholesale murder. "Blessed are the peacemakers." Tom Hayden and the SDS officers seemed almost dourly managerial as they laid out their blueprints of protest. Artie's eyes repeatedly drifted to the entrance of the room, but for all his anticipation he still blanched with shock when Pam finally made her appearance in a fur-trimmed jacket and maxi dress, muttering apologies for her lateness to the people in her row of chairs.

As if cued by her entrance, the speeches became more provocative. Jerry Rubin, the march's Project Director, short, stocky, with a Zapata mustache, shouted that he was ready for the Pentagon MP's with everything from sit-ins to ritual theater. They were now in the business of wholesale disruption and widespread dislocation of the American society. And the crowd barely knew how to react when Ed Sanders, his enormous mane of hair spilling over a G.I. surplus jacket, stated that he planned a group exorcism of the Pentagon, after which it would rise fourteen feet into the air. Artie checked out the audience reactions. Dad was poker-faced, Marcela had her hand to her mouth as if to stifle a giggle, but Pam, Danny, and even his sister seemed to hang on every word. The final speaker, Abbie Hoffman, expanded on the theme of the exorcism.

"Hey, when we get rid of a million tons of evil spirits, the fucker will just float."

The crowd laughed with relief, back at the intersection of politics and satire where they were most comfortable, but one German reporter huffily demanded what they hoped to accomplish with such a stunt.

"You mean is it fulla shit? Maybe. But people will see it's just a big ugly building and we humans around it are the ones who are beautiful. It's like if you hand a guy from Con Ed an ugly, grimy flower, and he goes, man that flower's polluted to shit ugly. And he thinks about that. We had one guy at Con Ed clean up his flower, look at it in a whole new groovy way. Adopt it. Think about what he's doing to its family. Mr. Businessman's involved. So in October we get Mr. National Guard into that same groovy frame of mind."

After the plea for donations the crowd mingled and transacted the business of protest, trading small cash donations for buttons or discreetly passing envelopes between jacket pockets. Artie hung back and stared at Pam, who was in rapturous conversation with Paul Newman. He worried that the feverish longings of a whole summer made him potentially ridiculous at any moment. He'd already stammered out a hello to Grace Slick, said how much he loved her songs, and gotten a pleasant smile in return—maybe he'd better call it a night. But Pam spotted him and bounded right over, hugged him as always, cheek to cheek, and said she felt stupid about being late but she'd been photographing a band and couldn't get away. He'd understand, of course. Artie could smell the hash on her breath.

"Such a marvelous idea, this ceremony for the Pentagon!"

"Floating it in the air?"

"Well, it's a symbolic action, Artie."

"That's gonna persuade people to help stop the war?"

He didn't want to criticize her and push her away… shut up, what are you doing?

"The point is to bloody take the battle to Washington!"

"I guess it depends on how many people they get."

"They've got Paul Newman already. They've got his blue eyes!"

No bluer than yours are green…

"He is very married though, isn't he… Well look, Artie, we

simply have to publicize these sorts of events! Some of my friends are thinking of starting a film collective to record the political and cultural scene, show the work at small theaters like the Film Forum. Have you ever shot film?"

"Just a Bell and Howell movie camera. But I could learn."

"Of course you could. Splendid."

This is the way it should be, must be, Pam doling out her enthusiasm to him as they discuss film and politics in a room full of like-minded strangers, with Dad and Karen a short summons away.

"God, it's stuffy in here. I've heard the roof of the club is open. Like to come up with me, Artie?"

Nate was about to call it a night. But Karen and Marcela seemed immersed in a tete-a-tete, and both Artie and a beautiful woman who seemed too old for him were nowhere to be seen. All around him was jaded conversation he was fast developing an allergy to.

"Well, if us over-thirties have lost our souls... another martini... "

"Hey babe, I'm H. Rap Brown and I've got you covered!"

Danny was engrossed in conversation with Grace Slick and her escort. Young royalty in hand-stitched leather. He'd enjoyed the Jefferson Airplane's hit tune, he felt he could hear Broadway in the vocals and a jazz walk in the flying bass. His glance rebounded between Marcela and Grace Slick. "Somebody To Love," Grace had sung. Had she been where he was, but in a different, more luminously assured way of knowing?

Nate went up and introduced himself to her. What wide, dark eyes, black hair, slim, almost girlish patrician loveliness. She could have been John Lindsay's daughter, and in fact, she'd been given a very upper class Manhattan education at Finch College, just a few blocks down Park Avenue. Grace in turn introduced him to bandmate Paul Kantner, who had a blonde stolidity behind his college boy looks that felt somehow reassuring.

"We should get to know Nate. He gets folks like us off."

"Not sure that's my kind of scene, man, but happy to meet you."

"I mean in the lawyer sense, Paul."

"Oh, yeah."

Nate grinned his way through, by now used to the patter of the put-on, the reverse etiquette of interactions with pop royalty.

"So it must be something, being at the center of the new music."

"Am I at the center of it? Too bad for the center, I mean, I don't know what's going to happen from one day to the next."

"Sometimes, from one minute to the next."

Their smoky, ironical voices signaled that the conversation had totally escaped him. He wished her a quick good luck and turned away, and saw Karen gazing with disbelief at the conjunction of her father and the princess of rock. Marcela came to his side and took his arm.

"I leave you ten minutes and you're after a beautiful woman."

"Strictly research, Marcela."

"And what did you find out?"

"I have no idea."

She folded against him, then looked into his eyes with a touch of sadness, as if she contemplated him from a growing distance.

"Are you all right?"

"I think all this people talking is too much. I'm thinking we need a moment away from this crowd, just for the two of us, Nate."

"You're shivering, Pam."

"Don't worry, I love the night air."

She leaned against the parapet and Artie looked past her toward Lexington Avenue, a jostled mob of hotels and stores banked up against the Chrysler Building. He'd always thrilled at city daytime views, muscular expanses of stone and steel cast in gunmetal-grey armor. Now New York was a hierarchy of brightly winking spires, above him a Presidential suite of offices, far below boutiques and restaurants, and rising to meet them the glimmer and the clamor of night traffic like an offering of bells.

Pam leaned forward as if to breathe it all in; the slim arch of her back hung in that spectral glow and she sprang all over again from the cloudy fluid of his dreams.

"You know, this is what I'm starting to miss in my work. The glamour of New York. Not that I'm not totally into documenting the Scene, but it would be lovely to take a Hasselblad camera, use some larger film stock to capture views of this city, get really big clear gorgeous negatives and—"

"Pam, I—I love you."

"What?"

"I'm sorry, I—I mean not in a possessive jealous way or anything like that, it's just—you're beautiful and fantastic and you care so much and—I have so many feelings for you… and… "

She walked over to him as he reined in his babbling and cringed at his own ludicrousness. She stroked his cheek with her cool, soft fingers.

"I know just what you mean. And I have feelings for you too, Artie. We're lucky to live in such a loving time, right? There's a lot of it going around, as you Yanks say."

He knew it from the lilting jocularity in her voice—she was handling him like all the others.

"You must think I'm… really young."

"Well, you are, but age is such a false value, Artie!"

His heart raced. She had a way of tossing off such propositions as if they were laws of physics. She drifted back toward the corner of the roof, and Artie followed her to catch every nuance of every word.

"It's just that I have to make my life sort of smaller now, not more complicated."

"Well, maybe we can take more photos together."

"Exactly, luv! I'm so tired of hearing, my God, why are you doing this when you still have a couple of good years on the runway. Or of course, let me take you away from it all."

"I know how you feel about that, Pam, I totally understand."

She gratefully hugged him again.

"I haven't seen you all summer. If we could just spend more time together…"

"We will, luv, we definitely will. We'll both join this film collective and it will be a smashing adventure."

They headed back to the roof entrance. Nearby a couple embraced and kissed. Artie felt totally brought down. He'd given away his feelings and only a vacuum remained. Some quivers of emotion had escaped from Pam's control, he knew it, but he didn't know how to raise that delicious uncertainty any higher.

He looked more closely at the folds of the amorous woman's dress as they approached the door. It was Marcela's. Suddenly, as the giggles of a flock of arriving couples startled them all, Nate and Marcela broke their clinch and locked eyes with Artie and Pam, and in the midst of the new crowd of night-seekers, Artie saw Danny and Karen. They were holding hands.

There were pleasantly offered greetings, mixed with nervous introductions and crosscurrents of scrutiny, and Pam, shaking hands all around, turned back to Artie and chuckled.

"Well, Artie—you have a very un-hung-up family."

They had ice cream sundaes afterwards at the neighborhood's latest turn-of-the-century-style ice cream parlor, and a cloud of chagrin might have hung over the whole evening, except for Marcela. She took the night over with her story of her escape from Brazil and her arrival in America. And as her lazy vowels and liquid consonants elided into a susurrus of welcome and friendship, Artie also wondered if his erection would subside before he got up from the table.

Later that night, as he watched Dad hug Marcela before he escorted her into a cab, he felt a weird jealous pang he couldn't wish away all mixed up with his memory of Pam slipping away from him beneath the skyline and the stars. Then came another thought he sensed he'd been evading, a dissonance struck off the erotic music that the women trailed behind them that unsettled him even more: why were Danny and Karen holding hands?

If he and Pam had been holding hands… no, he decided,

not after all the years he and Karen and Danny had known each other. Lil' bro. Lil' sis.

Still he was tempted to talk about it the following night with Karen as they watched *The Man From U.N.C.L.E.* together, spies and counterspies in a game with guns that seemed harmless as child's play and not as funny as it used to be. They sat quietly while Aisha lay on her back and with full-throated purrs received belly rubs from each of them.

But at the last moment he chose instead to ask her what she thought of Marcela.

She stared at the tv and yawned, almost like the cat would, to clear her head for paying attention.

"She's nice. She's like those Indian women."

"What?"

"At the World's Fair. With their great stories."

"Oh yeah… "

It was a little challenging to him that she could draw up that memory from that one lunch so long ago.

"Of course they were Indian, she's Brazilian."

"Well, I just meant she's nice, and from another country, and fun to talk to. I mean, yeah, India, Brazil, I know the difference, Artie."

"Yeah… and Marcela might be around a lot longer, don't you think?"

Karen looked down at Aisha. The two exchanged a long moment of mutual, exclusive fascination.

"He's known her almost a year, Artie, and this is the first time she's met us."

"So?"

"It's just weird, that's all."

Her seeming indifference pissed him off, and so he decided to press her on another subject during a commercial.

"Are you studying more?"

"I'm improving my grades. Look, I'm not a robot with the homework like you, Artie, but I'm doing better."

"Yeah, actually a B among the C's. Y'know junior year they'll hit you with all these tests, SAT's, college boards."

"Why do you think I even want to go to college anyway?"

"Of course you want to go to college."

"Why? I hate writing papers, I hate homework. I don't have to worry about the Draft. College is a grade grind."

"You want to just work in clothing stores all your life?"

"Yeah, maybe. Women can run and even own clothing stores. And you can have fun, you meet really cool people. Grace bought a shift in the store. Janis Joplin got some beads."

"That is so dumb. Do you realize how dumb that sounds?"

"Don't you ever think maybe you'd like to just take pictures and shoot film? Just be a photographer and a moviemaker if you really care so much about it? Or is that just with Pamela Huntington?"

"Shut up! God you're so obnoxious, I don't even want to talk to you!"

On the screen Robert Vaughn was sweet-talking an enemy operative in a black leather miniskirt. Aisha's eyes took Artie in briefly, then fixated on the picture tube. Watching the cat, and then Karen's impassive face lit up by the grey glow, he realized Karen had gotten what she wanted. She'd shut down his questioning of her grades, and he'd never even gotten to talk about Danny. My god, could his own sister throw him off too, just like these other women?

But then he realized she'd answered his most important question about Marcela.

"Karen's changing. I can see it in her taste in music."

Marcela drew the curtains on the window, paused, and fingered the pleats struck into relief by the courtyard light.

"She loves 'Society's Child' and the really serious Beatles tunes. But at least we can still sit together and laugh at a song like that Snoopy and The Red Baron."

"She's becoming a young woman."

"Well, I like that she still plays stuff like—what's that silly music hall tune? 'Winchester Cathedral.' She hasn't lost all the little girl in her yet."

"It must be a beautiful thing to see... all her changes."

"It can be tough to keep up with them though. Sometimes I so need a break."

He watched her thighs swish under her skirt, eager as a schoolboy. This fortuitous Saturday, Artie out helping his photographer friend move her studio, Karen away on a sleepover, had been delightfully unexpected. He got up, embraced her hips, kissed the back of her neck.

"God, between the kids and these planned demonstrations— it's so wonderful to get away to Carmine Street."

"This October march, I think it will be dangerous."

"It's normal American dissent."

"In Brazil we had normal dissent too for awhile."

"Marcela, we could never have the military come in like that."

"Oh really? It's getting crazy. Some of these people can't even talk about sex without talking about Vietnam!"

He almost laughed at her remark until he saw the genuine exasperation in her eyes.

"You know, Marcela, you're right. All this talk is getting too rough. Or ridiculous... floating the Pentagon... believe me, I want my clients to be less intemperate with some of their protests."

Marcela's hand moved in front of her face as if some mosquito had stung her lips into a tight little frown.

"This is all becoming a shadow on my life."

"What is, Marcela?"

"The city. The politics. I have to go to the country for awhile."

"We should take a trip to the country. You know, now that you finally met the kids, you should meet the rest of my family up in—"

"To Saratoga Springs, Nate."

Nate felt one of those gut-plummeting shocks he associated with a lying witness in the courtroom.

"Your old boyfriend?"

He got no answer. He tried to bring them to safer ground.

"Marcela, we all need a break from the city sometimes. You can ask the café for a few days off, and we can go to the country and spend some time together with the kids. They're very fond of you."

Marcela seemed to take that almost as an insult.

"Nate, how can that be? This is the first time I've met them. And do you think I want to... to break in on your time with them? Do you think I want to do that? I tried to tell you this before, at the antiwar meeting... I quit from the café."

"Marcela, let's just spend some time away from the city together. You'll see—"

"I just told you I left my job! I... I'm going back to Carlo, Nate."

"Just like that?"

"He knows me. He understands that I... "

"That every so often you take a lover and then discard him?"

He couldn't help the anger that rose to her abandonment of him. What a gross, paltry rejection this was.

"I already offered you help with the restaurant, whatever I can do. Do you want a green card? Is that it?"

She recoiled away from him, and hissed that her status was not threatened and that her friend knew very powerful people. Oh God, Nate thought, he hadn't meant to—

"Please, Nate, don't be this way, after all this time together, this... this is not for people like us."

"But... Marcela, I... like you said, after all this time... how can you just... "

She grasped his hand with a heat rapidly ebbing into the benediction of farewell.

Somehow they got through the final passage of a piteous embrace, a promise to talk later and stay in touch. It was all over in twenty minutes, and now he stood beneath the little sidewalk tree near her brownstone, on a normal afternoon, the shadows of the branches slate hard in the light.

She had said people like us, even as she'd banished him from her private country. The past month had been so easy, his rhythms with her so secure... what had gone wrong? Had he failed to be strong enough for her? He remembered how with Becky he'd tried to do what he could, but still laid a burden on her just by talking, talking about the disputes with the doctors, as if she were a colleague in this effort instead of slipping away from all effort except just to try and bear the pain. Finally she'd said: you'll just have to deal with it, Nate, and I trust you'll do the best you can. Becky had needed John Wayne or Gregory Peck and he could barely be Henry Fonda—and now in some way he'd made the same mistake with Marcela. Abruptly he was disgusted with himself—what could he have done for her, made his past, his children, all the troubles of the city go away? And it was profane even to compare her with Becky... a bargirl from Brazil... *how could he have even trusted this kind of "thing"?*... no, he wasn't about to fall apart, not with the stubborn memory of another woman, always watchful, always calling him home.

Still, women were women, and even if she was a girlfriend—and some of Ted Schomer's friends changed them like socks—she had lain so wonderfully by his side just a week ago...

Women were women, but some were his kind of people. With Marcela it had always been a dream. He'd tried so hard to stay with the reality of that dream that maybe what she said had finally come true: once he'd lost his detachment, he really was like her. She was trusting exile, and Nate, in looking for pleasure in the wake of death, and romance with one who was so different, had trusted an exile's uncertainty.

Nate felt he couldn't take another step. He looked back at the block he had walked, at Marcela's stoop foreshortened into a blur of wrought iron and concrete where two little girls played hopscotch under a nondescript row of shivering trees. There was no excuse for this agonizing fragility he felt now, and no way to deny that he had yielded to it with all his heart.

Pam set a hectic pace as she and Artie sidestepped furniture movers and transported her slide sheets and photo albums and boxes of proofs and negatives quickly to the moving van.

As they hustled her studio's contents into temporary storage, Artie learned about her business split with Nigel. It was all encouraging, especially when she tossed off that while it was always "tempestuous" between them, "that used to be what made it work." Almost twitching with irritability, she mentioned she had to score some grass, but God, I hope it isn't camel shit like last time. Ca-mell shitt. With her still crisp British accent she sounded like a rich woman having to take a dress back to Saks Fifth Avenue.

So many photos, the sheer daunting volume of minutiae in a professional's life. Artie glanced at them whenever he could. There was a pun in her collection "Paradise Trails," for every photo labeled with that title had a wispy edge somewhere, a blur or time-exposed tendril of light, a sublimation into energy on the border of every shot, as if the initial eruption of flames of the burned man at the U.N. had emanated to every corner of her work. When he saw the negatives and prints that had been early attempts at that collage, all her tenacious experiments, he felt closer to her than ever, and it was while he looked over one such print that he jumped at the touch of her hand, light but insistent, on his shoulder.

"Artie, luv, we really must keep slogging along."

But her green eyes archly forgave him. His heart lurched. Under her tie-dyed oversized shirt her breasts danced every time she brought a box to the van. She never wore a bra, and he couldn't help but constantly look at the cleft beneath the ankh peace sign that mirrored his own.

At last her studio was a bare white trapezoid littered with a few boxes. She paced its boundaries sucking on a jay she'd bought on a quick sprint to Washington Square, and then, without a look back at him, extended her hand with regal ease in Artie's general direction.

He plucked the jay from her hand, took a long toke, and saw how gravely she took in the blank space.

"I guess this is pretty sad for you."

"A tad, Artie, just a tad, but you know, one move after

another… our film commune is taking shape, did I tell you? We're calling it Truth 24, after Godard, you know, film is truth at 24 frames per second? We're going to be filming radical events all around the city. You'll join us?"

"Is it something you actually join? I mean, I have schoolwork and classes."

"Oh it won't be like being in a union or having a job or anything like that. But I thought you had some sort of commitment to these things."

"I'll do it. Sure."

She sat down on a box and once again reached out with the jay. Artie sat gingerly next to her and waved it off. He knew now he could sometimes get too high to hear someone properly. Pam gave a little chuckle.

"God, Artie, sometimes I feel like I really exploit you."

Had he reached that mis-hearing point already? No, he didn't think so, and he assured Pam that wasn't true.

"See, I really believe in giving, Artie. We're all here trying to be stars in our own movies and know the truth about our own existence and all that—but without love, it's all shit. Don't think I'd ever not respect you for what you said to me, and you must believe I feel love for you too."

Artie nodded, his mouth dry, the blank walls proclaiming how utterly alone they were with each other.

"But I do feel that there's a barrier between us, and it's just… it's not that you're younger, believe me, it's… actually, I feel you have an old soul."

"An old soul?"

"Yes, with a lot of beauty and wisdom to share, but you can't… let go."

"I can let go. Really, I can let go in… in any number of ways."

"I don't know, Artie."

"Well, you'll get to know me better as we work together."

"Yes, we'll be colleagues, and we should always be able to talk and learn from each other. There's so much you can take from me and there's sure to be something I can take from you."

"And you'll see… I can definitely let go, Pam."

He decided he would have one more toke. He took her hand in his grasp and savored her beautiful skin, which seemed to melt into his until his whole arm tingled.

"I think my fingers are going to burn."

He hastily apologized, tried to take the jay, and dropped it. She produced a roach tweezer from her purse, picked it up, and raised it to his mouth. He sucked it and, lips still pursed, bent forward to kiss her, and he was graced with a languid tickle of her lips before she pulled away.

"You know, Artie, I'm thinking of something we could do to narrow this distance somewhat. I had no idea I'd be in the mood to do this… but the mood is everything, Artie."

"The mood is perfect, Pam."

It sounded idiotic, but the moment begged for a response, especially since the tones of her voice were like foreplay.

"I think we should go back to my apartment, and then… "

She reached into her purse and pulled out a blue tab wrapped in cellophane.

"Do you know what this is, Artie?"

"Oh, of course, it's… it's acid. The blue acid."

"You've never dropped, have you?"

Her eyes burned with joyous anticipation.

"We'll do this. We'll trip together."

"But we're… we're already stoned."

"I know we're stoned, baby, but do you know what this is like?"

She pointed to the door.

"I've looked at this doorknob and watched it revolve and scatter rainbows."

"You mean, it's… like a prism?"

"Well, yes, but I also feel it. The image has weight, it has fire. I've looked at that doorknob for an hour. Or I'm listening to music, maybe Bach, maybe "Penny Lane," and it splits open, you can hear every line in it, strings, trumpets, a celestial orchestra… "

"And you can see it?"

"I can see the harmony of it… I listen to Stravinsky, and… you know, I used to be a ballerina, never professionally, not quite that good, but I danced the *Firebird*… "

"Really?"

"Now I put it on and the drums, the cellos, it's a thunderstorm over the mountains, it's woodwinds that light the edges of clouds, my God, it's a solar system. I saw the Music of the Spheres in Stravinsky. Swear to God, Artie."

She jumped up from the box as if she could cast those visions again all over the stripped bare ceilings and walls.

"It's so marvelous, it catches up all your senses. Think of it, Artie, all your verbal hang-ups gone, all the cultural conditioning swept aside… "

"I think I'll need those until after my college boards."

She laughed, as he'd hoped, but almost dismissively.

"You're funny, Artie, you really are."

"Can't we just get more stoned?"

"Artie, I really want us to be on the same register of consciousness. Think of it this way. Acid is the ultimate cool medium, you see, because when it most seems like chaos you are making all the connections. Do you understand that?"

He felt the need for the most sweeping answer he could dig up.

"Well, Jean-Paul Sartre said we're responsible for everything in our own life just because of our existence… even the war."

"Exactly! So you may have insights into the connections of the whole world. That's the ticket, luv!"

The flags of many nations…

She sat beside him and threw an arm around his shoulder. The box beneath them scraped the floor, and he knew, dizzy as he was, that they literally swayed in rhythm to each other.

"But, Pam… how long is… is the trip?"

"Oh, I don't know, four hours, eight hours, who counts? One doesn't time this out, it's the 'acid test' after all, it's… you said your dad and your sister would be away tonight."

"But what if I'm still tripping when I have to go?"

"Artie, do you think I'd throw you out on your first acid trip?"

She cupped her face in her hands, and her green eyes scored into his.

"I'll be with you, Artie. Everyone needs a ground person the first time to make sure nothing bad happens. We'll talk about photography and film and art and share all the beautiful visions that come into our heads."

"So just… in here?"

"No, God no, this is rather desolate. We'll go to my place, Artie."

Pamela Huntington's apartment. He imagined Persian rugs, silk curtains, honey-colored candles. She leaned so close, her willowy body half-bowed, expectant, a golden naiad offering him water from her cupped hands. He tried to be strong and masculine as he threw his arms around her; he felt instead like he was clinging to a life raft. She let him kiss her again.

"I'm offering a gift, Artie. You don't have to take it. But I'd love to see those pretty eyes of yours grow wide with wonder… if you just take a risk and… move forward."

In just an hour or so he could be lost in her arms, in her bed, his senses drenched with fragrances and images and music, it was all right before him, one lick of that tab away. But he'd heard over and over again that the whole point was a leap into… what? What kind of images? *Loving face in the grey rictus of death.*

What had sent his dad to Mount Sinai Hospital?

"You want to do this, Artie. I know it. You're advanced beyond your years."

She hugged him now, and he recognized that feral, musky smell from the body painting dance floor.

"We can feel very good together."

"Then why can't we be good together without this?"

"Artie, it's just if we're on the same wavelength, luv—"

"We're on the same wavelength now."

"Oh Christ, Artie, we're sitting in a defunct studio, you're getting nervous and I'm wondering where the next gig's coming from! I thought we could take a leap of faith and be free of all this, but of course not. No adventures allowed, right Artie? You just want to smoke some dope and head uptown and be cool, calm and clean clear through by morning."

Artie was so shocked he jumped off the box, and she responded with an accusing stare.

"You don't trust me."

"Of course I trust you, Pam! I just… maybe I don't want to take acid, isn't that doing my own thing?"

"So you don't trust yourself. Of course you're right, Artie, I won't make you do anything you don't want to do."

She took a quick hit off the ragged little roach and flicked it away.

"Go home, then. I won't keep you."

"Oh, I see. Now it's go home. You just wanted to use me as some experiment or something."

"What the hell are you talking about?"

The anguish snapped out of his clouded brain.

"You just use me! It's always a game and you don't care about me, you're always using me! Everything's about you! Even the burned man's about you! Screw you, screw your Truth 24! Like you could ever tell the truth at 24 or 48 or whatever speed!"

"Well fuck you and fuck your uptight bullshit you little schoolboy prick!"

"Take this back! THIS is bullshit! You're for freedom and peace and love but if anyone doesn't do exactly what you say you hate them!"

The ankh peace sign made an awful clatter as it struck the floor. He didn't have time to see if Pam was frozen in anger or amazement. He ran from the studio determined to hide from her how devastated he was.

After a long cold cab ride down Fifth Avenue, the radio droning a Yankee game that the cabbie kept commenting on, perhaps figuring what a young man in a cab alone needed most was baseball talk, Artie braced himself for the emptiness of his apartment, grafted onto the new vacancy of his soul.

When he opened the door he saw the lights on and smelled one of Dad's Chesterfields.

"Hello, son."

It was suddenly a regular night, Dad in his maroon bathrobe smoking and watching the news, motioning with his hand for Artie to lower his voice.

"Karen changed her plans. She's in her room asleep."

Artie took off his coat and settled beside him.

"How did the move go?"

"Oh, it was hard work. But every time I'm with Pam, I—I learn something."

"Good, good… "

His voice was gravely abstracted, a pitch and tenor Artie identified with impending loss. Aisha took the opportunity of the quiet between them to leap up and sink her claws gently into his knees. Artie chucked her under the chin, while nerving himself to ask a question he'd never asked before.

"How was your date with Marcela?"

"I don't think we'll be seeing too much of Marcela anymore."

"Already?"

He desperately wanted to snatch that blurt back, but Dad waved it off with a haunted smile.

"We'd been seeing each other about a year, Artie."

"It wasn't us, was it?"

"No, Artie, not at all. She was very impressed with both of you. It was… a surprise."

He glanced at his dad's fingers on the cigarette. They cradled it so loosely that it seemed the train of smoke might tug the Chesterfield away toward the ceiling.

"Women can be very hard to predict. They can change their minds very quickly."

"I know what you mean."

"Really, Artie?"

He deposited his cigarette in the ashtray, let it burn, and patted Artie's hand with a chuckle that was almost a sigh.

"I'll bet you do. You're getting older, son. I'll bet you do."
He turned back to the tv and reached over to scratch Aisha's ears.
"That's why it's so important... when they choose you. That's when it's special, when they really want to be with you for keeps."
"Dad, I... I'm sure it wasn't your fault or anything."
"It's not that anybody's at fault. But it was more me, Artie. Oh, she ended it, but—well, we were so different, and it just—went as far as it could go. I—I could never take the final step with her, and I think she sensed that. Because you see, no one can ever replace your mother. Never."
The tv segued to the bright, peppy suburban world of a floor wax commercial. They stared at the couple cavorting over their gleaming-just-like-new living room. Artie's hand found Nate's again over their family pet.
"You and Karen—if it weren't for you two, nothing in my life would make any sense."
Last week Dad had been the attorney in the ever-present black coat who had walked him around Columbia, masterfully introducing him to university officials to help contour his early admissions process. Drawing in a web of "business friends" to help Artie along, which made Artie feel grateful but somehow helpless—and Dad's visits to his "lady friend" had ratified the distance of that world.
Now Artie saw a man in a bathrobe who had also tried to find somebody to love. He would never feel closer to his father than on this night.

The Wabbit had his tunnels. Danny and Toby Varner, The Voyage's new lead guitarist, cracked up as Bugs popped his head up in China. Wrong toin at Albekoiky. Ain't no big thing, Bugs, ya ditched Fudd once again, burrowed your way to another universe. Wascally Wabbit.
Danny glanced over at Toby. There was something about his bulbous nose and greedy buckteeth that reminded him of the Wabbit. He played guitar with an impish grin of a magician

fascinating children with his chain of handkerchiefs. Look what I hid in the strings. He prowled the stage with leaps and cock-a-snoots. Albekoiky here we come.

The cartoon ended and it took five minutes until the slant of iridescent light on the metal window frame abated long enough for them to turn off the television. The acid ladder of choices and sensations. There was nothing that failed, within the flux of the trip, to find its own specific gravity, nothing and no one hitched a ride. Every flotsam of thought and action and light and sound and taste could stand clear and brilliant and enfold you in its spell.

Of course that could make it tough to decide even to get up and slap a record on the turntable. Danny was back on acid to dive under the Music again, feel it the way he did once before, now that the Voyage was newborn. Jimmy was not only gone from the band—he was gone. Danny had sweltered beneath the Jazzmobile, because word had gotten around Jimmy had been seen at an Archie Shepp concert and was trying to play those jet-propelled saxophone call-and-response riffs on the guitar. Or that he was in Harlem laying down some funk grooves, so Danny went to see the new electric purveyors of funk-rock-gospel, Sly and the Family Stone. Plenty of young black bloods at the Sly concert, but no Jimmy.

Once Danny started jamming seriously with Toby, he reveled in his new partner's ability to absorb and play all the new acid rock. Danny threw out his old violin phrases and starting putting them back together in more time-bending ways until he was shocking the hell out of himself. He fed the revelations by spinning the heaviest sides they could find. Big Brother's twin guitar supplication of Janis' belly throb of pain with feedback tracers that shed blood red firelight over the killing floor. The cavernous swirl of organ tones and fuzz guitar unleashed by Country Joe and the Fish's Electric Music for the Body and Mind. Quicksilver Messenger Service's guitar leads that dripped like candle wax, Jorma on the Airplane's "DCBA 25" playing like a trail of smoke… the Bent Note, the fullness of it, the shimmer of flight, the melding of surrender and defiance. He and Toby came up with dual runs where the guitar riffs and his glides on the violin were blown into endless purpling vines of sound. Their album-playing sessions always climaxed with the guitarist Danny now listened to more than any other, closest to the violin, closest to a whole orchestra, Jimmy James, back from London with a new name and checked Madras pants, floral shirt with a plunging neckline, goathair cape, a black hat with a purple band, and an interstellar gleam in his eye at all times. They said Clapton was God but Hendrix was a true electric messiah. What an unbelievable blend his Experience was of heavy bottom, thunderous jazz drumming, and Hendrix' amazing incantations of harmonics, bent notes, and overtones; it was as if the guitar had no frets, the motherfucker playing with his axe like a cat with a dying mouse, twisting it, chewing it, tossing it triumphantly in the air. Hendrix was the Music refracted through endless prisms. The guitar a hammer in "Foxy Lady," a deep red heartbeat in "The Wind Cried Mary," a march to an insane chime and its own shriek of higher wavelengths in "Are You Experienced." And what Hendrix celebrated in songs like "Love or Confusion"… nameless colors, heart burning, mind reeling… how could it be anything as mundane as a babe? Hendrix transmuted the vibrating planes and taffy time of acid itself straight to the guitar with those huge hands that splayed the springs until they bled octaves into feedback, and what he romanced was the trip, the cosmic fugitive run, the most intense bombardment of new musical and psychic messages, so lush and so free, to the suck and whomp of backwards cymbals forward march. Are you now or have you ever been experienced? Yes was the only answer, communistically and every other way.

Night crept over the windows and they decided to go out for a concert. It would have to be where there was a friend at the door, since Danny's total funds from his labors with the Voyage these days were some cash in his old Samsonite suitcase. At first it was okay on the avenue, burgers and Orange Julius hit the spot, but then Danny realized he was pushing his luck. The ebony and silver visage of Che Guevara shot its accusing stare at him from a hundred windows. A horde of images to replace the actual revolutionary gunned down in Bolivia, probably by the C.I.A. That's whom many of the freaks said had killed Linda Rae Fitzpatrick and "Groovy" Hutchinson in their apartment, but no, their lives had been beaten out of them by an insane black separatist, the climax of a streak of assaults by fanatics, mental cripples, and meth heads that had laid a whole other layer of bad vibes on the street. A reminder that the hippies and artists and Diggers and flower children were trying to grow utopia in a ghetto.

No the set and setting, as Leary had once put it, were not right at all for this trip. Danny felt the street was an uncoiled snake. Each step took him closer to ingestion. The waiting mouth might be a manhole, a gutter, or even that exposed base of a streetlight whose wiring betrayed a sneak attack by some urban squatter.

"Walk in the center of the street, Toby!"

"You see rats, man?"

No, it was worse. Danny passed a cage emblazoned with institutional white paint, he heard a crackle of electricity and read the warning sign: High Vulture. He leaped away from the huge black wingbeat as it soared over his head, shadow pinions flexing.

"Did you see it? Did you see it take off?"

"What, man?"

"The High Vulture. Look, it's circling… "

"Man we should go back to your place and you should write a song. You're on fire!"

He didn't want to write a song, he wanted to hear one. He passed some kids in the alcove of one of the head shops, Marty and Amy's Buzzeria, and didn't want to stop for a hit of their grass, because there were some sounds up ahead. The door had never looked more like an entrance to a church, a musical sanctuary…

The Velvet Underground was playing the Electric Circus tonight. There wouldn't be the usual mob scene, because the hippies and flower power types despised them. Danny had bought their psychedelic paranoid "Sunday Morning" single and had a long friendly chat with John Cale, whom he'd met at Scepter

Studios. Cale had showed him the mandolin and guitar strings on his rebuilt viola that he bowed to generate his Asian drones. Danny hardly wanted to go that far, but he'd taken advantage of some of what Cale told him when he and Toby had fused their separate wails together with a little downtuning on Toby's part, just as Lou Reed had done with Cale, and had gotten some truly eerie dissonances going.

You could barely see the Velvets on the bandstand. As he'd heard, the gorgeous living sculpture that was Nico was gone. That was a disappointment, but what was weirder was how Reed, Cale and Yule hung in the back. Shades hooded Lou's lizard eyes as he hit some bee buzz chromatic runs with his guitar over tom tom's and sirening viola, and then it stopped in an instant.

A slow chant to "Heroin" resumed...

The way they did that, so together, then changed to that dirge beat... like he and Jimmy had done on "I Don't Want This Life" but fuck it, better... he let the song's gritty mood swings speak to his darkness and bring him down to earth. He loved Reed's jaundiced tone, his sadness leavened with "I don't give a shit" that extended to the sound of the band. But in the back of Danny's brain crawled a growing dread and a bizarre mental counterpoint between the Velvets and his own new tunes, "Cruel Nights" and "Nothing From Nothing," filled with violin and guitar feedback and LaGrange's tintinnabulations of ouds and bells. Was his stuff anywhere near as together as the Velvets' paeans to street ghoul women and New York night vision? "White Light, White Heat," some old blues gone raw and thick and chunky and craggy and witty, so much what he hadn't quite pulled off.

Hey Danny boy, what are you doin' downtown? I'm a sponge, that's all, I strummed my folk and danced and sang my operetta, I went on a musical scavenger hunt, assembled a big pile of toys and shook it and it didn't mix. Nothing. "Nothing From Nothing."

The Velvets sank into "Venus In Furs." Danny's eyes adjusted to the bandstand framed in globular red wall crawl lights. The coarse jackstraws of humanity beneath the band, the cowboys and the addicts, acknowledged their randomness with daffy wisdom as they scrounged for advantage and pleasure. The violin mewed, the guitar chanted, and Reed stepped forward as black-and-white slides of his image and those of Warhol's superstars, pools of film amid the bolus of glimmering red, orbited and flickered like eyelids. A couple did a slow whip dance around the band. Black wings above the dives rendered simple and soaring. It all seemed such a purer distillation of what he'd been going for in his new songs, what he was coming to know about rituals of degradation amid the search for beauty and love. The song seemed to suck all the air out of his brain.

And then he knew... he KNEW... that the street had swallowed him. He hadn't taken anything from Lou Reed. Lou was the mouth, the High Vulture, and it was Danny's thoughts that were the prey. The red lights adhered to his skin and gnawed right down to his blood.

"Get out of my head, Lou!"

He was met by several bemused stares. Toby looked around like he had gotten the joke and was surprised the others weren't laughing. Danny broke free of all of them and headed past the whip dancers' slow gavotte right toward the bandstand.

"You can't have my thoughts! You can't have my music, fucker! Get out of my head! Stop it!"

Lou Reed's shades turned toward him, flickering with strobes, the barest acknowledgment—and then the big guys were on him in a flash, as a forearm went to his Adam's apple. Danny's feet kicked but he could no longer stop the ground. The crowd as it swept by looked on with amazement—just how fucked up do you have to be to be thrown out of a Velvets show?—and then Danny was down on his knees on the ice cold stairs.

"Danny, what the fuck's that about? We'll be non-gratis here now!"

"I've got to get away from the street, Toby!"

"Oh man, your head is in a real bad space... "

Toby bought them a fifth of Southern Comfort on the way home. They played *Fresh Cream* while Danny knocked back the booze. Toby tried to turn on the television but Danny saw a black suction warp in the glass as the electron bar widened out on the screen, and he begged Toby to turn it off.

Toby got him on the phone with the L.S.D. Line out of Chicago. The friendly baritone voice was unfazed as Danny told him about how hard it was to hold on to himself, to maintain the armor of his skin against everything that was trying to steal his thoughts away. The important thing to remember, the counselor told Danny, was that it was all within him. Nothing was coming from the outside to take him over. None of the good people around him would threaten him in any way. It was all signposts from the spirit. Hey, we all have our bummers, and sometimes they're trying to tell us something, and even the bad trips don't want us to have a bad end, so it'll all work out. Stay on the line, bro, I'm with you, Toby's with you, and that whole groovy scene in New York has been through this and is on your side.

Eventually he passed out with the phone in his hand. The morning sun when he blinked his eyes open seemed a heavy blanket he could barely throw off. Murmuring from across the street was the sultry croon of Bobbie Gentry. "Ode To Billie Joe." Number One on the top 40, straight from the heartland, tragic and sane. He crashed again, and at one o'clock the country guitar was much closer, somewhere outside his bedroom wall in the lobby. The reedy, slightly cracked voice gnawed at his memory.

Toby poked his head in, cheerful as always.

"You back? You okay? Wanna hear the new Dylan?"

"The new Dylan?"

Since the news had come that the Triumph motorbike Dylan rode had thrown him, had thrown him hard, the talk at concerts now wasn't "will Dylan show up" as "will he ever play again?" Is he a vegetable dying in Woodstock somewhere?

Donald, their neighbor, welcomed them to his bare Japanese-style pad, where the windowsill sprouted green traceries of marijuana under a purple grow light, the shades drawn to ward off the fuzz. They passed around his giant hookah of a water pipe and listened to *John Wesley Harding*, an album as strange as the winter-garbed forest dwellers that flanked Dylan on the cover and dark as the trees that gouged the white sky. In response to everyone else's communion with electronic phantasms, and maybe his own shucking and jiving and flight from fans and garbage scroungers that ended in a crash, Dylan was once again the honest outlaw with his guitar and harmonica around his neck, like the black troubadours in the Depression, with music utterly austere, spare, hammered out on the forge in the shed from basic folk, country, and blues. Out of his mysterious recovery period he'd conjured up a blend of desert boots and incense, cracked travelers, hobo drifters and outlaws, with so much left out of the music it was like a vanishing dream.

The album made Danny think back to Lenny and Dave and how he'd wanted to write music the lost patrol could embrace—and now, all through Vietnam, in every hooch and LZ, men trapped in the cowboy hat Dylan had borrowed, walking the perimeter and finding no line to cross or even trace, played his broken etched melodies and worn, fragile poetry over and over. The album's quiet melted away Hendrix and the Doors and a sliver of the Voyage right off the radios and tapedecks.

You want some SOMETHING to see, to target, some certainty to justify yourself, but you get only deep shadows and heat mirages, jungle and dust. The wind howls, fatal riders approach, and all you have is what everybody has, all you can do is suffer and refuse to judge…

Danny and Toby ventured outside, squinting even in shades into the chill leaf-beating blast of the first windy autumn day, and bought the album and played it straight through. Danny thought about it for hours—yes, Bobby D, I should never be where I do not belong. But with my music and my thoughts constantly moving without rest, how can I be anywhere else?

"You wouldn't believe it, Dorothy. I've got clients coming back shellshocked, stitches in their heads…"

"After that photo of the girl putting flowers in the National Guard's rifles?"

"Well, around the Pentagon, they beat the hell out of the poor kids."

Dorothy flicked the ash from her cigarette and leveled a subtly mocking glance at Nate.

"Y'know, Nate, it seems like you're defending these poor kids' right to get themselves in a lot of trouble, and driving yourself crazy doing it."

"They do have rights, Dot, and they do need representation."

"A couple of years ago, maybe they couldn't get a fair shake, but now they're all over the papers. You change your practice, they'll find skads of other lawyers."

"Well, that gets to the other point, which my senior partner never fails to mention: it's a well-off practice. You're not becoming a little conservative, are you?"

The question went unanswered, her cigarette arm immobile by the ashtray, the plume of smoke hovering above her head. He could understand her joining the throng of his friends bristling at news stories like H. Rap Brown calling urban riots "dress rehearsals for the Revolution," while in Ocean-Hill Brownsville parents had dropped ballots into taped shoe boxes, almost as if New York were a Third World country, to choose Rhody McCoy, a known black militant, as unit administrator for new local school board. So Nate assured her that he was still monitoring the Lindsay administration, where he felt his real future lay, and had gained confidence from how Lindsay, even after being shaken by the resignation of Deputy Mayor Bob Price, had loosened up the bureaucracy, and made a dent in problems in housing, air pollution, and the parks.

"Of course, Nate. He's Batman."

Dorothy coolly stubbed out her cigarette.

"It's over, isn't it?"

"How can you tell?"

"We're back at a steakhouse. Not Szabo's Continental Cuisine."

That was Dorothy's way: she never raised her voice, never grew petulant, just substituted the implication that he'd let her down by insulting her intelligence. Nate managed to sputter out that yes, it was over, for he'd been at Café Curacao twice and learned Marcela was indeed gone—and even as he told Dorothy that, he realized that the word "twice" was not the best way to grant a dignified finality to the separation. Now it was Nate's turn to retreat behind cigarette smoke.

"That's the problem with sophisticated love, Nate. It doesn't stick."

This was the moment he'd earned, the steely assessment of his ultimate unworthiness. As he tried to chew a suddenly dry piece of Bundt cake, he felt more than ever that he'd acted foolishly toward her and, by extension, both their families. But Dorothy instantly relented with a cozy smile.

"For Pete's sake, it's okay, we're still friends, and you'll always have me in your corner. Once a guidance counselor... "

Nate chuckled, perched his cigarette on the ashtray, and accepted their truce.

"So... how's your social life, Dorothy?"

"I'm seeing a guy on a kind of trial basis. A Park Avenue doctor. Dollink, such a deal. But look, Nate, I have something to tell you, the point of our little teatime, actually... "

She handed him a note handwritten on a Doctor Morris' stationery, a medical excuse, stating Nina Kempster had missed a day in school because of migraines.

"I had no idea your daughter had migraines. I'm sorry to hear it."

"Don't worry, she doesn't. What she had was some of Dr. Morris' stationery. The guidance counselor there finally got concerned enough to call me about all her headaches."

Nate let the implications sink in. Karen had been to the doctor's for the flu the past spring.

"Here's the part that you're really not going to like, Nate. I don't feel very proud about this, but I checked her chest of drawers. She had money there, far too much money. Then I checked her coat pocket."

The cat suddenly caromed past Artie's door as she sucked up Dad and Karen's latest shouting match into escape velocity, and finally his room was pierced by the cry that pulled him out of his chair.

"Don't you realize you could be arrested?"

He hustled out to observe the standoff in the living room. When he saw Karen fiercely hunkered down in a corner of the couch, he was shocked by her appearance. She was dressed in a miniskirt and what looked like a petticoat under a serape, her eyes ringed so black it look like she'd been slugged there. When Artie had first seen it he'd cracked a joke about raccoon eyes and she'd tartly responded it was kohl, k-o-h-l, and all the models were wearing it. But none of her other friends looked like gypsy waifs from the street.

"And then you go out looking like that and try to sell it?"

"Sell what? What are you talking about, you think I'm some teen prostitute?"

"No of course not! I'm talking about you and Nina and those new friends of yours selling drugs!"

"New friends? What's wrong with new friends? You have new friends all the time! Who's going to replace Marcela?"

It was seeing Dad so beaten, clinging so hard to the sanctity of their family, which impelled Artie to join the argument.

"Karen, did you sell drugs with your new friends?"

Artie instantly regretted his words as Karen turned on him with wounded fury.

"I'd never sell drugs! Maybe I tried grass, okay, but so did you, Artie, so's everybody!"

Now Artie truly regretted leaving his room as he faced his dad's outraged question.

"Is that true? Do you smoke marijuana also?"

"It's just… it's just around."

"Just around? You're both lying to me? I'll talk to you later, Artie. Now leave us alone."

No, he thought, I shouldn't do that, but Artie still backed obediently away, stopping just at the edge of his door so he could peek into the living room.

"Did you think I was that stupid, Karen? That I wouldn't find out you were constantly faking absences from school? Or did you think I wouldn't care?"

"I don't know. Do you? Or is it just embarrassing to you?"

"Did you really think you could keep bringing this into our home?"

It was almost funny to see his dad gingerly holding a roach between his fingers.

"Where did you find that? Did you find that in my coat? Did you go INTO THE CLOSET?"

The full-blown screech froze Artie in his tracks, and he barely had time to jump out of Karen's way as she fled to her room.

"Fuck you! You're an asshole! Get away from me!"

Dad was chasing her and Artie saw Karen recoil on her bed, knees braced against her chest, before Dad burst into the room.

"How dare you talk to your father like that? How DARE YOU!—"

"Get out of my room!"

"Your room? This is my apartment! I work and slave for it every day with endless clients! Do you have any idea what sacrifices I make for you kids? Do you have any idea how sick this is making me?"

As if three years hadn't passed, Artie once again hovered, listened to the fitful cadence of his dad's breath, helplessly waiting for the gasp and the thump and the long-feared moment that would make him the *man of the house* forever.

"Go away and work! You like your work! Don't sacrifice for me. Sacrifice for Artie or someone you care about!"

She was sobbing now and it broke the awful momentum. Dad couldn't restrain the quaver in his voice.

"Oh, Karey, Marcela's gone, and… and how can you say I… I don't care more about Artie. I love you both… maybe I love you more… "

That's good, Artie thought, that's the way to calm her down…

"But you're using and selling marijuana and that's got to stop!"

"I'm not selling it. If you love me, why don't you believe me?"

"Enough's enough, you're going to be home every weekend from now on, or you can go see Nina but only when Mrs. Kempster's there."

"Why don't you call her Dorothy? Or is she just Mrs. Kempster now because you fucked Marcela!"

"How DARE you use that language—"

Karen screamed she'd never listen to him again, and as Artie finally charged into the room, Karen took one of her books and threw it at Dad, hitting him on the leg, and Dad grabbed the nearest soft object at hand, a tissue box. Artie knew that this couldn't go on another moment. He stepped between them just as Dad, at his wits' end, meaning to throw the Kleenex box only out of frustration, smacked Artie in the head.

They both stopped and looked down at the dented box. Tissues scattered to the floor. It all would've been ludicrous except for Artie's broken glasses frame, which would have to be fixed, and the horror in Karen's stare.

"I'm gonna do my homework," Artie muttered. "You two can get back to killing each other."

Artie stumbled out of the room, on a trail of Dad's feeble apologies, but somehow he couldn't shut the door on his family this time, and so he heard Karen's footfall, light as Aisha's, as she slipped by. By the time they both realized what was happening Karen had her coat from the closet and was running out the front door. Artie tried to catch up but the hallway was empty. The elevator, usually so slow, had swallowed her up right away. He hurtled down the rear service stairs and sprinted to the lobby, but there was no doorman and no Karen. The street was empty, and he was about to check the basement when he heard Dad cry from the window above, heedless of any eavesdropping neighbor, that she'd gotten a cab.

She's really gone.

With Mayor Lindsay began on Channel 5 at 10:30. There was His Honor, dapper as ever, chatting about the ongoing school decentralization plan with MacGeorge Bundy of the Ford Foundation, whom he kept referring to as "Mac." He also addressed himself in the most congenial possible tones to Joe, Mary and Calvin as they called in with ever more venomous questions. Lindsay looked so uncomfortable trying to let his hair down and be palsy-walsy with random citizens on such a volatile issue. When is one of these callers finally going to scream on the air about blacks taking over the schools? What did John hope to accomplish with this? How could David Garth, big time media advisor, let this happen?

How could Nate even think about this with his daughter lost somewhere in the city? He told himself she'd been out before. She was basically a sensible girl. He'd notified the local precinct, barely able to keep an even timbre in his voice, then Dorothy, then that clothing store owner Eleanor—whom he swore he would have locked up if he found out she'd given Karen dope—then a couple of Karen's other friends' folks as well, just let me know if she drops by, diplomatic and judicious as possible, receiving sympathy and support as he bit down on the slow, acrid revelation of a family catastrophe.

Maybe Karen was right, maybe he really felt humiliated. Maybe he'd absconded so far from fatherly responsibilities with the work he believed was his justification and the paramour he felt was his well-earned bliss that his only genuine emotion was shame at being caught in the act of failure. How could he have let Karen shrink from him in her anguish, how could he have reached for that tissue box, when all he'd wanted to do was hold her, like he had with Becky in their few serious arguments? But perhaps that was because, just like with Becky, he felt he was not being truly respected. *When he'd threatened to leave Schomer, begged her to consider a move to Sag Harbor, he'd known she'd just wait him out, wait for his reasonableness, his weakness…*

He rigorously censored such thoughts of Becky. The holiday season was doing it to them worse than ever. This year it had gone beyond haphazard moments of shared gloom, spats over nothing, and Karen's determination to resuscitate old festivities in a month that mixed the tinsel and lights of Christmas with the sorrow of the Yahrzeit and the Mourner's Kaddish. This year the happiest time in America had risen up and torn them apart. He and Artie could only watch the endlessly caroling commercials while they waited for the phone to ring.

"I felt like I was gonna be sick. I practically puked in the cab. I don't want to throw up, I know I shouldn't be doing this but it really helps, y'know?"

Karen took a deep drag on the joint and huddled closer to the orange warmth of the space heater.

"He just won't believe me."

She talked about how she and Nina and the others had been hanging out by Gyre and Gimbel that night along with their new friend of the evening, Beth, a tough-talking girl from Yonkers in a torn off-the-shoulder dancer's V-neck and seam-splitting jeans. When the studley guy came along they all flocked together, shedding giggles. In his Cossack shirt with his blond bangs he had the perfect Ilya Kuriakin look.

"What a nice little trio of terpers you are!"

It was exciting to flirt with him and dope talk was a part of it, but when Beth suggested they sell him their stash so they could truck around with him, a door slammed in Karen's head.

"I told them no, that's stupid, that's wrong, and they thought I was being so goody-two-shoes or something."

When she'd refused to go along with her friends she'd had a brief memory of Mom in her hospital bed, propped up on her pillow, defying a surge of pain to help Karen with her multiplication table. Karen was also flexing a muscle in her mind, a tense levelheadedness that she was beginning to rely on.

"And it was awful after that. Nina went with Beth. I didn't want to go back home and have Dad ask me what happened. Like he'd ever get into my feelings anyhow. What an event that would be. He'd just say that I probably had schoolwork to catch up on, go to my room. Eleanor was still in the store, she served me cookies and tea and I could hang out and go home late enough so

Dad would just figure we called the sleepover off. Why did I even bother to fight with my friends? I should've just gone and taken my chances. I'm always guilty with Dad, always guilty, guilty. But it would be stupid to go off with that guy. He could be a real creep."

"He could be a narc."

"Exactly. They were crazy. I mean… I'm worried the smoking is making us all crazy."

The space heater had the glow of a jack-o-lantern, and Danny's was the grinning face on the pumpkin as he plucked the joint from her hand.

"You know what's a little crazy? Not bad crazy, but a little crazy? At fifteen years plus you shouldn't even be worrying about that, so maybe you are smoking a little too much."

"I'm not sure I can stop. I mean, it kind of just makes me tired half the time, like I don't want to do anything, but it seems such a part of me now."

"Oh, you can stop. I stopped acid again—well, mostly—when I realized it was screwing me up and eating too much of my life up… and besides I gotta stay in college to avoid getting shot for awhile."

"School is stupid. I just want to be out with friends and do beautiful things in the world before war and government destroy it. No really. What's the point of learning to be a part of America anyway? I don't like anything now except drawing things and clothes… unless I'm stoned, and then sometimes I still don't like anything anyhow. Sometimes I wonder if I'm still okay."

"Can you tell when you're stoned and when you're unstoned?"

"Sure."

"Well, you're fine."

She loved the way he eased her fears, that casual affection, his hooked nose like a clown's beak in the updrafted aura of the space heater. She loved his laughing eyes in the smoke.

"You're the birdman, Danny, you know that?"

"Uh-huh. Flying solo and trying to stay airborne. Let's get you home. I bet your dad's scared shitless, and he's one of the most righteous guys I know."

"Yeah, he really trusts me. Yeah, sure. You know something, Danny? When I say he never talks to me… he never even told me mom was dying? I never even could say goodbye. I didn't even know."

She bit down on her knuckles, as the urge to cry convulsed into shudders that banished all the heat in the room.

"Maybe that's what your mom wanted. Hey, maybe your dad listened to her about that. Maybe she just wanted you to be a little girl for awhile longer, and not be thinking about her but about yourself, so you could just be you and she could enjoy that as long as she could."

Karen wept, as she now realized she always could in Danny's presence. *At his concert she'd watched him at the center of that light show that was like blood cells on fire and felt him sing to every part of herself that Dad and Artie had exiled, the part that looked over her shoulder at the terrible threats from unseen machines, the part that craved some other landscape, some forest stream from her childhood to bathe in, the touch of a lost hand that offered nothing and withdrew nothing, that was just entirely there in the fullness of a caress…*

She struggled to compose herself.

"I'm not a little girl anymore."

"Very true. But we all have to report sometime."

Nate waited under the canopy with the doorman until Karen showed up, not having any idea that Danny would insist on personally escorting her back to the apartment. She glanced miserably at him, and Nate realized that was all the apology he was going to get that evening. It was Danny who seemed more contrite.

"Hi, Mr. Kovacs, I thought I'd better bring Karen home. I'm sorry you had such a bad night and all."

"I'm very glad you did, Danny. Thank you. What did the cab cost?"

"Oh, it's okay. She'll be fine now. She's calmed down."

Nate paid him anyway, then looked the boy over, his hands

shoved in his pockets, stiffly braced against the cold, underdressed and scrawnier and more sallow than he'd ever seen him. He knew he would have to relay to Bruce his impressions of his son.

"Danny, are you all right?"

"I'm fine, just a little cold. Haven't been out much lately, except to classes and to play and record. The album's coming out early next year. I'm just a music machine."

"Well you take care of yourself and… eat well, get some rest."

"Thanks, Mr. Kovacs. Say hi to Artie for me."

They shook hands and he rushed away like you might run without an umbrella in a nasty rain.

Karen went to bed quickly and uneventfully. Artie went out to get cigarettes for him, took too long and spiked Nate's worry, but he was in no mood to scold him. He had his smoke soon after Artie got back and went to bed, kept up for hours by cycles of terror and gratitude, and then a fearful wonder that a kid who he'd always felt was vaguely disruptive, and who now lived at the axis of a culture he was slowly coming to detest, had been the one to bring his daughter back to him, and had done it as gently and effortlessly as if a childhood game had ended, and everyone knew it was time for all the families to go home again.

Watching from the window, Artie had finally convinced himself that Karen had sought refuge exactly where he would have, that there was nothing wrong, nothing out of place. But he desperately needed some air.

He jumped at the chance to head down to the all-night drugstore and buy Dad's cigarettes—not that he would ever smoke tobacco, but he always relished how the simple act of picking up the carton from the druggist, who knew he was Nate's son, made him feel about three years older. He would bring the cigarettes back, everything would be fine.

But the insanity of adhering to that routine on a night like this drove him to the first phone booth he saw.

"My family's been really bringing me down."

"Well, that's what they're there for, luv."

Pam's lighthearted tone gave him hope.

"Pam, I'm so sorry for what I said. I just freaked out, I guess. I just feel so bad, and I'm so sorry."

"I should apologize, Artie. I was beastly to you. It was my fault... I can be that way sometimes, and it bloody sucks. So... you'll be at Truth 24's first meeting?"

"Sure."

"It'll be marvelous! For the price of a few subway tokens, we'll see history made every week, we'll film it all happening! You know, Artie, everything brings us down except our work."

Our work. Artie rushed to the corner of Park Avenue. He looked toward the old Grand Central Building rising against the hive of lights of the new Pan Am skyscraper, a superimposition that hinted at the migration of thousands of planners and workers and creators to the next level, the next highest point on Park Avenue in Manhattan, the next leap upward of New York City.

The way film had been cut to Simon and Garfunkel songs in *The Graduate*... movies could bring music to his photography, and he could ride that music to the next leap of his own new world. It would never be the same between him and Pam. He couldn't even imagine how he'd get the ankh peace symbol back. But instead she would give the city back to him, the Park and the streets, the glamour and the action, and beneath that rhythm his family would recede into the background, and become at last a passing shadow on the picture.

Now he really felt the loneliness, and it wasn't because Martha was away for a couple of nights. Danny was grateful at first she'd come back to him, but after the mechanism of seduction, oiled by one sweaty glide after another, he felt he was somehow losing himself too much, becoming permeable to her—as if he could measure the layer of skin cells that sloughed off every time they made it. He'd cleaned and rearranged the furniture several times so that once she was gone she was gone.

But Karen, with her pain held between them, that was welcome resistance. And when he helped take that pain away without joining her any further it confirmed him in himself, so he could give that self back to her with all his heart, performing his most honest music for an audience of one…

"Bullshit, Danbo. You want to fuck her too but you can't."

He whirled around but of course no one was there, just a pale trace of a bearded visage in a mirror, gone as quickly as a floater in your eye. Now his thoughts would race and soon he and Ed would be having one of their wrong-speed tapedeck arguments. After the last acid trip he'd just refused to leave. Too bad he wasn't Mr. Mxyzptlk and Danny couldn't trick him, like Superman would, into saying his name backwards so he could vanish back into the Fifth Dimension. How the fuck did you do that anyway? It would be hard enough with a guy named Steve or Harry, let alone Mxyzptlk, it would work with Bob, of course, well maybe if Ed said "Deh" or something. But no, this was crazy.

Strange days have tracked me down.

Well, when you're a hobo voyager, sometimes you pick up unwanted guests in the boxcars. Ed's mainly in the Phantom Zone these days, just a voice to debate until he backs off and it's time to grab some sleep. It reminded Danny of having an imaginary friend when he was little, and Ed sometimes had his good points. Or maybe by now it was like being a part of an old married couple, since he felt that Ed, though he'd only appeared this year, had known him forever.

Chapter 6
FLASH FRAMES

"Yeah, my dad told me about Randall. He passed the word."
"Why didn't you listen to him, Danny?"
" It wasn't Randall's fault."
"It wasn't Randall's fault? Then whose fault was it? Whose fault was it, Danny? Was it yours?"
Danny croaked out his weird, self-slicing laughter.
"It was nobody's, man. Nobody's. The group got together and— on the street what you decide, what you create, it can come back at you in a whole new way. Guess that's why they call it a revolution."

Changing film in the dark for years, Artie was used to at least seeing the penumbra of his fingers as he popped rolls of Ektachrome into his Nikon, or slipped negatives onto a film tank in the darkroom. This was as if his hands were in a burrow scratched and tickled by some creature ready to spring. Seated on a pile of paint cans in a walk-in closet in a Soho loft, he loaded sixteen-millimeter film into an Arri camera with a black changing bag up to his elbows. He worked only by touch as he threaded the film past the wheels and gates of the camera magazine. While Truth 24 continued its meeting he practiced loading the film over and over so that he would never fuck up in the middle of some big event—film jumping a sprocket, magazine jamming as the action went down, hundreds of dollars in scarce raw stock budget funds down the toilet.

He had plenty of time as the group argued just what it meant to create "an authentic people's film program of information and liberation."

"You're in the streets, after the essence of reality. Cut through the bourgeois bullshit!"

"And you have to perceive it into being."

"Yeah, shoot it without first bringing down in your mind what it is…"

They agreed to make two films a month and exhibit them not just in New York but Boston and New Haven. Create a "cinema of resistance" on the eastern seaboard. Truth 24 was Pam, Artie, Bill Lofton, and maybe fifteen other people, but they quickly divided up into committees: the anti-Vietnam committee, the workers' committee, the women's committee, and the music committee, which everyone signed on to as it became known as the sex, drugs and rock-and-roll committee.

Over the next two weeks Artie learned how to shoot with the two blimped Arris, the Éclair, and the hand-cranked Bolex. But mainly he was responsible for the Nagra tape recorder. They weren't quite ready to give their youngest and newest volunteer a camera—except to load the magazine in the changing bag.

To film in New York was to get very cold. And twenty-eight degrees became a lot colder after two or three hours holding a boom mike, adjusting a tape recorder, or loading film. Gloves could only thaw his fingers so far and it took him painful extra minutes to get the ribbon of film through the teeth of the camera magazine's maze, freezing his ass off scrunched beneath a stoop so he could capture some protection against stray sunlight. But as the crew discussed and re-discussed the purpose of every shot—once again, plenty of time.

Bill Lofton's film was about doctors going to the slums of Avenue B to meet with poor Puerto Ricans and help them secure basic health care. They were pleasant, determined, articulate men who made the footage almost suitable for network news—just like Lofton himself, with his rawboned Yankee hippie charisma and a buckskin jacket with fringes almost as long as the film strips on the editing bins. Artie kept stealing glances from beneath stoops and from the tape recorder to fume at Pam and Lofton's interplay behind the camera.

After the filming he headed for Gyre and Gimbel to buy Karen the scarf she wanted for Christmas. Eleanor told him how much she missed Karen and insisted he take the scarf free of charge. He rushed over to Geller Records to get *Their Satanic Majesties Request*, knowing Mr. Geller would let him have the record at the lowest possible price. The cover featured the Stones in a cheesy 3D picture dolled up in wizard's robes and framed in a motif of marijuana fumes one critic said they were running on. Yeah, maybe it was a rip-off of the Beatles, but the pounding riffs he'd heard on the radio, layered with tribal pipes, belled percussion and fanfares of brass and piano, promised as much of a banquet of sounds as "Strawberry Fields." Karen would buy him *Magical Mystery Tour* (Beatles plus Stones equaled Christmas). Dad had consented to give him a new light meter to replace the one Aisha had swatted down from his cabinet, which Artie purchased himself and Karen wrapped to sustain the ritual of a family holiday.

Winter was busy. Trips to Bookmasters to sneak looks at paperbacks by Regis Debray, Frantz Fanon and Herbert Marcuse so he could understand the jargon at Truth 24. Endless sex movies: the one about "the hippie revolution" featuring a strawberry blonde named Today Malone, or *Here We Go Round The Mulberry Bush*, where Judy Geeson took off her shirt and Artie almost choked. Films that needed no more advertising than the lubricious purr of the actresses' names—Joanna Shimkus, Mireille Darc, Anna Karina and Diane Cilento—and that incidentally introduced him to the cinema of Godard.

And *Romeo and Juliet*, where Olivia Hussey's breasts overflowed her gown and Artie feverishly speculated that maybe, just maybe, Truth 24 connections could lead to him and the actress actually meeting, perhaps at a movie publicity session, where he could introduce himself as a New York independent filmmaker.

That he was in the orbit of even the fantasy of such an encounter made him the envy of his schoolmates, and the combination of film and political activity, plus solid scores on his Boards, impressed his Columbia interviewer, who added with a kind of jocular desperation that anyone who still respected Robert's Rules of Order was welcome there.

His day at Columbia was a triumph, and the graceful statue of Alexander Hamilton seemed to lead Artie through the snowdrifts to his place in the University.

That weekend a draft resister took sanctuary with his supporters on the altar of the Washington Square United Methodist Church. The authorities arrived and threw the film crew out. But the pastor refused to close the church doors.

"I need height!"

Pam clambered onto the banister of the stairs and managed to balance herself, camera in hand, before several bystanders clutched her feet and steadied her. She held the Éclair above her head toward the open church door to shoot over the onlookers in the church. She rotated its angled eyepiece to look up through it, and stood straight as a ballerina to film the action as the cops forced their way across prone bodies over to the altar, and extracted the resister from the nest of all his comrades.

Somehow Pam on camera and Ernie on the boom mike held their positions for half an hour; Artie would have relieved them but they told him to stick with the Nagra and ride the levels on the sound echoing off the church walls. When the cops hauled the young man out, eyes closed and totally limp, his body disappeared from Artie's view behind the crowd, but as his back and the back of his head thumped against the concrete Artie heard a whispered mumbling. He turned the volume up on the Nagra and deciphered the words… a prayer… as the resister's captive body came once more into view on the way to prison. Artie saw he had glasses just like his.

In his heaviest coat and hat, Artie started to shiver and couldn't stop.

With anti-Draft protests in New York it was theoretically possible to establish well-regulated, tranquil defiance of the laws of the United States.

The police and the Administration all knew the players. Izzy, Nate and the other lawyers went through familiar paces as, on behalf of the Fifth Avenue Peace Parade Committee, the

National Student Mobilization Committee, and The Resistance, they negotiated the arena of the protests of Stop The Draft Week. The perimeter of the Army Induction Center at Whitehall Street would be legal, the steps would be declared off limits. One need only place a foot on the bottom stair to be arrested.

You could stage manage the march routes, the placement of police, the access and exit lanes, all part of the prep work of what Sid Davidoff called running the revolution.

Stop the Draft Week went as planned for about eight hours.

Eighty-six young men turned in their draft cards at St. John The Evangelist, risking five years in prison. Two thousand more demonstrators massed at Whitehall. The police guided Dr. Spock through sawhorses to the icy steps and then arrested him quickly at his request so that he wouldn't catch cold.

While Spock, Susan Sontag, and Ginsberg with his flowing orange scarf and finger cymbals, were being quietly detained, other groups convened on Peter Minuit Plaza and slowly assembled to face arrest in a predawn chill beneath the hooting seagulls…

… and no one knew why a police van charged, the cops flushed them into a panic. Manhandled them as they were dragged into paddy wagons. You could feel it curdling in the rancor of the cops and the workers in Lower Manhattan. Fun City breeding antibodies to itself.

The next day a younger, scruffier contingent tried to block the draft induction center's entrances and persuade draftees to join them. Construction workers lay in wait.

Hey, longhair faggot, fuckin' Commie.

The police ran the kids to the sidewalk and the hardhats attacked. Barry Gotteherer, trying to save one couple from being beaten, took the blows himself and almost got sent to the hospital.

Day Three and a march to the U.N. ran afoul of a squad of police furnishing security for the President. There were mass arrests. Lindsay was furious as he and his aides worked for hours to get the protesters out. Many wore wristbands with their lawyers' phone numbers, and Nate fielded endless calls and drew up procedural requests to drop the charges. On the final day's march to Union Square Gottehrer and Davidoff babysat the marchers past construction sites, but a bunch of kids squirted loose to charge a building on Irving Place that housed an Army Intelligence Center, and the police went into riot control. Marchers were beaten against brick walls and parked cars and dragged by their hair to the paddy wagons. Gottehrer and Davidoff were vilified by the cops for helping the marchers and almost lost their jobs.

This was not the time for Lindsay to fall off his moral high ground faster than he'd swan dived during his campaign on Rockaway Beach. His Water Commissioner and friend James Marcus was accused of taking a kickback from a Mafia chieftain on a reservoir cleanup job.

All the old pols chuckled once again about how Lindsay could send kids to kill rats in Harlem but couldn't smell one in his own backyard.

Lindsay was practically in tears on television. The Mayor who had been a national voice for urban reform and erasing ghetto poverty had become a local joke. Nate increasingly saw no purpose in aiming for a job from a man who, however admirable, would need another job himself in a year.

He was calmed by a holiday that fell less harshly than usual. Karen swore she'd quit smoking marijuana. Nate accepted his Christmas gifts of a tie and Sinatra album with good grace from Artie and Karen, and Aisha flew after her catnip ball gift and brought the token tree down with a merry crash. *When I was forty-eight, it was a pretty good year...*

Nate and the kids went to their first New Year's Eve party together at Dorothy Kempster's. It was a pleasure to watch Karen chatter away with Nina and Artie fraternize with students his own age as opposed to that racy blonde and whoever else he was shooting film with at that club or cinema co-op or whatever they called it, an activity Nate had permitted only because it so tickled the Columbia interviewer. Senator Eugene McCarthy and his largely symbolic antiwar campaign had the teens at the party all worked up. The kids seemed to get that their witty, very civil, but strangely diffident candidate could give them no more than a moral victory, but at least Karen was learning something encouraging about politics and Artie was no longer enamored of jokers who wanted to levitate the Pentagon or raise hell downtown.

As the glittering ball erupted in Times Square and the champagne circulated Nate got a drunken hug from Artie. He realized he might have to nurse his kid tomorrow through his first hangover. The glum headache of a different kind that the blue-and-white "McCarthy" button promised would come during Democratic primary season.

You can't even talk about sex without talking about Vietnam.

Nate wondered how Marcela was celebrating New Year's Eve. Perhaps in a warmer climate, where there was no Stop The Draft Week, no issues that couldn't be resolved in each other's arms. When the kids were in bed, Nate very quietly played Sinatra, not the new album but his classic *Where Are You?*, and stared at the drawing on the back, the singer clutching a curtain as he gazed outside the window, where the moon rose with a woman's face.

The film that began the eleven o'clock news was from Saigon—Artie knew that from the muddy hues, the green overhang of tropical shadows—but the image was not to be believed.

A hole blasted in the outer wall of the U.S. Embassy. A squad of Vietcong, having gunned down two MP's, attacking the headquarters. President Johnson had claimed just a few days ago that victory was coming and the war would not last much longer.

The McCarthy button on Artie's jacket seemed to flare up with history.

The big old drafty house in Great Neck, with its gables that creaked in the winter wind, its faulty heating system, its empty child's swing in the frozen yard and its spanking new ping pong table in the garage did not enhance The Voyage's rehearsal time as planned. The band tried to lay in accents like La Grange's trumpet voluntaries on English horn, as Toby and Danny worked out thicker, roomier solos behind Pete and Rick's thunderous backbeats. LaGrange cracked that if the sound got any more ecclesiastic they could play in a cathedral.

The female harmony end was sagging. Nell was tired. Nell wilted this way and that depending on how the acid trips buffeted her brain. Danny tried to win her back to some regular rehearsal routine, but she was always sneaking out with Rick for some sybaritic purpose or other. She'd gotten to the point where fucking everybody in the band had definitely become a distraction.

Danny was determinedly off drugs during this period of trying, as he told his dad, to "recompose" The Voyage before the album's release and the group's East Coast tour. With all the new stuff on the scene they had to whip their shit together fast. Cream had just put out *Disraeli Gears*. Where his friends like Artie saw magic, Danny saw stealing, the plucking of flowers from the old blues trees. The same way Clapton had used Buddy Guy's guitar attack and yelp on "Have You Heard About My Baby" he'd transmuted Willie Dixon's tune "All Your Love" into "Strange Brew," with a hint of delay on the beat, a vocal line more laggy and teasing, and raga rock turns in the melody. Still the album was a great mix of raw, tortured blues, blasts of drum and whirlwind bass, and cabaret melodies as regal and radiant as the purple and gold of the Atco label. Meanwhile there was word that the Airplane were cooking up a ridiculous motherfucker of an album at RCA, that the Byrds and Buffalo Springfield were going to recombine in some unknown fashion, and who knew what Hendrix would produce at Electric Ladyland, in his realm of guitars, mixing boards, paintings and the lovelies that gave the studio its name.

It could drive Danny batshit comparing himself to the top cats but it kept him sharp as he fought the insomnia of bargaining with Ed for some kind of quiet in his brain at night. But Danny finally had to admit that the plan to creatively sequester the band in his uncle's summer home had foundered. It was time to return to the city.

When the Voyage's debut album hit the New York record

stores, the band threw a party at the Bitter End, which became a two-day binge finally cut short by the review in Rolling Stone. The article began with a parody of the ad for the movie *The Wild Bunch*. "The Voyage's debut album comes too late and stays too long." The critic dissected gimmicky vocals, lack of focus, the lamented absence of Jimmy Hinton on three tracks, then tipped his hat to the "intoxicatingly strange brew" of the earlier tunes and of "Eden Is Here" before he branded the latest songs as "H.P. Lovecraft at the Renaissance Fair" and announced that lead singer and fiddler Danny Geller had careened into some sort of "Crazy World of Arthur Brown phase."

That was too much for Danny, who broke into a perfect imitation of Arthur Brown's "Fire" to prove he could do that crap if he ever wanted to, and then cursed the asshole critic for comparing him to that asshole with his black lightning bolt across his whiteface, and his songs which Danny called "cheesy horror music for teenyboppers." Rick yelled right back at him.

"Whaddya want, Danny? You put on makeup, stand at the mike and rant and rave during your solos!"

Yeah, okay, sometimes to cut loose from that flattening in his head, the bad spirits that inhaled the last sparks of his energy, he would trill on the violin and inveigh against the God of Body Counts and Freefire Zones that ruled the country, he would urge his fans to fight the ghetto outside and rise above the ghetto inside, to reach for liberation and peace and ecstasy and music. They'd shout in return and buoy his vamp and he felt like their psychic test pilot, even though Pete told him that maybe he had half the audience going but the other half telling him to shut the fuck up. Or as LaGrange put it, they cheer when Janis takes another belt of Southern Comfort too.

Creem, *Crawdaddy*, all came out with similar reviews, a lot of nautical language: rough sailing, way off course, lost the ballast of Jimmy's ear for the blues—even when one critic called Danny the "Captain Trips of the Lower East Side" it seemed a very tongue-in-cheek compliment. Danny paced past heaps of garbage high as plowed snow. The sanitation workers had made good on their strike threat. Fucking goombahs. Sometimes he wondered if he really was about to crash. How would he even know in a neighborhood where if a guy had horse's ears like something out of *Midsummer's Night Dream*, or started talking part Choctaw part Russian, it might or might not be a hallucination? Hadn't he just gone to Peace Eye and met Louis Abolafia, candidate for President of the Love Party, greeting well-wishers naked with an Uncle Sam hat on his cock?

For The Voyage's concert at the Anderson Theater, warming up for Big Brother and the Holding Company, a chance for a big rebound for them, Silver Records decided to pamper the band a little. One of their a & r guys, wearing a chocolate three-piece suit and love beads, brought them a bottle of champagne. The lights were so hot and the air circulation so poor that they drank it all. Rick and Toby tripped on the wires of their equipment as they came onstage wasted. Danny was sweating from the alcohol and the kohl smeared down his face like two soggy bruises. Over the next hour they fought the bad acoustics, the rhythm section thudding offbeat, LaGrange barely able to hear his oud and balalaika, and Nell blanking out to the point that Danny sang most of the gig solo.

But some Voyage fans would remember the night as one of Danny's most wrenching performances, his high-register wailing a foretaste of Robert Smith, proto-Goth in his swooning embrace of "Nothing From Nothing."

Speak… and the colors unfold.
Grab… but there's nothing to hold.
Embrace the sun… why am I so cold.
Nothing from nothing.

It felt terrific right up to the point Danny looked at the audience and saw that, while some waved and cheered and peace-signed him, most of the others, blasted by the theater's ragged, up-treble p.a. system, had stuck their fingers in their ears.

LaGrange, who almost never raised his voice, shouted backstage that they were no longer symphonic but cacaphonic, and he did mean "caca." It didn't help that Big Brother somehow tamed the sound and blew the place away, the double-barreled blues guitars right behind Janis Joplin as she lived the highs and lows of every song and the red and yellow yolk of the light show pulsed with every throb of her hips. Pete and Rick, not caring that Danny was seated nearby, talked about hooking up with a new band, Anteater, and finding a chick singer like Janis. Nothing but the blues.

Danny walked home chased by the newspapers that blew off the trash ramparts. He lay in his bath until his skin itched and he felt like some fifth-rate Marat in his madhouse.

He walked out naked, the better to feel the chill in his room give some dimension to his body, lit some incense, played *Axis* and danced with his hands waving like a conductor, while Hendrix' "Spanish Castle Magic" and its buccaneering electric roar reminded him there were still pirate kingdoms in this world.

The cardinal that returned every March to Vandemeer's cherry trees perched on the branches' last crust of snow, and fed the campus with a late winter restlessness there was only one place to take.

The Vandemeer Chronicle headlined that Mr. Thomas, who had suspended the school's hair regulations himself the previous year, would subject the school's conservative dress code to a debate in the assembly followed by a student and faculty vote.

"When young people have the power to exercise responsibility, when we show trust in their intelligence, sensitivity and good judgment, they will not disappoint us."

Artie would be the second senior class representative on the debate team that would support elimination of the dress regulations before the assembly. He would literally have the last word on the need to make a change in student behavior that was so intriguing to a portion of New York City that the *New York Times* was sending someone to interview Mr. Thomas.

The only disappointment came from Dad. The dress code change prompted a curt response Artie didn't expect, as Dad made a point of saying that he wore a suit every day at work. When Artie asked if that was simply a requirement of the court, and if he would wear the jacket otherwise, he shot back that someone has to bring some order to the table.

Still, when Dad heard that Artie was going to speak before the assembly he grinned and clapped him on the shoulder, telling him it would be a wonderful experience for him.

"You're really developing some debating prowess. I'm not saying I agree with you on this issue, Artie, but your participating in this assembly is terrific."

Artie's speech could be no longer than three minutes. This was different from a debate argument; this was one speech that had to tug his classmates along toward making a change that would affect them every day. Life at the school had the friction and glamour of events that Pam and Truth 24 chased after on the street. An A.P. history class on the Depression engendered a student antipoverty task force. English classes stressed Blake's revolutionary writings and even prodded *Our Town* for evidence of social injustice.

Artie practiced his speech over and over, his weapon in the fight against the vicious bastards that picked on other students, that wore their jackets and ties as badges of the endless, pointless strife that prepped them for business school and law school and smothered all the sparks of something better that he'd seen at concerts, at the Be-In, and at Pamela's side.

Russ suggested a way to clinch the debate for his team. His dad had landed a fortuitous interview, he was sure the great man would talk to a friend of his son—not to mention the son of Nate Kovacs—and Artie glimpsed a way to align the dress regulations debate and his leading role within it with the forces that battled, at the highest level, the Draft and the War itself.

Just what I need, Nate thought, an Abbie Hoffman coffee break. The denim-clad activist, rail-thin, faced carved into delicate, almost feminine planes that broke wide open to his clown's laugh, spread disorder the way *Peanuts'* Pigpen threw off dirt. Izzy and Abbie hugged, and Abbie scrutinized Izzy's new buckskin jacket.

"I dig the new look, Iz. Hymie on the Range."

Lefcourt was Abbie's lawyer but when Abbie got bored with Jerry he liked to visit Izzy and Nate and bounce his zanier thoughts off them.

"We could find the highest pile of garbage, plant a Canadian flag on it, ask Canada to recognize the ascent and grant us asylum, then give away dope from the top of the pile until they formally refused!"

Today Abbie came over to bring Izzy news he'd heard on WBAI. The conviction of Harold Solomon, former owner of the Café Au Go-Go, for putting on Lenny Bruce's performance had been overturned by the Appellate Court 2-1.

"You should be kvelling, Izzy. I think they even said something like it was in error to hold that Lenny's performance was without social import. It wasn't obscene. The whole case against Lenny was bullshit, and that's on the record, man!"

Nate could see that Izzy was not pleased, that his face had gone quietly livid. He moved into his familiar role of human junior partner bromide.

"Well, that goes a long way toward cleaning up Lenny's reputation."

"Yeah, that's great. Legal when you're dead. I'm sure that's a comfort to his wife and to Kitty."

"Main thing is to beat the motherfuckers, Iz."

"I got it, Abbie. It's not like Lenny helped himself by jumping bail and heading for L.A. But none of this shit ever should've happened, and they won the main battle, they shut him down in New York. He believed in the law, that's what was pathetic!"

Izzy was starting to work himself into a gutbuster polemic, but uncharacteristically he caught himself.

"A lousy post-mortem vindication… aah, I gotta siddown… I really gotta siddown… "

"Yeah, Iz, you look a little beat."

For once Abbie was understating.

Nate saw the blood abandon Izzy's face. The question of are you okay was a formality. He knew without even asking and his fingers instantly dialed police emergency.

Izzy, rueful and bewildered, settled into the chair, a buckskin-suited jellyfish trapped in a concentrated effort to breathe. Abbie in his own way was an effective nursemaid while Nate reported the heart attack. Iz, it's okay, just take a load off, you don't want the egg salad now, trust me. He followed Nate and the stretcher downstairs as the ambulance men huffed and cursed under Izzy's weight.

Izzy managed to issue a few scrambled whispers about one or two cases before they trundled him into the back of the truck and drove him away, sirens blaring, before the lunchtime rubberneckers.

Abbie shook his head toward Nate—what a bitch, what a ridiculous bitch.

Two kids rushed up and asked him for his autograph.

Sarah had served the Wednesday night butterscotch pudding and cookies, and Dad was well into his coffee and cigarette as Artie described the man's office, just like any other doctor's office but lined floor-to-ceiling with souvenirs of the peace movement. Photos of him with William Sloane Coffin, the Yale chaplain, and Martin Luther King Jr. A model of the Houses of Parliament. Wooden elephants from Africa.

Dr. Benjamin Spock was as tall as a basketball player and could barely fold himself into his capacious leather swivel chair. But once he did, in a voice that almost made the room shake, he'd heartily endorsed the removal of dress regulations at Vandemeer High.

Artie produced a signed letter that Dr. Spock himself had given him, in the same way he planned to reveal it to the student body after his speech.

Dad put his cigarette out, but his lips were pursed tighter than when he'd been smoking it. Finally he shook his head and let his hands drop weakly on the table.

"Artie, I don't understand you sometimes. Didn't I tell you my partner had a heart attack today?"

Artie, not knowing how or why, braced himself for a truly awful family spat.

"Yes, and it's terrible, and I'm really sorry about it."

"Dad, what does that have to do with what Artie just said?"

Karen seemed to be defending him, and that doubled his amazement at having to defend himself.

"I'm just trying to help our side win in the debate. I got an endorsement from Dr. Spock."

"And you think that's going to help? How stupid can you be?"

"Dad, he's just trying to do well in his—"

"This isn't your concern, Karen!"

Karen tersely asked if she could be excused, and Dad quickly agreed.

"No, Dad. She's right! Thank you Karen, thank you! I've just won Dr. Spock's support to help change our dress code, of course I'm going to discuss it with the team, and you know something? This isn't YOUR concern!"

"It isn't?"

"No, it isn't! You disagree with me, you disagree with me, but that's it, Dad, that's it!"

"Not my concern? Who pays tuition so you can be on that team? I'm your father, and—you're making me sick with this, Artie! Do you want to get me a heart attack too, is that it?"

Artie felt the familiar lash in his stomach and once again imagined his dad prostrate in the hospital...

... but this time there was a real flesh and blood figure he knew, poor Mr. Hamerow, in that bed, this time he couldn't imagine calamity coming neatly in twos, instead of all by itself out of nowhere.

"Why do you say that to me? Why do you always say that to me? How am I going to make you sick, how can I do that?"

Dad's voice sank to the level of a plea.

"You have more responsibility now. You're applying to college, for Chrissake."

"What does that have to do with—"

"He's going to be on trial, him and that chaplain from Yale, for counseling young men to avoid the Draft, for violating the Selective Service laws of this country!"

"Dad, you yourself said that it's seven steps from harm to counsel—"

"I don't want a debate, Artie! Give me that letter."

Artie clung to his evidence that a major public figure supported his side in his school's major debate that had been mentioned in the *New York Times*. He hoped his dad wouldn't lurch for the letter, and as he couldn't imagine what he'd do in response, he tried not to cry.

"Dr. Spock is a hero, he hasn't sold out and he hasn't been co-opted! He's a leader of the peace movement, of the sort of people you defend, Dad! And when the school sees that he supports us—"

"Know what'll happen, Artie? You'll lose! You'll lose because you brought a controversial figure into your high school's affairs! The kids who haven't decided yet will rally behind the conservatives in your school! But go ahead if you don't care about what I say, go screw it all up, I can't take any more of this!"

Dad finally waved his hand, his signal that he'd given up on trying to penetrate Artie's thick skull. He shut Artie out with the tv news, any cardiac threat clearly past for the night.

Artie took the garbage out, then walked angrily down to the street clutching his letter. Shivering in his pullover, he looked toward the East River, which floated in the five-block distance that ran opposite to his normal walks, icy and pale beneath a red-tailed cloud that seemed to sigh as it vanished into the dusk.

Two days later, he set out his papers on the rostrum and addressed an audience of his fellow students and teachers. The right to choose, he began, was the essence of democracy and so it must be the essence of education. He cited the Federalist papers and James Madison about how factionalism was the greatest threat to democracy, and all parties must be afforded a reasonable opportunity to join in and work together to make changes to the system. That line got him some cackles for being a pompous smartass.

FLASH FRAMES | 299

But he rescued his remarks when he stated that the new dress code showed trust in the students' good judgment. Conservatives can still be conservative as they want, but the rest of us will also have a choice, and that won't lead to some kind of Vandemeer High Love-In—and here he earned his laughs—because we'll all work together to make the system a reasonable compromise. Our normal work will continue, and our unity will be stronger when each of us can express our differences. As George Vandemeer himself had said, "the strength of a free mind is the strength of a free people."

The assembly loudly applauded him as he returned to his chair on the stage—and that night, the applause still ringing in his memory, he pasted Dr. Spock's letter into his souvenir book. Everyone on the debate team had seemed amazed that he'd pulled off getting Dr. Spock's support, until he'd nervously asked if anyone thought Dr. Spock might be too polarizing a figure to bring into the debate, and he'd seen the relief in their eyes…

Even Russ agreed. Your old man knows his shit about politics.

The next day the Vandemeer Chronicle put out a special edition to announce that after one-hundred-and-twenty years, the dress regulations code had been eliminated by a vote of students and faculty.

Dad seemed happy about Artie's victory, and especially its triumphant afterglow at his old Alma Mater. Headmaster Thomas wrote Artie an enthusiastic recommendation and he was accepted early admission into Columbia. Dad took Artie and Karen out for veal parmigiana and chocolate cakes and boasted about Artie to Leo's regular patrons.

"You did great, Artie. And see, what did I tell you, you didn't need the Spock letter!"

His cigarette hand waved grandiloquently in the night air, and Artie felt Dad had emphasized that last line with an awkward extra flourish because it was so unnecessary. They were getting along well again, but perhaps because he was now running the law firm with that black guy while Izzy recovered, Artie suspected that it had become important for Dad at all costs to win.

He seemed always ready to take swats at Artie over political issues. When McCarthy racked up 42% of the vote in the New Hampshire primary and stunned the President of the United States, Artie cheered and shouted that McCarthy now had a real chance—and Dad's reply was that Robert Kennedy would come in and beat him. *Now that McCarthy has done the hard work, the old Kennedy machine is going to swing into action.*

Artie didn't like hearing that—especially since four days later Kennedy was in the race.

Two weeks later LBJ announced peace talks with North Vietnam, and almost as an afterthought said that he would not seek, nor would he accept, the nomination of his party for another term as President. After they both sat amazed and Dad wondered aloud if he'd heard right, Artie laughed and applauded.

"Artie, this is serious!"

Artie was serious. He comprehended the enormity of the event, even within the giddiness of the moment, and once he knew his dad couldn't acknowledge his awareness, he fell away from sharing his thoughts with him.

In the new silences at the dinner table Karen reasserted herself, and Dad happily drank in her stories about her school plays and dances and even showed an interest in her new idol, Laura Nyro, whose alternately Gospel-heavy and spooky *Eli and the Thirteenth Confession* contested with *Disraeli Gears* in the acoustical stomping ground of Artie and Karen's shared hallway.

"Laura Nyro doesn't explain, she fills you with experience," the ad said. Artie liked her face on the album cover, with her raven hair and curled underlip. Artie was slowly filling with experience too, and he knew it, and the way Dad seemed to think it was there to be safely contained drove him deeper into secrecy. If in every discussion they had, Dad reached for some kind of defense, including the threat of his health, Artie would have to have defenses too.

How did all this craziness come by way of Doctor Spock?

You raise your kid according to *Baby and Child Care*, let him express his impulses, tell him he's special, steep him in the warm bath of liberal tolerance as gently as in a bassinet, and watch him gravitate to rebels and ruffians and ex-models filming anarchists, or at best an honored and respected Yale chaplain who wants to fill the prisons with draft resisters.

Nate knew almost as surely as if Becky's voice doubled his own: Artie must have no illusion he can take risks to himself or his future because of politics. He could never handle fasting in prison or being tear-gassed. He was no tough guy, there were no tough guys among the Kovacses.

That morning a real tough guy had invaded Hamerow and Kovacs. Detective Regan seemed to swallow up Nate's office as he handed him a series of flyers. The cheap yellow paper was scrawled with slogans and filled with tiny-type columns that excoriated the imperialist "warfare" state. The bearded faces in the corners that took credit for the battle cries were tiny smudges of grinning fury.

"Look like mug shots, don't they Nate? Too bad we can't arrest them. All this freedom of speech bullshit."

"Why are you showing this to me?"

"This guy here's been writing threatening letters to Draft Board members, this guy bodyguarded Abbie in Washington— yeah, good old smiley peacenik Abbie was scoring dope during that protest, and he was wearing a piece on his belt. Just keep the leaflets, Nate, and if you hear anything about these slugs, like maybe they're planning some kind of action... "

"You do know about attorney-client privilege?"

"Nate, once they become your clients it's too late. You know Lindsay and his Lower East Side urban task force group want to scout troublemakers and talk to them before all hell breaks loose? Well, so do we, Nate. Our own kind of dialog."

"I don't see what I can do."

"Just keep your ear to the ground. Help us out, help yourself out."

After Regan lumbered out of his office, Nate wished he'd

had Izzy to back him up, but who knew when that might happen? Nate had discovered that Milt, for all his hip lingo and acceptance of some black militant programs, also had the standards of gentlemanliness and decorum you'd expect from a Howard University graduate, and shared Nate's concern over not just Regan's intrusion but the firm's more raucous clientele.

They agreed to refer their more political clients out during Izzy's absence and search for new business in the burgeoning rock concert hall and festival scene. Rumors of partnerships going bust, light show operators getting unpaid, contractors screwing promoters, musicians getting shortchanged.

Gonifs, schnorrers, bad debtors.

At their favorite Spanish restaurant Bruce and Shari nervously watched as Danny, buttering his roll, laid it out flat on the tablemat. Shari, with a thinly reproving smile, moved his dish toward him and Danny apologized for being such a slob. He admitted he felt like he was coming out of a cave.

It must have been rough trying to hold the band together, Bruce told him, and Danny casually replied that when the breakup came, they all knew it. They were getting sick of the non-stop jostle for second and third on the bill with Leslie West's Vagrants, the Flying Machine, Scout, Rhinoceros, The Four Zoas, and Lothar and the Hand People. The last straw was bringing up the rear at the Westchester County Fair with the Savoy Brown Band and Kaleidoscope, whose bottom-heavy bozouki and blues music veered too close to their own style. Some bare-chested guy with a giant tattoo danced to them, and Danny shouted that there was a good citizen. The rest of the suburban audience didn't move, hardly cheered. Toby fucked up the changes. Danny appeared in a Victorian Aubrey Beardsley jacket with a white top hat, and used his vocal in "Nothing From Nothing" to attack the critics, to attack the audience for being fucking dead to everything except refried Clapton, and for good measure started singing "Fire" by Arthur Brown.

The rhythm section announced their defection that night to

some Moby Grape-ish biker band. La Grange absented himself and his musical caravan, thanking Danny for an enjoyable quest. Nell was in detox.

"Couldn't you start a whole new Voyage with Toby?"

Danny, between chomps of paella, waved the idea off with disgust. What's the point now, it's all everybody doing the same thing, a lot of blues rock like that up-and-coming band Creedence Clearwater Revival played.

"It was great work, Danny. You're not done yet."

"I don't know if I want to lead a band again. Maybe I want to do studio work. Find some gig with Al Kooper. Yeah, Koop thought I was a pretty mean fiddler."

Danny speared a piece of chicken.

"Or maybe I'm just a fucking actor."

Bruce assured Danny that there was nothing acted or artificial or pandering about his music—which was more than could be said for Miles Davis. Bruce had accompanied a friend of his backstage where he was interviewing Miles between concerts. A chance to speak to the great trumpeter he would have given his proverbial eyeteeth for a year ago. But now he saw before him not the sharp-dressing cool jazz maestro but a wild-eyed Afro-topped bandleader in a patchwork coat of animal skins. Miles talked a good game about his new band's guitar blues voicings and dueling electric pianos that doubled the bass line. Everyone knew Miles had checked out Sly and the Family Stone at Newport, that he envied the young guys and especially his lady friend playing the funk. He actually told his buddy that jazz was an Uncle Tom word.

Miles had now joined all the sellouts who went yakety-sax in the '50's to try and catch the rock-and-roll wave, he was noodling, he was becoming—excuse me, Shari, these were once Miles' words—a no-playing motherfucker.

Danny shrugged and retreated into silence until suddenly they all jumped at a china clang from a nearby table. A waiter apologized in a spate of two languages for dropping the dishes. Danny sank back into the banquette and laughed.

"Someone's holding."

"What?"

"Oh not me, Mom, not me, promise. But that's a signal for a bust. They'll probably wait and do it outside in the street."

After they put Danny in a cab, Bruce agreed with Shari there was something to worry about and that it was time to persuade their son to move back in with them now that the band had run its course. All Danny's shuffling and fidgeting and frightened looks around the restaurant... to settle his own nerves, Bruce took refuge in what he still convinced himself was his job. He left Shari by the tv, donned his headphones, and calmed himself by listening to the latest Simon and Garfunkel record in his bedroom. *Bookends* enchanted him, such exquisite technique, even if the pair's latest work was infected by all the current stereo trickery, like bumping furniture on one tune from speaker to speaker—but listen to the perfectly blended menace of "Mrs. Robinson," whose staccato guitar and percussion lines ran through the tune like the dividing line on an L.A. desert highway.

Where did you go, Joe DiMaggio? Where have you gone, Miles Davis? Where have you gone Beatles, with gurgled flutes and foxhorns that follow the gallop of horses hooves pointlessly across the stereo? The fragrance of the first youth of the music and Bruce's second youth following it had been blown out by the wah-wahs and music roaring backwards through sonic vacuum cleaners. The charms of his son's band had succumbed to that same grandiose overproduction. Bruce went to the head, checked out his paunch in the bathroom mirror, lifted up his lip on a yellowing tooth. Tempus fuck it indeed.

It was time for Danny to catch up with his studies to make sure the Draft couldn't catch him. It was time for everyone to catch a break.

He heard a cry as if Shari had dropped a dish, but there was too much anguish in it, and so he raced into the living room and saw her crouched before the tv... at the same time an aide raced to John Lindsay's Broadway theater seat, whispered in his ear, and prompted his immediate exit from the theater… while the Kovacses were stunned by the freeze-frame jump cut of the tv news bulletin and the tombstone dates under the photo of Martin Luther King Jr.

And as Danny, back in his apartment, tried to create a quiet space around the confused tangle of his own thoughts with the acoustic folk jazz and feathery female vocals of The Pentangle, he heard chain reaction shouts trailing police sirens, like when Tompkins Square Park had gone up.

He stuck his head out into the April wind as a black guy's voice shouted fuckin' uptown, motherfucker, fuckin' A train uptown!

With the somber ignition of the streetlights the windows start to crash. A guy hit with a plank by some looter crouches dazed by the curb, amid smoke of burning plaster and rotted wood.

Same fools, different city? Maybe on some blocks, but no, Jimmy knew he was right to have moved to New York. The proof was the loudspeakers. All the radios and stereos by the thrown-open windows, all the music store speakers that would normally blare out Aretha or salsa or jazz to proclaim their wares or simply their ornery swagger now spoke with one voice. The street was booming with "the sacred rights of man" and "color of their skin" and above all, the dream, the dream, and you couldn't run off like a crazy man in that web of sound and memory.

Couples hugged, men stood in the streets and sobbed, or they just walked together, grim and silent, to the meeting place, 125th and 7th, and Jimmy could just feel it. He had the same hurting in his gut they all had, but also the awareness that he had moved to Harlem for a moment like this.

Fanon in *The Wretched of the Earth* had talked of the second phase of the revolution against the colonialists, the mobilization of the masses under the idea of a common cause, a national destiny, and collective history. Martin Luther King had been all of those. Jimmy remembered how he had taught that what affects any one of them affects everyone.

Tonight is the night to find out, as Stokely had cried, if all the scared niggers are dead.

The wall of people moved forward. Everyone talking about MLK, personal memories, or just what they'd read in the news about how he was getting too close when he linked southern bigotry, northern poverty, and that fucking white man's war, which he'd called an abominable evil.

That Memphis garbage strike had turned violent, provocateurs hard at work, and so he'd stuck around another day to do it right, and everyone knew where King was and where he would be but now all over again you hear the lone crazy man with a gun bullshit. King had drawn damnation and rocks and bricks from the white mobs, now at last had come the shots.

Jimmy walks in lockstep with the people all around him, they're converging on the block from west to east, and that balding Mayor's man is frantically working the walkie-talkie by the Glamour Inn, where there's no table stakes poker and drinking tonight.

Jimmy can read the Mayor's man's lips: no go, no go.

Cops stand by and let looters run, agitators scream. Black Panthers in their leather jackets walk the crowd ready to organize, knowing this time it won't be ditching cars in the middle of the FDR drive to stop traffic, or a peaceful demonstration for community control of schools—if you're wedged in solid with a righteous crowd that adds up to too damn many for the pigs to scare or to hit, this can be the night you take the schools, seize key intersections, have some real leverage once the frenzy was shaped and focused.

No more dead black leaders, someone shouts, we want to be heard!

Jimmy raises up on his toes, and he sees two official city sedans pull up with the triple antennas. Police vehicles... *and the crowd surges suddenly, it's roaring now, you can't even make out the words, everyone speaking in tongues of defiance, no speaker at the speaker's corner needed when everyone knows the path to take, even if it's right over every white cop in Harlem...*

Jesus, there he is, like some long thin ghost, the pale visage towering above the crowd. Only a couple of cops with him, frantically scanning the rooftops. Where'd Mayor Lindsay come from? Frank's restaurant, someone mutters. His two pasty-faced aides huddle beside him, and the Borough President greets him, his mahogany face sweating in the cool night, normally pleasant and unctuous, now scared shitless.

With the lights pouring out of the suffocating darkness to converge on him, the Mayor is the embodiment of a moving target.

He resolutely heads toward Lennox, where you can still hear the sirens and burglar alarms and the bricks felling sheets of glass. His hands are raised up to take in the crowd. He embraces a woman as she sobs. Clasps a storekeeper's hand. He stays out there, surrounded, and over and over he says how sick at heart and how sorry he is.

Like a huge moan the crowd sways toward him. This is a sight they've come to welcome over weeks, months, years. The Mayor in Harlem.

Jimmy can see that this gathering in the streets has now become a funeral, and the City itself, at grave risk, has officially come to mourn. Only gangsters fire at a wake.

There's a jostling in the crowd. Jimmy recognizes the skullcaps of the Five Percenters. They seem to want to help protect the Mayor, but Frank Overton's labor union guys, who've taken a position beside Lindsay, shove them away, and now the craziest fight starts over who'll be Lindsay's guardians. The Mayor is quickly run to a city car that pulls away from the sidewalk.

"Bwana Lindsay."

"Hey brother, least he remembered where Harlem was!"

Jimmy could hear the voices, mainly older ones, saying let's hold it together now. This is our city.

Lindsay stayed in the streets for three days. His people organized a memorial at the Central Park bandshell where black radicals could address the crowd. To Jimmy's amazement, even Sonny Carson wound up preaching peace.

When Mayor Daley in Chicago threatened to shoot looters,

Lindsay declared that New York places a higher value on innocent life.

That week, Jimmy had to admit it, New York was different from all other major cities, never sustaining a full-scale riot, and mainly because a white man had gone into the black street and put out all the moral force he had, and not just in the sunshine flanked by his advance men, but in the no-go territory of the night.

"So you still talk to honkies?"

"Yeah, Danny. I still talk to honkies. I'm no fuckin' reverse racist. Man, you're the same joker you've always been."

Danny grinned and shrugged off his provocation. He hadn't meant to tease him, but the jab had leaked out from force of habit and because he really didn't know how to handle this new Jimmy.

His old pal had literally adopted the stance of the black militants he'd joined, tamping down the energy that had once sent his gangly arms in all directions to illustrate a musical point. Now he was coiled and watchful and seemed to move to the sinuous fittings of the funk, the new backbeat laid down to the struggle of his people.

They sat in the West End Café over their Cokes and bowls of spaghetti and Jimmy caught Danny up on his new life in Harlem. While taking classes at CCNY, he also worked with the Panthers, helping to coordinate donations from local merchants to the breakfast programs.

"Man, the Panthers are militant."

"Yeah they're militant. But Eldridge Cleaver, Minister of Information, he's put out the call for white allies. And hell, man, we all can see that Lindsay is at least trying to do some things right."

… though he couldn't make it right forever; every black man had to be prepared. On a field hidden behind a street of auto body shops along the Expressway, with makeshift targets provided by some black GI's from Vietnam, Jimmy had shouldered and shot a rifle for the first time, and thrown himself to the ground from the

recoil of firing a handgun. The instructor picked him up, dusted him off respectfully, let him keep trying until he least put a hole in the target... but there'd be no telling Danny about that...

They talked about what Jimmy was listening to. Archie Shepp, Ornette Coleman and Albert Ayler's free jazz, fragments of music as launching pads in a flight toward shamanic energy and political liberation. Stax, Aretha and Sly.

"Even Miles is listening to the funk."

"Miles Davis?"

"You know any other Miles? Yeah, you'd have to get into a whole other bag to jam with us."

"Hey, the Voyage is over. The Voyage was about nothing."

"I tried to tell you, man, but you didn't want to hear about the blues."

"It's not just that. The whole scene's fucked. With politics, you deal with the pigs, man, but you don't have to deal with the critics."

"I don't see you in any kind of politics, Danny."

"John Sinclair says a rock-and-roll band should be a total self-sufficient revolutionary production unit. Earn enough for self-reliance and spread it around to help serve the people. It can all work together, the bands, underground newspapers, theater groups, health clinics, the Panthers. The problem with the Voyage was we didn't do that enough, we got caught up in the hype and the record company capitalistic bullshit."

"So start a new band."

"I can't. I'll just do the same shit. It's like... I became this false self, you know, this guy under the control of the audience, the rest of the band, the a & r assholes. It's like they were swallowing me up."

"Man, you don't need the Movement, you need a shrink."

"Jimmy, just tell me where you need some backup. This is authentic shit, Jimmy. You want honkie allies? Just tell me what you're working on."

Jimmy pointed a fork over his shoulder at the window.

"Columbia? But you're not a Columbia student."

"This isn't about Columbia, Danny, it's about Harlem. It's about the black community where I live. Columbia has all these building projects and land purchases and they're gonna evict longtime tenants and storeowners. The gym they're building on Morningside Heights with the one entrance in the back for the community? We call it the 'apartheid gym.' See, Lindsay means okay, but he can't do shit about this, and MLK's gone. It's time for us to break it down for ourselves, take direct action in our own neighborhoods."

"I want to get involved."

"Yeah, well involvement arises out of commitment, see, out of conviction transformed into action. You ready for that?"

The ripe pink balloon sailed over the audience seated on the floor of the little Union Square office until bare-chested Jerry Rubin grimaced like a silent movie villain beneath his walrus mustache and snared it to general hisses and laughter.

Artie framed the new leader of the Yippies grinning at his prize and let the Arri run a couple of beats. He decided he didn't like Rubin much. For all his sympathy for society's victims, he looked like the kind of guy who was gonna sneak up behind you and viciously rank your bookbag, really stomp the shit out of it.

The Youth International Party, organized by Rubin, Abbie Hoffman, and Paul Krassner as a "drop-back-in for dropouts," had posters of the United States with a little "Yippie!" shout painted on the state of Illinois. They'd put out ads in the *Voice* and *Rat* and *The East Village Other* about their planned protest at the Democratic Convention in Chicago—but still they endlessly debated the need for a press conference. Rubin glared and punched away the balloon.

"Forget the press conference! Let's all do our own thing to publicize this, not put out some party line! We're not leaders, we're cheerleaders!"

Giggles and applause.

Artie looked at Judith Rosecrans manning the Nagra, a plump woman with wispy bangs and softly drawn-down eyes.

Pam had introduced Artie to Judith, asking him to break her into Truth 24. They worked well as a team, and now she shrugged off Rubin's cry in a way that echoed his feelings perfectly. Artie knew that Rubin, Hoffman, and their comrades had pulled off some wild stunts—bombarding the Stock Exchange with dollar bills, sending city leaders Valentine's Day cards with joints—but now this "merry band of freaks" wanted permits to nominate their pet hog Pigasus for President and march on the Chicago Convention.

People sprawled on the floor on each other's laps, nursed their babies. You could get a contact high off the room.

The balloon sank to the floor. The meeting quickly wrapped up with a no vote on the press conference. They decided to create a tactical committee and then call Tom Hayden for help.

"Our lifestyle is the Revolution!"

"The President's war on LSD is bullshit! All it does is create more bummers!"

"We're against all the merchandisable insanity, man! Free food, free politics, don't need a credential to be a Yippie."

"Everybody come to the midnight Yip-In at Grand Central. A spring mating ritual for the Equinox! You are invited!"

The whole thing ticked Artie off—he'd envisaged the meeting as an ideal opportunity *to pick a girl up* but he and Judith had been way too busy recording, as it turned out, aimless bullshit.

When Artie shut off the camera and told Judith to cut the sound, they could at last take a hit of one of the joints traveling the room. They emerged into a burst of spring sunshine that lit up the pavement of the square like an asphalt pond of tiny dragonflies. The trees were budding and St. Mark's had shaken off its winter slumber in a tumult of hawkers' cries to buy T-shirts and buttons and beads on black velvet backdrops. There were handclasps and kisses on the sunlit stoops.

Judith bought a hash pipe at the Psychedelicatessen, then surprised him by inviting him upstairs for some wine. Her studio overlooked an ivy-walled courtyard and glowed from red balloon curtains and the yellow bulb of a paper ceiling lamp. She got her bong from the bedroom, and came back having exchanged her jeans for harem pants that gave full play to her thighs.

The day had borrowed the absurdity and the high of the Yippie meeting to fly off in another direction altogether —"Dark Star" on the turntable, roseate curlicues of Garcia and Weir's guitars, incense for the ears, blending perfectly with the slow bubble of the water pipe and the lambent warmth of a high that coaxed him effortlessly into Judith's arms.

"Yes… you're so sweet, Artie… "

Yes, they'd shot film so harmoniously together, and the words sighed with the guitar that circled the corona of the organ as they pulled off their clothes and pulled open the sofa bed. Artie hesitated as she stretched out before him. The Dead sang of a world a New York kid could only imagine, a summer night's forest, a mild and verdant place of rest seen through dappled guitar harmonies…

A flare of sunlight broke loose from the curtain and he blinked at Judith. She opened her shirt. Her cinnamon eyes glowed as she pulled him down, and her breasts swayed apart like fleshy gates. She wanted him to kiss, then suck, but then just when it all seemed right the intimacy of the moment ambushed him. He felt his hips trying to pilot the residue of his opportunity to an impossible destination.

He was shocked at how groin to groin felt, the conjunction of hair and bone and desire gone askew, and it was like that first toke, where you miserably wait for something, anything to happen.

He rolled off Judith and apologized, and couldn't believe the peevishness in his own voice. She shrugged and stroked his hand. He felt it would be totally stupid and shameful to get up and leave. If it made her feel better he would just lie there and listen to the album. The guitar, organ and double drums relayed silken messages to each other; the bass stippled against those lambent filaments of sound. Join the music at your own speed. Her breasts rose with her breathing and exhaled a scent where he'd sucked them. Garcia's lead guitar languidly surfed the beat, the bass undertow surged, Judith brushed her nails across his ribs, and Artie's pelvis brought him back like an arrow. With the glide and suck of her belly he shot forward, pushed harder and harder, at last not thinking about anything at all, and bubbled like a peach turned inside out.

For the next half hour in her arms, he savored the pleasure and the triumph that the bridge to manhood was behind him. He felt nothing but fondness and gratitude toward Judith even as the gust of passion for her subsided into quiet satisfaction at an experiment gone well and anticipation of more experiments to follow.

Such a beautiful accident.

That night he felt he had grown manhood just like he'd grown his second teeth, he was entitled to let a whole range of new choices into his life. And his plans for that future, more than ever before, glowed with black light.

They gripped the cold chain link metal. The shock of fifty other bodies lashed through Danny's muscles as the Cyclone fence peeled away. After the march from the Columbia sundial and all the chants of "Gym Crow must go!" and "Columbia out of Harlem!", the grit of rust that cut through his thin gloves, the snap of the gym construction site fence as it coiled down, felt like sheer vindication that the people united will never be defeated— right up to the point when the police charged.

Danny looked over his shoulder as the first wave of students was pried off the fence and arrested. The fence thrashed and almost flung him into the construction pit. Later he would ask himself if he'd been a coward but it wasn't much of a decision to let go and start to run.

Their march rapidly unraveled down Morningside Drive. He could see the neighborhood's junkies dressed in filthy jackets and overalls as they perched on the ramparts past the pavement, beyond which the ground sharply dropped off into the crater of a park littered with windblown paper, broken glass and syringes, the first green of spring on the trees as thin as a gauze bandage. The junkies grinned at the students as if they were all in on a private joke. But some residents raised their fists in solidarity with them as they made their way back to Columbia.

The marchers trailed onto to the campus, sweeping up some students headed for classes. Power to the people. Gym Crow must go. Let's just march in our usual disorderly fashion.

Danny and Jimmy hung back with the other sympathetic CCNY supporters, waiting to see what steps the SDS and the Student Afro-American Society would take.

"We're going to Low!"

The plan was to present demands to the Vice President of the University. But security guards and testy administrators blocked them from any chance at a meeting.

The Afro-American students' Cicero Wilson and SDS leader Mark Rudd decided to keep the momentum going.

"We're gonna take the petition to the Dean!"

Danny roared back in approval and raised his fist toward Mark Rudd. The guy had eyes almost popping out of his head and a ton of energy. A natural frontman. He and Wilson led the students down College Walk to Hamilton Hall, up the marble stairs flanked by stained glass windows where they instinctively silenced themselves, but only for a moment, until they consummated the ultimate disciplinary infraction, sweeping past the astonished secretary and into the Dean's office.

"Columbia out of the Park! Columbia out of IDA!"

The mob backed up and collected on the stairs and in the halls. When Dean Coleman, a crewcut ex-athlete, strode through them all and entered his office with an air of bruised dignity, silence fell again, until Rudd defiantly set the tone of the next eight days.

"We've got the Man where we want him!"

There was a stream of onlookers, an audience that wouldn't quit. Students who gathered to look through the barred windows of Dean Coleman's office to see him held hostage. Students who came to protest, and then to protest the protest. The Student Afro-American Society put a cardboard sign on the outside door of Hamilton Hall, "Malcolm X University, Founded 1968

A.D.," right in the face of the bust of John Howard Van Amringe, "Dean of Columbia for many a day." Right in the frozen path of Alexander Hamilton himself.

"Yeah, we got the Dean in an extended dialog."

The black students solemnly hung posters of Malcolm and Stokely on the walls while the whites bounced beachballs down the stairways. Streetlamps gave way to the lights of the news crews, over a quadrangle packed with students, reporters, campus police. A swarm of flashbulbs popped.

Cheers and boos in equal measure went up from the crowd— the flag of the Vietcong flew from one of the windows.

Somewhere in the building a mimeo ground away and by the time Danny was munching on trail mix and one of the Drake's coffee cakes sent in by well-wishers, the students' demands were circulating. Amnesty. Shut down the gym. "Disaffiliate" from the Institute of Defense Analysis and its support of the war machine. The party had become a political occupation.

Meanwhile the whole black contingent seemed to evaporate upstairs.

Danny tried to join them, and J.J., the building's new Defense Minister, pleasant but implacable, told Danny it was a private caucus.

The hungry, empty hours sank down to a thin blue light and a few diehard reporters against the massive doors. Walkie-talkies crackled and broke into Danny's fitful doze, as Rudd and the other SDS student leaders paced the gallery.

"We got 7000 dues paying members in the SDS! We won't let you down!"

The crowd shuffled to its feet, one girl already in tears, pricked to uneasy wakefulness by the rumor that the whites were being asked to vacate the building. Danny looked for Jimmy and found him leaning over the banister peering directly down at him.

"Hey man, are we getting the bum's rush?"

"Not my call, Danny."

"What about what Eldridge says?"

"You want to be our allies? Do it your own way."

"What do you mean?"

"This was our action. Come up with your own."

Danny reached up his fist and Jimmy quickly looked over his shoulder, then they touched fists together.

"Right on."

The white students spilled out into a frosty dawn wrapped in blankets. They straggled across South Field, the shimmer of red, white and yellow tulip beds mocking their grey exhaustion, students distracted from all-nighter homework sessions in a few waxy yellow dorm windows watching them, and no other audience except the stone lion and the Alma Mater statue with her arms raised as if to shrug off their very existence.

The march continued up the stairs of Low Library, and Danny blearily gazed at the immense Doric columns and was ready to pack it in… it wasn't until the plank shattered the glass of the Library door that Danny realized they were about to break and enter the President's office.

He threw himself into the headlong rush as five hundred war-whooping demonstrators blew past the bewildered security guard and penetrated the deepest, hoariest grove of Columbia University.

So much just outside the scope of the lens, but Artie knew the trick was to keep the focal length distance as he handheld the camera down the walk, and keep Pam with her mike and her interviewee in the frame.

"It's all related! If you're into day care, food co-ops, tenant issues, you're also against White America's racism and imperialism."

The subject was one of the hatchet-banged, leather-jacketed, horn-rimmed SDS big men on the counter-campus. He turned ardently toward the camera.

"We want to break down the walls of people's little jail cells and hangups. Get into their hearts and minds and shake up their bourgeois values."

After a few more endorsements for himself and the Columbia

SDS and repeated invitations to Pam to join them, he took off, and Artie and Pam were free to pan the knots of demonstrators before them, and the full-blast discourse from bullhorns that vectored the greensward into little townships of protest.

In Avery Hall architects had taped over the windows with plans for a humanist city project. The wood smoke vocals and barrelhouse organ of the Band's *Big Pink* album boomed out from Fayerweather. And at Mathematics Hall, rumored to be the most radical of the "liberated" buildings, the red flag that hung from one of the windows seemed to lift in response to great blasts of Hendrix.

Leaflets. Strike manifestoes. "Create two, three, many Columbias!" Walkie-talkies tried to stitch a narrative to the exuberance of students who stood on windows to shake out blankets, catch sandwiches and fried chicken from supporters, and hang banners that said LIBERATED ZONE, SOLIDARITY FOREVER, JOIN US!

"The Administration knows the facts, they just refuse to see them! We see the facts and know their lies and oppression are over! Power to the people!"

Artie focused on the signs: HELL NO WE WON'T GO, STOP THE MARINES. SPRING HAS COME (WE ALL DO SOMETIMES). He panned, rack-focused, and there were grinning skull faces in the lens. He pulled back on the street theater troupe as the death's head figures pinned a Vietnamese down with a rifle while a man with an LBJ mask looked on.

"Mah f'luh Amurricans, ah come to yew with a heavy heart..."

"And a BIG ASS!"

"We tryin' to achieve peace with annnuhhh... "

"Pow! Ten farmers down! Peace is underway!"

"But the North Vietnamese wunnnt unnnerstand our resolve!"

"Pow! Twenty! Fifty!"

The camera didn't falter. Artie's grip was flexible but sure, and he moved tirelessly across campus. He was where he most wanted to be doing what he most wanted to do with the woman he most wanted to be with. He was in his college-to-be at the heart of its evolution, at one with the changes he was shooting. A new Vandemeer rule gave him two "socially relevant" excusals from classes and that took care of the days. Nights were covered with the phrase "I'm going out with Judith." Dad was pleased in a sheepish, comradely way that Artie's virginity was behind him and was a total good sport about his nocturnal disappearances.

"We act because of what we know and what we believe and we will stand by this protest!"

SDS officials toured them through the offices at Low, the windows crisscrossed with duct tape and blanketed against tear gas. Student strikers camped on the rugs beneath a giant Rembrandt and smoked dope in the room where Artie had had his interview. The room was being kept clean and orderly so no one could accuse the students of vandalism, except for the jimmied file cabinet locks—the strikers boasted of liberating files that revealed President Kirk's dismissive attitude toward Harlem community leaders and Columbia and IDA's battlefield research for the war in Vietnam—all sent to *Rat* and *The East Village Other* for immediate publication.

They displayed for Pam the President's liquor cabinet they'd raided. Pam looked down at the row of bottles.

"Didn't you liberate any olives?"

At Math Hall there were student strikers on every windowsill. Artie knew this was the center of the action when a window opened and out onto a first floor ledge stepped a figure who'd been all over the news. Tom Hayden, SDS founder, who'd drafted the Port Huron Statement, stooped down to help a coed climb up into the window, and as her leg crooked and her thigh bunched up her miniskirt, cameras clicked and a cheer went up from the crowd.

Artie could only imagine what would happen when they helped Pam up, and sure enough he was jostled almost to the ground by hollering guys trying to climb in and follow her. Artie didn't want to risk the camera in a scramble through the window but he saw the door was barricaded by a heap of firmly wedged sofas and chairs.

Pam shouted out to him and soon she and several other students hauled him up through the first floor window as he tightly clutched his Arri.

"We have moved from symbolic civil disobedience to barricaded resistance! We stand for the transformation of this university and the society itself! We are guerillas in the field of culture!"

Kids were seated everywhere; no hippie flamboyance, just take-to-the-streets workshirts, dungarees and boots. In the basement there were boxes of sandwiches, and big pots of spaghetti were on the stove. Some rooms were drowsy with pot, some filled with communally petting couples, some echoed with acoustic jams, some were hung over by a Berlin bunker mentality.

At last they found Tom Hayden and cornered him for an interview. The SDS leader was antsy and overtired and he joked that maybe they'd prefer to cover Abbie Hoffman, but at last he unwound for the camera.

Revolutionary politics was tied to a willingness to teach, to raise consciousness, and that meant showing the students their links to the poor, and to the people of Harlem and the Third World, so that they might someday join the larger forces working for a classless society, equality, and solidarity. Pam asked him if he thought Mark Rudd was being a bit of a cowboy, not performing the teaching function. No, Rudd and the Columbia chapter are free to exercise spontaneous action… a peaceful rally isn't a cop-out, but it's also true that there's no contradiction between organizing people and getting into heavy shit… but yeah, busts do get in the way of programs and teach-ins.

And as he cast an eye over the dope-smokers and tambourine-bangers and bull sessions, he added that he still wanted people to go to school and learn how to think creatively and critically, that Castro believed in educational as well as political guerillas. With a rueful smile he stated the New Left was a work in progress.

Pam grinned and told Artie to cut the camera, and after Hayden left the room Artie, savoring the conclusion of the day's work, was suddenly caught up in a bear hug.

"Hey lil' bro! Look at you on the film crew, man! How's it goin'?"

With one arm clamped around Artie, Danny threw another around Pam and gave her an enthusiastic kiss on the lips. She pulled back, laughed and asked him what he was up to.

"Oh, talkin' about politics and jammin' and running down strategies for if there's a bust. It's a full day."

Down the hall there was another outburst and Artie saw Gabe Pressman's film crew zero in on high school students seeking help from the strikers for a protest of their own. A skinny red-haired Barnard girl blocked the cameraman, shouting at him that they hadn't gotten the kids' permission and would get them in trouble with their parents. In a demonstration of the quick, loosely-knit response to local conditions Hayden had emphasized, a directive soon circulated to banish "oink pig media pollution" from the liberated buildings.

From now on only the guerilla press, Newsreel and Truth 24 would cover the strike. Artie thrilled to the exquisite realization that, with Danny and Pam by his side, he was in a charmed circle of youth, education, political rebellion, and the focal length of his camera lens.

That night, after leaving the footage with Du Art Labs, they met at the Truth 24 basement to watch rushes of the Grand Central Station Yip-In.

Tom Fenster, who had shot the footage, insisted on screening it dressed in the shirt he'd worn that night and his makeshift Truth 24 press badge. Both were caked in blood.

Tilt down from the Kodak Colorama widescreen mural where an American family frolicked in big pine country. Zoom in and out of what WBAI had advertised as "the participatory event of the year. A theater with YOU as performers and audience." The main terminal swarmed to the balconies with heads and freaks who'd brought blankets, pillows, recorders and guitars, clearly planning to stay the night and greet the commuter mob in the morning.

Dancing together and alone, flashing peace signs, smoking, groping... while a hundred or more police ringed the entrances.

Every shot signaled by a flare.

"Fuck You" spray-painted on the Grand Central walls. Abbie Hoffman and a guy from the Mayor's office, Abbie grinning, the city flak horrified.

Then slowly, as dreamily as the lazy ascension of balloons, kids crawl up the information booth clock tower. One holds up a banner. "Up Against The Wall, Motherfucker."

The clock has four faces, and one is suddenly blank as some kid waves the disembodied minute hand over the cheering crowd.

Another flare, a second frame fragmented by the aura of a sprocket hole.

"Abbie didn't have a megaphone. The city and New York Central wouldn't let him talk to the crowd on the public address system. They all fucked up!"

When the police charge it looks like a great grey slug ingesting its fill as the cilia of its clubs flick over the little cells that scream and try to run. Scraps of bleeding finery catch in the frantic camera amid slashes of silver glare. One kid yanked off the clock and beaten.

Cop's face in a white blur, lips like slits, as the offscreen voice swept up in the action cries why are you doing this, what are the charges? The club hits somewhere the Arriflex doesn't film and the floor and trampling feet annihilate the frame, and now the very persistence of vision that makes film flow is eaten up by the smashed, impacted stutter of flecks of white burning foam, film trying to develop itself second by second in celluloid whiteouts.

They all try to calm Fenster down as he screams you don't cut this, you don't cut this at all, man, this is what tells you it's really happening!

The old Alma Mater statue held up a sign that said PLEASE STRIKE. SUPPORT LIBERATION CLASSES. In the windows of the beautiful colonial red and beige-pillared halls of learning were pictures of Marx and Lenin. VIVA LA HUELGA. SMASH THE STATE.

Worse of all, on South Field there was a long brown stripe that ran from a ragged gap through the hedges across once pristine grassy lawns that generations of students had skirted out of tradition and respect.

Thank God, Nate thought, the tulips were undamaged.

At the rally that loudmouth Rubin was hectoring the crowd that their parents were dictators teaching capitalism in consumer school concentration camps.

"Columbia must stop the Institute for Defense Analysis because they killed Che! Che was killed by University research!"

Nate wanted Rubin and SDS and the strikers punished for what they'd done to his University. But for now he needed to walk the grounds with Barry Gottehrer on a mission of mercy, on a lovely spring day when Lindsay's top aides were doing their best to stage-manage this nightmare away from disaster.

At Hamilton Hall, the Vietcong flag had particularly infuriated Nate, but Gottehrer had pointed out that the black students had had the good sense to release Dean Coleman after a day, and that while they'd received Rap Brown and Stokely Carmichael they hadn't responded to their more fiery rhetoric. They were adopting the posture of serious negotiators for their community.

It was the white kids who had the idea they were going to live like hippie revolutionaries on Columbia property and transform the city. They were aided by liberal faculty trying to broker a deal, who whined about don't hurt our children, shrill and hysterical, until SDS told them to butt out because anything short of general amnesty was total bullshit.

"This kid Mark Rudd know what he's doing?"

"Rudd's like the kid who put a frog in Grandpa's bed and now doesn't know what to do about the stroke."

"What about the Mayor?"

"First he said the students had sound grounds in logic and conscience for rebelling. Now he says the occupation exceeds even the most liberal right to dissent—he's caught in the middle on this one."

"But if he just came down here—"

"Oh yeah, the trustees want him to walk around like he did in Harlem and work a miracle. But they won't give him any authority to negotiate on their property! So what pull does he have with stoned-out right-on kids from Great Neck?"

They arrived at the quadrangle of Avery, Fayerweather, and St. Paul's chapel. Students in jackets and ties from the conservative Majority Coalition sat on the shoulders of more muscular students in sweats and held up garbage can lids to knock down food being thrown toward the strikers in the windows. The strikers hurled abuse and water balloons down on the Majority Coalition while they caught the few snacks that made it through the cordon.

It all seemed to Nate like some bizarre kiddie color war. One boy held a sign that said "Please Don't Feed The Animals."

Sid Davidoff, burly and thick-necked as the college wrestlers of the Coalition, was slowly convincing the jocks to hold off on any premature punch-outs or invasions of the premises. He agreed to pass Nate's message on to the two occupied buildings. While they waited, Nate listened to a bullhorn voice from the rally that Gottehrer identified as Rudd's.

"To say a scholar who works for the IDA is not involved with military violence and oppression, that's total hypocrisy! The University must face the consequences of that scholarship! I consider our actions here to be defensive. We have risen up in response to the violence of the University against the people of Harlem and the people of Vietnam!"

As Nate and Gottehrer walked across the campus, the shaded nooks echoed with frantic debates. Call in the cops. Don't call in the cops. Everywhere were the armbands. Green for peace with amnesty, blue for the Majority Coalition and an end to the occupation, red for strikers, white for sympathetic faculty. The statue of "The Thinker" was festooned with blue, green and white armbands. He seemed as confused as everyone else.

When they reached Mathematics Hall, Nate was relieved to

spot, amidst the reporters, someone he knew he could talk to. Hayden greeted him courteously and agreed to take his note inside. Gottehrer had a quick whispered conversation with Hayden and did not look reassured, and so before Hayden climbed back up to the waiting arms at the window, Nate asked him what he might do if he heard the police were coming.

"We'll be nonviolent, Nate. That's all I can promise."

Nate watched him clamber back up the wall, his supporters hoisting him in through a window that seemed like a crack in a cliff wall, where a chattering bird's nest clung by the thinnest of twigs.

He thought back to Elaine's the previous night, the well-lubricated writers' table arguing the pros and cons of the student strike. When the Revolution comes, Avery had cracked, they won't attack the Russian Tea Room. Bruce had quipped that at least '68 was a great year for Corvettes. His robust form sagged as he mentioned Danny's prolonged absence. The shrink treating Danny had assured them, within the bounds of psychiatrist-patient confidentiality, that his son's political rhetoric, his fear that he needed to get to friendly territory to avoid being followed, might be only a temporary reaction to all the drug-taking. Under the pressure of some of the new drugs, and some of the ugly new urban realities, what appeared to be conventionally paranoid remarks were actually a new language invented to describe resistance to social norms. An attempt to communicate an altered personal reality when no other way could be found. Try to understand and really listen to what Danny is saying.

Bruce and Shari had done that and then implored Danny to move back home. Danny hadn't been heard from since.

It had occurred to Bruce that maybe Danny was in one of Columbia's occupied buildings. Nate had suggested Bruce write four identical notes to Danny and promised to go to Columbia and pass them on.

Now as Nate waited and his eyes traversed the bewildering array of candles, plants, placards, and shouting students that jammed the windows of Mathematics Hall. Danny at last appeared in one of the top windows. He flashed the peace sign. It was clear he wasn't coming out and there was no way to retrieve him.

He hadn't looked as happy to Nate in a long time.

On Broadway, where a large Negro crowd held signs like STOP COLUMBIA and COLUMBIA GET THE HELL OUT AND STAY OUT, Gottehrer watched them march back and forth, and commented to Nate that as long as they move they don't cause trouble. The kids in Math Hall used ropes of bedsheets knotted to buckets to lift food donations from students and neighborhood supporters up to the windows. Hayden addressed the crowd through a megaphone from the third floor.

"Morale in the liberated areas is high! We're storing plenty of food. The barricades are built firmly and strongly. We will achieve our demands. Vietnam has come to America, and if those who claim to be the Administration call in the police to protect them from their own people, we will resist until the end!"

The crowd gave Hayden a half-hearted cheer. Gottehrer shook his head.

"If the trustees agreed to stop that gym and tolerate an amnesty the blacks would be off the streets and the kids would be out of those buildings and throwing Frisbees. Instead they're thinking of calling in the police. One guy told me they had to do it to get classes back to normal by Monday. They'll be lucky if it's normal in a year!"

Nate looked more closely at the news contingents filming the crowd. The golden hair, the profile of the perfect English lass triggered the pull of recognition, and he certainly recognized the boy holding the shotgun mike with a resolute stillness he'd never displayed before.

Artie sat hunkered down on the couch next to Karen while Sarah hastily set the table. To Artie's surprise, Karen once again took his side.

"He's just filming, Dad! That's all he's doing!"

"Oh really, kids? Did you know that the strikers have ejected what they call the establishment press? Which means they believe Artie's film club is part and parcel of what they're doing, and so will the police! Or do you have information that Barry Gottehrer and the *New York Times* don't have?"

"Maybe they're just sick of the *Times*! The *Times* calls them a destructive minority with hoodlum tactics!"

"Artie, listen to me. They are destructive! They're destroying an Ivy League campus! Your campus! They won't compromise! No one will compromise! Teddy Kheel mediated the transit strike and he's getting nowhere! How long do you think the trustees and the authorities will let it go on? Or do you really think the students are going to win their demands this way?"

"WKCR says they're still talking!"

"Christ, Artie, do you want to wind up in the hospital? I've seen the kids who come back from stuff like this and—"

"I'm not going to get in trouble, dad. I'm not part of the student strike. I'm on a film crew."

"Yes, you're on a film crew with this Pamela Huntington and from what I hear—"

"What about 'this Pamela Huntington'? She's on the crew with me, that's all! You defend free speech, right? Maybe I'm speaking with a camera!"

"Look, Artie, I have information that you don't have, and my information is that things are not going to turn out well up there. I'll make it easy for you. I appreciate your loyalty to your friends, I understand and respect your beliefs, and I especially support your photography, but you're not in Columbia yet, you're under my roof, and I forbid you to go back there. Understand?"

Artie stood and swallowed down his outrage. He lowered his voice.

"Dad, I wasn't planning to be there tomorrow night anyway. Judy invited me over."

"The trick is to be clear and not to get into a kid's stuff head. You've rejected what your parents taught you but you're still on a children's crusade."

Randall Soles wore those granny glasses that made his eyes look as if they peered down at you from a crevice at a great height. He had a case of acne that could have been battle scars, thick black hair swept back in a ponytail, and a low ominous voice, capable, after all the goofing and pot smoking, of engaging you in the kind of three a.m. bull session that could change you forever.

"You believe liberation has to happen. All will be well. You're conditioned to that by easygoing parents, material wealth and peace, television and music. So you transfer your faith in all that to this scene here, but it's closer to war than you ever thought, and it scares the piss out of you. It could go all to hell and on your body, your skull. It's like your mom's cocker spaniel in a fight in the alley. Most of these people here, after all this shit goes down, they'll cling to head victories. Feed their heads with music about liberation instead of trying the real thing. Slay the dragon in a movie or a song."

"But guess what? Kids our age are in the tunnels in Nam, setting booby traps, getting fried by flame-throwers. You heard the radio. The pig power structure knows this university right here and now could be a leverage point, that revolutions have started in smaller places than this. Cops are on the way. Are you prepared for that? Are you prepared for what comes after?"

"I thought we're gonna be nonviolent."

"We got no choice. See any weapons? Trust me, though, you'll feel it. You'll wish you had a gun."

The student strikers no longer sauntered through the rooms or lay under tables in reefer-hazy conversation. They had drawn together on the staircase in their long wool scarves, pom-pom hats, ski caps, and bulky coats shapeless from being sat on or slept in. Randall was cheerful, but all around him the kids within earshot had sunk into a pallid silence. They were fidgety, nauseated, knowing they'd just filled buckets with soapy water and poured them down the stairs, and wedged even more desks onto the first stairwell.

WKCR had broadcast the trustees' decision. They knew what had happened to the protesters that had sat on the steps of the Pentagon in 1967. They tried to talk about their favorite Monday night tv shows, they passed around a *Village Voice* with news from the other world they'd left for a few days. Demonstrations for Local Community Control of Schools. Rally for Eugene McCarthy at Hunter College. Censorship battles on *The Smothers Brothers Show.* Tom Paxton, Ars Nova, Joseph Heller.

Pick up the right paper and it seemed everyone was on your side, a comforting bulwark of the likeminded, even Lindsay had come out against the war in a speech in Central Park. Everyone wanted to stop the military madness, fight racism, smoke a doobie and meet a chick at the demo. The problem is you were wedged in on the stairs at Mathematics Hall and the Tactical Police were coming to send you to the hospital or the Tombs.

It didn't help that the only food circulating was Familia. Someone cracked that it could be used to incite a riot. No one laughed.

Danny knew he had to do something for the people he'd shared the past two days with, and he asked someone to pass him a guitar. He'd gotten into plenty of music bull sessions. A great one about how Winwood might not be Clapton but he played lead guitar in chunks of repeating riffs, like an organist, and that was cool too. The Jeff Beck Group, on the other hand, with their album *Truth*, that was really boss. Beck had Rod Stewart on vocal and Nicky Hopkins boogying on the piano, his leads were like poured electric paint on canvas, he was even better than his days with the Yardbirds, the way he could slide like a violin, power down like a freight train and roar through an arena. Beck had always been a fuckin' fountainhead of guitar. Someone had asked Danny if he played, and he said once he'd been in a band, but he was a little rusty.

Now he strummed the guitar softly in the light that fluttered from the candles on a windowsill above him and sang "Eden Is Here." Whispers migrated up and down the stairs, and he heard his voice multiplied on the chorus from the kids that surrounded him, then the floor above singing along. When he finished his tune applause came down in waves from the building. People were thrilled to hear Jimmy Hinton was with the SAS. Spirits lifted. Down the stairs through the linked hands came "Strike!" leaflets for him to autograph, one after the other.

The New York City buses marked "Special" rolled down Broadway. Cops filed into the lights that glinted off their helmets and visors as they massed along the curb. Artie's shoulder ached with the Nagra strap and he felt the weight of the extra battery pack on his hips.

He suddenly had a moment of stepping out of himself and watching himself. He saw a small astigmatic young man weighed down like a turtle standing next to a British ex-model with a movie camera while a hundred cops in military formation prepared to charge. He began to shiver violently.

"All right, luv?"

"I think so. I mean, I hope I'm not going to be sick."

"Look, Artie, perhaps you shouldn't stay here. I can put the Nagra on my shoulder, call on the radio for some help. The group's out in force tonight, we have too many people, actually."

She was right about that. Strictly speaking, Artie hadn't lied to his father. Judith was here tonight as well, they all were. He shifted the weight of the kit on his shoulders. The fading light caught the last flecks of green in Pamela's eyes.

"It's all right, Pam. I can do it. I'm ready."

She kissed him gently on the cheek.

"We won't get near the arrests. When the cops make their move, we run to the edge, I'll use the zoom, open the stop way up, it'll all be soft focus anyway. It's not like we can get any more than a general impression of the bust, but… we don't plunge into that crowd, we can't try to save anybody from what's going to happen. We're there just to put it on film."

At 2:30 p.m., the phone lines to Math Hall were cut. Students began to frantically introduce themselves to each other, hi, I'm

Bob, how the fuck did you get into this? Girls took their earrings out of their pierced ears. They put kerchiefs and blankets over their mouths for some protection against tear gas.

They tried to bolster each other's resolve by remembering the quote from Mario Savio. There comes a time when the machine is so odious, makes you so sick you put your body on the gears and the wheels to make it stop. Or Daniel Berrigan. This is the act demanded of us, to take one choice that includes many other choices.

They checked each others' intonations, even each others' eyes for the opaque fire of true believers, the hardness on which to forge resistance.

Hayden's voice echoed from the top of the stairs, asking for and getting a vote of nonviolence, reminding them that meant going limp, not resisting arrest, in an act of morally justified civil disobedience. The crowd joined in a song, "We shall not, we shall not be moved," while they waited for the wheels and levers and gears and clubs that would yank them out of the building and hurl them into jail.

The cops marched onto the campus, and Artie saw within their formation men out of uniform wearing orange buttons. Pam was filming them, and he wondered if their images would come out. Barely identified plainclothesmen who could mix with the students in a melee, ambush them, do whatever they wanted.

He wondered if his mike was picking up the tramp of the cops' boots. He knew it was picking up the shouts of abuse from the students milling on the grass.

"Go fuck yourself, you pig!"

"Your wife sucks cock!"

"Get off campus, motherfuckers!"

They railed helplessly from the lawns as the cops headed down South Field. Pam was clearly in their line of sight as she shot her footage. Perhaps she hoped her presence would help keep them from lashing out at the bystanders.

My god, Artie thought, all those cops, they all can see Pam.

The police army split up at College Walk and Artie and Pam followed the contingent to Mathematics Hall. Artie couldn't believe it, the windowsills on fire with candles, the faces like red cinder masks whose features dissolved in smoke, hands waving the peace sign as if they could chop the police down where they stood.

"Strike! Strike! Strike!"

The cops held in place. What were they waiting for?

Maybe, Artie desperately thought, maybe after all this they'll just be the local police...

"Your sister sucks off your mother!"

"Who's fucking your wife, pig?"

"Hey black cop, Uncle Tom asshole!"

The cops had probably absorbed this kind of loathing and disgust all night on the street. Now it sharpened directly before them in faces as confined as a row of targets. Artie could feels the cops stew in their own rage. He heard one cop spread the word that a bucket of piss had been hurled at the police from another building.

Artie dared not bring the mike closer, but he heard their muttered imprecations: yeah, give me that look, you rotten cunt, I'm away from my wife for this shit, spoiled pricks, you'll pay for this overtime, you bitch.

Artie remembered the eyes of a neighborhood patrolman when he'd been mugged once and a bystander had made him talk to the cop when he'd just wanted to go home and nurse his humiliation. The cop had been polite, helpful, but too case-hardened to be all that interested.

These cops were wide-eyed and hungry.

Pam repeated to Artie to stay back, don't try to interfere, there's nothing we can do. But he could hear her quavering voice catch the panic in the air, and it finally infected him until he felt close to tears.

"Why don't they stop? They're just pissing the cops off! And what the hell are the cops waiting for?"

A comforting hand fell on his shoulder. A man in his thirties with a white armband. Sympathetic faculty.

"Don't worry, son, they won't go in busting heads."

"How do you know?"

"Because they don't dare attack the blacks in Hamilton Hall. And they can't treat the white sons and daughters of the Ivy League any worse."

In front of Hamilton Hall, Assistant Chief Inspector Eddie Waith, chosen for the task because he was black, fumbled with the keys to unlock the massive double doors. They apparently didn't fit the lock. Fifteen minutes later he was still trying to open up the Hall while the crowd behind him jeered, hissed, laughed.

The decoy worked. Downstairs near the janitor's quarters, Jimmy Hinton turned to where SAS leader Cicero Wilson, observed in a formal capacity by black Human Rights Commission Chairman William Booth and Distinguished Professor Kenneth Clark, acquiesced to the terms of a peaceful arrest. Wilson spoke to the squad leader of the two hundred police who, while Waith had created the diversion, had secretly headed through the tunnels beneath Columbia and opened the door to the basement of Hamilton Hall.

As Jimmy marched out beneath gurgling rusted pipes and ducts with the members of the SAS, he wrestled with the contradictions of a heroic action that was ending in a clandestine flight beneath the University, an acceptance of this getaway in the hope that daylight would reveal them as empowered negotiators for their community. Finally amid the tramping of feet through the puddles came the shout of discontent they all harbored.

"If we'd stayed, Harlem woulda backed us!"

Wilson turned around and shouted down the line from just in front of Jimmy.

"Man, Harlem doesn't back us, we back Harlem, and we're no damn good to them anymore in Hamilton Hall!"

Jimmy kept his question almost under his breath.

"What about the whites?"

The answer came back from one of the leaders ahead in the tunnel.

"They'll make their own damn deal."

The barricades flew apart with unbelievable speed. It took just a couple of seconds longer for the hunched blue shapes Danny could see through the banister to break through the desks and the filing cabinet.

They were leaping in the windows now, and they dragged Hayden and the first limply acquiescing wave of students by their hair and shoved them out through the door. They weren't using the clubs, but Danny's stomach turned over as a flashlight cracked one student in the lower back and he screamed.

Danny watched the cops come up the stairs. The strikers who went limp were dragged out so that their heads bashed along the steps. Those who even flinched got the flashlights. They were better for short-range action, threshing blows that cleared the stairway as if the students were knots of weeds. The longer the police fought their way up the stairs toward Danny and his friends amid curses and screams and cries of "we shall overcome!" the harsher the blows became.

The students in front of him linked arms. The cops had to pull the whole chain of them down; they clubbed their backs and the sides of their ribs and shoved them in a tumbling heap down to the gantlet below.

Danny wouldn't let that happen to the girls behind him who had asked for his autograph. The frontman caught the light and took the heat. He stood up and spread his arms.

"Love and revolution, brother!"

The nightstick caught him flush across the temple. It was only because the startled cop stood below him that the force of the blow didn't fracture his skull. Danny saw the blinding fissure of pain and then blood from the head wound sealed up the light. Another blow chopped into his belly, and he coiled around the shape it left in the fetid air before he sank to his knees. He crumpled against the banister and then to the floor, his fingers slid on blood and soapscum, and he collapsed into the machine of kicks and blows and curses that drove the wriggling bodies, who somehow found each others hands, down the flight of stairs.

The first students were shoved out, the next were carried out. Kids with bloody heads flashed the peace sign as they were dragged onto the quad. Others tumbled out perilously close to the broken glass and still smoldering wicks of candles the cops had swept off the windowsills. Some spun away from the cops and rushed into the arms of the anguished onlookers, and it seemed the cries echoed all the way back to Avery and Fayerweather.

Pam backed herself and Artie farther and farther off, anything but stupid, somehow keeping an eye on all the chaos, but even she wasn't prepared when twenty of the cops spun around and began to pick off their tormentors in the crowd.

Artie raced away as fast as the Nagra and magazine kit's weight would let him. He couldn't see Pam, but he could hear her scream that she was from the bloody press before he saw her being dragged away. She caught sight of Artie, and before he knew what was happening he was opening his arms as the Arri flew and hit him in the chest. He hugged the camera like a football, stunned, mike dropped onto the ground, Nagra spinning. He had one last sight of Pam as the crowd surged and the police muscled them into the night.

"Damn it, Artie, keep filming!"

Artie threw the mike over his shoulder, got the Arri attached to his battery pack, and shot the black squirming mass of cops and students as they headed toward Broadway, now banked with floodlights and whirling cherry tops. He shot as if the lens could somehow pluck Pam out of that police mob the size of a small army.

The hum of the motor against his cheek settled him down, and the adjustment of the zoom carved the images without him having to get too close. He played his distance from the cops like a fishing line. Planning to get to the gate and document the mass arrests, he started to run while hooking the mike to his waist to pick up the hubbub and be as far as possible from his gasps for breath.

The gate was a heaving barrier of people. Students under arrest signaled and exhorted others on South Field who screeched and yelled at the cops. There was no chance of spotting Pam or Danny, and he hadn't realized how quickly a scene like this could degenerate into total havoc.

But he kept filming. Somehow the police arrested and processed the students and got them into paddy wagons. Artie took as wide a shot as he could, closed in on portions of the mob even though he knew they'd be a mass of phantoms on film. The image needed some definition, whatever he could get. He had to get closer, and so he hid the camera under his coat and figured he'd better not run, just try and slip out through the gate and hope the overwhelmed cops didn't spot him.

"They're charging!"

Artie saw the whole blue army fan in through the gate right toward him. He spun around and ran as hard as he could, tripped, shielded the camera as he went down and fell to the campus lawn on the Nagra. Something cracked as he went down, he was scared it was his rib, and those few moments of shock sprawled on the grass, boot heels flying past him, kept him out of the cops' hands. When he next lifted up his head the cops had run by him and pounced on the students who had never seized the buildings, only taunted the police from the sidelines. A plainclothesmen pummeled a kid with a rubber truncheon, then his fists. Two cops tore off a kid's jacket and beat him over and over with their nightsticks.

Artie couldn't believe all the clubs flailing against the floodlights, the screams, three cops on one student, six on two others—and he was shooting now all alone on the lawn, not thinking of his safety, as if he could pin down the savagely violent police and annihilate the protective darkness that they trusted with every frame he ran through the camera. The students scurrying away, chased down, hit with the clubs and coiled on the grass, dictated the rhythm of pan and pull focus. He found the shrubs along South Field, crouched behind them, and captured one beating after another. He kept filming and adjusting the lens purely on instinct, and his zoom lens was nimble and lucky enough to catch the faces of the cops who finally spotted him from sixty feet away.

Artie ran for the gate with a hurtling mob of other students and somehow avoided getting wedged or trampled as the crowd forced the gate open and broke through. Stumbling out across the curb and into the street he heard a stone-breaking sound that was weirdly ancient and unnerving and that he couldn't place until he looked back and saw past the paddy wagons the mounted police gallop across Broadway. He froze, unable to comprehend the sight of horses, actual horses, bearing down on him.

Someone he never saw yanked him back on the sidewalk. As the horses ran down the students still in the street and the cops reached over and swung at their heads Artie took off and didn't stop running until he saw the Truth 24 van on 114th Street and his comrades hauled him bodily into the back.

Walkie-talkies were crackling, and as he caught his breath he inhaled familiar perfume and was buried in Judith's embrace.

"I fell on the Nagra."

"It's okay, you just cracked the visor. Let me have the Arri. Artie, you can let go of the camera."

He felt as near to fainting as he ever had as Judith took the camera, Lofton the Nagra, and the van gunned away from the curb, but he still shouted for Pam.

"We heard from her on the walkie-talkie. She's headed for St. Luke's. A medic at Fayerweather thinks she cracked a rib."

"At Fayerweather?"

"Improvised medical center. The cops threw kids out of the windows there so that's where the doctors set up. Fuckin' cops went batshit."

He finally looked up at Judy and saw she was bleeding.

"Oh, it's nothing. I was running and I came up behind this gardener and he whirled around and whacked me with part of the rake. Jesus, I guess I could've lost an eye, but it was nothing really.

All this… this going on, and the poor man was so apologetic. But God if I'd been hit by the wrong part of the rake… "

She clutched Artie's hand and couldn't stop sobbing.

The sign that now hung on Alma Mater read RAPED BY COPS. Beneath the statue beer cans, broken glass, blankets and shoes littered the Low Library stairs.

Behind Nate and Bruce, the hedges were splayed open and the flowerbeds trampled, except for one patch of white tulips unimpaired and jewel bright in the sun. Bruce just shook his head and muttered that they overran the place. It was unclear whom he meant.

"Fayerweather's this way, Bruce."

"I never realized how beautiful Columbia was. You were lucky to go to college here, Nate."

Nate led his distracted friend down the walkway, past students on the benches who looked shellshocked, holding hands, muttering some sort of revolutionary encouragement.

"Dig it, the war's not over, but a lot of people are growing in awareness… we've exposed the university for the monster it is."

Nate thought of the Tombs filled with hundreds of students about to face charges of criminal trespass, vandalism, "dis-con," and resisting arrest. Artie had come back home early. They'd been too angry about what happened to make it a date night, he'd said. *But he hadn't been angry, just frightened and silent, except for, hours later, nightmare cries from his bedroom…*

At Fayerweather the windows were demolished. In a room with two coffee dispensers students with bandages on their heads lay calmly next to each other. Another demonstrator with his arm in a sling talked about how Seaver, Koosman, Gentry, and Cardwell were going to win the Mets a pennant. Nate asked the medic if he'd treated anyone named Danny Geller. The name sounded familiar, he might be at St. Luke's, that's where they sent the injured students, but no one kept a record in all the chaos.

Nate remarked sympathetically about the demands on the University staff, and the medic told him he was a volunteer. The

University facilities hadn't treated anybody.

As Nate and Bruce came out into the sunlight, a student with a bruised face in a torn peacoat with a patch of inside-out lining hanging past his zipper glared at them. Good morning, he muttered, good morning. Nate was startled as Bruce walked toward him with open arms, but the kid cursed at Bruce and jogged away.

Just entering a hospital threw Artie back into a numbly efficient protective shell. Judith sensed his uneasiness and stuck by his side, not knowing what to tell him.

They turned a corner and speeding gurneys almost knocked them aside. The fifty or so Columbia students still being treated were raucously pushing each other's cots in hospital corridor drag races. Judith laughed in relief, while Artie kept looking. Past three students stealing hits off a concealed jay in the presence of tolerant orderlies, and in the middle of the fracas, cheering the racers on, propped up on pillows as casually as if the overflowing emergency room were a cabana, Pam delightedly waved to the Truth 24 contingent.

Her nonchalance and the bedlam of jostling gurneys amid stoned-out defiance at least ended Artie's fear that she or his other friends were badly injured. Pam looked like she was actually enjoying herself.

But he was still dreading the outcome of this visit, waiting for someone to take him aside and tell him his reel was a disaster. He hadn't even thought about focus or exposure or even paid that much attention to the zoom the whole time he was panning and shooting the police attack, he hadn't really paid attention to anything at all, he was just trying to take the camera and film where it had to go. But for now they all welcomed him gratefully as Pam held court before them.

"They're checking my X-rays now. I didn't get hit, someone else got hit into me. This one cop was so freaked out he swung at everything that moved. Judging from the scream I heard behind me, I think he hit his partner!"

"Hey, Arturo! M'man!"

Artie drew in a breath and winced. Danny had a black eye, torn lip, and a massive bandage beneath his long black curls.

"Danny, are you okay?"

"Yeah, got ten stitches though. Head wounds are really ghoulish, man, they bleed a lot. Scared the 'rents half to death, but… great for the camera."

Artie was relieved to hear that the students brought to the Columbia medics and relayed to St. Luke's were not only all recovering, but would face no charges.

"The pigs arrested too many students to bother with us. But in the long run their fucking dragnet won't do them any good."

Tom Fenster and Pam both beamed at Artie.

"Artie, didn't anyone tell you?"

"I was at school."

"Your film came out beautifully, luv. Well, very much shadows and soft focus at times, but the framing was spot on. You caught the whole event."

"Yeah, and it makes it even scarier, police phantoms beating on student ghosts. And it's all there for everyone to see, the whole scope of the police riot, the screams… "

"I didn't break the Nagra?"

"No, baby. You made it all happen."

She languidly extended her arm to drape his shoulder and pulled him closer to her.

"Let's hear it for Arturo! You really brought it home, bro!"

Danny pounded him on the back, and Pam, even though she sucked in a painful breath, bent Artie down to her with a resolute embrace, as he was bathed in her warm breathing and the cheers of the hospital hallway. He was mindful of Pam's ribs, but he sensed his life had momentarily opened up onto one of those golden sunbursts that would never arrive again, and he laid his head against her breasts as long as he could.

Myocardial infarction. Izzy's every step, a beat too long, betrayed the clotted rhythm of that word. He shuffled around on knees of glass and his wheezing was inescapable. But Izzy was not abandoning his business, and Nate knew he had to brief him in order to get his blessing for Hamerow and Kovacs' new profile.

Nate had kept the case of the nude dancers at the Stock Exchange who claimed they had the same rights to public nudity as any number of actors in new plays—right on, Izzy chuckled— and of course they'd take a share of all the defense work and police brutality suits that would come out of Columbia. But the main body of clients had now become, as Milt dryly described them, the kind of business types who love to talk about Abbie Hoffman. Like Barry Hitchcock and Mort Pankow who grew up friends and now called each other "fat kike" and "goyische fuck" over some international rock festival that didn't happen. Minus the suits and ties, it was a professional caseload that harked back to when life was still recognizable to Nate. Rock acts suing promoters; all sorts of unpleasant professional divorces as good vibrations went bad. It all could get the firm, which fell behind during Izzy's illness, back on solid financial ground.

Milt headed off to the bathroom and Izzy finally managed the ghost of a smile.

"So Nate, sorry you ran away and joined the circus?"

"Izzy, you should have seen Columbia. It's not as if we need to win them any more rights. Maybe they need less of them."

"Sez you, bubby. You didn't happen to notice the conviction of Father Berrigan and the Catonsville 9?"

"They got convicted on very narrow grounds. The whole question of their rights never came up."

"Kunstler got the judge to admit that it's reasonable for Americans to believe war was illegal and immoral."

"But the criminal intent in defying the draft law stands."

"Unless one juror has reasonable doubt. Fuck it, Nate, if you break a window to save someone it's not criminal intent! He got the judge to admit he was antiwar, they prayed together in the courtroom—"

It was just like all their old arguments, until Izzy stopped just short of making whatever point he was going to make as his breath came harder and he raised his hand to quiet himself. Something else was arguing with him now that he had no answer for.

Nate tried to find unshakeable common ground.

"I'm just looking at the retainers a little more these days. I bought a summer house."

"Good for you. Well, we could all use a little more security. Not that there's any such thing."

Over the next couple of days, Izzy began to show an interest in the new crop of clients. Gone were the exuberant egg salad lunches, as Izzy carefully consulted the new diet printed out for him by his doctors, but the spark returned to his phone calls, his arguments with his ex-wife to not be so gloomy about his condition—you know, honey, the one fucking Jewish sin is despair, and you nail it every time—and his recovered belief in establishment Democratic politics.

Yeah, McCarthy and Kennedy might deadlock the nomination on the first ballot, force a peace plank down Vice-President Humphrey's throat.

Nate was grateful for Izzy's acquiescence, and he felt a wave of fellow feeling and pride in his partner as they shifted to a lower gear of optimism to keep themselves going up a very steep hill.

They listened to Traffic's English rainbow garden of guitar, sitar, organ, and flute as Judith fluttered her fingers in his hair. They edited raw footage of the Columbia bust, and as Pam watched his first attempts at cutting and splicing in the dim editing room she hugged his shoulders.

Back home Artie read profiles of "The New Rock" sanctified by *Life* Magazine. On the cover, at the peak of a pyramid of Plexiglas cubes, Grace Slick in some kind of Southwestern garb ruled over Jefferson Airplane in their cowboy hats and shades and berets. Photos of the new bands chased into the meager center of the magazine the ads for a "wifesaving" Frigidaire. May and June were a Lew Friedlander double-vision photograph, the store window glass supered over with the mountebanks of counterculture boulevard.

The carnival had now tented in the East Village, reflecting its motley visions off the mirrored walls of an old theater. Sneakers and sandals trod a carpeted hallway to a burgundy-shadowed interior with a chandelier above the lobby. There the Music was no longer a third-class sideshow at colleges and Forest Hills and the Singer Bowl, no longer on *The Ed Sullivan Show* flattened in creaky, washed out sound, the groups posed like dioramas of themselves on sets that were swatches of paste-on psychedelia. It had found its new sacramental space, a home where the posters that announced its coming and going, whorled and glowing like melted stained glass, could stay on the walls. For $5.50 a ticket Artie could catch Santana or Blue Cheer or whoever the warmup act was, run upstairs for popcorn, doughnuts and a hit off someone's jay amid the collective fumes, then watch Jim Morrison prowl the violet stage as the rest of the Doors brewed their organ and guitar thunder behind him, or, from way in the balcony, see Hendrix in musketeer dress command a vortex of sound, briefly enthrall, then complain about the amps and cut the set short.

Artie thought that was an unnecessary bummer. Bill Graham's Fillmore East had the best rock concert sound he'd ever heard, backed by a full screen light show, steeped in the freedom of dancing in the aisles and no set time to bring down the curtain.

Rat and *The East Village Other* published the Columbia files revealing the University's Vietnam War connection. The counterculture press interviewed Artie and the rest of Truth 24. Artie, stammering a little with fear and pride, talked about shooting the police riot on South Field while men and women many years older than he took down his words.

He and Judith balled between movie dates. Judith adored *Yellow Submarine*'s luxuriant pop animation, but Artie told her it seemed nothing more than a Beatles promo, a glossy sellout. *Fantasia* was better, a part of their childhood reclaimed with a cube of hash, like reports from Disneyland of acid-trippers taking the boat through the "It's A Small World" exhibit over and over and over.

Still he was glad he reserved *2001* for a night with Russ, Dad and Danny on his birthday. It wasn't a regular film so much as a Cinerama /World's Fair/Expo '67 exhibit at first, and then it became an event, an environment, a tone poem, and we want you all to sing along. Director Stanley Kubrick lived in an English castle with a beautiful mod wife and he invited everyone to engage the movie in his own way. What's your interpretation? Everyone knew what the end of *Bonnie and Clyde* was about, who and what was getting shot to bloody pieces by the police, but what was the monolith? Artie and Danny and then Artie and Russ, intoxicated by the film, talked for days about HAL, the film's curving Lucite surfaces that embraced and chilled, the final space-time warping cosmic ride, the shattering of all the forms in a blaze of color and the hope of rebirth.

When Dad told Artie he really didn't get it. Artie wished Mom could have seen the film with all of them. She would've dug it. The Conspiracy of the Brainy let loose on the Ultimate Trip.

Only national politics bummed him out. Senator McCarthy, who had cheerfully slighted his Presidential chances before mounting a real campaign, now was about to be proved right after all. New York pulled through solidly for McCarthy in the primary, as did Oregon, but California was too close to call, right up to when Artie finally turned off the little television he now had in his room and went to bed.

He woke up to Kennedy's voice echoing in the courtyard, one Kennedy speech after another. It was obvious who'd won—McCarthy was finished, his dad had been right. Artie found it hard to go back to sleep, not just from gloom at McCarthy's defeat, but from the oddly lingering presence of the tv echo in the courtyard, the dark solemnity of the newsman's cadences. He felt a creeping unease and it felt familiar.

Artie went into the living room, took his usual spot on the couch, and turned the television on.

The camera was caught as if hypnotized, nothing more than an instrument of the progress of the train, and the lines of people went by, town by town, all along the route the coffin was taking from St. Patrick's Cathedral to Arlington National Cemetery.

Lindsay, in all the starkness of his honesty, had said that the country had lost its way. And Lucas Oxley, who had cracked a joke to a black crowd after Andy Warhol had gotten shot, *we're ahead,* now told his audience *I was wrong to say that. We're all equal now in this country. We're crazy. We're all goddamn crazy motherfuckers.*

The country had lost its way. But there it was by the railroad tracks.

Once again came the pictures of the brothers playing tackle football in sweatshirts on the surf, sailing the Cape, hair tousled in the wind. You could almost hear "A Summer Place" sigh in the background. Karen was sitting in Becky's old chair.

So many black faces by the tracks. Robert Kennedy had been for years so evasive on the cause of civil rights for which John Lindsay had stuck his neck out. As Attorney General he'd weighed the votes of the "democratic South" against the rights of Negro citizens. Nate's whole Republican Club knew the awful story of how the Kennedy administration had coldly played politics and hung Martin Luther King and the Freedom Riders out to dry to the point where King had almost lost his life to a white mob surrounding a church. But then Bobby had worked the phones in socks and shirtsleeves all night to get King out of that town in one piece. Speaking to the kind of Southern officials Lindsay had never spoken with. Speaking to everybody.

There's Kennedy again, giving the victory speech. Charming, elusive, haunted. So tired he can barely speak, hair in his eyes, he flashes an awkward peace sign, then leaves the rostrum forever.

Lindsay versus Kennedy in '72, a Lindsay aide had once told Nate, and Nate had entertained a doozy of a daydream, a Washington office, a home in some leafy glade in Maryland. But when Nate thought of Lindsay trying to debate Kennedy, he remembered when Kennedy, announcing King's death to a crowd in Indianapolis, had actually remembered and quoted words from Aeschylus.

The man could improvise.

Lindsay believed that White America had created the misery of the Negro, and in the same way he showed up to walk the ghettos, Lindsay made damn sure the Koerner Commission declared that America was headed toward two societies, one black and one white. But Lindsay divided the voters the same way. He couldn't make a move to please the blacks in Harlem without infuriating the whites in Queens. Old pols cackled at his misfortune even while their sons and daughters cheered him in Central Park. But Bobby Kennedy... there in the gaze of the unmoving moving camera from New York to Washington, there they all were, white, black, the poor, the working class, students.

Lindsay versus Kennedy in '72. Had to hit, has to happen. Nate watched the people by the tracks soon to be sundered into their different ghettoes and suburbs, he glanced at Karen in the armchair, and not only did he know that Lindsay could not have beaten Kennedy, and maybe Nixon couldn't have either, but he knew that nothing has to happen, and only God knew what would.

"On to Chicago!"

"Politicians lie, Vietnamese die!"

"Pigasus for President!"

The slogans hectored Artie from wall-plastered and streetlight-slathered broadsheets all along the walk to the Fillmore. McCarthy was telling his supporters to stay home because his delegates were almost sure to go to Humphrey on the first ballot. But Tom Hayden had taken over a phrase that Humphrey used to describe his campaign, thrown it back at LBJ's handpicked successor, and used it as a rallying cry.

"We're going to Chicago to vomit on the politics of joy!"

Artie waited on a long snaking line to buy tickets for the Airplane and listened to the echoes of Abbie Hoffman on a bullhorn from a rally the few blocks away.

"Hell no, pig won't go! We took nine polls, and the American public wants a pig for President! Pigasus is the only candidate who gives the same speech in every state!"

Echoes of laughter swelled beneath the speech, the sun came out over the line, and the only tension was whether Artie would get to the ticket booth before the concert sold out. He sat down with the others on the sidewalk and leaned back to get a face full of heat, strangely exhilarated just by the act of stretching out on city pavement. He read his Zap comic of Mr. Natural bamboozling poor old shithead Flakey Foont. Fillmore staff members emerged, tossed out Hershey kisses, and threw buckets of water on anyone who wanted to be wet.

Artie gazed out onto the avenue, spotted Danny walking by, and shouted to him to come over. When he sat down along the brick wall Artie flinched from his matted hair and rancid smell. He could see scars of stitches just below his hair.

Danny clutched in his hand leaflets from the Revolutionary Action Vanguard.

"You wanna see the Airplane? I'm getting tickets for a bunch of us."

"The Airplane? Dunno, Arturo, maybe if they do a free gig in the park."

"I can get you a ticket. Pay me back later."

"It's okay, thanks for the offer, man."

Just as well, Artie thought, that would barely leave me money for the subway—but Danny so obviously needed some kind of lift.

"You working on your film with Pam?"

"She's editing it now and I'm helping out."

"She's the greatest, man. Great to work with… "

He brushed his hair from the new stitches in his forehead. His eyes knowingly gleamed Artie's way.

"And let me assure you… fantastic to ball."

"You—wait a minute, you… you had… ?"

"Yeah, didn't you? I dunno, in the hospital you seemed awfully familiar with those tits."

All the times Pam had rebuffed him, and Danny seemed to have won her as if it were natural as breathing.

"But I thought she was hurt."

"Well, we were both hurting—but at least intact in that department."

"But I mean... where did you?... "

"After the hospital, Arturo, at her place."

"Pam's apartment? What... what was that like?"

His helpless curiosity defeated the urge to just stop the conversation.

"Kind of functional. Like photographer's lights everywhere and a beanbag chair and a couch bed—yeah, you kinda figured it would be like Scheherezade or something... "

Her long limbs so pale, green eyes flashing with welcome lust, she wriggles playfully out of her dress with quick movements the toss of her hair can barely keep up with...

"I mean I felt kinda weak, I remember my scar was going crazy, but I stayed with it, I mean, I'm fucking every boy's dream. That English skin, Arturo. And I guess all sex hurts good, y'know?"

"Yeah, great... congratulations."

"You never balled her? Well, you've got a treat up ahead, man. She's probably just waiting for you to age, or maybe it's different when you work together, she's gotta put that aside one night and—"

"All right, Danny, could you just get off it?"

"Look, Artie, I mean, if we share her, so what? That jealous bourgeois crap doesn't mean anything anymore. Don't worry, you'll get the gig. I want you to, man. I'll help make it happen!"

"Yeah, well, thanks for the generosity, love god!"

"Well, hey, sorry, Arturo. Really, didn't mean to bring you down. Here, read about these guys, the Revolutionary Action Vanguard, they're right on, and... when you get the ticket, stick around for the rally, okay?"

Artie was thankful when Danny shambled away from the ticket line, and happy he didn't buy him a ticket. He wondered if Danny smelled that bad when Pam took him to bed, or maybe they were too stoned or tripped-out to even care.

Once he got the ticket, he decided to storm right past

the rally but Tom Hayden was addressing the crowd, and his measured seriousness demanded attention. He announced that the Seed, local Chicago activists, who'd originally denounced the New York Yippies as dilettante ego-trippers, now welcomed their participation. Hayden had brokered an agreement for both groups to unify on a joint application for a permit for Grant Park.

"Saigon will fall! See you in Chicago!"

The ovation surged behind Artie as he turned away, and as he walked to the Astor Place subway station his mind opened like a shutter on *a cop felling a protester with a nightstick.*

Images that sometimes appeared behind his shut eyelids, that woke him up with a gasp, that wouldn't quit his dreams lately… and now faintly, impossibly…

Pam and Danny together. Limbs reaching through the pain Artie had escaped… to intertwine and to caress…

Back on 86th street he walked past the old Loews marquee headlining yet another sex comedy, *Prudence and the Pill.* The flyer from the Revolutionary Action Vanguard seemed a foreign souvenir. His Upper East Side neighborhood, as always, was insulated from the real and imaginary phantoms that followed him from the East Village down the IRT.

The wound mixes with the embrace… licking Pamela's throat, kissing her breast, fitting himself to the glide of her thighs… bury your face in her hair after the battle…

The apartment was cool, quiet and deserted, with Dad and Karen away for a picnic with Mrs. Kempster and Nina. Artie wanted to toss his Zap comic, keep the lights off and play *Crown of Creation.* Suddenly he had no appetite for Mr. Natural savaging Flakey Foont, for the chaser as the chump, the striver as the fall guy, always eluded and always a fool.

Amid the gentle acoustic guitars he heard Grace's silken invitation to love on the song "Triad," that maybe they could go on as three…

No, that wasn't helping either. He lifted the record off his turntable and laid it back in its place in his closet, dark as a grotto in the weak aura of the courtyard sun, where a pair of shiny plastic amphibian eyes met his.

Odd Ogg, Odd Ogg
Half turtle and half frog
He's the greatest toy of all
Odd Ogg plays ball.

He fled to the lobby to retrieve the mail, and plucked out an envelope from Columbia. He was almost grateful for more Freshman Orientation procedures, a dose of back-to-normal collegiate sanity. He flicked on the kitchen light and read the one-page letter.

We regret to inform you that we have withdrawn our offer of admission to Columbia University...

The train thudded to a halt, the signals frozen on red, the car sweltering...

Dad had looked almost pathetic, in his grey suit and burgundy tie, trembling as he clutched a copy of the ragged underground newspaper.

"I didn't know they'd print my name, Dad! And I sure didn't know the Columbia trustees read *Rat!*"

"Artie, the contents of stolen files were printed there! You didn't know that?"

"Do you think I wanted this? Do you think I wanted to put myself in—it was an accident!"

"Artie, here's your name. You gave them an interview, you gave them your name!"

"I—I filmed what happened, Dad! I didn't take part in what happened!"

"Filming the cops like that? After I told you what was going to happen? After I told you not to? And on that day? Lying to me, Artie?"

"Columbia called the cops on their own students!"

"Enough, enough Artie, I'll do my best, I'll talk to people, maybe I can beg forgiveness for your stupid mistake, and—"

"Is that it? Because of your Columbia connections, I have

some sort of obligation to—"

"There are obligations in life!"

Dad's cry compelled Artie into silence.

And you never knew when the train could be stuck in the tunnel for an hour, when there might be another blackout... or you shut your eyes... the cop, the nightstick...

"There are obligations to yourself! I tried to protect you! Don't you see what you've lost here, Artie? My god, do you realize what can happen if you're out of college for a year?"

His shout at last provoked an answering cry from Karen, perched at the edge of the living room.

"Dad, stop tormenting him!"

Down in the darkness, where we wind up with nothing...

The machine had arms like the antenna of a huge insect. There was a reel on each one: film and magnetic tape trailed down to loop through meshes of gears on a rattling path from one arm to another.

"Artie, luv, come watch for a minute!"

She was seated by the Moviola in a saffron minidress that hitched up over her thigh, luminous in the light shed by the machine's projector, and she tapped a foot pedal to advance the film. The machine clacked as if it would peck the film to shreds but somehow with the lightest toe pressure Pam eased the dangling celluloid through the gate until a frame with a red x appeared in the viewer.

Artie stood miserably behind her as she lifted the film clear, whipped it into the pins of a splicer, and in one efficient motion disposed of a rejected segment with a two quick chops of the blade.

She tape-spliced the butt ends of the film strips, inserted the segment back into the Moviola, and worked the two pedals until image and sound were in sync again.

"And voila! You know Nicholas Ray once said about editing, it's all in the foot!"

"It's all in the foot. You mean like this?"

He kicked her film bin hard enough to send it rolling and

smashing across the room as it shed filmstrips all over the floor.

"WHAT is fuck all wrong with YOU?"

He jumped back as she reared up from the stool as if she might hit him.

"What do you care?"

"Christ, are you throwing another jealous snit? Get the fuck out!"

"I don't care about you and Danny!"

"Me and Danny? My god you are such a child!"

"They draft children!"

She sat back slowly on the stool, and Artie thought he saw a flash of painful shock, if only for a moment. He let her think about it for awhile, let a hint of his plight snip from the reel of her brain her fucking footage and Truth 24, and replace it with the awareness that the boy in front of her might get drafted, processed into the War, that that might be happening right this minute. Then he finally explained the details of what had happened to him.

"Oh God, Artie, I'm sorry I—why didn't you tell me straight out? Those wretched informers!"

"What?"

"Remember Jack Bugliosi? Some creep with his own Bolex, popping off all militant with the students, even used the camera to smash a window during the bust? He's disappeared. And no doubt some of those people interviewing us—"

"You mean the police might have given my name to Columbia?"

"Artie, it's not as if you have an arrest record."

In the darkness and the heat amplified by the Moviola lamp, the smell of film, cigarettes and perfume made him almost dizzy.

"I was just shooting the film... I'm in high school... "

"It's horribly vindictive, Artie, like killing the messenger for the bad news. Disgusting, really. I'm so sorry."

"I'm sorry for kicking the bin."

She switched off the Moviola and reached for a cigarette. Even her unconscious movements, he thought, have such precision and style. He grabbed her lighter and lit the cigarette for her. She laughed, rolled her eyes, took a drag and put the cigarette down, and after she expelled the smoke (he had seen THE GRADUATE, after all) Artie jumped forward to kiss her full on the lips. He tried to make them part and caress, and when it didn't work, he backed away to see her curiously watching him.

"Be with me, Pam. Be with me now."

She flicked her eyes to the ceiling.

"Oh Artie, Artie, Artie. You know, I did introduce you to Judith. I'm not sure it would be right."

A part of Artie wanted to protest, a part wanted to burst out laughing at the revelation of just why she might have led him to Judith in the first place—all he could do was sag down onto the stool at the other end of the table.

Pam watched him ruefully and parked her cigarette in an ashtray.

"I'm in trouble, Pam. It's too late to convince them I'm a Quaker or something. I hear you can't even be a conscientious objector if you're the type who hits back in a fight. I'm really screwed."

"No, you're not, you merely have a problem. Let's put our heads together and—"

"How did I let you get me into this?"

"You're saying I led you on, Artie? Because you hoped I'd sleep with you? That's bullshit and I'm not going to apologize, Artie. I don't feel the least bit sorry. Do you know why? Because you wanted to do this. You chose to be there, to express yourself, to help document the struggle against the system, and you were beautiful. You had balls behind that camera. You shot the key footage in the middle of a police riot! Sometimes there are consequences, and it's not fair, it's not fair at all, but don't you fucking try to weasel out of such magnificent work!"

The dim light over the editing table was barely brighter than a candle, but it still wafted toward the accusation in Pam's eyes. He knew there was no defense against it, nor any protection within it, not any longer.

"Artie, think about it, no more gym, no more war research. The students stopped all that! They fired that fucking Grayson Kirk. The strikers pulled it off! They won, Artie! Even though the police did what they did. And we filmed that together and that will help the students even more!"

She took his face in her hands and drank him in with her gaze.

"What a brilliant way to begin!"

It seemed forever before he could get his voice back.

"Thanks, Pam... I know all that, I know, I understand... but I... I have no time to apply for other colleges. Dad says even hiring an attorney won't necessarily get me a draft exemption or postponement. My eyes aren't all that bad. I could be classified 1-A. What am I supposed to do, go to Canada?"

Pam butted out her cigarette, flicked on the Moviola, and gave him a triumphant smile.

"Baby, there are colleges in Canada."

"If the ruling Democratic party doesn't represent you, confront the warmakers in Chicago! Demonstrate determination to stay in the streets until every G.I. is home from Vietnam! The people, yes!"

More ominously, Bruce saw an ad in an underground paper for bus rides to Chicago that read, "turn your desires into reality." Danny would be sure to fixate on that. He decided to take time off work and drive Danny to the country to make sure he was nowhere near those buses' staging area during the week of the Democratic Convention.

Even Danny's tolerant-to-a-fault shrink expressed concern about how political activity might affect Danny that week.

And then there was the call from Nate about the leaflet Danny had given Artie. It had been distributed by a group that the police were intent on investigating. Nate had wanted to make sure to warn Bruce about Danny's connection with a group that might just graduate from militancy to violence.

Danny agreed to the mini-vacation, because for once

he agreed with the shrink. The August heat and the shadow of Chicago had injected a new fix of paranoia into the Lower East Side. There were so many ghost-eyed motormouths on 2nd Avenue near the Eaterie it was called the Speederie. Mind vamps, burnouts, and hoods hung out near the Fillmore, the What-Not Shop and the Naked Grape. They lured girls from the boroughs into tarot and body-painting sessions, and soon enough they were getting raped in alleys, crash pads, the confessional booth at the Holy Trinity chapel.

The Diggers tried to bring everyone back into the fold.

"Revolt, resist, tell the man to go fuck himself! Drop out of this system and join your brothers! We love each other, we give away food, money, drugs. Everything should be free so stop ripping off our fucking store, okay? How can you rip it off if it's free?"

Free food could only stretch so far with so many runaways in the East Village that even Abbie Hoffman had been funded by the Lindsay administration to create a guide to services and resources. Abbie joked that he was a city father now, show him some respect. When his guidebook hit the street it was called *Fuck The System*.

Fuck the system. Chicago. Yip-pie. Like metal pins the phrases stuck to Danny's brain, and when they passed through the subway they picked up an electromagnetic charge, drew down voices right through his scar that never seemed to harmonize, only vie with each other in one great hum like hatching insects. Ed, of course, and a new one, the Motorcycle Black Madonna. Codes from within, the shrink said, his brain conducting its own LSD regression therapy.

If he could only understand the change of signals as the train barreled through. He looked at his fellow passengers, riding the subway to glean some clues. So many faces under faces, erased sketches, the selves they buried, should have been. Like The Voyage should have been, could have been *had he not, like the voice in "Mr. Tambourine Man," but not Dylan himself, followed and disappeared into the smoke of romance, picked the mind-spinning over what Jimmy Hinton had found: the dark, unquenchable, undisdainable thirst for the blues... or even the folk music purity he'd forgotten when he'd synched his imagination to the one shots, the offshoots, isolated brilliant singles by bands at their most imaginative, experimental, drugged-the-fuck-out...* and now his world was like the eroded hieroglyphs on Cleopatra's Needle in the Park, do you even know which direction to read?

Taken higher... and higher... to be left so lo...

Mom and Dad talk politics and music. As the wasteland of auto body shops and factories and a pointless profusion of suburbs passes before him the discussion pleasantly bats about like moth wings on glass. Offerings from the liberal Democrat catalog of outrage. Danny at last joins in on a discussion about Billboard. Blood, Sweat and Tears at Number One, can you believe it? New York Julliard studio cats throw out Al Kooper, add a beefcake Canadian soul singer, and get to the Top of the Pops.

Gotta envy the timing, though, Dad chuckles. Kids' ears getting opened to jazz and along comes Jazz 101, all over the car radio, tasty drum fills, a nice skip in the bass, horns with a ton of harmony. Yeah, they threw out Koop, who'd taught them that combination of blues and Broadway belt, but hey, you can't argue with Number One.

Yeah, can't argue with fucking Number One.

Hayricks and glittering lakes shone upon the hills of Stockbridge, Lenox, the old town colonial brotherhood on the road to Mount Wilcox and Lake Otona. *Calling up to mom in the front of the station wagon, an only child trying to entice someone to a game of "Cows."* The black and white Herefords, the horses in their corrals—no time had passed for them. The clapboard house with the dormers, bay windows and brick fireplace was a little musty, his old room at the top of the stairs a little damp, but he wouldn't be spending too much time there anyway.

He only had to thumb two rides to find the Crystal Lake commune where he spent most of the next three days. Through the mist brightly dispersing over the water he saw a log cabin and a couple of teepees. They started the day with a Buddhist gong.

They planted truck farm vegetables, split logs whenever possible to store firewood, and hitched or rode in a van to the Pittsfield area where they worked in a day care center, a health food store, the lumber mill. Danny petted the pig and goats they kept as pets; they were still working on milking the goats.

The clothes they made for themselves were amazing. A drifter had a western denim shirt adorned with dyed handmade laces and Indian head cotton. Where the white weft threads showed through the surface warps of the shirt, they'd been embroidered into a vine of fantasy flowers, pointillist knots that swirled into fish and *honu*, sea turtles.

The guy told Danny the shirt had *mana*. Been to Hawaii? This shirt has power invested in it. Endless circular energy, his old lady's sewing, his poetry and pictures. The clothing had music and stories. He asked one girl, Alicia, about the butterfly on the breast of her pleated blouse, and the astral and crescent patches on her jeans. They were woven in New Orleans during the Mardi Gras. She had a merry, cunning smile joined to a curt flick of an eyebrow that suggested she knew her sexual worth in a free love market. He could tell an ex-New Yorker, and he definitely wanted some nookie.

But instead she stitched a yin-yang symbol onto his shirt—you'll sing better next time—and softly advised him to follow the commune's prohibition against any drug stronger than hash.

"My acid trips are gone… but definitely not forgotten."

"Acid doesn't make people loving and gentle, it just throws their own head trip on a bigger screen."

"Yeah. Cinerama."

"Only love makes love… "

They didn't want to change him, except for one Jesus freak passing through who tried to hit on him for the God squad. They just wanted to cast a net of fellowship. Make it, grow it, share it. He watched them read their kids fairy tales by the light of a kerosene lamp. He imbibed the night's fleeting tranquility. He threw the shrink's Valium down the toilet. Had he dropped in on another transformation? Buy land so money manifests trust.

Plant a garden. Sanford Ives, the group's unofficial leader, calmly rapped to them by a campfire whose faint glow made the teepees seem papery yet enduring as birch bark. When we learn to survive, discard electric technology, and become responsible for our food supply, we don't just take and take and rape the planet. When we meditate and become a medium through which a language of affirmation materializes, the energy we get in return from ourselves is atomic, it's cosmic, it's bliss.

They drove Danny back to Lake Otona, Sanford sympathizing with him in a rare flash of humor—hey, confronting the situation in America is a full-time job and I guess I took a full-time vacation. Alicia kissed him and made the peace sign over him. Hope you get into a better space. This Ed sounds like a scary guy.

The truck carved a vanishing trail of light and Danny felt dropped into a well where his parents could only peer over the rim and shout good wishes from an impossible distance. Still there was no way he wasn't going to hang with them in front of the tube and watch Chicago. At the last Village rally Jerry in his red, green and yellow wampum-beaded headband and war paint had proclaimed the explosion of love and drugs and anti-imperialist politics they were going to bring to the city. In Abbie's arms was their squealing candidate Pigasus, as some dude pretended to assassinate him.

The crowd had gleefully marched the would-be assassin to the East River and thrown him in. *Exorcism. Theater. Yippie!*

But Cronkite in his press booth seemed determined to keep the real theater off camera. The Convention herd in suits and ties and straw hats prevailed, cranking their red-white-and-blue signs on oversize lollipop sticks. Julian Bond, one lone black face, talked about McCarthy. He gave the truth, he cried, to people who were starving for it.

His mom and dad talked about Adlai Stevenson, another wise man, another loser, while Humphrey savored his impending victory on camera. "The politics of joy? I get a lot of razzing on that, but I think there's joy in politics, there's joy in my family…"—the camera cuts to the front of the Hilton Hotel as if, in disbelief, it registered something before any explanation could be scripted. Police facing demonstrators in a floodlit nocturnal battleground Danny knows well, breaking past the barricades to mow them down. Danny's scar rages in sympathy. "There's joy in my job, joy in American citizenship…" and it's Columbia times a hundred, the cops breaking formation, an engorged mass of uninhibited violence that jettisons its shock troops into the unarmed demonstrators to bury them with boots, clubs, and fists.

His dad shouts at the screen how the hell can they let this happen? Senator Abe Ribicoff, seconding George McGovern's last-minute nomination, cries out that if McGovern were President we wouldn't have police using Gestapo tactics in the streets of Chicago. Mayor Daley shakes a meaty fist at him and yells something which Danny's years of trying to lip read band members on stage translates to fuck you, fuckin' kike. "Any laws by which Mayor Daley can be compelled to suspend police state terror?" No more than you can stop the ballot count to the backbeat of the students and yippies and McCarthy supporters getting fed to the police meat grinder.

The kids keep coming, their signs reading SIEG HEIL and WELCOME TO PRAGUE… arrests, beatings… his mother is crying don't the bosses realize that's their future in the streets?

The streets of France, paving stones torn out and hailed against tear gas and guns. The streets of Prague, blood of young men with long hair and women with brazen short skirts run over by tanks. Kids just like him. That's the motif Ed comps and vamps on, his bullhorn lodged deep in Danny's flashbacks to the stairs of Mathematics Hall, the smash of the billyclub on his skull, *Kids Just Like Him. But you're not there, are you?… the police lights lay the dark right open and they're smashing them up, Danny, your friends, the woman you held in your arms, all the women you've kissed and sucked and fucked Danny they're bashing their brains out in the streets of Chicago… you cowardly little cocksucker… and when it happens again in New York you'll write a tune, wail on your violin…*

Next day on the ride back, when the city's skein of electricity could be felt in the antennas on every rooftop, Danny exploded at his parents. He didn't even know what he said, something about the false hype and the false self he'd been forced to live out for their pleasure.

His mother silently endured his tirade and gazed out the window. Did she really have nothing to say or was she just being secretive? He needed to have something to read them by, and fortunately his dad, as always, obliged him.

"Danny, don't you think we're all horrified by what we—"

"No, it's just law and order, right?"

"Son, that kind of law and order is . . . is practically Nazi Germany! You should read Lindsay's article about repression in *Life* Magazine."

"Fuck *Life* Magazine! Fuck Lindsay, fuck him and his do-good promises! It's like your promises. You'll get a primo contract, Danny, you'll—"

"Son, you were on your way, and you still—"

"You're the greatest, Danny, the top of the pops. Can't argue with Number One! Fuck it, I'm number zero, man, I'm nobody!"

"Danny, where is this coming from?"

The tearful bewilderment of his mother shut him up fast. It was her signal she could not control what could happen. A drive to some facility, perhaps. Bellevue's Ward Six if he was lucky, or worse.

"I'm sorry, Mom. I guess with what I saw on the tube I got carried away."

The words felt thick and squishy, the cold clay of his former self, and he tried to mold his replies as carefully as possible so that Mom and Dad would be reassured. But what Bruce and Shari saw was their son turned blandly robotic, muttering words he clearly didn't believe. His voice was so toneless that Bruce thought he was mocking him.

"Look, Danny, I still have a right to be concerned—when you tell me about some dangerous group like this Revolutionary Action Vanguard—"

"Why are they dangerous?"

"Well, the police are after them."

"How do you know the police are after them? HOW DO YOU KNOW THAT, DAD?"

"I—I—I read the papers! They're investigating all those groups down there!"

Shari quickly changed the subject, telling Danny how much they'd enjoyed having him with them again. Could he just stay with them a couple of days?

In that same quiet but affectless way he complied. But his own room unnerved him, particularly the bathroom, alien soap and shampoo and hairbrush which they told him a guest had used. Danny hurled them into a wastebasket and buried them with trash. He froze to the bed, engulfed in the afternoon shadows. He was worried he'd talk to himself about Columbia and Chicago and then the bugs his parents had been compelled to install by the police and the FBI would pick that up and relay his opinions to some Bureau listening room.

Columbia, Chicago… flashpoints of history, events colliding into a mestasis of oppression…. It wasn't the 'rents fault, the pressure on them to comply was great. But he didn't feel guilty about slipping into the hallway and putting his ear to the crack in their bedroom door the way he'd done years ago to overhear their fucking.

Shari, you'd think after all these years you knew nothing about artists and musicians. Jesus, Bruce, his mom replied, stop treating him like some kind of high priest.

"Did he even listen to you, Bruce?"

"Shari, maybe he's just continuing to experiment and he'll—"

"He isn't experimenting with his music, or his style this time, he's experimenting with his life, and he has no idea where he's going!"

At Shari's insistence they went to see Dr. Loudon, an old friend of hers, a wiry, aging, strict Freudian psychiatrist with close-set weak eyes that could muster a shrewdly piercing stare. When Shari hinted at how Danny was being psychoanalyzed for acid flashbacks, Loudon's eyes honed in on them and his lips curled in a dry, Oxford-donnish smile.

"If Danny's well into acid, he's been engaged in a bit of spot rewiring up there, I'm afraid."

They explained the current doctor's theory of treatment and he shook his head.

"What did R.D. Laing say about schizophrenia? 'The cracked mind may let in light which has not entered the intact mind of people whose minds are closed.' Very popular now, Dr. Laing."

"Do you think Danny's schizophrenic?"

Shari's hand flew to her lips as if she could shove the word back into her throat.

"Of course I won't know until I talk to him. But I do know there are a quite a few acidheads being told that freaking out against our politically oppressive environment is the only authentic response, and that ego death is a good thing. If Danny is getting that sort of advice, he needs immediate help."

When they got back to their apartment, they found Danny's violin and guitar and a note requesting they take care of them for awhile. When they arrived at Danny's apartment, he was gone.

As Regan hung up he had to laugh at the way Nate Kovacs had talked to him, like he was guilty of something himself. Regan had assured the squeamish lawyer he was doing the right thing in reporting to him that Randall Soles had formed some new radical group. Probably, Regan thought, Nate had found the group's leaflets on his kid's dresser—that tended to shove some sanity back up your typical liberal's ass.

Of course, now he had a phone call ahead of him he'd enjoy about as much as Nate relished talking to him. It was never any cakewalk to try and cooperate with the Feds.

The FBI and the freaks deserved each other.

Escrow finally closed, and Nate took Artie and Karen on their first visit to the little cedar shake two-story house in Centerreach with a white front porch and quarter-acre front yard. Everything that had charmed Nate pleased the kids as well: the old staircase with its polished newell posts, the second-story terrace shaded by maple trees that couldn't quite mask a pale blue glint of ocean. They walked past their mailbox and an old helmsman's wheel bearing a name that would soon change to "Kovacs" and headed down a sand road to a pond with a thin fringe of pebbles and sedge, where they could watch the birds gather—a flock of Canada geese, then a sudden and magnificent great blue heron, perched on a log with wings like sails. He watched Karen sit on the embankment while Artie skimmed stones through a gap in the rushes.

When he couldn't protect them anymore, when, for all he knew, their world might fall apart, this haven would at least pass on to them.

That conversation with the Columbia admissions officer had been a tortuous embarrassment conducted between two men who'd normally be talking politics over Dewars and water.

"Well, he was in that film group and he—he participated, Nate. You can imagine I was shocked."

"Who saw the film? Who made that judgment?"

"I don't know. But we know Artie was on the crew, he was interviewed. And they used one of their cameras to smash a window!"

That damn Truth 24, that damn addled infatuation for that Englishwoman. What a waste. Artie could've found a way to combine his political, journalism, and film interests at Columbia, the intellectual hub of the greatest city in America. With his resourcefulness and pluck, he might have gone so far. He had no idea what he was missing. And so Nate couldn't punish him. What could he mete out that was worse than the consequences of his actions? And from his inescapable mediator's perspective he had to acknowledge that to make a mistake, to suffer, as Artie called it, an accident, was not the same as to be wrong. Had Columbia not handled the crisis the way it had Artie might have filmed its' successful resolution. The Administration itself might have proudly screened his work during his freshman year.

You tell me you admire my boy's combination of academics, politics, and art, but when, in the throes of some adolescent crush, he at least tries to serve all those masters the best he can…

In the end Karen had said it best: stop tormenting him. Just face another moment when the icy window is open, the cat is gone, the woman is gone, things are broken and the old manual is useless. Nate flinched as a mob of noisy grackles scattered through the trees.

His children stood together by the pond. They watched the antics of the birds as they darted through the branches. Nate had tried to pull some strings at other colleges closer to home, but damn if that Englishwoman hadn't called up a few of her connections and wangled Artie a successful interview with the stateside representative of McGill University. The man was amazed by Artie's Truth 24 experience and promised Artie he would meet members of the National Film Board of Canada in Montreal. There was a financial aid package of sorts. Artie said something about having missed Expo '67.

Nate looked at Artie, so lean and fit these days from constant soccer games. Soccer, with its longhaired players, its T-shirts and bandanas, was hip among his friends. As were cats—he'd mentioned he could actually talk about cats with his buddies and not get made fun of. Nate had read somewhere that cat ownership was pacing America's love of dogs for the first time in its history.

His boy had a whole new confidence. And somehow he had found it in himself, for a half hour very late one night, to act the part of a war correspondent.

Next to him Karen clearly was saying something fairly serious. She no longer wore the kohl around her eyes that made her look, as Avery had said, like a lost raccoon. She had disciplined herself to practice guitar and piano and flute regularly and keep up with her studies. She seemed ready to pass on to Artie some useful advice before he left for Canada.

Let her talk to him now, by the home he would pass on to them. He could no longer hear even a hint of their voices across the cove.

Roadies adjusted the wiring on the banks of amplifiers and

popped the mikes, while the sparks of joints seemed to flank Artie everywhere, signals that totally bypassed him. He felt the weight of the past month in their fugitive glow, like the look of his Vandemeer pals who had been all set to be his Columbia classmates, and who now grinned uncomfortably at any news of his McGill University plans as if trying to be polite about a lousy joke. His classmates were a border of future strangers, like the Fountain in the Park and the whole New York skyline would be in a couple of weeks. Even Dad and Karen sometimes glanced at him as if he were fading away.

Don't worry, Artie, Montreal will open your mind. New perspectives. You'll transfer to Columbia when the furor dies down—they're going to lose a year anyway. You'll do well no matter where you are. Dad and the adults were all good sports, but Dad was in such a fog of worry that he almost vetoed Artie going to the eleven o'clock Fillmore show, until Mrs. Lansing told him, oh please Nate, he'll be with my son, he'll be okay.

At last Russ and some friends of his Artie barely knew finally made it, so stoned they simply tittered and lit a joint for Artie so he could catch up.

The Fillmore went dark and the blackout kindled cheers. Red amp lights peered through the backlit tune-up ritual. The audience hollered the names of Grace, Jack, Jorma, and their songs as the Airplane one by one took the stage, staking their territory with a drum fill, a bass thunk, chiming guitars. Artie borrowed some binoculars to catch the moment Grace drifted in, dark eyes piercing the blue shadow.

Spencer blasted out the drum rhythm from "She Has Funny Cars" and the entire crowd leapt to its feet to dance. Paul guarded his rhythm guitar corner, while Jack prowled behind him, bass jutted out to hurl the sound right through the bandstand as he pouted to the beat, gulped it down with the air. Jorma, tall and skeletal, uncoiled his guitar leads off the bass line, and Grace and Marty swayed toward each other, voices entwined in a spiral, Grace stretching a line like the long shiver when you're stoned or fucking, Marty's wail just a step behind her until he strutted to her mike and they met in the full cry of harmony.

He'd never seen a band bring it home like this.

In their rests between songs they were still into it, the rhythmic patter, Grace above all—hey, it's all right, people, you can get ants in your pants and dance, you can get anything in your pants if you want—and the crowd pressed toward the stage, overflowed the aisles. "Watch Her Ride's" galloping guitars… Artie hadn't liked the way "Baxter's" was recorded, as if it was buried under a blanket… but live at the Fillmore the songs yanked him out of his seat. Yes, we can say I love you. We. I. Everything that had tricked him and blindsided and determined and inspired and crazed him, the way he'd dropped Columbia and caught obsession in a zoom lens flash of blonde hair, it was all both outside him and part of him now, welcoming, rising, loving… By the third hour Grace's hair was wet and sweat sparkled on her neck and her white minidress. We're gonna play some new stuff for you lucky dogs. The drums exploded, the guitars rang out with "We Can Be Together." The light show's jaguar-spotted oils bled and throbbed into each other, and their ghost trails mixed within pinwheeling bands of red, green, blue. The crowd as one tried to sing along thought it could only pick up fragments of the words.

Grace got her breath back, clutched the mike and shouted "Love you PEOPLE!"

Over the next few days there would be many embraces. Karen's hug would come after they looked at photo albums of the World's Fair and she thrilled to his going to a foreign country. Your first Flag of Many Nations. Judith would stroke his hair in bed and provide him with her address in Pennsylvania. Pam would take him in her arms with a fervor he'd never felt from her before and go on and on about how he'd be speaking French and having bouillabaisse in the Old City, and he'd get to Expo '67, which of course wasn't there anymore but the buildings were beautiful to photograph—and then she'd sear him with a gentle, fleeting kiss on the lips, her hands around his neck—and the ankh peace sign once again dangling on his chest.

Dad would hug him close and tell him he was sure he would make the best of it.

He'd feel the welcoming current of the drive north with two new friends from the city, pastures and hills and elm groves rinsed with light, cloudbanks buffed to a foreign shine, here and there a maple leaf flag flying over the road down Route 9 past towns like La Prairie, the St. Lawrence Seaway, the Ile Notre Dame, and at last the Buckminster Fuller dome's hemisphere of geodesic facets glinting like a diadem.

And the whole journey would be lit by the walk back from the Airplane concert, the sun coming up through a veil of pink clouds on the East River—God's light show, Russ' friend Tony said—the Manhattan dawn shining to the cries of the Fillmore and the Music.

The soundtrack at Revolutionary Action Vanguard headquarters depended on whose drug was kicking in. When Randall Soles was juiced on some bennies or *bombidas* from the Speederie, the JBL's rang with "Kick Out The Jams." Roger, the scag freak, a medievally bearded 140 pounds of black Irish emaciation that tapered toward a hooked nose and watery, deep-set eyes, liked to spin The Byrds' "Sweetheart of the Rodeo." He slouched in from the bathroom, his rubber tourniquet still wrapped around his arm, pored over the Swedish sex film ads in the *Other* or simply stared at his big toe, and as he began to turn into some kind of mineral, the dappled sweet country Byrds' music splashed over him.

Bitsy Harker, a lithe, jumpy, straw-haired woman who was a girlfriend of at least a couple of members of RAV, toked up and lost herself in Country Joe and The Fish and memories of Berkeley. And Caleb "Colt" Borden, who had recently joined the group but now pretty much led their merry band of brothers and sisters, alternated between Blood, Sweat and Tears, "Jumping Jack Flash," and even an album by Paul Revere and the Raiders, the governing principle of his tastes being the male lead singer's priapic roar.

Colt seemed to take particular pleasure out of evicting Roger's records from the turntable. Enough of that Christian country-rock shit. Roger would just shrug and laugh. Once when the scrawny nineteen-year-old neighborhood half-blind cat that Colt was fond of paid a visit, Roger repeatedly asked Colt where does this cat come from, where does this cat come from, until Colt slapped him in the face.

Danny didn't second-guess himself over why he'd moved in with RAV. The group had rented a storefront and a facing apartment across a tiny courtyard, which meant natural air conditioning and a sunlit patch of stone planters and green shrubbery where Danny could seek refuge from both the four walls and the street—and Colt, who had military experience, claimed he regularly swept the place for bugs.

RAV was planning an action. Colt had a copy of "The Anarchist Cookbook" and its recipe for Molotov cocktails. Randall had once driven a sound truck to the West Village apartment of a Draft board member to demand he stop condemning the neighborhood's sons to death. He was constantly issuing pamphlets that promulgated support of black liberation schools vs. the United Federation of Teachers, and the freeing of all political prisoners, especially the Conspiracy 8 in Chicago.

But as the weeks wore on Randall mainly yelled at the landlord to fix the radiator and hawked used paperbacks. He tried to preserve revolutionary consciousness by sending everyone to see *Battle of Algiers* as a "revolutionary training film." Or the play *Che!*, where the true revolutionary endured psychological oppression from the President and reprimands from Castro, played by a half-naked red-haired woman smoking a cigar, and responded in every liberating way he could, which included anal sex, group sex, fellatio and (so it appeared) group fucking. Danny appreciated the turn-on, but when was something going to happen?

Sometimes Danny and Bitsy, to be as useful as they could, helped out at SRO's and the Free Store and walked old people with welfare checks home. Otherwise the Revolution came down to Colt and Randall squabbling over whether they should still support the Yippies—hell, man, Colt roared, dope and free love are revolutionary necessities—while Roger played "The Christian Life" and waited for his pusher to show up.

As the Lower East Side fermented in the late summer heat and curdled in the wake of Chicago, Colt kept their spirits up by "cattle rustling" at the local A & P so they could occasionally have hamburgers and steak without busting their budget, and by somehow scoring friendly, mellow grass at a time when when Mexico had napalmed its crop in advance of the Olympics, and the drugs sold or copped on the "panhandle" from Cooper Union to the Fillmore were coke and speed. Danny got to like Colt, especially when Colt threw his arm around him and said he'd played in a band once, though not like the Voyage—a "banana band," he guffawed. After three months on the East Coast Colt still had the red leather skin from what he called his time getting rid of his old life in the desert.

And when the time was right Colt showed Danny the handgun he had concealed in a pouch in an old armchair upholstered with a flounced slipcover. I know you get the willies, Colt told him. Here's the willies medicine.

In a mass meeting at the Fillmore—which, with the curtains open, the light show screen blank, and two standup mikes on the stage, reminded Danny of a woman padding around in a ratty bathrobe, nowhere near dressed for her lover—a Panther came to the mike to ask for bail money for six imprisoned brothers. When he got into the white race's history of killing and plunder, and used it to justify whatever muggings were happening on the street, most of the white kids started to exit the building.

Randall fumed that the Movement was becoming a paralyzed mess of contradictions.

Colt lit a cigarette and grinned at Soles' anguish. He never announced his final plan of action. One night he just drove up in a battered unmarked van from a public auction with numbers still chalked on the windows. He'd furnished the van with a giant pair of pliers, a crowbar, and a satchel of tools. Joined by two local radicals, Bill and Julie Schmidt, the RAV members sat on the rattling floor as the van headed toward Long Island. Finally when they reached Suffolk County Colt announced they were going to break into a draft board, go batshit, trash it. Put it out of business.

"If we want it to work, man, it will have to be dynamic. Don't let your mind cloud, just keep it in our heads we want to do it and that'll be the way it is from now on. From now on, take no shit from each other or from yourself!"

Danny grinned. Lenny and Rick, all you lost soldiers, here we come.

At the iron gate it took three of them working the enormous pliers to snap the padlock and chain. They raced to the offices and Colt got down one knee and poked into the lock with a toothpick-sized sprig of metal as he slid a Diner's Club card into the crack of the door. With a metallic squeak it lurched open and Uncle Sam pointed at them out of the shadows.

They slipped in between the banks of desks, beneath a phalanx of fluorescent lights, as Danny imagined the hum of each metal lozenge, the clack of typewriters and clamor of telephones, as the hive all around him processed young men into amputees, wheelchair victims, corpses. Tonight they were not going to just lay hands on the machine, but assault and batter the fucker. They went at the file cabinets first, Danny gleefully applying what he'd learned at Columbia to busting open the locks. Out came the records, and after Randall carefully separated dupes and cross references to be spirited away in bags so the board could reconstruct nothing, they tore and stomped the other files and drenched them with blood-colored paint. The latex gloves Colt brought for them gave them the freedom to tear apart all that crap, then steep their hands in the paint and smear it on everything, the walls, plates, cups, the Mr. Coffee machine.

Randall wrote a note about exacting reprisals for the bloody imperialist war while Danny and the others posted *Life* Magazine photos of dead G.I.'s on the bulletin board. And Bitsy and Julie came up with the most ingenious tactic of all. Using needlenose pliers they made a collection of extracted typewriter keys, all 1's and A's.

As they left they ripped out typewriter ribbons, tore out the phone lines, and even though it made atrocious noise, smashed the glass doors. Danny felt like Townsend in his auto-destruct finale, or, as he busted a phone with the crowbar, like the apes in *2001*.

Like a virgin acid trip, the high lasted for days. They were worried they might get arrested just for the goofy smiles on their faces when they saw the draft board raid condemned in the *Daily News*. Their rundown little compound between the carniceria and fortuneteller's store hummed with the residual ferocity of the action, and its heat seemed to draw an errant firefly: Cornelia Gunderson, ex-teacher, with flushed, perfect skin and auburn tresses that tumbled down to a denim jacket lovingly embroidered with appliqué flowers and Ali Baba castles. One of those refugees from middle-American wealth who'd migrated to the big town to be possessed of a truth she'd admired from a distance.

Colt predictably lavished his cowboy charm on her, Bitsy just as predictably froze her out, and Danny wondered at the timing of her arrival. Sure she was a tasty gift of the night—ethereal cereal to be sure, but the legs on her (too bad Colt had a jealousy hangup, putting out the hands-off)—but still Danny was unsettled, couldn't get it out of his mind. Why was she here now? Some rumor seeped out, Roger maybe couldn't keep his mouth shut?

Their Revolution had just escaped into reality, and here, tempting them from responsibility to protect their secrets, was a walking dream.

The French guy next to Karen in the crowd called them "Le Living". The allure of that Gallic phrase made Karen all the more eager to see them, while two kinds of anxiety tightened her breathing: the fact Danny might not show up at the Columbia theater at all, and the fact that he would.

He arrived at the last minute, dressed in clean denim, a little pale and unshaven, but hardly looking like the bum Artie had described. After he hugged her, the crowd began to file into the theater, backed up at the door, and left a long silence for Karen to fill some way or other. At last she asked Danny if he'd heard any new Beatle tunes.

"Nope, they haven't done anything since 'Hello Goodbye.' They just release those silly tv clips. Kinda lame."

"Yeah, it's like they don't even care anymore. Think they're breaking up?"

"All groups break up."

When they got to the door they were handed charts of a pyramid inscribed with Hebrew lettering and various pronouncements. There were eight sections, each with a rite and a vision. The Chart is the Map, it proclaimed, The Plot is the Revolution. Karen mock-wrinkled her nose.

"God, I hope there isn't a quiz afterwards."

Danny smiled and gave her a comforting pat on the shoulder, and Karen, despite being surrounded by an adventurous Manhattan theatergoing crowd, despite Danny's effortless trust in her maturity, felt in the sweat beneath her choker and her wool miniskirt like she was twelve years old again.

As they settled into their seats, there was a disturbance in one of the front rows. A man drifted into view, frail, arrow straight, hair thick as ropes hanging in a tonsure from his temples.

"I cannot travel without a passport!"

Danny grinned and Karen shared his excitement at being shocked into the opening of the play, with no dimming of the lights, none of the usual rituals of a night of theater.

"I can't travel freely! I'm separated from my fellow man! I can't travel freely! Governments I never see set boundaries!"

Other nondescript bearers of all sorts of laments wandered through the crowd. The tiny woman who walked up to Karen's row seemed to look past her and through her as the group screamed as one and froze everyone in the theater.

"I can't stop the wars!"

They were dancers that made their moves not just in the crowd but right through their tingling nerves. A man in a cashmere jacket backed away from the woman who cried you can't live if you don't have money, you're not allowed to live! A skinny teenager with a rat's nest of hair threw his arms to the sky. I'm not allowed to smoke marijuana! The crowd, most not yet seated, cheered that line, welcoming the comic relief. The Living Theater was not about to allow them that respite. I don't know how to save the earth! I can't stop the killing! Now the man in the sweater was trying to debate one of the entranced actors, point out it was easy to just say these things, to just piss people off, while others screamed the slogans back at the actors, and added their own angry shouts.

Karen didn't know what to say, only that she felt her emotions crystallizing on her skin, and that if she wasn't careful they might spill out to everyone in the auditorium.

Suddenly the actors turned their backs on the confusion they unleashed, walked at last to the stage, faced the theater as one.

"I am not allowed to take my clothes off!"

A roar of relief shot through the crowd as they stripped down, but the hopes for any kind of sexy public freak-out were dashed again by the sight of their scalloped ribs and breasts beneath dun-colored body leotards, under lights that blazed down to their bones.

"The Gates of Paradise are closed to me!"

Le Living was after another kind of nakedness. In the Rite of Prayer, they touched hair, clothing, even noses with members of the audience, muttering the word holy, holy, holy. To be free is to be free of money… hatred… punishment… violence. Danny was up and shouting with the rest of the audience.

"Paradise Now! Paradise Now!"

Karen was silent, amazed at how the simplest of spoken phrases could infuriate or harmonize so many people. The man in the cashmere sweater was hugging someone next to him. To those who didn't walk out, the theater became an oasis of unleashed emotion—and as the actors clambered back onto the stage, fell into each other's arms, and writhed across the floor, it seemed the most natural thing in the world to walk onto the stage and join them. There was no play. There was no audience.

"They look like they're really…"

"Well, no, Karen, but they can get to the point… where they can feel…"

Just like that the action changed, and one of the actors whipped free from the collective embrace, in the grip of some private demon. Danny seemed to have caught the sickness—clutching at his temples, breathing so hard…

The group shook and tore at the sufferer in their midst until he calmed down, the rictus of his face slowly settling back into joy and contentment. He told them he felt free of all temptations to wield power, to give in to power. The sacrificial sufferer was gradually revived and regained in the Rite of I and Thou. A return to the world with deep breathing, collective chants, a laying on of hands…

Standing with Danny, Karen felt a slowly mounting surge of pleasure, the sense of a potential lifetime of joy and freedom within her and within everyone around her if they could find it behind the locked doors of themselves, spring it loose, make the world answer to it.

Paradise now.

The performance didn't end, but instead migrated out into the street, and overflowed into argument as the actors stayed behind, trembling in the chill air, their leotards beaded with sweat. A black man lashed out at them that they created a situation but they're not dealing with it. They responded that they didn't want power shifts but an end to power, not a share in the money system but getting rid of it, not better marriages but no marriages. And you gonna do that with nonviolence? Man, you gotta change up!

Some spectators hugged them and begged them to take them with them to Europe.

Karen and Danny headed for the 86th Street crosstown bus. They stayed close to the stone embankments of Central Park, so Danny could slide behind a tree to light up a jay, cup the flame, and share it with Karen.

"Such a quiet night."

"Uh-huh."

"Don't worry about muggers. You're with me. They won't attack a crazy man. Though I dunno… right now I'm feeling so sane, I guess they might. That was righteous."

"It was amazing. I heard Julian Beck, I think, talking about them going all around the country."

"Yeah, he and Judith Malina are like the founders… amazing, though, it's like there's no authority… he keeps it a heavy head trip, but lets the others have their freedom… he just never lets it get into a bad space… man, how do they do it, how do they keep that going?"

"Well, it says they're a 'creative Collective,' part of a cooperative group called Radical Theater Repertory, and they were formed in March 1968, 'to sustain and extend the radical community in this country,' and they're all communal groups sharing voluntary poverty and experimental collective creations… "

Danny snickered and she realized she'd recited the pamphlet like she was answering some question in school. Why couldn't she just relax into the night, under the golden moon, with the one person who dealt with her without explanation or judgment, as if there were no age difference, no barriers?

"Are you okay, Danny? I heard you moved out of your apartment."

"Yeah, I'm living in a group scene now. Very political."

"What do you do?"

"Well, last night, we set fire to some heaps of trash, and when the firemen came, we threw stuff at them."

"But that—that's awful, Danny."

"Well no, next time they'll send the pigs with the firemen, and the… the thinking is we'll attack them, we'll get the pigs. We're trying to stop them from harassing our community."

"By attacking firemen?"

"Yeah, well, I'm not sure our fearless leader was right on that one. We were getting some shit done, and then… I don't know, now nothing's happening, and the living situation's weird, the sexual politics. This new girl's come in and Bitsy, Colt's unofficial girlfriend, is spying on her. Kinda bringing everyone's trip down."

"That's weird."

"Yeah, but Caroline's pretty weird too. Of course, Bitsy may just be possessive. But she says Caroline's trying to get Colt to split on us. She followed them to a restaurant. They were talking about Colt's birthday. None of us know Colt's birthday."

Danny's squinched his eyes as if somewhere a bright light turned on that only he could see. They started walking again and Danny started kicking at the sidewalk.

"What do you have to do? Take apart history? Undo a thousand years of fucking up?"

Relieved, Karen understood he was talking about the Living Theater again.

"If you can't do it with a guitar, a violin, or a gun, maybe it's about being ultimately honest. Peel away all the bullshit selves. Do you hear the voices?"

Karen hoped he meant that in a poetic way, and couldn't find an answer. He searched her eyes, desperately looking for one.

"I want to do it but I just can't see it."

"Maybe you can join one of these theater collectives, Danny. I mean, you're a beautiful actor."

She had meant to say terrific or groovy or something more lighthearted.

"Naah, that's just kid stuff, the way I did things before. You ever hear *Electric Ladyland?*"

"I don't like Hendrix much, that's guitar jock music."

"Yeah, I guess. Everyone asking about his Fender Strat and wah-wah. But y'know, he can make the guitar sound like the gods having a… well, a good time on the cosmic scale and then he can make it sound like what it would be like to live under the sea with different senses, or just lay down this easy funk groove… so free… and he's been everywhere, the chitlin' circuit, the Army, acid, London, the blues, but still he says a musician is like a child who hasn't been handled too much by man, touched by too many fingerprints, like a child, so he can be a messenger, a heavy of heavies… "

"Danny, you—you play violin like no one else, you should get together with new musicians. Maybe I can help, I—"

"I can't anymore, Karen. I got so many fingerprints across my noggin, I can't hear even my own music anymore."

He tapped his forehead.

"It's too crowded."

Suddenly he slowed down again. She followed his gaze up to where the moon hung in the fork of a tree, its aureole clinging to the branches, dimly visible through the autumn leaves.

"You make it quiet, Karen. It's like they said when we were all hanging around the theater, you're outside the gates of Paradise when there's too much noise in your brain. You make it simple."

Eden is here…

"You know, when the Living Theater on the stage looked like they were getting down… there's a way to be touched… many ways… and I can show that to you… "

She couldn't take a step toward him or flee, she just watched his lovely musician's hands travel to her hair, her shoulders, her waist. The boy who had graced her highest moments…

"I'm not putting you on. I don't want there to be any falseness between us. I mean… maybe it's kind of early for you to ball someone, I know… but maybe that's just a false rule. I mean, wouldn't it be amazing, like in the park? Where we grew up? Just free and… but only if we both want it. Other girls it's like… I just like the different feel of them, but you're Karen, you're Karen, and I want us to be… I mean, if two people want to be naked before each other… really open without all the cruel pretentious making it kind of crap… because they know each other already and trust each other… and they care about each other… then it isn't just balling, it's… "

"Why do you say that? 'Balling'! That's such an awful, stupid word! Stop saying that to me!"

She had never imagined a moment like this could be like this. She felt like she was being plucked like a guitar string in a riff he relied on.

"I don't want to talk about this anymore, Danny! You're a

musician, can't you hear how awful this sounds?"

He laughed, a laugh she flinched from, a drug-laced bray.

"All right, big deal, right, big deal, more bullshit… "

"Danny, I'm—I'm just going to get the bus, okay?"

"Hey, I'm sorry, really… Karen, please, let me at least walk you to the stop."

He followed her across Central Park West and as the bus clattered into view she suddenly realized she might be his last tenuous connection to the world he once knew, that he might just vanish into the Lower East Side. Even as she clambered up the crosstown bus steps her pity and fear for him poured out of her.

"Danny, look, why don't you just give me your number?"

"No, it's okay, I'll call you."

"Really, it's okay, we can talk, I—I want to talk to you, Danny—"

The bus door opened and Danny backed away flashing the peace sign.

"Stay cool, Karen. Have as much fun as you can without being a jerk, okay?"

She wanted to run after him as she let the bus take her across the Park.

Jimmy Hinton is exhilarated. He describes to Danny kids going to IS 271 in the middle of the teachers' union strike against their school, even though they're flanked by hundreds of baton-wielding cops and scanned by hovering choppers. Les Campbell teaches Intro to African American history in a black and yellow daishiki with a Jomo Kenyatta staff in his hand. "The cradle of civilization. Oldest continent on earth, three times larger than the U.S." There's a child's painting of Nefertiti towering over a blonde Helen of Troy.

Voices real and unreal. Did someone really say The Band was capitalistic revisionist rock music, put on the Last Poets? Bitsy's chipmunk patter, that's real: it's getting heavy, everyone laying down heavy shit on each other and getting burned… lot of down vibrations, maybe I should go back to 'Frisco…

Karen's cry in the Park in the night...
"I can't travel without a passport!"
No, that's not real, not the Living Theater in the ratty living room, not the Voyage audience shouting for more when he has none, not Motorcycle Black Madonna or Ed, who smells like sour cheese, saying *what are you waiting for...*
Jimmy is furious. The teachers' union accuses the decentralized schools of vigilantism. Of not teaching the kids. Not teaching the kids? Drama, photography, art, African American history, First Aid, Swahili, the history of people's revolutions, building a black political machine—and since when is there a law against decentralized schools creating their own curriculum? And the union saying their teachers were kicked out of the schools without "due process"—since when is there a law against making teachers transfer out? When you're black, it's always someone else's law and order.

Jimmy and four other Panthers come down to the Lower East Side to help organize solidarity and a revolutionary response to the local police. Eldridge Cleaver says white kids schooled on civil rights who are breaking with their elders over the war in Vietnam are worthy of any black man's respect.

The jive divides. Let's fight the common oppressor from the local pig precincts to the White House. Bring the revolution home.

And while in France the people's revolution, which had spread from students to Renault workers and brought millions into the streets, was short-circuited by the old Communist Party because they didn't organize it, the New Left would shed that bullshit party line dictatorship, and work through individual guerilla cells. In separate communities.

They emerge from their basements and storefronts shouting free Huey Newton, John Sinclair, Ahmed Evans and Martin Sostre. The National Liberation Front's flag flies from the Washington Square arch. An alliance of freaks and Panthers make the Common Ground Coffee House on 6th Street between First and Second Avenue their meeting place, and the area between the Fillmore and the Gem Spa on 2nd Avenue their battleground. LSD, the Lower East Side Defense organization, and ACID, the Action Committee for Internal Defense, go out whenever the police arrest loiterers and break up spontaneous demonstrations; they wear red headbands, witness arrests, take down badge and license numbers, mount bail fund drives.

By October St. Marks Place is the hot zone of the Lower East Side's war. Random fires are breaking out on street corners and kids throw bottles at patrol cars. Sometimes they even hold the corners. If there are black militants in the crowd the Panthers know it, and they scope the roofs with binoculars for cops, they get right in their faces when they come down to the pavement.

Randall wanders the streets and acts like he's supervising the action, but mainly he's a sidelines provocateur. Colt hangs around in a surly funk while Cornelia serves him dinner.

RAV remains strangely silent.

What are you waiting for?

One night Danny's doing his bit, watching an arrest for "discon," distributing the leaflets with bail fund numbers to outraged onlookers. Jimmy comes by to take him for a walk.

"You should get your ass out of here, Danny."

"What do you mean? Things are just getting started."

"I mean your living situation. Randall's lost, putting out these freaky pamphlets with incorrect goals, and Colt is just a Lone Ranger Custeristic asshole. Just another cracker crazy about his guns."

Danny, sworn to secrecy about the draft board action, can't change Jimmy's mind, so he grins and tells him we're just working our tactics and strategy out, just jammin', like in a band.

"Yeah, but you don't engage in self-criticism. Colt's got no education in the struggle, and Randall's forgotten what he had."

Jimmy, three inches shorter than Danny, grabs his shoulders and pulls him down toward him, as if ready to peer down into his brain.

"Listen, I still feel bad that I couldn't come to Mathematics Hall and tell you what was happening, warn you about what was gonna come down. Well now I'm telling you. I'm warning you."

How do you silence Jimmy's contradiction?

Getting hairy among the heads.

Danny tries to angle more of his waking hours toward the sun. At the League of Spiritual Discovery the floors are carpeted and set with tables of scented candles and Moorish handicrafts. Ginsberg and a swami and a downtown rabbi lead the crowd in meditation and tell them the natural state of man is joy.

At Washington Square guys with turtlenecks and shades, a woman with Capri pants, still watch stringy-haired folkies with guitars and recorders. A winsome girl wears a white button with a weeping flower to support rescuing the environment.

At Times Square there's still the sign advertising 100% pure beef hamburgers, two for a quarter, in a store that sits beneath the Coca Cola and Castro Convertible neon billboards. He wishes he could afford to see *Rosemary's Baby* or *Casino Royale* with all its silly James Bonds chasing all those broads. The guy at Colony Records tells him the *Casino Royale* soundtrack album represents the peak of Hi-Fidelity Stereo recording.

He follows a kid carrying a guitar case into the the Brill Building, to the golden woman still reaching out through the brass elevator gate.

Four guitar voices in Hendrix' cover of "All Along The Watchtower." The lead guitar line that attacks with bent notes and stabbing jumps. The warped vibrato tones that pour over the choruses like veins of rainfall, a deep chromatic undertow. The tiny echoing wa-wa strain, a cat paw on the glass, faint cry of life in the watery murk, and then the chug of the last funky guitar riff that drives the break home.

That night he once again finds a phone booth and thinks about calling Karen. What if Mr. Kovacs answers again, so kind but so careful, and once again Danny clicks the phone back on its cradle, because the voice will signify what he already knows in his heart, that they're speaking to him out of duty, that he's shunned as a pervert that made a pass at fifteen-year-old Karen. Little sis'…

But where are you, Danny? Can you tell us where you are?

Cornelia headed out the door on some errand. Danny nodded and greeted her, and then came the muttered incitements from Ed, and he knew that to shut Ed up he would have to finally take advantage of this opportunity to follow Cornelia. He ducked in and out of alcoves to keep hidden behind her until she slipped into a phone booth.

She constantly looked over her shoulder as she made the call, weirdly secretive, and it was weird in the first place that she would use the phone booth when this was one of those rare weeks when Ma Bell hadn't disconnected RAV's number.

Danny came back to a darkened storefront and apartment and Lassie, Colt's new Doberman. Her simmering growl was more than enough protection—so why was he reaching into the back of the covered chenille chair? The gun in his hand—what would it take to wave it not at the walls but one of the pigs that hassled them in the street? Or this beautiful apparition that appeared so coincidentally after the draft board raid? He whirled around, covered one corner of the room, then another, and felt a hand grip his shoulder.

"Easy, bro, don't turn around."

He recognized the voice and let the red, calloused hand take the gun.

"Even know if it's loaded, partner? I mean, it's good, primo, that you're ready to defend the fort, but we're cool now, we're copacetic, right?"

Colt had the gun in one hand, a bottle of Chivas in the other.

"Tomorrow's Election Day. Bars are closed."

"Sorry I messed with your piece, man."

"Hey, it's cool. Just don't want you to accidentally put a bullet in the wall and get us evicted."

From his suede vest he pulled a jay and poked it through his clenched lips.

"So what's spookin' you, Danbo?"

"Well, okay, I—I hope you don't mind my sayin' this, I mean,

I don't want to rag on your old lady, if she is your old lady, it's just that Cornelia dropped in right after the draft board raid, I mean, I've always wondered about that, and now… I just saw her go off and make a phone call, and I mean, if you're tight with her, I don't mean to bring you down, but—"

Colt chuckled, put a hand on Danny's shoulder and wagged his index finger between their faces.

"Eyes to see and ears to hear, right bro? Let me show you something."

He yanked a broadsheet from the cardboard box that collected their mail. There was a scarab on the front with a phrase "The Siberian Beetle can talk."

"Jesus, what is that?"

"Man, look at you, Danny. That's too much, man! Your eyes bugging out. That's what the FBI and the cops want, man! Get the heads real paranoid over stupid shit like this. Some bogus revolutionary into the occult will really freak out over the fuckin' Siberian beetle. Plus, I got a letter from a guy wanting radical troops to help him blow up the Brooklyn Bridge."

"So this is like undercover creeps trying to fuck with our heads?"

"And when do you think all this shit started stinking up our mailbox? After Suzy Homemaker appeared. Don't worry, Danny, we're cool. Fact is, we should share our thoughts more."

It was one of the privileges of supervising the poll-watchers; coffee and apricot Danish from Dumas Patisserie as he welcomed the usual roster from the Republican and Lexington Democratic clubs. As the impromptu breakfast ended he slipped into the voting booth in the quiet of the morning.

Nate quickly pulled down the levers for the local Republican candidates while avoiding the Nixon-Agnew square.

Tricky Dick, whose victorious followers had so atrociously booed Rockefeller at the convention. Anti-Rockefeller, and probably anti-Semitic.

The way all those sharpies kept Nixon away from the public,

traveling the whole country but almost never leaving television panel shows. Humphrey at least faced the public, he'd answered questions live on the telephone, the man of the people, the man who genuinely cares...

... then why did he give his Convention over to the thugs? Nixon had stood up to the Russians once. Humphrey couldn't stand up to a lame duck President. He sold out to the South to win on the first ballot. He said nothing while the kids got tear-gassed and got the crap kicked out of them. Humphrey's politics of joy was the politics of the labor union leg-breakers and goons, the aging vicious muscle at the shipyards, the hardhats, the greasy, corrupt, brutal Democratic machine. Nate reached for the Nixon-Agnew button, flicked it down, ready to certify his vote by levering open the curtain...

... and they must be wondering why it's taking me so long... Nixon keeps secret how he'll deal with the Vietnam War, and never gives a straight answer about how he'll deal with ghettoes... talks about America's fear of crime and it's a mealy-mouthed version of George Wallace's racism... pandering to the "forgotten Americans", the "silent majority"... hates Lindsay, that's for sure... can't even crack a convincing smile saying "Sock it to me?" on Rowan and Martin's Laugh-In.

How far is Nixon from Wallace? But how far is Humphrey from LBJ?... the damn war every night on television... the War in Vietnam and the war in New York... howls of creeps, Commies, pigs, ofays, honkies, faggots, Reds, hoodlums, bums, motherfuckers... and then the beatings in the streets...

... and Artie in Canada because the violence and drugs and lawlessness that had invaded those streets and his chosen college campus had derailed his future, just as it had swept his friend's son away into some radical protest group in the East Village underworld...

He swiped the lever. The curtain yanked open and the machine ratcheted Nate's votes into place.

The older residents of his Harlem tenement clung to the

memory of when Nixon was more pro-civil rights than Kennedy, but Jimmy and his militant comrades knew better. Jimmy imagined no-knock searches and the Tac patrol breaking the door down at the Panthers' office and coming in hot.

It was eight in the morning, the wind had kicked up outside, and the feeble heat in his apartment could no longer fight off the cold slamming the windowpane. Jimmy threw on a coat, cursed the radiator, made his Frosted Flakes and instant coffee, and tried to write yet more letters demanding a restoration of job funds for antipoverty centers, a resumption of food donations from grocers and owners of local diners. The Panthers knew Jimmy could write a good letter, but that was only the first step. Next would come showing up at the grocers' and restaurant owners' doors in force. Some called it a shakedown, but Jimmy figured it was more like driving a hard bargain before Nixon was inaugurated and the law-and-order Republicans came to power.

None of the usual hints from the streets, whistles and catcalls that signaled the recognition of unmarked cars on the prowl or cop cars driving with the siren off—and so Jimmy was stunned by the pounding on the door. He waited for them to identify themselves but there was only silence. Jimmy shoved his writing back into a desk drawer and hurled his hash pipe out the window. He hung close to the wall and waited for the door to splinter, then heard an inarticulate moan whose register he knew in a second.

When he opened the door Danny almost fell into his arms. For a moment he was angry about losing the pipe but Danny's terror chased those thoughts away.

"Jimmy, I—sorry, I—I think I really fucked up."

They called it the "infinity trip."

3000 mikes, and Danny was almost halfway there. By now there was no way to quiet Ed, only overwhelm him out of the way with a blizzard of sensations. Danny fell through them, mired in them one after the other like quicksand—until the trip was suddenly yoked to another of Colt's action plans.

Colt had been building up to it all night with the hash, the acid, and then some speed snorted off a chewing gum wrapper that Randall had bought. We're gonna bring Cornelia back into the fold. We're gonna have a little talk with that bitch. Roger was too far gone to go with them and Bitsy, terrified, refused. Colt had commandeered another unmarked van. They were going to see Cornelia at her new private apartment. Isn't that your gig, Randall had joked, and Colt had grabbed him by his jacket and pulled him to his feet. You are gonna shut up. You are gonna help Danny and I and for once just shut the fuck up!

One step outside and Danny didn't want to go, but Colt had gotten him in the van. He seemed to be wearing white racing gloves. Now Colt had a helmet, the horn of a scarab, and the spiders were coming after them, and flying over the roof of the van, the crackling wingbeats of the High Vulture.

"I didn't want to follow them there, Jimmy. I tried to get out."

He begged to be taken to Ward Six. Colt cursed at him but headed for First Avenue and swung by the big stone fortress. Danny saw the sturdy brick building fortified against the demons, and over the admissions door the marble flagons overflowing, Greek youths bathed in moonlight that flashed from the stone, gods at the fruit bowl... beautiful view... Bellevue... but there was a guard at the gate and his no's slid into the murmur of ozone hiss and crackle and Danny heard a yell like you hippies should just get off the fucking drugs! Randall knew what to do. He took out a ten spot and handed it to Colt, who handed it to the gatekeeper. Soon they were all popping a vial of dexies like candy.

Now the riptide of the trip had an undertow that slowed him down, despite the flares of apprehension that jumped from a skidding curve around the street, the stairway of a walkup. He couldn't even move, not really, someone else in his body floated to the voices and that epileptic wah-wah from Hendrix' "Burning of the Midnight Lamp." Cornelia's place was so weirdly neat with her blond wood desk, Tensor lamp, some of her knitting on the dresser, the kind of apartment you figured a telephone operator might have. But the yelling tore through the tidiness and when they thrashed out of the room Colt had scratches on his face. She clawed again and the gun flew to the floor and shone on the rug.

"Grab it, Danny! Shoot!"

"I didn't, Jimmy, I didn't!"

With a smack of Colt's fist she crumpled down into her chair, and then, a few seconds later, with a roar the room telescoped into itself, crumpled down like burnt paper around the black crackling buzz where she had been alive, the red gallop of all that blood.

"Did he shoot her?"

"The gun was so warm."

"What?"

The slamming of the van door jolted Danny to alertness. The van almost collided with a truck as it screeched away. Colt's white scaly hand was at the wheel, Danny's like some alien graft was welded to the gun.

"Toss it. Toss it!"

Danny threw the gun in the dumpster as Colt pulled over, and then he tugged the lock up, shoved against the door, and threw himself toward that same curb. His shoes hit the street and he ran desperately for the sidewalk. He kept running and thought he heard Colt's footsteps behind him, imagined being shot in the back, but then he heard the van door slam down the street, the van pulling away.

All the time seeing a black swamp of blood, white mask framed with red hair...

"Was she still alive?"

"I dunno, don't think so, but I couldn't've killed her, that's impossible... "

"Yeah, Danny, yeah, this truly is fucked up."

Jimmy had a program. The program didn't condone murder. It also didn't allow him to send a friend away. He looked at Danny closely and saw no blood on his hands, denim jacket, the cuffs of his filthy jeans. He briefly remembered the ruffled shirts and sorcerer's robes Danny had worn when he'd led Jimmy to the threshold of fame.

"You come all the way up here from that apartment? Anyone see you?"

"I just got on the subway, man. I figured I was goin' batshit and I'd get too much attention on the street, so I've been hanging out on the trains all night, riding back and forth. At least the trains are warm."

"Are you okay now? Think you can be on the move again?"

"Yeah... yeah maybe I gotta go to the fuzz, turn myself in... I guess I gotta do it... "

"Yeah, well you don't want to do it here. You gotta go back up to your parents' place."

"No, I can't—"

"Man, you want your parents to call the cops and be present when they take you. If they come for you here—"

"Yeah, okay. You're right, I... with Mom and Dad as witnesses... thanks, man."

They settled into an awful silence, each trying to imagine the future until it clarified with the blows of a fist on the door. The police i.d.'d themselves. Danny's eyes said let them come. Jimmy raised his hands above his head as the lock blasted loose and the cops charged in and threw them down. When he realized Jimmy was also being arrested Danny shouted he didn't do anything, he just wanted to help a friend. Shut up while I read you these fucking rights! The cop had them on a card. They heard the words harboring a fugitive, conspiracy, and murder. Danny screamed he didn't kill her and that made the cop yank his wrists harder as he cuffed them. Yeah, some other stupid prick's fingerprints all over the gun.

As Danny was dragged to the police car, the handcuffs that pinioned his arms behind him tipped him forward into a helpless, drunken gait. The cops had to push his head below the police car roof to fold him into the back. But disoriented as he was he saw no trace of the pulse of blood on fire, no giant wing against a sickly yellow moon, no omega of violet shadows—just Harlem stoops in the grey armor of ice and tarnished snow, and a few grim brown faces in the watery morning light.

He knew he'd finally come down.

It was Henry Lerner, the expat friend Artie had made the long night of Nixon's election when the Illinois votes hadn't come in until two in the morning (where's Mayor Daley when you need him, Henry had cracked) that handed him the paper. Artie read the story from the States—the phrase he'd already begun to use in common conversation—about a New York radical group and two rock musicians charged with a grisly homicide.

Last night he'd been with his new girlfriend, Celeste Bloom, angular, raven-haired, sharp-witted, and surprisingly mischievous in bed. He was learning the "second tongue" from classmates and her "Pepsi" friends—the Quebecois were known for preferring it to Coke—and thanks to Celeste's parents, a well-known writer on politics and a French teacher, he had met not only members of the National Film Board of Canada, but, briefly, Pierre Trudeau, the Prime Minister.

His friends talked politics all day… calmly. In France, where students and workers had gone on strike together, an alliance was shaping up among them and the socialists that could change the future of the country. That seemed to Artie a lot more like peaceful, functioning democracy than the clanking joust of political machines that had delivered Tricky Dick to the White House.

And Expo 67, though the party was over, was a feast for his camera.

Artie walked past the massive stone buildings of McGill University still bearded with the gleaming drifts of a winter snowfall and framed by huge, spreading trees. Would there be any point in calling Truth 24 about this? Pam had taken off. He'd called her studio. An assistant had answered and said Pam was in Los Angeles for two weeks, and was then thinking of going to Mexico.

"Hey, I envy you, man, in Montreal, wish I could get up there, or maybe Guadalajara, the scene here is definitely going to shut down for awhile."

It was after that call that he'd started to think of even New York as "the States." And after his Canadian friends told him about The

Living Theater and what they represented, Artie hadn't been able to stop thinking about what Karen had told him, what it meant that Danny had taken her to see them. Danny now seemed some kind of thief of sensation, skuzzy and wasted, prowling the edges of their lives for whatever he could get. Pamela. Karen...

Still... they were calling him a murderer...

He knew he needed to speak to Karen and to Dad. But instead he scribbled away at an English paper, smoked an old roach he had lying around until he tossed it in his old "Arthur" ashtray. Then he lay on his cot and shut his eyes.

The whiteness of a football field, laughter and a long black coat. His own busy hands swathed in black. The whip of a nightstick in the corner of his lens. Eyes shining under violet light, under the spotlight...

Threaded blind, caught on instinct, the memories jumped between his dreams, erupting in the dark until they faded out against the window of dawn-blue snow.

Chapter 7

RESOLUTION

D issociation. Fugue states. Lost time.
Bruce had recited these terms over coffee at the Automat,
the only clues Nate had to decipher Danny's illness. So far as Nate
could tell this was the reverse of a blackout; in the schizophrenic
state, the interruptions were the coherent memories, the few
moments where the person you once had been could hold its
own.

The Haldol at least calmed Danny down, but he leaked
drops of spittle out of the corners of his mouth when he spoke.
Nate offered him a Kleenex but he waved it off, letting the side-
effect of the drug run rampant so long as he could speak without
interruption.

Hearing Danny's determination to get his story straight, and
his relative lucidity under the medication, Nate came to his final
decision.

"I'm so tired. It's like everything is so slooooo."

"How are they treating you, Danny?"

"They treat me no different from anybody else. I'm finally
learning how to deal with the babble."

"The babble?"

"My cellmates, Mr. Kovacs, on either side of me. It's hard to
sleep, it's weird, but, I dunno, I feel less lonely… sometimes it's
almost like they're a chorus. In stereo. They ever find Colt?"

"He's officially wanted for murder."

"He killed Cornelia, Mr. Kovacs. Randall was in the car,
and I threw away the gun when Colt told me to. But to say we
all conspired to murder her, and to say I shot her, that's bullshit,
that's just wrong."

"You know, Danny, I don't pretend to have a thorough

understanding of what's happening to you, but from a legal standpoint here's what I think. You were on these terrible drugs."

"Yeah, I was on terrible drugs, I had blackouts, I was drugged out and brainwashed, and so I killed her."

"Danny, hear me out. I think Colt knew what would happen once he gave you a combination of acid and speed. I think he made sure you had enough drugs to take you over the edge."

"He almost left me at Bellevue."

"But he didn't, did he? Instead he got you more drugs. I hate to put it this way, but I think he was out to make you his patsy."

"I threw the gun away for him. That's where he made me the patsy, so my fingerprints would be on the gun. But I never picked up the gun at the apartment, and I didn't kill her."

"The voice that tried to get you to pick up the gun, was it Colt's?"

"Well, who else would it be? I mean… "

He caught himself, stymied.

"That's what schizophrenia is, from what I understand. It's an illness where you can't really see or understand what's happening to you. You hear these other voices. And I think one of them might have compelled you to… to join in this killing in some way."

"So you think I'm guilty?"

Nate explained to him in laymen's terms how the legal system defined being mentally ill and not responsible for one's actions.

"I'm of course willing to represent you, Danny, but I believe the only way I can do that is if you plead not guilty by reason of insanity. I don't think you know or can clearly testify as to what you remember, what you saw, what you did. You're not capable of murder in a normal state, I don't believe that for a moment. You were in a schizophrenic state, you were being dosed with drugs, and I'm convinced that an insanity defense is the only way I can save you from life in prison."

"So I spend my life in a mental ward for the criminally insane?"

"No. I'm not saying it might not take years, but the idea is to cure you, not keep you incarcerated forever."

He could feel how his words inducted Danny into the psycho ward. He remembered discussing with Becky surgical options that seemed like medieval torture.

"Mr. Kovacs, you have to believe me, I didn't conspire to murder or plan any murder or commit any murder, and I'm not insane."

His eyes drifted away, almost prayerfully, toward the blank wall.

"I mean, when I saw that black bloody..."

For the first time in the interview, Danny eyes shot straight back at Nate.

"You've seen stuff... I mean... you know what I'm talking about..."

Nate had that ghastly crawl now in the pit of his stomach he'd feared he would feel... *no, this is not good, not good for me...*

"There's no way I could... be it, create it, be behind it... I never wanted that, Mr. Kovacs..."

Nate loosened his collar, took a deep breath.

"I know, Danny, I know..."

... no good at all...

"I damaged myself with all the drugs. I did things I hate, most of all when I talked to Karen the wrong way, and that's all I did, and please, please forgive me for that, Mr. Kovacs. But no one can say that because of too much acid or dexies or Colt's bullshit or even schizophrenia that this person that I am, that I know I am, a musician, someone who wants to see change and love and peace in the world, just fell apart and went to shit and was replaced by what they say I am. I know who I am."

Nate promised he would think it over, he let Danny clasp his hand for a long time before they led him away — but he was already preparing for the torment of telling Danny he couldn't represent him, and even worse, repeating his decision to Bruce and Shari.

He was already framing the words: that he was ethically enjoined not to take on a client who rejected his counsel and prevented him from offering the best possible defense.

When he explained to Karen that to argue the case the way Danny wanted it, with no chance of bringing up his mental illness, would risk life in prison, and so he didn't think he'd be the right lawyer for Danny, at least he didn't get the rancor he expected, though he could see barely masked behind her disappointment a deep and lingering reproach. But that could hardly prepare him for his meeting with Bruce, in the cramped little back room piled floor-to-ceiling with boxes of albums and singles, Bruce's face grey in the shabby fluorescence over his sales desk.

"You're going to turn away from him? From my son, Nate?"

"How can I be your son's lawyer, Bruce, when he won't take my advice?"

"And you call yourself a friend?"

"What about you, Bruce—did you even listen to me?"

"I've always listened to you! I tried to tell Danny that Randall and those other creeps were dangerous! It was hard to get through to him!"

"Well now I'm giving you another warning. An insanity defense, in my best judgment... Bruce, just listen... "

Bruce shut his eyes and waved him out of his office. Nate trudged past the rows of candy-colored album covers and the hectic chatter of two teenage girls and felt as if his very presence could poison them and drain all the bright colors away.

What if, as his classical Greek literature class had taught him so many years ago in college—and which he'd never forgotten— what if madness could be a contagion, a communicable disease? How could you deliberately put yourself in its path? What *The Bacchae*, the most fearsome of all Greek tragedies, had intoned— this would not have happened had you understood your mortal natures—how could you so *willfully* misunderstand? All the pills Nate took to stave it off any hint of such a disease and kids like Danny *invited* it...

The only comfort he drew was from his phone call to Artie, who agreed with him one hundred percent. He had no choice but to walk away. Nate thought he detected a budding lawyer in Artie's response, and genuine support, but also a desire to maintain a strict distance from not just Danny, but the whole New York world he'd once known.

Hanging up the phone he felt lonelier that he had in years, his old friends soon to be estranged from him, his son comfortable with what Nate had hoped would be a transitory exile in Canada, his daughter once again nursing a solitary anguish behind a closed door.

Karen had hoped that the woman named Bitsy would be at the RAV storefront so that she could duck in and out of the neighborhood during a bright Saturday afternoon while pushcart vendors and button tables brought a fringe of humanity to this block of tenements and abandoned construction sites. But there was only Roger, a man who looked like a derelict and spoke in a high hissing voice as if the air was leaking out of his lungs. He tried to sell her something out of his bin of used records and books, and mumbled unhelpfully that Bitsy would be back at night if she hadn't split the city. Karen fought her dread, walked back to St. Marks, and prepared to wait Bitsy out.

You couldn't analyze this situation the way Dad and Artie did. No weighing of pros and cons. She was boiling over with what had to be done. Maybe it was because of all the writing she'd been doing in her diary, all the sensations she'd imprinted on those pages. You had to really see, smell, touch, *feel, listen.* You had to listen to the words. A sentence fragment Danny had heard and that she'd remembered, one sprig of hope. To clutch it she needed the half-crazy woman who lived on that devastated block.

She bought a tuna sandwich and Fresca at Ratner's and lingered by the Fillmore. Along the strip, everyone was buying buttons, posters, love beads, Zig Zag papers, the Movement now a bazaar, each booth trying to outshout the other. She decided to check out the Free Store, but the junkies, street people and Hell's Angels had beaten up the Diggers and Yippies and ripped off the place one too many times. The doors were padlocked, and where once the word "Love" had been painted the shattered glass was boarded up and the word "Hate" was chalked on the slats.

She got faintly nauseous as it got colder, the sky darkened, and the smoke trails of the Con Ed plant melted into the twilight. Sodium lights grazed the corners and doorways of the street. She saw fumbling lovers and dope dealers. You tryin' to score on me, motherfucker? Second Avenue was lined with spare change panhandlers who could've come from her high school. Other kids, dressed in slightly better vests under their coats, and bell-bottom jeans from Different Drummer and Paraphernalia and the Tomorrow Shop, drifted toward the Fillmore. Scalpers hawked tickets for ten bucks. She wished she could buy one. Instead she turned once again toward Avenue A as the lights died on the storefronts and the windows dimmed to the glow of yellow paper eyelids. The street was now watched by men bent over the stoop railings holding paper bags, and the occasional skinny kid who roused himself to a sprint to a Jaguar or Maserati that pulled over to the curb looking for a drug deal. She'd been taught to run for an apartment house canopy if she thought she saw muggers, but there were no canopies on this block and she wasn't about to run for those cars.

She clutched her stupid pink purse to her side. How dark it was in that brick-and-glass strewn vacant lot across the street, where you could see the moonlight on the huge abandoned pipes… at last she was now passing the fortuneteller but behind the red neon palm a face dismissed her as if she were just another part of the street. The bodega was full of men and one called to her. Eh, Chiquita. She walked as calmly as she could to the RAV storefront and saw a light way in the back. She jumped as a tree caught the wind and she thought it was footsteps. Hitting the buzzer over and over again until it almost fell from its wires she grew short of breath, and at last she almost cried out in relief when she saw a woman with straw-blonde hair grope her way to the door.

"Bitsy?"

"Yeah, man, do I know you?"

Karen got in with a story that she was a friend of Danny's and that he'd told her to come by if she needed a place to stay.

"Yeah, well, guess I can't let you stay out in the street—God, you're young. I guess you know what happened, everyone does. At least no one's evicted us yet, so if you want to stay here, even though the vibe's kinda trashed, I mean, I have some mellow weed... "

Karen couldn't even hold this woman's eyes steady, and so she decided the best way to make her understand was to shock her.

"Bitsy, I don't need a place to stay, at least not here. What I really need to do is to help Danny, Bitsy. I need to know everything Colt said to Cornelia at the restaurant. You told Danny you saw them there together."

That knocked the bleariness right out of her, as she stared at Karen like a snake that had crept under the door.

"You overheard them at that restaurant, right?"

"Listen, I'm sorry about this, honey, but you better leave now."

"Bitsy, all I need to know is, did Colt know Cornelia before she came here? Did you overhear something like that? Because Danny said she knew Colt's birthday—"

"Man, I dunno, I dunno... "

She sank into an armchair and lowered her face in her hands, then looked up again at Karen.

"You can't be a narc, right?"

"I don't think you can get that job when you're sixteen, Bitsy."

"How long have you known Danny?"

"Since I was little, here in New York."

"Wow. Look, I dunno anymore, maybe Cornelia was Colt's old lady before she got here—see, like maybe Danny told you, I couldn't hear everything because I was keeping myself away from them? But they sounded like they were gonna go away together. I mean, I felt really burned, man. He said he would stick by us and lead us, but instead he might be splitting with her... then suddenly he says to Danny and Randall she's narcing us, you know, an infiltrator?"

Karen's mind raced ahead of Bitsy's dragging memories.

"Then he had to be lying at some point, Bitsy."

Bitsy stared helplessly at the ceiling.

"How can everything be happening so right on, man, and then get so heavy and bad for no reason? Maybe most of us can't handle the Revolution."

Karen went for the phone and grabbed it off the table.

"Bitsy, I need you to call my dad. He's a lawyer. Tell him you're doing it because Danny gave you the number if you ever needed legal help."

"I don't need legal help."

"It's just to get to talk to him. Then tell him what you told me."

"Wait a minute. I don't talk to lawyers."

"He'll want to help, Bitsy. He'll want to help Danny and all of you. If the… what if the police or the FBI are watching you because of what Colt did? You'll need a lawyer, Bitsy."

If she comes for me, Karen thought, I'll throw the phone at her and run. But instead she weakly nodded her head. Karen dialed the number, handed the phone to Bitsy and lingered nearby as Dad asked how Bitsy got the number.

"I'm… I'm like a friend of Danny's, and he said you're a lawyer… in case the pigs are spying on us… I… I don't know what to do, man, I—"

Karen grabbed the phone and took over the call.

He stood over the coffin and he couldn't recognize the features. The aquiline nose had too sharp a ridge, the eyes weren't as somber and deep-set as he remembered. The rouge was so thick. She smiled a little too avidly, a coquette's grin, a bizarre whim of the embalmer. They'd changed his Becky, or perhaps because his eyes were blurry, fading in and out… where were his children? He reached out for Karen's pudgy little hand and it clasped his, but then slipped away. She threw a tantrum, he couldn't make out the words, and when he tried to speak to her, it was as if his jaw was thick and slow and he couldn't force out a word. She ran across the sitting room and it vibrated with an oceanic roar. When he tried to chase her his legs went stiff and he was instantly out of breath and there was no way he could overtake her.

He woke up still trying to catch his breath. How much wood would a woodchuck chuck—he couldn't utter a single word. This was definitely his room, and he was in his bed, and he'd stopped dreaming, but he still couldn't move. His breath couldn't make it past the pressure on his heart, and the terror sank down to his loins.

This wasn't a panic attack then, this was it.

All the times he'd said to Artie and Karen they might get him sick, and it was a nightmare of having to chase after Karen, his exertions among ghosts in the brain, that had brought on the stroke or the heart attack that was pinning him to the bed.

He couldn't swallow, couldn't speak, but then he realized the duration of all the thoughts that had run through his head without the situation getting worse.

His heartbeat slowed. He looked at the grey light in the window and then at the alarm clock. Other sounds began to calm him, the hum of a faucet, the clang of dishes from the kitchen. Karen was up a little earlier than usual, making her breakfast.

By the time the radio alarm went off a few minutes later, he'd settled his breathing. This was simply not a day he could call for the doctor if his body was even fitfully under control. He got into his slippers.

She was still eating breakfast when he came into the dining room. Those carnelian eyes of hers warily probed his for clues to how he would punish her. He watched as Aisha clambered on the table and she poured out some milk. The cat stuck her face in the glass and licked until the milk spattered her nose. He patiently waited for the cat to finish her drink, but when the words finally came, they tumbled out of him.

"Karen why didn't you come to me first? I have the means to bring this woman in for questioning. I think you know that. Why on earth did you go down there into that dangerous neighborhood?

Why do you kids think you can take the subway and do what you please down around St. Mark's Place or wherever the hell you go and nothing will happen to you?"

The last sentence leaked more recrimination than he'd intended but he didn't care. Karen stared down and petted Aisha.

"I don't think that, dad. That street RAV was on was really bad. I know that. But Dad... if she'd gotten some kind of paper from you, Dad, she would've split. She wouldn't've cared if it was a legal paper. She would've run off to Canada or California. She's a big baby, and she needed someone to talk to her."

Karen looked at him and as he met her gaze a shock of recognition stunned him. He was faced with the unsparing conviction of the woman he had lost five years ago. He pulled a chair up and laid his hands on her shoulders.

"Listen, Karen. Please listen. This trial, whether this woman might run to Canada, that's not what's most important to me. Ever since your mother passed away, there's not a day that's gone by when I haven't thought about what it would take to keep you safe. Understand, darling? I—I'm trying to be a mother and a father at the same time, but I—I can't possibly understand you like a mother would. You need to talk to me. You're very brave, but from now on, you mustn't do anything like that without telling me. I couldn't bear it if anything happened to you... and when you don't trust me... you break my heart, Karen. I'm not saying I'll always agree with you, I'm not saying I'll never try and stop you, but everything that you care about is precious to me."

As she clung to him, his shirt collar was warm and wet with her tears.

"I promise, I promise I won't do anything like that again, Daddy. I knew it was real stupid as soon as I got down there. It's just that—"

"I know darling, I know. Please, just... believe me, Karen."

She pulled back from him and he held her shoulder with his left hand and stroked her hair. Her eyes were red but somehow hopeful. Just two minutes ago, he hadn't known how he would answer her, but now it seemed inevitable.

"You know the term railroading, Karen? When they railroad somebody?"

"Like they put him on a track and push him so he can't get off?"

"That's it. I have to try to get Danny off the track, Karen. He got about as raw a deal as you can get."

Izzy sat in his armchair now like a stone idol, accepting the density his illness had given him, and when his breathing grew labored he smiled, as if pretending it was a joke played on him by his body would make it more bearable. He gathered a couple of more breaths and then doled out his advice.

"Christ, Nate, he should cop a plea, insanity, manslaughter… if Colt and Cornelia were tight, I don't see how it helps, just the opposite maybe."

Milt had already gotten Izzy's blessing to represent Jimmy Hinton, and so when Izzy grew difficult about Danny, Nate knew he probably had a point.

"Iz, Bitsy said Colt and Caroline were arguing. Both Randall and Danny remember Colt saying, his words, they had to go talk to the bitch."

"So they all agreed to talk to the bitch, which gets us back to the conspiracy charge. You know, they came to a mutual understanding to accomplish an unlawful blah, blah, fuckin' prosecutor's utopia."

"Unless two of them thought it really was going to be a talk. If Colt has a prior association with the murder victim, and the rest of them don't… "

Izzy stoked up some harsh, long breaths. He waved his hand at the office.

"You know, like the immigrant father says to his kid, some day this could all be yours, Nate. Or maybe Jesus comes back in a Porsche and Lindsay gets a second term. This'll be a tough case, nasty capital case, beautiful woman with her head blown off. This isn't the Oxley case or the Hicks kid. The press and the public won't be on your side. And everything you've done to boost the firm's income, which I appreciate now that I got a disease to support…"

He leaned to the table to slowly sip a glass of water.

"Funny to hear the old outrage in you, though. You voted for Tricky Dick—don't bother arguing, I know… hell, now I'm the one who feels like copping out. Milt's got a black militant client accused of stealing fifty grand in city poverty funds, you got a rock musician alleged murderer… Christ… y'know Jerry Rubin once worked for Adlai Stevenson? And I remember Tom Hayden telling me he was in the audience at Ann Arbor when JFK announced the Peace Corps."

Izzy lowered the glass and took another breath.

"He was so damn proud."

Behind the judge's bench rose a painting of a massive woman draped with an American flag and flanked with expectant children. The brood dwarfed Danny as he emerged from the detention area through the door the bailiff opened and took his place by Nate's side for his arraignment.

Prosecutor Ron Kagan, a lean, six-foot former track star with a tensely corded neck and the stare of a sparrowhawk, fought the bail request hard. He'd expressed professional sympathy to Nate over Danny's refusal to plead insanity, but now, even though it was inevitable the Gellers would bail Danny out, Kagan took off the gloves early just to show Nate what they were in for.

Nate's fear quickened when he ran into Detective Loomis Regan in the men's room.

"Whaddya know? Greetings, Esquire."

Nate's groin froze and he zipped his fly, trying to nonchalantly conceal that Regan had literally scared the piss back into him.

"Still on the same beat, Detective?"

"Yeah, I stay put. You're moving up though. Capital case. So much for peace and love. Know why they call it a movement, Nate? It's a load of crap."

"You're entitled to your opinion."

"Yeah. You know these aren't your usual bleeding heart sob sisters or soul brothers. These are killers, Nate."

"I know this boy, Detective."

"You think you know this boy."

"Thanks for the warning. I'll see you on the stand."

"No you won't. I'll be on the trail of Colt Borden. Got the Captain and the Feds on my ass. You watch your own, Esquire."

There it was again – Regan's mention of the Feds.

When Danny had assured Nate he hadn't been mistreated by the police, he also mentioned they did scare him with the threat of Federal jail time. According to the people he spoke to at the National Lawyer's Guild, FBI and police undercover agents were swarming into New York's New Left community. So much of what Nate heard dismayed him with its delusions of conspiracy, but there was a history here he couldn't ignore. The Communist party had collapsed in the United States in 1956, and J. Edgar Hoover still put several times more FBI agents into domestic spying and internal security squads than he threw at organized crime.

Cornelia Gunderson... the FBI... no, he had no evidence, it didn't make any sense, and he couldn't even unearth one specific prior instance of a Movement recruit revealed as an FBI plant in a trial. All he had were anecdotes from groups like SDS, Liberation News Service, Radio Free People, and Artie's old Truth 24 about "students" arrested at college demos who'd never showed up as enrollees, infiltrators spouting rhetoric about "pigs" and the "Establishment" while wearing wingtip shoes, mysterious thefts of film footage and tapes.

There was no substantive connection between the FBI and RAV that would establish Colt's motive for murder and take the gun out of Danny's hand. He found it tough even to defend the case to Artie. This year wouldn't see the normal buildup to a fractious holiday season, for Artie would be joining Celeste's family in Montreal this December. But Artie seemed more than willing to step up the holiday tensions early at the dinner table.

404 | CATS' EYES

"Can't you work out another deal, change the plea back to insanity? I mean even if he wasn't strictly insane, he sure as hell could act it. He was a pretty good performer once."

"Shut up, Artie."

Nate was glad Karen had confronted him, for along with Artie's new confidence and better grooming—Canada had given him the confidence to fight his age group's slovenly fashions and dress a little "preppy"—there was a knife-edge to his insults that got Nate's back up quickly.

"He's just bullshitting you guys. He's a total con-man."

Karen grimly excused herself to go to the bathroom, and the silence hung after her. Nate knew there was no way to win his son over. Artie needed to find a way to accept the course the family had taken.

"How's Truth 24 doing, Artie?"

"Pam's gone. Left no forwarding address. Nothing. She's just gone."

"Well, you have a steady girlfriend now, and she sounds wonderful."

"Yeah, Dad, Celeste is something else."

He bent toward Nate, his pleading eyes belying his attempt at calm persuasion.

"You really shouldn't be defending him, Dad. He's so crazy he might have actually done it. Then he pulls people into his trip and his mind games... yeah, okay, I feel sorry for him, but... Danny could just drag us down."

"Son, you can look at this as a legal case with a great deal of reasonable doubt."

"Fine, get Danny off. I'm just glad Karen didn't."

"Shut up, Artie! That's a terrible thing to say!"

Artie didn't apologize, but simply hunched over, turned away, and ended the argument.

Nate knew there was no way to dismiss his resentment, just as there never had been any way to deny the risk inherent in this case. In one step Nate had reversed a well-timed withdrawal from a cause that he could predict was guttering out. If Artie was right, Danny was nothing more than one of the rag-ends of a faction lost in sleaze and violence, and the reputation and bankbook of his law firm might never recover. But Nate also had a sense that the past five years had worn him down to the nub of himself, and if there was anything that obstinate fragment of faith in the defensibility of reason, of the social contract, of the law was good for, it was to see past the cynical write-offs, the reflexive invocations of chaos and decline, and to bring into the light of judgment just whom he'd come to believe Danny Geller really was.

The dinner scene could've been 1966, Danny and Bruce talking about music while Shari served her famous paella by candlelight. But you couldn't ignore how languorously Danny held up his end of the conversation. The new mix of Haldol and Chlorazil, the constant experimentation with the right blend of pills to retune Danny's reality, left him with tremors sometimes, or a dry mouth, or a ringing in the ears, and every so often he quickly excused himself to run to the bathroom.

Bruce saw in their musical conversations proof that he hadn't totally lost Danny yet. Yet sometimes when he peeked into Danny's room as he listened to new records he worried for the first time about what thoughts the songs catalyzed. All his life Bruce had felt the underside of music's mysteries and always welcomed them as seductions and arousals for the body and mind. Now, after music had passed like a storm through his home and the life of his son, leaving albums behind like fragments of a broken room, he felt like some idiot censor from the '50s wanting to snatch the records away, worried they'd lure Danny right back into his private maze again.

Hendrix' guitar shrieks, the ghost-wails of Albert Ayler's sax, the street rhymes of the Last Poets, all the stuff he'd listened to at RAV—worst of all the new record by the Velvet Underground, creepy rock for opium dens. Lyrics that sounded like I hate my body and I want to walk away from me. Why couldn't he just listen to the Stones' guitar fusillade and full strut return to R & B like everyone else? Music was becoming big, brassy entertainment again, Bruce could sense it, but Danny was still being lulled by ingenious perversions of the kind of late '60s music he'd once been a part of, by that little girl voice… *close the door and I'll never have to see the day again.*

He watched Danny sit by the turntable muttering to the album and to himself.

"Just writing songs, Lou, just keep writing songs… "

On Christmas Eve, after they'd set the electric menorah next to the little tree they called their Chanukkah bush, they watched Borman, Lovell, and Anders orbit the moon in Apollo 8. The space missions were rare touchstones in their lives now, a timetable adhered to, wonders on schedule, a promise being kept. How could all not be right with the world when both God and the astronauts were in the heavens? The words of Genesis were read—*and God divided the darkness from the light.* But the astronauts and their words were offscreen, and what the television showed were the phrases of geologic time scrolling across the capsule window: the moon stripped of its marble glow, revealing itself, with the ghostly precision of an X-ray, as a march of valleys and craters blasted from vistas of unremitting day and night, plains of scarred rock, airless, alien, and alone.

Darkness and light. Isn't a critic supposed to know the difference?

Starts great, ends shit, one of his friends and said about a musician's life. Miles gone sour, Coltrane dead, Mingus evicted, raving on a stoop about the white man over and over among his possessions. Now Danny, sitting right here next to me, damaged far beyond where I can reach any longer…

"Just keep writing songs… "

At the Kathy Boudin trial, the streets were blocked off by barricades and forty helmeted police. Marksmen were positioned on rooftops, choppers backed them up from the skies. The defense, besieged by the local press, was ushered to the courtroom each day by a police escort.

Still Nate wasn't really prepared for the crowd trying to shove his way toward him, and aim their curses as much at him as at Danny. Commie. Pervert. Murderer. He found himself ironically grateful for the close presence of men in blue with sidearms.

The *Daily News* had weighed in with a predictable article about a wannabe rock star turned vicious, then had gotten the maximum law-and-order bang for the buck out of the *Voyage's* black militant lead guitarist in a separate but related trial. They were especially tough on Hinton, even though the case against him was the weakest.

No, Nate told one reporter, who shoved the mike practically into his mouth, no, he didn't see this as a political conspiracy trial. We're going to prove my client is innocent of the charge of murder.

Conspiracy. Everyone was being turned into conspirators. Tom Hayden, Rennie Davis, David Dillinger, Abbie Hoffman, just because they had led the Chicago demonstrations together. The Panther 21 had apparently conspired to blow up the Bronx Botanical Gardens. Law enforcement saw the New Left as a whole subterranean network of conspiracies, and why not, for as Izzy had pointed out, it was a prosecutorial dragnet par excellence.

But what parts of that shadowy interplay came from the prosecutorial imagination, what parts were real, and what parts were aided and abetted by law enforcement itself? These invisible strings that so many of his friends and allies thought were threatening them brushed at Nate's thoughts as he walked to the courtroom, and compounded the usual pretrial anxiety. He'd disparaged the paranoia of some of the people he defended—but as he headed for the courtroom, he felt the rising elevator in his brain that signaled his own panic. Just recently he'd refilled his prescription for Valium.

As he and Danny took their seats Nate looked back at a painting of three serene Roman Senators draped in their togas and laurels, the aegis of the Roman Republic. Beneath them reporters and spectators hunched and fidgeted, the fluorescence from above glinting on their flash cameras and hair tonic. He'd never had an audience like this for an opening statement. The elevator in his brain climbed another floor.

Kagan laid down his case: a deliberate, planned conspiracy by Caleb "Colt" Borden, Randall Soles, and Daniel Geller of the Revolutionary Action Vanguard to murder Cornelia Gunderson, with Danny pulling the trigger. He threw his body forward like a football player delivering a block, and crooked his finger at Danny and Nate.

Nate began to take umbrage at Kagan's needless chest-thumping and cornball theatrics, and out of that anger came one of the strategic insights he needed. Kagan was trying to make this group sound like a radical equivalent of the bank robbers of *Rififi*. But the members of RAV didn't have the foresight or discipline to conspire with any sort of efficiency. They were panicky footsoldiers that Colt was able to dose with his own fury.

Nate tempered his opening statement to his new insight, and also adopted as low-key an approach as possible, treating the jury as equals rather than unruly schoolchildren.

"Ladies and gentlemen of the jury, when you dispassionately examine the facts, you'll see that there's no conspiracy, and that the real criminal, the sole planner and killer, has fled justice. Daniel Geller never contemplated killing Miss Gunderson, and even in the heat of the moment, a moment more terrifying than any of us are likely to ever experience, did not participate in her murder."

"We came together to reject bullshit materialism. To make it in our neighborhood by selling books and records, making candles, whatever we could, and sharing food, clothing, the Music… to fight a system of imperialism and corporate fascism that makes 90% of us poverty-stricken nonpersons… and we were in a community where just about everyone on the street is your sister, your brother, your lover."

Randall Soles was a good salesman, and his conviction and strength of will bolstered Kagan's case that RAV was strong-minded enough to organize itself and eliminate anyone they thought was a spy.

This was a trial where the initial police witnesses hadn't meant much. There was no way Nate could deflect the evidence of Danny's fingerprints on the tossed gun that Detective Damrosch had found, although Nate had elicited from him the admission that there was also no way to determine from the prints if Danny had actually fired the gun or merely dumped it. Nate had also established that no gunshot residue had been found on Danny's clothes.

Soles was the first truly vital witness, and he testified with devastating effect that Danny had brought up that Cornelia was possibly "narcing" them, that Colt had joked with Danny about his playing with his gun, that Danny had accompanied Colt up to Cornelia's apartment.

There was only one way to shake Randall's testimony, as Izzy had warned him, and Nate steeled himself to do what had to be done.

"And then what happened?"

"They were both freaking out. They'd just killed somebody."

"Do you remember what they were talking about?"

"Just craziness."

"Craziness? There was no strategy for disposing—"

The objection about leading the witness came like clockwork.

"Do you recall either you or Colt telling Danny to toss the gun?"

"No."

He received permission to treat the witness as hostile.

"Are you telling me that you and Colt were supposedly the leaders of this group and you had no strategy for even disposing of the gun?"

"It was Colt's gun, man!"

"But you say Danny decided to dump it?"

"It's his fingerprints on it!"

"So Danny told Colt Borden what to do with his gun?"

"Hey, we're a functioning revolutionary unit! We work together!"

"Mr. Soles, if you were all working together, did you ever

once tell Colt that you thought the idea of murdering Cornelia Gunderson was wrong?"

"Man, I didn't know he wanted to do it until that night."

"So you didn't really conspire with him?"

"Well no, but I—but you have to maintain unity and combat threats!"

"What kind of threats?"

"The whole fascist power structure!"

By now, Soles didn't know whether to defend the conspiracy, break away from the conspiracy, or deny the conspiracy. Nate had succeeded in triggering his mania and degrading his testimony.

"We're in a battle on the street every day. We're not allowed to peacefully assemble, we're not allowed to put our truths out in the public place! We have to meet aggression with self-defense! Like Mark Rudd said, organizing is another way of going slow!"

Kagan was eyeing the judge helplessly as he cautioned the witness to sit down. Nat shouted out no further questions, but Soles wasn't about to stop.

"We're part of all of it, man! The battle of our black brothers and sisters and the F.A.L.N. and the Native Americans and the NVA freedom fighters in Vietnam! RAV was established to support these struggles and to provide a revolutionary alternative for the neighborhoods of New York City! We're not killers! The cops are killers! The FBI are killers!"

Amid all the tumult, Soles thrashing in the bailiff's grip as he was escorted from the courtroom, Nate looked over at Danny and could read in his eyes a flicker of sorrow.

Loomis Regan had to go through the national BCI files to finally uncover Caleb "Colt" Borden's fingerprints from an arrest in Philadelphia for drunkenness and disorderly conduct. He learned he'd met bail with the help of a Miss Cornelia Gunderson, and he figured all his suspicions that Gunderson was a confidential informant for the Bureau were on target. Couldn't the Bureau have shared that fucking tidbit, he wondered, couldn't they have gone beyond the usual clannish bullshit in the interest of taking this cowboy hippie trash off the streets?

Then again, maybe they didn't want to find him all that much. Clamming up like this went beyond the usual turf war crap. Maybe when Cornelia went sweet on Colt she'd talked to him about the Bureau's bag of tricks: the poison pen letters they sent to break up New Left marriages and relationships, the "snitch jackets" they put on black nationalists in prison so other militants would ice them, all their "disrupt and neutralize the target" tactics. Suddenly Colt isn't a head case cockroach, he knows some shit.

Loomis got permission to spend two days in Philadelphia. He visited his favorite hoagie joint in the City of Brotherly Love and got tickets for a 76ers game. Then he poked around for Eric Lasky, a biker he knew who had been a bodyguard for Jerry Rubin and who had once joined Colt in Philadelphia, where they'd been suspected of a string of drug deals. But when he ran down one of Lasky's last known contacts, a Buzzy Riegert, the greasy little freak laughed and gave Regan a number in Washington D.C.

Back in New York, Loomis placed a call to Agent Ed Lazarus. After some initial reluctance, Lazarus agreed to review the photos and prints of Caleb "Colt" Borden. After that, the connection went dead. Regan's phone calls went unanswered. Finally he called his Lieutenant, who told him to cease and desist calling the fucking FBI.

Loomis took a walk around the block and bought a Sabrett hot dog and a Coke. He strolled past the Washington Square arch, looked at the usual bunch of dopers and the hot numbers in tight jeans they were lucky to get within sniffing distance of, let alone bang. Guitarists, tambourine-slappers, conga drummers with Afros, ocarina players for Chrissake, Hare Krishna glassy-eyed chanters, the whole bunch made him want to puke. But as long as they didn't cross him, he'd pledged to serve and protect those assholes along with everyone else.

You could know the rules. It wasn't that fucking complicated. Unless you're the fucking FBI.

Nate gave Bitsy Harker the legal equivalent of hand-holding a toddler through her first tiny steps. He had her carefully describe how she'd followed Colt and Cornelia to a restaurant and eavesdropped on their conversation. He allowed her to freely admit her jealousy of the new, strikingly attractive woman in their midst. That Bitsy appeared so drab and furtive only made her seem to be a more sincere witness.

She also vibrated with a cloistered paranoia that Kagan took full advantage of to pay Nate back for his treatment of Randall Soles.

"Was that the only reason you followed Cornelia? You were jealous of her?"

"Well, yeah, and I was right. She wanted Colt to run away with her, and—"

"Please stick to the question, Miss Harker. Didn't you and Randall Soles also consider her a threat to the group?"

When Nate promptly objected, Kagan rephrased and asked if she felt Cornelia was such a threat. Bitsy, who was too scared of the court to be anything less than honest, but not so dimwitted as not to know where the cross-examination was heading, gave a sad shrug and mumbled that yeah, she guessed she thought she was a threat. Did anyone else? Yeah, she thought maybe Danny did. He got her to state on the record once again that Danny felt she might be narcing on the group. But we're a target, she insisted. We're authentic, we're on the front lines. Kagan dropped that line of questioning and then got her to admit that at the dinner she spied on Colt didn't seem angry, that they didn't discuss politics, only personal matters, yes, they were relaxed, probably stoned. Wasn't she stoned too?

"So you were under the influence of drugs, scared stiff, jealous, and angry about the threat you thought Cornelia posed to the group and your relationship to Colt Borden when you heard the conversation you're relating to us today?"

After shambling her way through a few more questions Bitsy slunk off the witness stand. Nate glanced over to Karen and could see how Bitsy's ordeal had repelled her—my God, Karen had been responsible for bringing her into this, and now she had to watch as Bitsy, and perhaps their whole case, began to crumble.

The bus rattled down York Avenue and Nate wondered if he was becoming as crazy as any of them. No, maybe he was just trying to get all the anxiety, and his own anxiety, in a judo hold. Use the anxiety's power against itself.

Gottehrer thought Nate had a fighting chance. There was already scuttlebutt the case against the Panther 21 might not hold because two of the conspirators urging on the plot had been undercover cops. Cornelia Gunderson had been a librarian in Philadelphia drifting in and out of the hippie scene, waitressing some nights at the Mind Game, a folk rock cabaret. That's where she'd apparently first met Colt Borden on his long trip from the western desert to the east coast. The FBI might have latched onto her and turned her into a confidential informant— but Nate knew he couldn't use that suspicion alone as a reason to go trolling the FBI.

But what if his conjectures about FBI infiltration tactics had echoes down the halls of the very government of the City of New York? Barry Gottehrer thought he had a leak in his office. The Feds knew what radicals he was dealing with, Gottehrer was sure of it. Based on his own suspicions, he would definitely consider the idea of testifying, of putting his worries about leaks and Bureau infiltration into city political groups and even city offices on some kind of record. But of course he needed permission, he needed Nate to make inquiries at the highest possible level first.

The Mayor leaned his impossibly tall frame back into his chair and swiveled to face the East River, a busy waterway now empty and curdled with ice.

"Oh, I don't think your client is particularly paranoid on that score, Nate. Anyone who's been in public service in the capital any amount of time knows about J. Edgar Hoover's tricks."

Nate's lower back was starting to kill him, but he didn't dare move as he watched Lindsay swing around to his desk and absent-mindedly fumble with his cufflinks. His face had gotten leathery since they last spoke, or perhaps that was just the wind and the cold.

"Still, when you talk about Barry testifying to FBI interference in his office in court… the timing of it… look, I have great concern about this, especially with Nixon in the White House. New York is trying to choose its own destiny, and we get enough resistance from the state, let alone the Federal government. Now to have a city official testify in court… "

On the shelves behind him were photos of Lindsay meeting black leaders after his triumphant walk through Harlem. Only a year old, but still a distant reminder of the great peacemaking days before the teachers' strike had ruined everything. The Mayor had vacillated between defending the decentralized ghetto schools and urging respect for the teachers' union and the Board of Education. His stumbling path toward compromise had alienated those black leaders, all the women like Dorothy who'd once taught in city schools—just about everyone.

"This damn weather, Nate."

Lindsay didn't have to say another word. The blizzard that had paralyzed Queens for days thanks to poor planning and sanitation equipment upkeep had given the final blow to his reputation. Lindsay had done a walking tour in the outer boroughs far lonelier and nastier than his trips to Harlem, and had been greeted with boos, jeers, and accusations that he was uncaring and incompetent.

Nate knew the meeting was over as Lindsay's eyes drifted back to the river.

"You know housewives in Queens cursed me on the street? You try to do so much in this job and then… snow."

As he walked away from Gracie Mansion, the ice caked beneath Nate's boots. Yeah, snow. He kicked at it like he used to when he was a kid, then packed a snowball and flung it against a tree. Still got some aim. Take that. He watched a squirrel hop across the snowdrifts. The ice is freezing again… better know where those acorns are…

He had to stop for a cup of coffee to keep his mood from

bottoming out altogether, but first he wanted to place a call to his office. He fished out a dime from his pocket, called from a phone booth, and instantly got the word from Milt that Detective Regan was looking for him.

Twenty minutes later Nate was scanning the throngs of hippies and NYU students on MacDougal Street. He wondered if Detective Regan had gotten second thoughts about a hush-hush meeting with him, if he should take an Anacin for his headache, find another freezing cold phone booth, check in yet again and get the message that the detective had cancelled. Then suddenly a hand clapped his shoulder and with a brusque greeting he was shuttled along the pavement as fast as he could walk. Regan wanted to keep moving.

"Lemme tell you, Esquire, from where I sit, the world's gone fucking nuts."

"It's not easy being a cop now, I understand."

Loomis cocked his fingers into the shape of a gun and aimed them at Nate's head.

"You've got a split second to decide if you're gonna draw your weapon and open fire. If it's a fist, or a knife, you've got maybe a half second more. But if you react like you're trained to do, like you have to do to get out alive… police brutality charges, investigations, Lindsay's little twerps all over the news, maybe you even lose your badge."

"So how can I help you, Detective?"

"How can you help me? That's rich. Well you can start by getting it through your head that no one from the force was spying on the Revolutionary Alternative whatever the fuck they call themselves. We got no time. I mean, we got the Panthers, the P.R. crazies in the Young Lords, the SDS Action Faction, the Redstocking feminists kicking shit, some Oriental group, even the goddamn fags now have a liberation front! Jesus!"

He shook his head like a horse infuriated by gnats.

"The RAV doesn't even show up on our radar."

"What about the FBI?"

"Fuckin' G-men. We're after the same fugitive and there's no give-and-take from them, they don't give us squat."

"So you believe Cornelia Gunderson was a confidential informant?"

"Oh, Christ, Nate, use your head! I don't have much time here. She's dead! Why would they bother to hide that now?"

Nate felt the gooseflesh begin to creep up his neck. Loomis took his arm in a grip somewhere between a collar and a plea for friendship.

"Look, a few years ago you caught me on that minor bust. Okay, I was careless. But then I turned out to be dead to rights about that Cornelius Hophead, didn't I? I don't feel proud about the way I planted evidence, and I don't do that shit anymore, but I never did it unless I knew they were guilty."

"What did you say?"

"It's not like I was dangling smack in front of that sax player's eyes. I wasn't entrapping him, I wasn't leading him to break the law. A junkie's gonna cop, a hitman's gonna kill again. But I don't know as some punks are gonna declare war on the United States. Fuck!"

The mustard from his hot dog flew on Loomis' trench coat. He splashed some 7-Up on it and dabbed at it with his napkin; his anger seemed divided between the mishap and Nate not getting his point. But Nate got it. He understood why his hope that someone might nab Colt in time for him to be questioned on the witness stand was useless. He knew how he had to proceed.

"I'll need the name of whatever FBI agent you feel might be the best… "

"Target?"

Nate swallowed hard and nodded.

"Fuck it, cooperate with the Feds and look what you get… "

"You cooperated with them? My god, when I gave you the name of that guy in RAV, did you—"

Regan was suddenly in Nate's face again, as livid as when he'd swept Nate up in his arrest of Cornelius Hill. Nate stepped back and almost fell over the railing of the frozen park lawn.

"Listen, I don't know or care how the Bureau came into this, all that is water way under the fuckin' bridge! Understand one thing, Esquire. You're alone in the dark on this one. My name comes up I might lose my job. And then you'll have to deal with me as a very pissed off private citizen. Anybody asks, you say it was an anonymous phone call."

"I think I understand, Detective."

Regan backed off, and collected himself with a shrug.

"By the way, sorry about what happened to your kid."

"What?"

"Artie Kovacs, right? The d.a.'s office had us infiltrate showings of films about Columbia to see how damaging they were. His name was on the Truth 24 film, he was interviewed by the underground rags, nothing I could do."

"You passed his name on to the University?"

"The d.a.'s office, and then they probably—look, for all I knew he was a Columbia student."

Nate let the righteous anger in his voice bleed out.

"He might have been, Detective."

"I'm sorry about that. Honest. Just doin' my job, just doin' what I can until a wave of law and order comes down and buries all this shit. You know his film was the ballbreaker? When that judge dismissed criminal charges against all those Commie students, and some of my buddies were chewed out as police rioters… your kid's footage, Exhibit A. Tell him. He'll probably get a kick out of it."

Regan didn't even try to shake Nate's hand.

"Just remember, you heard nothing from me."

He waved his soda in Nate's direction and shouldered his way into the crowd.

If acid was a gleeful saboteur detonating roadblocks in the mind, Haldol was a thief. The pills stole Danny's appetite, muscle power, desire to fuck, and all to make him normal, which left him even more frightened and defenseless.

The blackouts, the lacunas in Danny's memory, were a form

of protection after all. When his memories thinned out, when Ed's babble and the roar in his ears was gone in the vapor trail of sleep, he was back in Cornelia Gunderson's apartment, like a detective following the trail of himself with deepening dread.

Colt shouted at him to get the gun—*and he's never seen it so bright and harsh, the red hair mixed with darker gouts of blood, almost black, her last shriek a grey silence as she empties out down to the chair.* Her hand felt cold—yes, he rushed up to her to check she was alive, he knows that now. Colt had to drag him out of there.

Her hand felt cold, and there was something else that had felt even colder, in the moments before Colt opened fire…

After Nate asked to call FBI Agent Ed Lazarus to the stand and demanded a recess so that he could be sent down from Washington, Judge Cranston adjourned the court for twenty-four hours. Next morning Nate met with Kagan and the judge in the robing room, little more than an anteroom with a desk, a few chairs, and a flag in the corner, dominated by the bland, thickly muscled presence of Agent Adrian Khan.

"Agent Lazarus is in the field at this time, Mr. Kovacs. You'll have to direct your inquiries to me."

The conversation hadn't even begun and Nate had the feeling he was being set up, allowed the barest courtesy of speaking his peace before they took him down. But this time there would be no stopping him.

"So Cornelia Gunderson wasn't the first one the Bureau sent in, was she?"

Khan settled back with a look of barely patient scorn.

"You're already on the wrong track, Mr. Kovacs. We didn't send her in at all. She had a thing for desperadoes. Let's just say we kept an eye on her."

"Not very well, it appears. I don't understand how you could do it. How you could watch her go in there and—my God, how the Bureau could set up a leader of a violent radical group in the first place, and then let him entice—"

"Mr. Kovacs, Randall Soles founded the Revolutionary Action Vanguard."

"Yes, but Colt Borden, if that really is his name—he took it over!"

"You might say it took him over."

Khan hitched up his pants, and tried to maintain his button-down certainty with a dismissive toss of his head.

"He turned out to be a rotten apple. Bought into all the hippie bullshit in California and Philadelphia. Took all the drugs, who knows? We send him in on a strictly limited assignment, he goes off the reservation, becomes the group leader — well, they wanted action, he had the training to give it to them."

"So you didn't pull Borden out? You let one of your own agents tip the group toward his kind of violence to the point this young woman got killed?"

"They were headed toward violence anyhow. Violence, degeneracy, it's the name of the game with these creeps."

Cranston, sleeves rolled up and smoking, frowned at Khan, and Kagan stepped in.

"Your Honor, what purpose would be served by calling Agent Lazarus to the stand, and compelling him to reveal this rogue agent's identity? It would impede the manhunt for him and threaten ongoing operations that are part of America's internal security."

Nate was so taken aback by Kagan's question that he could barely veil his outrage.

"To establish this rogue agent had a motive for murder! He felt he was in danger of being exposed, that Cornelia would ruin his new life! Colt had the gun, the plan, and now he has the motive!"

"Your prosecutor's right, Your Honor. Any revelation of the fugitive's connection the Bureau will jeopardize Bureau operations."

"Like what, Agent Khan? Entrapment? Inciting kids to riot? Taking drugs at the taxpayers' expense?"

Cranston at last lumbered to life, cautioning Nate to moderate his language. But Agent Khan felt no such restraint.

"Mr. Kovacs, I admit, this is a rough, dirty business, and some of our techniques may seem pretty dicey to you, but I can assure you, these techniques have been used with success against Soviet Communist operations in this country. We're damn well going to use them to prevent a second civil war and Mau Maus in America!"

"Agent Khan, shouldn't we both be trying to bring a killer to justice? Isn't that what the Bureau is supposed to do?"

Cranston raised his hand to quiet Nate, butted out his cigarette, and seeing that Kagan was trying to get a word in, let him have the floor.

"Look, Nate, we know Borden is a fugitive from justice. You've established that he's a cowboy with a propensity for violence and the owner of a concealed weapon. We've already let some of his previous record be scrutinized, despite the fact that I could've objected that such past actions could be highly prejudicial to my case against Danny Geller. Now you want to get an FBI agent on the stand to reveal Colt's true identity just to help you with a fishing expedition? We don't know if Cornelia knew anything about Colt's FBI background. How do you know anyone told her that? How do you know Colt feared her because he thought she knew that, given how off the reservation he was? You're building castles in the air! What purpose is served by calling this additional witness, given that it might impede an FBI investigation?"

"I tend to agree, Mr. Kovacs. You've made your case about Borden, and we all agree on the need to catch him as expeditiously as possible. Once we hear he's been apprehended, I'm willing to reopen this conversation. But for now I'm not going to allow you to call Agent Lazarus to the stand."

Nate finally felt the kind of anger at Judge Cranston that made students seize buildings and get themselves clubbed and arrested in front of draft boards. In just a few seconds all the old misgivings swarmed his brain… *what happened to King and the two Kennedys, what's really been happening ever since…* Thoughts blasted in his head about how he could go full-out confrontational, even at the risk of disbarment, get Borden's real identity as a former FBI agent into evidence somehow, blow the whole thing up into a mistrial. If he could just pounce on this opportunity, shake it and tear it in his teeth like Kunstler would...

He once again protested that the decision made it impossible for him to fully and fairly represent his client.

"You'll just have to do the best you can, Counselor."

When he was called to the stand it was if he were dressed in his flowing robe and bringing his violin to the stage, a performer's readiness in his eyes. Nate wondered if Danny had sufficient awareness of just how serious the exchange between them would be, how much it would weigh in the balance of the trial. Certainly Karen, pale, leaning forward, clutching her purse, knew the import of it, and Shari, who'd lost fifteen pounds since the trial began and looked like a cancer patient, and Bruce, trussed up miserably in his black suit.

Nate's worries had begun after he'd transmitted the D.A.'s offer to Danny to reduce the charge to manslaughter. Kagan had conceded Danny might have been drugged, frantic, under Colt's thumb. Danny had refused with such serenity that Nate hoped his confidence didn't come from some bizarre inner conviction that had no bearing on the facts of the case.

"What did you think would happen when Colt said they were going to have a little talk with her?"

"That we were going to check if she was straight with us. If she was for real. But by that time I wasn't thinking too well. I was having a bum trip, the worst ever. Acid and speed, one lousy combination."

Nate had him describe how he tried to commit himself, but the group had bribed the Bellevue guard with money for Dexedrine so that they could bring him down a little and keep him in the car. As Nate led Danny through the ride in the van and the upstairs walk to Cornelia's apartment, his face recaptured the dread of that night.

"What happened when you were waiting?"

"Their argument got worse and worse. Finally they came out of the room, she's slapping and scratching at him."

"Did he try to shoot her?"

"I think so, but—but then she knocked it out of his hand. I heard this voice saying 'Get the gun!' But I didn't give it to him."

Kagan lurched to attention just as Nate, stunned, tried to recover himself, glancing reflexively at Karen, Shari and Bruce. No one else had picked up on the disaster. Nate knew he had no choice but to continue his line of questioning.

"So what did you do, Danny?"

"I don't know. I don't remember. But the next thing I saw was… was Colt shooting her and all the blood. I remember going up and taking her hand. But she was dead. Then they must have got me out of there. Next thing I remember was I'm in the van, and Colt is telling me to dump the gun. So I did, and then… I dumped myself… right into the street… I busted ass out of the van and spent all night running… "

While Shari sobbed, Nate fought the pounding in his head and forced himself to keep questioning Danny until he'd described the long circuit of subway trains he'd ridden, his visit to Jimmy's, his decision to go to his parents' place to turn himself in just before the police apprehended him. Danny made sure to emphasize Jimmy had no part in any of what happened.

As soon as Nate concluded his direct examination, Kagan was out of his seat, cornering Danny into his chair.

"You claim that all of you were uneasy about Cornelia? Did you ever discuss just throwing her out of the group?"

"You really couldn't get thrown out of—"

"Answer 'yes' or 'no,' Mr. Geller."

"No."

Kagan took the jury through the details of the drive to Cornelia's and forced out of Danny the admission that, no, he didn't try to flee the van then and simply get himself admitted to Bellevue. Nate could see the current of pursed lips and eyebrows flit across the faces of the jury. In their minds, Danny was at least willing to go along for the ride.

"You remember a voice saying 'Get the gun!'"

"Yes."

"Now Colt had once let you hold the gun? Aim it?"

"Well, yeah, I'd done that and he'd let me. He even warned me it might be loaded."

"Did he ever discuss with you your experience with a gun?"

"No."

"So for all he knew, you could use a gun."

Nate objected and Kagan promptly withdrew the question.

"In your previous statement you said you never picked up the gun at Cornelia's apartment."

"Yes."

"But you just said under direct examination you didn't 'give it to him'."

"Well, if I didn't pick it up... I couldn't give it to him."

Danny didn't reply with resentment or sarcasm, he didn't make light of it, but Kagan received permission to treat the witness as hostile.

"Well, what is it? Did you or did you not pick up the gun? Did you ever have control of the gun, Danny?"

The cold impression in his hand...

"I didn't have control, I couldn't control it."

"Couldn't control what, Danny?"

"I was so... so scared... of him... of HIM... he was in my head... just to shut him up... "

"Did you pick up the gun?"

"But I didn't shoot her."

"Did you throw it out the window?"

"No."

"Did you run away with the gun into the street?"

"No."

"Who shot Cornelia Gunderson?"

"Colt."

"Then how did only your fingerprints wind up on the gun?"

Nate objected as much has he could, but Kagan still managed to steer his line of questions where he wanted, getting Danny to admit he didn't actually see Colt wipe his fingerprints off the gun, and he thought maybe Colt had latex gloves, but no he didn't see him put them on, and yes, yes he did dump the gun.

Nate tried one final rebuttal question. He asked if to the best of Danny's knowledge, Cornelia knew anything about any criminal action undertaken by any member of RAV, and Danny replied with a firm "no." That would at least establish that Danny had no concrete motive, beyond a vague feeling of unease, for killing her. But Kagan demanded a final redirect. He asked if Danny considered any of RAV's actions to be criminal. When Nate objected, Kagan told Judge Cranston that it went straight to the defendant's state of mind during the whole time he was a part of the group with Colt and Randall Soles. Nate's objection was overruled.

"No, I don't think what we did was criminal. We were trying to stop racism and an immoral, illegal war. We were trying to protect our community, our music, our way of life, and we never hurt anybody. How can that be criminal?"

Nate could see in Bruce and Shari's stricken faces, even in Karen's, where there was a flush of pride beneath the dread, how Danny had walked into the trap, branding himself as a loyal henchman of the group, possibly even giving the impression, should he be convicted, that he felt no remorse for his actions. The miscalculation was complete, and Nate knew that he'd lost him.

An early spring had coaxed out the gold-green shimmer of the boat pond's willow trees, and the throngs were back at Bethesda Fountain when Artie took it in for the first time in a year. Watching the child-of-the-Universe girls in their pioneer dresses with their endless falls of glimmering hair, he thought of the latest Traffic album, murmurs of plaintive woodwinds and guitar, piano chords that burst like ripe fruits in tunes with a music hall lilt. "You Can All Join In." And they had.

He took his usual walk around the basin. A photographer mounted a camera on his tripod to snap the scene he imagined as fresh and new, while all around Artie heard the bent note scat of the wandering blues harpists. An incredibly fat private school kid in purple velvet bell bottoms and a Paraphernalia jacket was dealing—hey man, you can get ups or downs or both, it's all in the individual I guess—and the kids buying looked as stoned as the R. Crumb potheads whose heads liquefied to ectomorphic gunk in their hands. They all seemed to have identical ragged field jackets, peasant shirts, hod-carrier jeans and leather boots.

They were multiplied by the thousands next day for an antiwar demo in Sheep Meadow, lying in the sun, kicking up their feet in flat-heeled shoes and sandals, toking up and listening to Judy Collins and the cast of *Hair*, ignoring a black labor leader urging workers to unite against the war. "Whaddowewant? Peace! Whennawewannit? Now!" Nixon still dropping thousands of tons of bombs on Vietnam. "Pee-snau! Pee-snau!"

It was even harder to revisit the Village and Columbia, knowing that Pam was gone. Not even dad's relaying Loomis Regan's news to him, not even knowing the film he'd shot had helped free so many students, could make him feel better when he observed the desolate sheer normalcy of Math Hall, or could calm the hopeless quiver on his skin when he thought of himself by Pam's side that night. He had to laugh when he got the news that SDS had actually seized Math and Fayerweather again, only to abandon the buildings in disgust when no one had shown up. The student troops were probably off buying clothes and accessories at the Legal Front, or the Conspiracy, a boutique that advertised with a gas mask.

Dylan and the Byrds, one critic in the underground press had written, had "gone muff diving into the womb of country music." The Beatles' new album sounded gorgeous — the bass on the knife-edge of the drums on "Birthday", the silver circles of guitar chords on "Julia"— but never had the group he once thought sounded like four bands in one sounded more like four bands. He wondered if *Bless Its Pointed Little Head*, *Uncle Meat*, and *Tommy* would also be disappointing, but he bought them anyway, although it was already kind of a bummer to buy them at a store other than Geller Records.

Artie welcomed a weekend at the country house. By tacit agreement Danny and the case were never mentioned and Dad was left alone to compose his summation to the jury at the patio table. On the newly growing lawn the grass was saturated with raindrops, each a little bead of prismatic colors. Life seeped from the trees. When he wasn't reading *Portnoy's Complaint*, and laughing his head off, Artie walked with Karen by the water and had surprisingly adult conversations with her about books and movies.

"Yeah, my friends told me *More* was fantastic, so I saw it and it was just… they were putting me on. There's a scene where Mimsy Farmer shoots heroin under her tongue."

"Ewwww!"

"Yeah. Now I got that shot stuck in my head for I don't know how long."

And *Easy Rider*, Peter Fonda and Dennis Hopper wind up martyrs on their burning motorbikes—how could you forget that right in the beginning their journey had been tainted by heroin sales to the snarl of Steppenwolf's "The Pusher"? How could a movie about corruption at the heart of the Revolution be embraced as a battle cry by the young moviegoers of Manhattan? Karen agreed, and Artie was heartened to see his sister joining the Conspiracy of the Brainy.

"Sometimes the States seem so stupid to me, so backwards."

"Then you really want to stay in Montreal, Artie?"

"Well… gotta finish the term… "

This is what he really hadn't wanted to talk about, now that he felt closer to his sister than he'd been in years—how the vandalism in Central Park made him yearn for Montreal's green spaces, how the bedraggled Fountain made him miss the sculpted nudes at McGill's "Three Bares" basin, how he welcomed not being compelled to dress in the latest clothes all the time, shout the latest slogans, milk your convictions for all it was worth. How nice it was to speak two languages in one city.

"You're not even going to wait around for the verdict?"

"I can't. It could be weeks."

That night they played *Bless Its Pointed Little Head*, which finally caught the splendor of the Airplane live. Artie forced Karen to listen to two sides of *Uncle Meat*—what was it with girls and Zappa? What the hell did Karen mean when she said "loveless"? When she'd finally had enough of that they put on *Tommy*. Everything Artie had loved in The Who from "A Quick One While He's Away" to *The Who Sell Out* seemed to come together in the French horn clarion call, tremulous ring of guitar chords, delicate harmonies on the edge of an abyss, and Keith Moon's Cinemascope drumming. Normally he wasn't so grabbed by an album when he first heard it—not just the music, but the story that mixed the rush of liberation and messianic delusion, the acid queen and the pinball wizard, and took dead aim at the stupefaction of mobs at rock concerts and churches when the ultimate pervert Uncle Ernie became the head counselor of Tommy's holiday camp. The Who doing to religion what they'd once done to advertising.

As the tonearm drew toward the end of the record he noticed Karen in front of the speakers, her jaw clenched, trying in vain to hold back tears. For Karen the album was more than brilliant scatterbursts of colors and emotions and ideas, an artifact that gleamed so brightly for the camera or the collection. The deaf, dumb and blind boy trapped in the loop of his darkness until the mirror is smashed… the abandonment, the lonely launch to some kind of power and all the hurting in its wake… the front man… as soon as he understood what associations this other dimension of the album had set off within Karen, he knew he couldn't deny them either…

Artie walked away from his new album with the listening-to-you chorus ringing in his ears. He didn't want to hear the Music anymore.

It's right that it's called a plea of not guilty. As Nate's eyes passed over the courtroom, he saw Karen, bearing up with poise beyond her years, Danny, hanging on his every word like a supplicant, and his loyal son Artie, in his suit jacket and new shorter haircut, looking at him so intently he had to flick his eyes away. He projected his best lawyerly authority, but his plea, like any prayer, contained an admission of helplessness, and standing beneath the flag and the judge's bench, looking into the orbits of twelve pairs of eyes, trying to keep them in the pull of his words while his family and friends watched him with the same intensity, he had never felt so much like sinking to his knees.

Like any prayer, this plea had at its heart a mystery. Nate's first words to the jury were about gaps and absences. No evidence Danny actually fired the gun, even if, as the People had stated, he'd held it in his hand. No eyewitnesses. No powder burn residue. No evidence of a planned conspiracy in the chaos of that night. No motive for Danny to shoot Caroline Gunderson, except a general paranoia that, because of strenuous police and FBI undercover work, was shared by almost everyone who lived between Second and Fourteenth Streets.

There was enough reasonable doubt for the believers' act of faith.

As the jet rose toward Montreal, New York veered beneath him like a huge circuit board of winking signals. Artie wondered what tiny nest of windows marked the sequestered rooms of the jury. If Pam had returned to the city without telling him, what swath of glamorous illuminations was right now framed in the lens of her new Hasselblad camera? And somewhere along the tracks of lights that emanated from the Empire State Building, Dad was resting after his courtroom speech.

He'd laid the facts out so logically, in perfect debating style, and rounded it off with a perfect summary. "This is a young man with no criminal record, and the facts do not show that this young man committed murder. He couldn't prevent the murder but that's not the same as committing it. And he stands before you on trial today, unlike the fugitive from justice who possessed the gun, Caleb Borden, who instigated the confrontation with Miss Gunderson, who led the group, but who, the People want you to believe, was only a co-conspirator, and didn't even pull the trigger of his own weapon."

And then Dad had taken an extra breath, Artie was sure of it, and split off a whole other chain from the argument.

Almost as if he were improvising.

"To support their conspiracy charge, we've heard some of the prosecution's witnesses talk about a 'war' for law and order. It's true the Revolutionary Action Vanguard's rhetoric and some of its deeds went beyond the limits of reasonable debate and protest. But when the word "war" is used, we're asked to alter our concept of justice, take extraordinary measures, no longer give young men like Danny Geller the benefit of the doubt."

Dad's cadences rose and the rhythms got stronger.

"What is the war here? Are we really at war with young men like Danny Geller protesting another war that millions of Americans now say they can't support? Are we at war with young men like Danny Geller who joined the civil rights movement? Who joined activities to increase the standard of living of poor people in their neighborhoods? Who joined other students to demonstrate for the right to express themselves and shape the course of their studies when they could've focused on a getting into law or business school and stayed silent? Who tried to make a change? Who try to help protect the city, the country, even the planet? Is that where we've come to in America? Putting on the other side of the law anyone who wants reform and dares to exercise their rights as citizens of a free nation?"

"I've had to answer this question, ladies and gentlemen of the jury, because the prosecution raised it... "

Yes, legally that was so, but Dad, you raised it... you raised it the way I did when I gained and lost Columbia... Karen in her trip to the East Village... Danny on the stage flashing me not the twinge of recognition I could barely return in the courtroom, but that comradely welcome-to-the-show blessing from his temple of darkness beneath the spangled lights that made me so proud, so ready to follow... let's see what we'll all make of it together, the spaces between, the nights underneath...

"Ladies and gentlemen of the jury, this is the principal issue before you today. Before you take away from this young man all that he has and ever will have, you must consider: has the prosecution even remotely met the burden of proof that Danny Geller conspired to murder Caroline Gunderson, and that he is the one and only person who could've committed that murder? They have not met that burden, and so you must acquit on the standard of reasonable doubt."

"That is the true and only justice."

Artie's departure time at the airport was so soon after his dad's speech that they'd had their goodbye hug during a brief break on the stairs of the courthouse. For a moment he'd laid his head on Dad's chest, and then he stood back, composed and distinct, efficiently putting New York behind him. Along with praise for Dad's performance, the only words he could find for all his jangled emotions were "You did the right thing to defend him."

And then suddenly Dad was hugging him again, and telling him, to his amazement, how proud he was of Artie, that he could never have done what Artie had done at Columbia, or even what Artie was doing now, so that Artie had never felt more the man of the house, even of his city, than when he was about to leave it…

Bookended between two strangers in his flight above New York, he stared at the red light winking on the icy wing of the plane, and he realized that now the city was a hundred miles behind him; a part of him was lost beneath that skyline, another waiting in Canada, and the third nothing more than a signal detached from from all the other signals in a darkening sky.

A week later, during the cab ride to 100 Center Street, Nate couldn't keep one logical thought in his head, but grasped for an omen. Jimmy Hinton had been acquitted. The case had been weak from the start, and Jimmy, thin, fragile, soft-spoken, coached well by Milt to play his compliant part, had clearly won over the jury.

Danny and he waited for the elevator, and as the numbers

counted down to the main floor Danny touched Nate's arm and said he had a confession to make in the last few moments they might have of attorney-client privilege. He knew Colt was wearing latex gloves when they drove away from the murder because Colt had once outfitted them all with those gloves on the night they'd raided and vandalized a draft board on Long Island.

It seemed absurd to be angry over such a confession at this point but Nate felt he had to tell Danny that such an action was unacceptable and, of course, a crime.

"But how do you stop the war if you can't even do that?"

Nate recalled the issue of *Life* Magazine he'd just read, and the hideous photos of the American soldiers' massacre of Vietnamese civilians, including women and children, at My Lai.

"Thank you for being honest with me, Danny."

"Thank you, Mr. Kovacs. For everything."

The twelve pairs of eyes he'd communed with so often in the courtroom were now shielded by their decision, in the same way Nate kept his eyes averted from the Gellers and from Karen. He patted Danny's hand in an avuncular way, but otherwise kept his eyes fixed on the altar, bound to the ritual to which he'd dedicated his service.

When judgment was announced, the blood rushed into his head with the force of a snapping spring, and he almost didn't hear the second verdict on the charge of conspiracy, the fail-safe, the prosecutor's utopia. Not guilty, not guilty of all charges. Danny was in his arms as soon as the gavel rapped and then Bruce and Shari caught them up in their twin embraces, and Izzy, after he slowly got up from his chair, insisted on hugging everyone. Nate broke free to catch his breath and watched as Karen rocked in Danny's embrace. Finally she rushed to him, and he held Karen until her sobbing flowed away.

On the courthouse stairs the noontime sun scoured into his brain, and with all the racket of a normal afternoon came the questions of the reporters and a quick peacemaking handshake with Kagan, with whom he'd have to deal another day.

The reporters took off for their next story and the Kovacses and the Gellers were suddenly once again just two families in front of a courthouse trying to flag down cabs in Lower Manhattan. Karen was speaking to the Gellers and, as Nate and Danny found themselves alone, Nate remembered a question he'd always wanted to ask Danny.

"Danny, have you ever heard the expression 'watch my horn'?"

Danny smiled and turned his face up toward the nearby skyscrapers, welcoming the sun back into his life.

"It's kind of hard to explain, Mr. Kovacs. It's like, if you're a sax player, your horn is a total part of you. Maybe the most important part."

"I don't follow you, Danny."

With a directness and an intimacy all the more intense from someone normally so furtive and distracted, Danny looked into Nate's eyes.

"It means 'take care of me while I'm gone'."

The half-written letter about the Black Panther breakfast program was still on his desk, his pen laid down where it had been six months ago when Danny and then the heat had come in through the door. Jimmy stared at the desk, sprawled onto the couch, flicked on the tv, and stared at the desk again. Two months passed.

The Harlem summer crawled outside his parchment-colored shade, the loans from his family ran out, his old friends tried to entice him or shame him back into working for the community, but the Panther's ten-point program, a ticket to Muhammad Ali on Broadway in *Big Time Buck White*, the words of Frantz Fanon, nothing could get him out of his room. He couldn't dislodge from his head a story he'd heard from some guy in the holding pens. He'd cackled away as he talked about how they'd squirted some kike teacher at Franklin Lane High School with turpentine and set his coat sleeve aflame with a cigarette lighter.

The guy boasted like it was a war story, and a memento

of a victory, ignoring the fact that in April the New York State Legislature had passed a "Decentralization Act." Despite its bullshit name, the law had submerged the black decentralized schools into larger districts run completely by the Board of Education once again. Community control of schools was dead, and these cats didn't get it. Long as they kicked the ass of some Jews who had nothing to say about their union and might have even been on their side.

Some kike teacher. Some kike like Danny Geller.

Huey and Rap and Imamu Amiri Baraka were in jail. Alex Rackley had been killed and Bobby Seale charged with the crime. The cold hands of the pusher and unemployment were clenching down on the ghetto, and all the powerless could do was fight each other until they were even weaker than before. Headed for the jail, the hospital, the morgue.

One day Jimmy lay back on his throw rug, toked up, watched a bevy of cockroaches lay down a line of manic reconnoitering beneath his couch for whatever bits of corn chip he'd spilled the night before, and reached for the phone to call Danny. It was the first time he'd spoken about music with anyone in weeks. Danny wanted to know if Jimmy was into the Afro-Cuban band, Santana, and Jimmy replied Dizzy Gillespie and Machito, that was Afro-Cuban. There was a weird lag in Danny's speech and Jimmy asked if he were taking drugs. Danny told him he was on too many pills to take drugs.

Jimmy shambled out of his apartment, blinking in the fervid glare off the concrete, took a walk to the bodega and saw a storefront he didn't recognize. Jesse Jackson had brought Operation Breadbasket to the community. Asking around, he wound up at the local A & P, where Jackson, with a blustering joviality, led pickets around the store to broadcast the need to hire more Afro-Americans. Jimmy decided he needed the walk.

Food was the great unifier, and you couldn't outlaw it. He remembered Les Campbell at IS 271 honoring Africa's agriculture. "When we were in Africa, when we had different gods, we farmed our own land." Jimmy spent more and more time in community gardens. From the Breadbasket people he got soul food recipes and found he was a pretty good cook. Feed yourself, feed your own, protect the little plots of land from the city, maybe think about your own little place where the food and the music and the rap can go on...

I only lost six months. Some of these brothers lost years in the joint.

First he needed to discipline his life again, and that meant taking care of the money situation and fast. He had to go with his old standby job, food delivery, but as he slotted himself back into the route he thought he'd left behind years ago, he found that at least it still ran by the music studios.

"Play this sound like a spiral goin' up... a circular situation... yeah, throw in that drum rhythm you practiced in New Orleans... yeah, I'll take it, I'll take it."

At Studio A, Miles had thirteen musicians trooping in and out of the session. Three keyboards, a guitar, two basses, four drums, Wayne Shorter on soprano sax, a bass clarinet, and a ton of percussion. Jimmy was always bringing in his pastry cart to the thunder of an ostinato bass line and a maze of electric piano chords that rang like a clutch of African kalimbas.

Miles in the booth pointed to Benny Maupin on bass clarinet to slither below the drums, to the pale, skinny white guitarist John McLaughlin to dart through the mix and tickle the high end. All the electronic textures made you forget how simple the harmony was, just a framework for all these eddies and streams and waves of exploration and emotion. No one really knew Miles's plan, but they were working with it, they trusted it, and it pulled in every one of them.

There was a break and Jimmy slipped in to hand Miles a Danish. Miles gave him the barest flicker of recognition.

"Good to see you're still at large."

That sandpaper croak was all Jimmy needed to keep him going—that and a couple of more stolen hours watching Miles command his major dudes, push the buttons he had to, taunt his producer with whispers of "Teo... Teo... " as Macero patiently recorded the jams that Miles sculpted. When he came out of the booth Miles was the Pharaoh who harnessed the ensemble with trumpet fanfares that swept up the rogue licks of rock guitar, talking keyboards, strutting drums, and Asiatic soprano sax. The ardor of the Fillmore and the sagacity of the jazz clubs and the fire in the streets were all lashed to the peals of his horn.

Got the bloods, an Irishman, a Puerto Rican, a Hungarian, and one fat old hippie holding down the electric bass... yeah, I'll take it, I'll take it...

No, Miles didn't own the tape, not yet, but still the reel spun from what he saw and what he heard... a circular situation... and there was no question whose axe convoked that uprising of African and New York and black and white spirits that came to harmony in the final mix.

Yeah, yeah, I'm sellin' out jazz, Dylan sold out folk, Hendrix is lost in space...

Gotta have a session with that cat. We could lay down some terrible shit.

We're gonna scare the shit out of all you motherfuckers.

Chapter 8

THE FESTIVAL

"It's a free concert from now on."

When the huge disembodied voice made the announcement Artie took the wet dirty strips of paper that he'd paid eighteen dollars for, ripped them up, and tossed them away. All the torn Woodstock box office tickets in the spotlight beams looked like a swarm of midges above the crowd's heads. Artie's eyes swept the stage that rose like twin rocket gantries rigged with carnival lights, the huge speakers on the eighty-foot towers, and the shadowy mass of a World's Fair-size audience cheering through the night on the slopes of the pasture. The main thing in the concert promoters' heads, the Voice assured them, was everyone's welfare.

"But if we're going to make it, you better remember the guy next to you is your brother."

The closest he'd ever come, Russ Lansing, was at his side —along with buddies Tony and Kent and Chris, eight of their friends and girlfriends, and 300,000 students, hipsters, freaks and heads all around him in whom Artie now placed his trust that, despite the predictions of the *New York Times*, the Festival that held them in an open field for the next three days wouldn't wind up a catastrophe.

He hadn't even meant to stay in New York in July more than a week, much less buy tickets to a mid-August rock festival whose chain of evictions from the original Woodstock site to Wallkill to White Lake spelled disaster. But then, as if he sensed the improbable victories on the way, he'd put in some hours at Lindsay Volunteers as Mayor Lindsay admitted mistakes, reminded voters how he'd kept the peace, and headed for a second term. He'd caught two games at Shea to cheer on baseball's longest-running joke as they charged toward winning the World Series. And he'd remained in the States for one last convocation of the decade before its television sets, as Neil Armstrong, in an image as ghostly as the most ancient photographic plates, trod and scurried like a crab upon the lunar shore. That night, on the porch by the pond of their summer home, he and Karen had looked out at the moon and she'd joked that the man in the moon now had a zit, but soon they were holding hands and their chuckles dissolved away at the thought of the Eagle and Tranquility Base, at the sight of the tv sets in windows across the road that shared those images with every living room in New York City, and with the awestruck gaze of the entire planet.

Then came "blast off sales" and Jim Dooley holding a can of Tropicana Orange Juice against the Cape Kennedy sky as he intoned "aren't you proud you're an American?" Madison Avenue and Richard Nixon took the moon landing back.

They could never get their hands on this.

The sheer craziness of it, the Bizarro-world accident-ness, the ultimate Camp Saco trip gone wrong so the kids take over the forest-ness of the Festival, began when the New York State Thruway funneled into the "quickway" to White Lake, and a twenty-minute drive became almost as many hours. Artie had around his neck his camera and Pamela's ankh peace symbol, while slung off his left shoulder was a water container in the shape of a Basque wineskin sold by a hip camping store. He disentangled the straps, pulled out his Nikon from its case, and snapped pictures of the procession of cars with day-glo hoods, flowered VW microbuses, and gaily decorated old bread trucks. Through the crush of cars and vans threaded Harleys and hitchhikers who finally just kept walking when they realized they were moving faster than the cars.

Radiators hissed all around him, vehicles were pushed to the side of the road and abandoned, and Artie knew the guys in the front of the van were flying on acid when for the third time the question "are we moving?" came from the driver. He wondered sometimes if they'd miss some of the acts, maybe a whole day of the acts—and he didn't care. The road was now part of the Festival. The procession was punctuated with shouts to share food, dope, wine, peaches, Hershey bars, and chewing gum, and orchestrated to countless guitar, flute and harmonica jams on the roofs of the line of traffic. Thursday night was perfectly clear under a full moon, lush pine woods and homey Catskill cabins revealed by single light bulbs in cool country darkness, and the way the ruby beacons of the vehicles ahead lit the road and the headlights swept the trees reminded him of the '65 blackout. Don't complain, get a kick out of being part of a benign apocalypse, extend the good cheer to others. As the reaching out to strangers became almost delirious, Artie was called beautiful and called others beautiful back, he leaned from the side of the U-haul to give skin to passing drivers.

At four a.m. they parked the van at the outer fringes of the Aquarian Age Parking Area, waved on by personnel in red day-glo shirts embossed with peace symbols who were as sleepy as they were. The sun turned the cool damp to pea soup heat. Artie and Russ headed toward Hurd Road with a mob of sweat-smudged hikers, most of them kids dressed in jeans and workshirts, sweaters belted around their waste like Artie, but also djellabas, a red toe ring, American flag slacks, amulets, serapes, and caftans.

It reminded Artie of the Be-In but after that traffic jam pilgrimage all the garb looked dusty and settled-in. Normal mufti for a normal day in a new community.

They filed through a silent corridor of woods toward the top of a hill. Through the leaves that meshed with his lowered eyelids Artie made out a nude guitarist strumming gently under the trees, next to a little makeshift bungalow with a single-word banner, "Smoke." Noticing that one of the red-shirted peace symbol officers was comfortable with the whole scene, Russ promptly bought an ounce of grass for fifteen dollars. At Movement City vendors hawked underground papers and Vietcong flags, while at a string of booths and tents and paper pavilions that were pitched between stone outcroppings and cowshit other salesmen shouted they had psilocybin, opium, hash, sunshine and pink mescaline.

Russ and Artie paused at a gap torn in the hilltop's fence, sidled through the broken chain-link metal and joined the crowd. Over the next eight hours Artie shot another roll of film, but mainly he developed a mental picture of what almost half a million people looked like, the pennants, balloons and Frisbees defining a boundary that receded to the edge of the pasture and beyond. He took a walk to buy some lousy burgers and endured an hour-long piss wait at a Port-O-San, after which his body shut down the need to shit. He just managed to find his way via a thread of tents, balloons and mini-geodesic domes back to Russ. As they kept staring at the bare stage and its impossibly golden, freshly hewn scaffolding and piles of lumber, Artie finally stopped worrying about how the tickets would be collected.

Richie Havens hammer-strummed his guitar and the giant speakers thundered across the pasture to the loudest swell of cheering Artie had ever heard. Havens paced the giant stage he shared with only one conga drummer, and as he blurted his inarticulate amazement at the crowd, he could have been anyone of them, stunned by the creation of the third largest city in New York on the foundation of small cash transactions, barter, peace, friendship, and the Music.

Friday night was a big hootenanny around the Woodstock campfire. Tim Hardin, balding, shirt soaked with rain in a blue spotlight, did free-form picking in the bridges of "If I Were A Carpenter" so he could stay a little longer with the crowd. Arlo Guthrie chortled his way through his sing-alongs, Joan Baez and her guitarist invoked the Draft Resistance movement. It all seemed a prelude to the real celebration, the kinship, the cheers at every recognition of a tribal presence so enormous that no one had any choice but to leave the rest of the Festival in its hands. *Agape, darshan*, as speakers intoned between the acts—that night it all added up to being able to sleep together where they were and be left alone by the world. From the great dark breathing presence sounds rose up like fireflies, winking across the huge encamped pasture—shouts, harmonica chirps, guitars like katydids—and Artie, wrapping himself in his poncho around his camera, said goodnight to Russ as he had in so many sleepovers before.

Four hours later, Artie stumbled awake to a chilling rain, trembling violently as his poncho drained on his sneakers, and looked at a pre-dawn wasteland the color of mildew, crammed with patchily waterproofed people sluggish and pale but unbelievably cheerful. Somehow, as on a camping trip, breakfast materialized from wet dirt and rocks. There was oatmeal cooked on Sterno cans here, a bag of gorp trail mix and an orange there, candy bars and peanuts provided by Artie, Russ, and their friends.

Danny woke up a little warmer, crammed under a blanket with five other heads from the Ken Kesey Oregon contingent. The little communities around Phillipine Lake, not content to just wait for the Music, were busy with all sorts of schemes. The SDSers and Motherfuckers set out to rip off the higher-priced concession stands of burgers and pizza and bring some back to the campsites. They later persuaded the stage announcers to broadcast the location of free food until the concessionaires knocked their prices down. In the rain people walked naked and laughed at radio disaster reports. A network was set up to report any broken water lines.

Danny joined in the languorously paced work details of the first free dope territory in America, where people walked around with joints dangling from their mouths. Meals were prepared over hibachi stoves and in beercans hung over wastepaper fires. In lean-tos sheltered with scraps of clothing, teepees, wigwams, and a treehouse, amateur swamis "Ommmed" and the smell of hash and reefer, smoked with fifty-cent pipes and free cigarette papers, was everywhere.

He caught a light for his spleef from a red-jacketed guy who admitted he was an off-duty cop... *got a light, groovy man, peace brother...* and floated through the bull sessions, not minding the last drizzling mists of the rain at all... *this is the highest and absolutest most beautiful trip ever and maybe every head in the world will be here to join us... all bullshit and barriers gone... no government and authority and business and cars... just the Music and us... no Lavoris or Ice Blue Secret... maybe one day Hendrix will play and no one will go home because we'll be home...* He looked for Ken Kesey but never found him, and instead lay in the grass and watched chickens and rabbits a commune had brought just for fun, and kids frolicking at a teepee with a flat stone hung from ropes to swing on. He gazed for what must have been twenty minutes at the Meher Baba followers, and their banner. "We Are All One."

All his political and artistic work had somehow come to fruition on one weekend. When he had filled up at the Hog Farm free food tent on dollops of boiled wheat, raisins, and honey, and drunk some water in a plastic cup, he felt nothing but gratitude, gratitude to the farmer who had let him fill his canteen at a pipe spigot on the way, gratitude for the liberation of White Lake and the Catskill Mountains, enough gratitude to his parents to wish he hadn't had to sneak out on them to hitch to the Festival, above all gratitude to everyone at Max Yasgur's farm this brightening day, where the tunes of John Sebastian floated from the pasture into the breeze. To welcome all this into him cleansed him. He stopped worrying whether his mind had been permanently stained by RAV, or memories of a crime of which he'd been proven innocent, or the disease that doctors claimed had wormed itself so deeply into his head. Caressed by the miracle all around him, he put a cap on the pills that made him half of who he was, and one quarter of the man he might come to be.

When the sun came out the speaker voice announced playfully "we'll see who can outlast whom." Artie smoked a joint with Russ and fell into a series of naps, blinking open his eyes in hazy, drowsy sunlight for crooning from John Sebastian and Celtic keening from the Incredible String Band, finally awake for good when Country Joe turned the "Fish Cheer" into a glorious canyon-span cry of "Fuck!" from 300,000 throats, and Santana's conga and guitar jams got everyone on their feet.

Helicopters swooped in with the evening performers, their rotors becoming part of the serenade, and when an occasional Army or police chopper passed over the crowd, it was greeted with thousands of peace signs. One speaker announcement jolted the crowd, a warning that the brown acid might contain strychnine. Later, when someone else at the mike defended the acid, Russ and Artie agreed it was the strangest commercial they'd ever seen.

By the time Canned Heat took the stage, Artie, having spent Keef Hartley's set sharing coleslaw, cashews, salad and fruit while lying in a woman's lap getting his hair stroked, was happily ready for the greatest lineup of acts he'd ever seen. After the Heat's wallop of smoky barroom blues, Mountain, whose obese orange-lit guitarist with equally gigantic hair played blues-rock through jet engine feedback, was a weirdly thrilling optical illusion. Creedence Clearwater Revival's set, with one ferocious hit radio vocal after another, sprinted with clean, rough-hewn grace through the deepening blue-green of the country night. The Dead spun their moony improvisations and Artie felt a pleasant rush of remembered sex until another spurt of rain had the amps crackling and the group evacuating the stage—but then came Janis Joplin and "Can't Turn You Loose," shaking her ass in front of a line of horns, the climactic howls of "Ball and Chain," and then Sly and the Family Stone hurled out the greatest seesawing, foot-stomping, singalong chorus Artie had ever joined. Sly, a black caped crusader dressed in white, waved the peace sign instead of a fist and the spotlights swept out from him and snatched up the entire audience into his spirit-raising funk.

Canned Heat, Mountain, Creedence. Dead, Joplin, Sly, Green Lantern, Flash. Futurama, Kodak, Wonders of Life on Earth... so much richly classifiable abundance...

When The Who hit the first chord of *Tommy*, Artie and the crowd stood up and didn't sit back down during the entire set. They lit matches that seemed to be the only energy powering them at five in the morning. Artie stared at a sight he could not have imagined ever seeing, rock concert spotlights over The Who fading slowly in the glow of a vast blue dawn. During the encore there was an odd kink in the procession of sun and music... did he really do that?... Abbie Hoffman took the mike, shouted "I think this is all a crock of shit while John Sinclair rots in prison!"

and Pete Townsend jabbed Abbie with his guitar and knocked him offstage. But Abbie seemed to bounce up to his feet, a cranky cartoon character, and the crowd murmured its acceptance of the burst of emotional interference that you might find at any demonstration, before giving the band a triumphant sendoff.

The Airplane came on to close the show, Grace a ribbon of white that almost hurt the eyes, the vestal non-virgin of the ceremony. Artie cheered at the cry to tear down the walls. "Volunteers" was kickass, and he made it through a riotous "Somebody To Love," he tried to import the sanctity of his favorite band closing the greatest seventeen hours of music ever through his fog of sleeplessness, but when Jack Casady began his bass solo, the ground rose up to meet Artie, and the next thing he saw was a gap-toothed, bearded hippie bending over him.

"Want some raisins?"

The off-duty cop turned Woodstock patrolman whom Danny had befriended lit another joint for him and told him he and his buddies had refused to leave even though the police commissioner had warned them about moonlighting. He courteously directed one barefooted girl who had stepped on broken glass to the medical tents just behind them. She headed toward a strange but not threatening scene, shaky and jabbering bum trippers waiting to get comforted. Hugh "Wavy Gravy" Romney had just announced on the Big Speakers "if you get confused, come to the Hog Farm tents and we'll help you see the humor in the chaos..." Nearby a guitarist led a sing-along of a Byrds' tune... yes it was a strange gathering of tribes...

Danny bought a soy and vegetable macroburger for fifty cents from a woman named Sheila, who listened to the guitar and, her long dress totally open, swayed like a frail branch in the wind, the indolence in her thighs and yaw in her breasts reflecting his own surrender to the day. He and Sheila went to a picnic where they shared fruit, cheese, cucumbers someone brought from California, and Boone's Farm Apple Wine. When they swam nude in the lake her ass-length hair trailed behind her like seaweed flecked with sunlight and Danny swam through it before he stroked her temples, kissed her, dived to stroke her all over. They ran out onto the shore and a lean-to that was thankfully empty, with plenty of quilts and blankets to wrap themselves under, and beneath their cocoon they clenched each other until the shivers stopped and they could let all the lust and affection of the day explode out of them in a rush of gasps and laughter.

When they emerged and stared at the glimmering lake Danny knew the set and setting, as Huxley and Leary used to say, couldn't be more perfect. He remembered a line of Yeats: *the ceremony of innocence.* They shared one tab of acid, then another. Danny wanted to be sure that, if anything went wrong, he was near the bad trip tents, and so he volunteered along with Sheila for the Hog Farm open air kitchen. He and Sheila tended to the simmering oats, rice, and bulgur wheat, passed out cups of water, and shouted right on as a naked man rushed out of the LSD tents announcing he was "cured" and was headed back out to the "space pasture." As Danny stood at Sheila's side dicing the salad the Farm had prepared for lunch, he saw, like the turning colors of an opal, the faces of men, women and children as prismatic reflections of unending heartfelt bliss.

After his next hike to the Port-O-Sans, Artie found the way back to Russ and his friends definitely trickier, now that the field was more dun-colored and embedded with crushed ponchos. He wound up talking with one of the movie cameramen as the crew set up for Day and Night Three. Yeah, lot of great political flicks, real Chicago police violence in *Medium Cool*, and Z, a movie whose imminent release was wild-posted all over New York with the slogan "He Is Alive." Films like *Midnight Cowboy* were shooting all over the city, they told him, and a lot of the crew members and guys working on postproduction were coming out of N.Y.U. Canada's pretty cool, he knew a couple of guys who had to flee there, and yeah, sounds like you got really burned by Columbia, but you might want to check that out....

Artie located Russ and the others and his relief at having

found them swelled into an ecstatic welcome for Joe Cocker and the Grease Band. Cocker's "Let's Go Get Stoned" sucked the steamy murk right out of the air, and he did "With A Little Help From My Friends" like a soul song until, in a headlong finale, he corkscrewed his body so wildly, fingers clawing in a non-stop spasm, that you could almost think that he could beat back the massive thunderheads that were coming up over the hill. But despite all that musical bravado and the lusty cheers that followed, the wind blasted and tore at the tented stage, and as Artie wrapped himself in his poncho the worst storm he'd ever experienced came down on his head.

How had he gotten lost? Sheila and the Hog Farm tents were right behind him, it should've been a very simple turn… instead Danny was now alone with this fucking rain, whose silver swells had at first captivated him, but now drove into the quilt, the ragged blankets, and the poncho he'd wrapped around him like freezing nails. Where had he gotten those from? Had he stolen them from people now totally exposed to the storm? There was the lake, but where was this barely sheltering tree in relation to where he'd been? Something was making his hands cold and he realized he still had the knife from the Hog Farm. The mood dived down fast; there had been people singing beside him when the rain had started, but now Danny heard whispers, even though he could've sworn he was alone.

Artie and Russ, who stood side by side under the slats of wood that the group took turns holding above their heads, debated above the rattle of the rainfall about staying versus going. Russ pointed out that, even if they could convince the two guys who rented the van to head back, it would be a total drag to hike to the parking area let alone drive back to New York in this shit. It's like at a baseball game, you just wait it out, and hey, there won't be a rain delay on this event ever. Artie shivered as the wind drenched him under their makeshift shelter. He couldn't even put on his second sweater; it had gotten so soaked he'd wrapped it in some plastic sheeting. When someone finally took his place holding up the wood, he saw that everything he could sit on had been sucked into the mud—his sleeping bag, now ruined, looked like a sodden leaf—so he succumbed to the urge to sit in a puddle, curled around his camera case. Russ was amazingly good-natured about it all, just as he'd been on that Camp Saco Kezar Lakes canoe trip when the cold rain had hit one morning, but all Artie could think about was "Sloop John B": might this be the worst trip I've ever been on? As his ass soaked and froze, he wondered if they were the ultimate idiots, if the musicians had already gone home, if the speakers were short-circuited and no one was even able to tell them it's over, get the fuck off my land.

The insane cheerfulness around him, choruses of "Help!" and shouts of "No rain!", kept falling with the showers on his poncho hood, until slowly the clouds moved on, and sunlight the color of mercury wafted over the stage. Someone passed around plastic cups filled with tea brewed over Sterno cans. Artie watched as filmmakers approached wrapped in ponchos, hunched over their cameras. They wove through the crowd, determined to record every change of scene, and Artie realized from their haggard, dirty, but alert faces that they'd been working all through the storm. As the sun baked his limbs loose, he took out his camera, thankful it was perfectly dry, and shot the Festival coming back to life.

A drum hitting a fast four-four brought everyone to their feet, dancing to shake off the rain like wet dogs. Country Joe, playing a second gig with his bandmates the Fish, gave the crowd a tongue-in-cheek entertainer's rap—we're certainly delighted to be here today—that masked the affection and relief that surged across the field as the band segued into its straight-ahead "Rock and Soul" music. The musicians had not, would not abandon them.

Artie kept busy with his camera as the Festival became a banquet of instrumental and photographic contrasts. Alvin Lee and Ten Years After's blizzard of Brit blues guitar was followed by The Band, black-suited minstrels and historical ventriloquists bringing into the fold hymns, bluegrass, even square dances. The silver horns and soul keyboards of Blood Sweat and Tears gave way to Texas country blues down in the darkness that shrouded the black hat and indigo backlit white hair of Johnny Winter, and his slide guitar that reminded Artie of embers being poked into a flame. But it was Crosby, Stills, Nash and Young's set that really brought it home to the new home they'd all spontaneously created. The set turned from blithe harmonies and impossibly dextrous acoustic melodies, the golden loneliness of three guys with guitars in a pool of light, to blazing folk and country rock. Three hours plus of buckskin, giggling charm and earnest faith, songcraft and supergroup power. By the time Artie fell into the rhythm of a girl's unbundled hair that shook just before him, and swayed shoulder to shoulder with everyone else to "Long Time Gone," it seemed that California and Canada, London and New York were all woven together in the minor key that hinted at the struggle coming down and in the high harmony and backbeat that rocked the sunrise.

After that Paul Butterfield and the genial grooviness of the "Love March" was an anticlimax. Artie was just too exhausted to feel sweaty and sultry, to rise to the bear hugs of loose jams and squealing horns. And in the sleepless glare of morning fueled only by granola and canteen water Sha Na Na's mock-'50s greaser antics went from a good laugh to a comic strip hallucination.

The crowd had thinned out and many of the diehards were zoning into comedowns, drunken wastedness, and private trips. As people picked up their filthy camping gear and headed back to the parking area, Artie heard all around cries of "Don't leave!" "We can keep doing this… aah, see ya next summer, man…" Others moved up to fill the gaps and huddled together, all splattered by the mud that had rutted and stratified everywhere. Artie felt wiped out, caked with mud, a rash under his arms and on his neck under the camera straps, but Hendrix was coming soon, the crown prince of the Festival. The pyramid's point. *Don't miss a thing.*

He looked at the film and sound island in the midst of the crowd, to see if they were setting up, a good cue that the act was about to begin. A woman with a red bandana on her head and a flash of blonde hair perched on the platform and started taking photos with that poised swooped-forward stance that Artie could never forget.

Without a word to his friends he darted through the crowd, past clumps of people seated in the mud and others trying to trudge across them. He didn't get very far before she'd utterly vanished, like a bird flashing away from a tree in the space of a missed glance.

Had Pamela even really been there? It made sense that she'd somehow make this ultimate scene, but after all the hours of shared joints and intermittent food and almost no sleep, Artie couldn't be sure. The only thing he did realize was that with one set to go before the trek back to the van he'd completely lost sight of his friends. Trying to orient himself, he gazed at the stage and suddenly the Voice seemed to be speaking directly to him.

"Danny Geller, please come to the platform. We have a number for you to call in New York City. Your folks and your friends just want to hear from you, make sure you're doing well. Some old musical comrades are here as well, so come join us backstage, Danny, we'd love to see you."

All that weekend, whenever he'd wanted a glimpse of the Music, Danny had followed Gentle Path or Groovy Way or whatever-the-sign-said from the campground to that amphitheater lit by Christmas lights. Now, as the weird '50s greaser act brought their set to a close, all those glimpses ignited and fused and rushed back to him.

The wood of that skeletal stage was sprouting branches. The boards that had lain there all through the weekend soared up and formed a giant overhanging lattice, and to flee the mud that sucked down at them, all the fiery spirits were going up in the tree. Entangled and frozen... The Who in suits of white ice, Johnny Winter white haired and trapped in the blue spotlight....

He tried to get closer to the stage, to see the one last act that maybe could break through the *mindfuck madness here... the*

*fuckin' choppers droning over the tunes… webs of wire and wood…
the tree would become bigger and bigger and encase them all…
right at the gates of Eden shut out of Paradise forever…* and then
the tree called out to him. *Called out his name.*

He could join them, he could be there… *but the wood was
creaking, the tentacles were forming…*

Maybe Danny had lied about spending the night somewhere
and not come back, and his mom and dad had figured that of
course he had to be here. Dad or Mr. Geller had found some
way to communicate by phone or helicopter pilot or walkie-talkie
with the stage itself. They'd made the call, and now Artie could
feel Dad and Karen reaching out to him and urging him to be *the
man of the house* even here, even at Woodstock.

When the Jimi Hendrix Experience was announced,
Artie was swarmed by kids who rushed the giant platform and
shouted themselves hoarse. Hendrix appeared in turquoise
velvet pants, a studded turquoise belt, a grey suede fringed shirt,
and a jade medallion on his headband. Knowing he could get
a medium shot from where he stood, Artie quickly fired off two
pictures while at the same time he realized that his side-to-side
vision was blocked so thoroughly that finding Danny might
be hopeless. Still he could glimpse an access path to the giant
platform, which looked like his best bet for finding Danny and
bringing him to the stage.

"I see we meet again… I've got mine, thank you… I've got
mine…"

Hendrix and his new lineup, Gypsies, Sun and Rainbows,
broke into "Fire" and the crowd split up to writhe by themselves or
gambol in tight little couples, and in the interstices of the dance
Artie kept looking for Danny. He once again used the longest
lens of his camera as a telescope. He swept the crowd and kept
refocusing, as the horde subdivided into different planes of focus,
the faces coming closer…

"You've proved to the world what can happen with a little bit of love, and understanding, and sounnnnnnnds..."

The jam built and built and Danny wished again that Jimmy Hinton was here to groove to what Hendrix was laying down. His torrent of guitar was like Coltrane on sax, the spirals of furious motifs that dove down and soared up in whole new configurations as Mitch Mitchell's drums laid down the rhythmic barrage that spurred him on. Danny got close enough to see Hendrix' face, eyes closed as he savored and flinched from his own music in a kind of wakeful REM sleep... *but the band was being swallowed up in the branches of its own creation. The tree drank their energy and sprouted higher...*

"Danny?"

He was standing in that access path, entranced by the music, in a filthy congelation of blankets and quilts.

"Artie! L'il bro! You actually made it, man! Beautiful! Does this blow your mind forever or what?"

Artie inched closer to Danny.

"Is everybody here? Karen, is she here?"

"No, Danny, just me."

One arm emerged to hug him, the other stayed hidden under the blankets.

"How long have you been here?"

"Seen a couple of acts. Not sure I dig Butter with horns. Remember 'East-West' when you first got high?"

"Aren't you going to the stage? You can say hi to people, be up there with Hendrix... Danny?"

"In a minute, man... let him play..."

As Hendrix went into "Voodoo Child, Slight Return," it was so hard to talk to Danny above the crowd noise that Artie resolved just to stick by his side.

"... let him wail..."

"Gimme the gun!... FUCK!"

Now the cold is gone. Unstoppably gone. Snatched out of his hand.

Now the blackness isn't from his mind, it's from his shut eyes as the shot explodes.

"Wake the FUCK UP or I'll leave you here! Jesus!"

He sees her and the blood. The white plastic hand grabs him, hustles him out the door until he finds his footing…

"Did you throw the gun out the window? Did you run with the gun out into the street?"

" I wish you peace and happiness, happiness, happiness…"

Yeah, right, peace and happiness, right motherfucker, Experience band of Gyps, ragged ass fucking sellout. He's selling a dream, Danny. You know it's really chaos. But this chaos into dream, it will become a permanent dream, a fucking lie. To come back and come back again, yeah, right, everybody can be okay in a big wet grassy field in the Cats-kills. Turn it into fire to burn that tree down. Fuck it! Let them know the truth, the reality, and that reality is what will come back ten, twenty, fifty years from now. WAKE THEM THE FUCK UP, DANNY!

Danny knew the tree had grown, trapped Hendrix himself in its branches, and Ed was right, he, Danny Geller, was at the fulcrum of the fulcrum, he was the prime mover. There were no guards, just a man playing his guitar. He'd been invited to the stage, they'd all welcome him. Everyone was exhausted, hungry, blissed out. He could run up and move the great lever with the knife in his hand, cut a black jagged chasm of reality all through the era, bounding up just like Abbie tried to until Townsend jabbed him off the stage, but unlike Abbie Danny would really DO IT, so everyone wouldn't be lost in this dream, but would know and see the nightmare all around them…

Artie looked at Danny, and he saw his arms stir under the quilt, and, as it slid away, the hasp and the blade of a knife. Behind him Hendrix and his band created a roar that made it almost impossible to think.

"What's that, Danny?"

"Hey, man… listen… you're right, I gotta go up to the stage, see whoever wants to see me."

"What's the knife for?"

"It's—it's—I was eating something, Artie. I was cutting up salad, what do you mean? Look, I gotta go..."

"Can I see it for a minute?"

"Artie, get the fuck away from me!"

At the first hint of hostility two bearded strangers were on them, pulling them apart, saying peace, man, we're all brothers, peace, over and over again. Danny backed away from Artie toward the access route to the stage as the two smiling intercessors calmed them down. Artie nodded everything was cool, and tried to keep Danny's attention, hold him from running away.

"Danny, let me just hold it while you go up there. I mean, you're going to be seeing people who care about you, old friends from the Voyage days, or maybe the top people in rock, they all remember you. And I mean, everyone's walking around with mud on them, but you don't want to be walking around looking that weird. Hey, I'll go with you!"

Danny wasn't listening to him, but was holding still. It looked like Hendrix had once again hypnotized him. Hendrix had dismissed his own licks with "we're just jamming that's all," but then hit three rippling notes over and over, struck the "Voodoo Child" refrain, and climaxed with a classic blues ending that climbed and climbed through ascending tremolos to... "The Star Spangled Banner."

The crowd went nuts. Mitch Mitchell did drum rolls and fills, Billy Cox laid down a few spare bass notes, but everything else was Hendrix, alone with his guitar, crying out with endless vibrato above a furnace of sound...

... come rockets and bombs... squeal, my strings... sing a song brother... all my brothers caught in the War... jump again into thin air... chute on my back, gunners and Spanish dancers behind me... I got mine, I got mine... it's all freedom...

"Man, how can the motherfucker play that? How can he sell out like that, man?"

Only Artie heard Danny's cry of despair, and, as fascinated by the music as Danny's stillness, he crept up behind him until the two were standing next to each other. Danny gazed at Artie helplessly. "How can Jimi sell out like that?"

He was still clutching the knife, Artie knew, but he seemed transfixed by the shock they all felt at this one black man firing the national anthem through an electric guitar, through the feedback of engines running hot and bombs exploding, sirens and rounds of incoming mortars. The refrain of "Taps" bled through it for a moment, and then, as Hendrix played the final bars of the anthem, Artie at last knew what to say to Danny, a reply that came from the Vandemeer High School Debating Society, but also the ground of the Festival itself.

"He's not selling out, Danny. He's taking the other side."

Artie's reply created a silence for Danny, free of all the images and the shrieking voice of his vision of the long slide down. He heard the anthem end on four majestic chords, then jolt into "Purple Haze."

Fuck it, there's the hit, as always, gotta have the hit, can't argue with Number One, the machine cranks on, the tree grows and grows... Ed's screaming something, but I'm so tired... tired... Danny felt the angle of the knife turn in his hand...

"Danny? Come on, let's go to the stage. You know, this could be really great, we could get high with Crosby or Butterfield or whoever's still there, come on, Danny..."

Artie's voice, like the chirp of a bird, tugged at his attention, and then Hendrix launched a cyclonic run of endless bent notes and attacks and jumps into a whole other vein: the malaguena, Spanish flamenco strumming. The Near Eastern and Andalusian and gypsy and blues and raga music howled and spiraled and flashed and soared.

"Danny?"

The tree inhales the sunlight, breaks up into fresh golden shards of wood, and in the delicate, newly gleaming mesh, a golden woman with green eyes reaching out her hand...

"So fucking beautiful. So FUCKING GREAT! HOW IS IT SO FUCKING GREAT?"

Danny collapsed to the ground and lay in the mud.

Onlookers quickly gathered. He was bent nearly double, tearful eyes closed, his blankets tangled around him, and under one fold of the quilt, Artie could see his hands spasmodically loosen and clutch at the knife.

Artie backed everyone away as best he could. He's okay, he's going to be okay. Then he stood over Danny, kneeled at his side, watched his fingers clench and unclench until he thought the moment was right, and grabbed for the knife hasp. He couldn't believe how quickly the knife was in his hand. He shoved it under his belt and turned to the alarmed onlookers.

"He's fine, he's gonna be all right."

Danny's eyes burned into Artie, and then he gave him a smile, heavy with resignation, but also, it seemed to Artie, touched with pride.

"Fuck me, right, lil' bro? Fuck me."

Artie let him lay still on the ground. Hendrix was playing gentle farewell music. The crowd was already dispersing amid hundreds of pairs of shoes, swaths of plastic, and trodden sleeping bags.

"Danny, do you have any medication with you?"

Danny clambered up to a crouch and he and Artie looked around them. The departing Festival-goers harvested the endless trash. They were taking it away as they left, so the amphitheater could be a cow pasture again. Hare Krishnas passed out peacock feathers. The SDS sold "New Left Notes." Soon it would all vanish as if the heaviest of the heavies who played there and all the celebrants had just been a dream.

Danny pulled a bottle out of his pocket, popped the cap, and took his pills.

People held up makeshift signs scrawled on cardboard flaps. San Francisco. Portland. Los Angeles. Montreal. Just beneath the stage, Artie's friends were waiting for him and offering rides under a magic marker placard that said New York City.

Time to bring Danny home.

ACKNOWLEDGMENTS

My deepest thanks to Susan Stein, my sister, for her love, support, and counsel; for helping me with our mutual memories of the period and sharing some of her own; for the musical knowledge she also shared as a singer/songwriter, and for providing me a Manhattan perch while I researched the book.

To Dr. Michael Tanner, my oldest friend, for also helping me with our shared memories and with his own—and for, along with his mother, Louise Tanner, opening up a world of art and entertainment to me at that time.

To Kurt Griffith for his excellent work on the interior design and cover of this book.

And for their marvelous insights regarding politics, culture, and music: civil liberties lawyers Martin Garbus and Ron Kuby, former owner of the Village Gate the late Art D'Lugoff, former Deputy Mayor Robert Price, former Lindsay administration urban affairs aides Sid Davidoff and the late Barry Gotteherer, film editor and former Newsreel member Lisa Rutchka, former off-Broadway actress Valentina Rutchka, and, on the musical end, guitarist-songwriter-singer Charlie Karp, guitarist-songwriter-singer Lenny Hat, bass guitarist-songwriter-singer-bandleader Tony Conniff, and Doane Perry, who as a young drummer idolized Clive Bunker of Jethro Tull, and who later became Jethro Tull's longest-serving drummer—all proof that, despite some opinions to the contrary, many of those who most embraced the arts, ideas, and spirit of the period not only survived it but lived well.

Made in United States
North Haven, CT
02 May 2023

36170024R00251